PENGUI

AUTHOR

David Lodge is the author of twelve n⸻
Places, *Small World* (shortlisted for the Booker Prize), *Nice Work* (also shortlisted
for the Booker), *Paradise News*, *Therapy*, and *Thinks . . . .* He is also the author
of several works of literary criticism, including *The Art of Fiction*, *The Practice of
Writing*, and *Consciousness and the Novel*. He lives in Birmingham, England.

Praise for *Author, Author*
from America and England

"A bold new departure . . . Lodge handles his hero very tenderly—shows us
James's sensitivity, his kindness, his constant fear of appearing a vulgar Yankee, his
good sense, his mantle of worldliness, his need for both friendship and solitary
withdrawal. . . . His portrait of the man explores an interaction of fragility and
strength, delicacy and force."
—Rosemary Dinnage, *The New York Review of Books*

"Lodge combines wit and erudition here to produce a cunning, audacious portrait . . . [his] greatest achievement, perhaps, is to present the master not only as
mortal—helpless and delusional towards the end, dictating letters in the voice of
Napoleon—but also as a failure. . . . This reverent portrait of literary genius and
human frailty allows us an intimate, but never prurient, view of James's vanity
and desolation."
—Anna Mundow, *The Boston Globe*

"Lodge is very deft in two aspects of his reconstruction: the sexual and the con-
textual . . . [he] recreates the little world of London's West End stage with great
charm and care. . . . I knew what had later happened to James on that night of
nights, and it says a great deal for Lodge that he kept me in suspense for a considerable time about a denouement that I understood in advance, and then made
that climax into something more shattering than I had anticipated."
—Christopher Hitchens, *The Washington Post*

"You need not be a fan of Henry James's mannered novels of manners to be cap-
tivated by this fictionalized portrait of a gentleman. . . . Lodge delivers warmth
and comedy, even suspense."
—Kyle Smith, *People*

"Lodge, a master of smiling sympathy, always has excelled at dialogue and scene-
setting. Here he re-creates the provincial and London theater worlds with delight.
. . . Deserves to reach a wide audience."
—Kerry Fried, *Newsday*

"Breaks fresh ground in its innovative approach to creating fiction in the form of
biography . . . it turns the rather stuffy figure of Henry James into a lively character of endearing complexity and resolve whose struggles with authorship are
part of a deeper design in life."
—Michael Shelden, *The Baltimore Sun*

"Reads like a cast list of nineteenth-century creative superstars, with Henry James at its head. . . . *Author, Author* comes off not as elitist but as full of integrity . . . Lodge's homage resounds with faith that genius can and will indefatigably pursue truth."   —Sarah Cypher, *The Oregonian* (Portland)

"A riveting portrait. . . . Lodge uses his novelist's skill to reveal a dramatic pattern of crisis and recovery in the artist's middle years, when an ill-advised venture in the theater led to his most humiliating defeat. . . . Those who want to experience life, at least for a little while, through the mind of one of America's greatest writers, won't find anything better than *Author, Author*."
                    —Thomas Bontly, *Milwaukee Journal Sentinel*

"This is a compelling book, which reads seamlessly, organically, as a novel. Never has a character—Henry James himself—been so well served by an author."
                    —Anita Brookner, *The Spectator*

"Nothing I read in 2004—and I read a lot—came up to David Lodge's *Author, Author* . . . it takes an enormous talent to do what Lodge has done."
                    —Ruth Rendell, *The Mail on Sunday*

"This superb book is the best of a run of novels based on Henry James's life. . . . It's a unique achievement, very different from *The Master*, and for my money offering a more biographically persuasive picture of James the artist as well as a more imaginatively lively and profoundly moving one . . . as well as being marvelously sure-footed in treating late-Victorian culture, Lodge knows the ultimate practicalities of being an author, the sensitivities, aspirations and near-suicidal despairs, and taking James as his hero allows him to evoke from the inside what an apparently successful career feels like. . . . *Author, Author* is a poignant, magnificently shaped expression of affection for a great writer who was also a great human being."   —Philip Horne, *Daily Telegraph*

"[Lodge's] imaginative flair flickers brilliantly over a rich accumulation of research. . . . This book is a superbly vitalizing addition to James's thriving afterlife."
                    —Peter Kemp, *The Sunday Times* (London)

"A fascinating novel. . . . A new and surprising venture [for Lodge]—the novelist as biographer of a novelist. . . . Lodge follows [James' life] with the rigor and delicacy of a moral bloodhound, but also with the instincts of a born novelist."
                    —Anthony Thwaite, *Sunday Telegraph* (London)

"Beautifully conjures the pathos, farce and misery of the lone writer tangling with the dragons of showbiz. . . . *Author, Author* paints a picture of an urbane mid-career writer, not taking part in the erotic arena, but watching closely from the stands. Throughout, Lodge sticks to established facts in a virtuoso blend of the truth of biography and the authenticity of fiction."   —Boyd Tonkin, *Independent*

"Lodge has settled Henry James more comfortably into his own skin than any other biographer, or novelist, to date."   —Jonathan Heawood, *Independent on Sunday*

DAVID LODGE

Author, Author

PENGUIN BOOKS

PENGUIN BOOKS

Published by the Penguin Group

Penguin Group (USA) Inc., 375 Hudson Street, New York, New York 10014, U.S.A.
Penguin Group (Canada), 90 Eglinton Avenue East, Suite 700, Toronto,
Ontario, Canada M4P 2Y3 (a division of Pearson Penguin Canada Inc.)
Penguin Books Ltd, 80 Strand, London WC2R 0RL, England
Penguin Ireland, 25 St Stephen's Green, Dublin 2, Ireland (a division of Penguin Books Ltd)
Penguin Group (Australia), 250 Camberwell Road, Camberwell,
Victoria 3124, Australia (a division of Pearson Australia Group Pty Ltd)
Penguin Books India Pvt Ltd, 11 Community Centre,
Panchsheel Park, New Delhi – 110 017, India
Penguin Group (NZ), cnr Airborne and Rosedale Roads, Albany,
Auckland 1310, New Zealand (a division of Pearson New Zealand Ltd)
Penguin Books (South Africa) (Pty) Ltd, 24 Sturdee Avenue,
Rosebank, Johannesburg 2196, South Africa

Penguin Books Ltd, Registered Offices:
80 Strand, London WC2R 0RL, England

First published in the United States of America by Viking Penguin,
a member of Penguin Group (USA) Inc. 2004
Published in Penguin Books 2005

1   3   5   7   9   10   8   6   4   2

PUBLISHER'S NOTE
This is a work of fiction. Names, characters, places, and incidents either are the product
of the author's imagination or are used fictitiously, and any resemblance to actual persons,
living or dead, business establishments, events, or locales is entirely coincidental.

THE LIBRARY OF CONGRESS HAS CATALOGED THE HARDCOVER EDITION AS FOLLOWS:
Lodge, David, 1935–
Author, author : a novel / David Lodge
p.   cm.
ISBN 0-670-03349-9 (hc.)
ISBN 0 14 30.3609 2 (pbk.)
1. James, Henry, 1843–1916—Fiction.   2. Chelsea (London, England)—Fiction.
3. Americans—England—Fiction.   4. London (England)—Fiction.
5. Authorship—Fiction.   6. Authors—Fiction.   I. Title.
PR6062.O36A95 2004
823'.914.—dc22   2004053590

Printed in the United States of America
Set in Bembo

To Danny Moynihan

'We work in the dark – we do what we can – we give what we have. Our doubt is our passion and our passion is our task. The rest is the madness of art.'

– Henry James, 'The Middle Years'

Who was to be lucky and who to be rich,
Who'd get to the top of the tree . . .

– Felix Moscheles, *In Bohemia with Du Maurier*

Sometimes it seems advisable to preface a novel with a note saying that the story and the characters are entirely fictitious, or words to that effect. On this occasion a different authorial statement seems called for. Nearly everything that happens in this story is based on factual sources. With one insignificant exception, all the named characters were real people. Quotations from their books, plays, articles, letters, journals, etc., are their own words. But I have used a novelist's licence in representing what they thought, felt, and said to each other; and I have imagined some events and personal details which history omitted to record. So this book is a novel, and structured like a novel. It begins at the end of the story, or near the end, and then goes back to the beginning, and works its way to the middle, and then rejoins the end, which is where it begins . . .

PART ONE

LONDON, December 1915. In the master bedroom (never was the estate agent's epithet more appropriate) of Flat 21, Carlyle Mansions, Cheyne Walk, Chelsea, the distinguished author is dying – slowly, but surely. In Flanders, less than two hundred miles away, other men are dying more quickly, more painfully, more pitifully – young men, mostly, with their lives still before them, blank pages that will never be filled. The author is 72. He has had an interesting and varied life, written many books, travelled widely, enjoyed the arts, moved in society (one winter he dined out 107 times), and owns a charming old house in Rye as well as the lease of this spacious London flat with its fine view of the Thames. He has had deeply rewarding friendships with both men and women. If he has never experienced sexual intercourse, that was by his own choice, unlike the many young men in Flanders who died virgins either for lack of opportunity or because they hoped to marry and were keeping themselves chaste on principle.

The author is dying propped up in bed among starched sheets and plump pillows, attended by three servants and two professional nurses working in rotation, while the young men are dying in the mud of No Man's Land, or in squalid trenches, or on jolting stretchers, or on camp beds in field hospitals amid the groans of their wounded comrades. But of the little group caring for the author only his manservant Burgess Noakes knows what dying on the Western Front is like, and he doesn't want to talk about it. He's happy to be out of it, is Noakes, with a Blighty wound – thirty small wounds to be exact, thirty bits of shrapnel from a German mortar bomb that had to be painfully winkled out of his head, body and legs – and with his hearing permanently damaged by the blast; glad to be on convalescent leave extended by special dispensation so that he can attend his distinguished master (who has friends in

3

high places – as high as the Prime Minister himself, Mr Asquith) and hopeful of a discharge on medical grounds in due course. As for the others – the cook/housekeeper Joan Anderson, the parlour-maid Minnie Kidd, who both live in, and Mr James's secretary/typist, Miss Theodora Bosanquet, who has a small flat in nearby Lawrence Street – the drama of his dying is inevitably more vivid and involving than the carnage in Flanders, because it is personally present to them. As it happens, none of them has lost a near relative in the war – yet. Of course they are depressed by the long daily lists of casualties in the newspapers, and share sympathetically the grief of bereaved friends, but they cannot really imagine those deaths.

In fact it is Henry James himself who, if he were *compos mentis*, would be better able to imagine them, up to a point, being a novel-ist whose job it is to imagine things he has never personally experienced. Stephen Crane, for instance, once briefly his neighbour in East Sussex, wrote the best novel ever published about the American Civil War though he wasn't even born when it took place. Henry had at least some experience of that war to go on, having been as a young man an anxious and uneasy spectator of it, exempted by an obscure back injury from taking part himself, but with two younger brothers who served gallantly on the Union side. He never forgot visiting seventeen-year-old Wilky at his training camp with the 44th Massachusetts, one of a crowd of sunburnt smiling confident young men in smart new blue uniforms, and then seeing him brought back months later to the family home in Cambridge on a stretcher, half dead, with terrifying stories of battle to tell when he recovered.

Perhaps it was because he had lived through the first major war of the industrial age, the first with casualties on an industrial scale, that Henry foresaw the catastrophic consequences of the European conflict sooner than most Englishmen. Only two days after war was declared he was writing to his friend Edith Wharton, fellow Anglophile and Francophile (not knowing when or where his letter might reach her, for she was motoring somewhere in Spain as the armies mobilised and the ultimatums expired), to say 'I feel all but unbearably overdarkened by this crash of our civilisation', and he has been in a state of handwringing mental anguish ever since. Not that he has been a passive, or pacifist, observer of the conflict. On the contrary, he is convinced of the iniquity of German aggression, and has done as much as a portly, valetudinarian, expatriate American of his years could possibly do to help the Allied cause. He has visited wounded soldiers in hospital (his fluency in French was appreciated by the Belgian Walloons, though what they or the Tommies made of his convoluted style of utterance was a subject of amused speculation among his friends) and been active in charitable work assisting Belgian refugees in Rye. He became Honorary President of the American Volunteer Motor Ambulance Corps. He has urged American participation in the war on his compatriots by every means, even to the extent of granting an interview to a journalist from *The New York Times* to promote the cause, in spite of a lifetime's aversion to this form of publicity. (He did however insist on seeing the text of the article before publication and completely rewrote it, so that he was, Theodora Bosanquet reflected with quiet amusement, in effect interviewing himself.) And in the summer of 1915 he made the biggest commitment of all, taking British nationality in a gesture of solidarity with his adopted country.

'The old toff could hardly do more,' Burgess Noakes remarked to George Gammon, the gardener at Lamb House, in October, when Henry James went down to Rye for what proved to be the last time, accompanied by Joan Anderson, Minnie Kidd, and Burgess himself. 'The old toff' was how he and George usually referred to their employer in private. It implied no disrespect, but rather admiration for the style with which James played the part of a gentleman – his impeccable manners, his elaborate verbal courtesies, his dashing waistcoats, the carefully discriminated collection of hats and sticks for all occasions in the hall at Lamb House. 'Put a lot of Yankee noses out of joint it did, when he got himself nationalised,' Burgess said. 'The family weren't none too pleased neither.' He had overheard Mr James dictating letters to Miss Bosanquet about the critical reaction in America to his change of citizenship. 'And he sent me socks,' he added reminiscently.

'Socks?'

'When I was at the Front. Socks and ointment for me feet.'

'What was it like, Burgess – at the Front?' George Gammon asked.

Burgess smiled and nodded and stared into the burning coals behind the grate of the kitchen range – its door left open to shed a cheerful glow on the flagged floor. It was evening, getting dark, and they were sitting in the parlour kitchen of George Gammon's cottage, tucked away behind the garden wall of Lamb House. George waited patiently. Since Burgess came back from the war it was difficult to know whether he hadn't heard your question, or didn't want to answer it. 'Did I ever tell you how it was between me and him when I joined up?' he said at last.

'Aye,' said George, nodding. But Burgess told him again anyway. He was itching to join up as soon as war was declared, but hung back because he knew how dependent on him the old toff was, especially now his health was so poor, and he didn't want to seem ungrateful to the man who had taken him on as a houseboy and trained him up to be a gentleman's gentleman, travelling all over England, staying in the grandest houses in the country, Scotland and Ireland and America too, and always in the same railway carriage, no first-class and third-class tickets like with many masters and servants. So for two weeks, while more and more Rye lads took the train into Hastings to enlist in the 5th Battalion of the Royal Sussex, Burgess suffered miserably in silence as he went about his duties at Lamb House, until he could bear it no longer and told Mr James he wanted to join up. 'And what d'you think the old toff said?'

George shook his head in pretended puzzlement.

'Well, he couldn't have been more pleased. Not that he wanted to lose me, like – said he didn't know how he'd manage without me. But it turned out he'd been hopin' I'd volunteer ever since war was declared. So we'd both been of the same mind for two weeks without—'

An urgent knocking on the cottage door made Burgess break off his narrative just short of its conclusion. It was Minnie Kidd, a shawl thrown over her head and shoulders, who had run the few yards along West Street from Lamb House to the cottage. 'You'd better come, Burgess,' she said. 'Mr James 'as been took bad.'

Burgess wasn't surprised. Ever since they arrived at Lamb House his master had seemed restless and unhappy, wheezing and sighing to himself, raising his hands as if about to utter some lament and then letting them drop to his sides in mute despair. He was dismayed to see in the garden the stump of the ancient mulberry tree that had been blown down in the great gale of the previous winter. It had been reported to him at the time of course, and he had authorised Gammon to cut off the boughs and branches for kindling and to saw the hollow trunk into sections that could be chopped up into logs. But actually to behold the dismembered corpse of the beloved tree under whose dense rustling shade he had so often sat in summers past was a different matter. 'It's a symbol, Burgess,' he said mournfully. 'A symbol and a portent. First the poor old mulberry tree, next poor old HJ.' Burgess received this pronouncement, as he received all of his master's utterances other than instructions and questions, in respectful silence. Long experience had taught him it was the best policy. 'You don't want to bandy words with the old toff,' was always his advice to new servants, 'or you'll get more than you bargained for.'

The house had been let or lent to a number of transient tenants over the past year, looked after by temporary servants, and it had a shabby neglected air which caused Joan Anderson to frown as soon as she entered the front hall, and to emit audible signs of distress when she reached the kitchen. While Joan and Minnie worked away with brooms and dusters and scourers and dishcloths to restore the house to something like its normal order, their master ransacked his drawers and cupboards for private papers, letters, photographs and manuscripts, and made a bonfire of them in the kitchen garden. He stood grimly over the curling, blackening sheets as they turned to ash, poking them occasionally with a stick, like the staff officer of a retreating army destroying documents lest they fall into the hands of the enemy. It reminded his servants of a much bigger bonfire back in 1909, when Mr James destroyed the accumulated correspondence of a lifetime in what was obviously a mood of black depression, though what had triggered it they didn't know.

'What's the matter with him now?' Burgess asked Minnie, getting to his feet and hastily buttoning up his army tunic. He continued to wear his uniform although he was on indefinite sick leave – it saved having to answer pointed questions, or fend off accusing looks, from people keen to hand out white feathers. He was barely an inch over five feet, but muscular and well proportioned, an amateur boxer who had once been Sussex bantamweight champion. Minnie Kidd admired the silky moustache he had grown on his deep upper lip while he was in the Army, its lustre faintly reflecting the glow of the fire. She was a buxom, pleasant-featured young woman of thirty-three, and stood a head taller than Burgess Noakes, much to her regret.

'Gastric,' said Minnie.

'Eh?'

'*Gastric*,' she repeated, raising her voice.

'Aye,' said Burgess, fastening his belt buckle with a click. 'All that Fletcherising done it.'

Ten years earlier Henry James had been converted to the teaching of the American dietician Dr Horace Fletcher, who recommended that every mouthful of food should be chewed and masticated until it was reduced to liquid before being swallowed. One memorable day Fletcher had visited the author at Lamb House, and their lunch was a solemn ritual in which priest and acolyte vied with each other for merit. The servants could hardly keep straight faces as they watched the two men virtuously chewing each forkful of their roast beef sixty times. The tempo of conversation was necessarily slow, and the meal inordinately long. It was the opinion of many in the author's circle besides his manservant that he had ruined his digestion by this faddish regime, though he no longer practised it in its full rigour.

Burgess stamped his boots on the flagged floor, the reflex action of a soldier before going on parade. 'Let's go then, Minnie,' he said.

Outside it was dark, and a sea mist had crept up the steep incline of Mermaid Street from the quays. The gaslamp bracketed to the wall of the Garden House at the elbow of West Street, turned down to a mere glimmer because of lighting restrictions, was hardly visible, but a slab of light shone across the cobbles from the front door of Lamb House, left open by Minnie when she dashed out.

'You'll get us fined,' Burgess teased her. 'Attractin' the Zeppelins.'

'Sorry, Burgess,' Minnie said meekly. 'I was that flustered.'

They found their master slumped in an armchair in the Green Room on the first floor, haggard and gasping for breath, a hand pressed to his chest, or his stomach (it was difficult to tell where the one ended and the other began under his waistcoat), papers scattered at his feet where he had dropped them. Burgess got him undressed and into bed, and dosed him with the physic he usually took for gastric attacks. But the breathlessness continued, he spent a sleepless night, and the following morning Doctor Skinner was summoned. Skinner detected an irregular rhythm of the heartbeat through his stethoscope, diagnosed intermittent tachycardia, prescribed digitalis, and recommended that Henry should see the heart specialist Sir James Mackenzie as soon as possible. So the whole party had to prepare to return to London after only three days in Rye.

Minnie Kidd brought him the papers she had picked up from the floor when he was taken ill. They were letters, all in the same hand, with little sketches inserted into the text of some of them.

'Ah, thank you, Kidd,' he said. 'Poor Du Maurier! I was going to burn them, but I fatally began to read them.'

'Shall I burn them for you, sir?' said Minnie

Henry smiled faintly. 'No, no, thank you, Kidd. Let them escape the – ah – holocaust. They escaped the last one, somehow. And, after all, they can do no harm. There was no malice in poor Kiki.' And he put the letters away in a drawer in the Green Room.

Sir James Mackenzie confirmed Dr Skinner's diagnosis, which seemed to give the author a melancholy satisfaction. He had consulted the great physician once before, in 1909, convinced that he was suffering from a cardiac complaint, like his brother William, only to be told that there was nothing wrong with his heart – indeed, nothing wrong with him at all that couldn't be remedied by a sensible diet and regular exercise. The news had been a relief, of course, but also, the patient felt, cast a slight aspersion on his character, the imputation of being a *malade imaginaire*. Now it appeared that he did have 'a heart' after all. He dictated letters to his friends to this effect, and basked in their concerned replies. He played the part of a certified invalid assiduously, rarely going out, and never in the evening. His London doctor, who bore the exotic and suggestive name of Des Voeux, attended him regularly at Carlyle Mansions. He managed a little work in November – finishing off his elegiac introduction to Rupert Brooke's *Letters from America*, a task over which he shed some tears, for he had been deeply affected by the death of the handsome, gallant young poet, whom he had met once at Cambridge, as an undergraduate of exceptional charm and promise, and whose literary career he had subsequently followed with keen interest. The fact that the manner of Brooke's death – not from a battle wound, but from blood-poisoning on shipboard, en route to the Dardanelles – had so signally failed to match the proleptic sublimity of '*If I should die . . .*' only intensified its pathos, only made it more eloquent of the tragic waste of so many young lives in the War at large.

Having dictated the final revise of this piece, he found that he had no inclination to go on with his novel-in-progress, *The Ivory Tower*. This caused him some uneasiness, since Scribner's had paid a surprisingly handsome advance for it, but the War made any fictional subject seem trivial. He read through the manuscript of another unfinished novel, provisionally entitled *The Sense of the Past*, which he had sent Theodora Bosanquet to fetch from Lamb House earlier that year, hoping that perhaps this blend of ghost-story and period piece would be more take-uppable, but he lacked the will, and the strength, to resume work on it. In late November he suffered a succession of restless, wakeful nights which deprived him of energy for anything more demanding than correspondence during the day. On the first day of December he finished a letter to his niece, Peggy, in America, with the phrase, 'the pen drops from my hand' – a purely rhetorical flourish, since the letter was dictated – but, as it turned out, a prophetic one.

The next morning Burgess Noakes called his master at eight o'clock as usual. Half an hour later, as Minnie Kidd was laying the dining-room table for breakfast, she heard a cry from Mr James's bedroom, and found him sprawled on the floor in his nightshirt, entangled in the cord of the electric lamp, which he had pulled down from the bedside table in groping for the servants' bell.

'Oh, Mr James, sir!' she exclaimed, kneeling beside him. 'Are you hurt?'

'It's the beast in the jungle,' he murmured, 'and it's sprung.'

'There's no beast in here, sir,' she said, looking round the room, wondering if the caretaker's cat had somehow got into the flat. 'You've had a fall, that's all.'

Minnie called Burgess and together they got him back into bed. He leaned heavily on them and dragged his left leg, which seemed to be paralysed. Des Voeux was summoned and Minnie ran round the corner to the flat Theodora Bosanquet shared with her companion, Miss Bradley, to tell her that Mr James seemed to have had 'a sort of stroke'.

'Can he speak?' was Theodora's first question.

'Oh, yes, Miss. But his mind's wandering. He said something about a beast. A beast in the jungle.'

'It's the title of one of Mr James's stories,' Theodora said. 'One of his finest.'

'Oh, I see, Miss,' said Minnie, though she didn't really.

'I'll come round as soon as I'm dressed,' said Theodora. She was wearing a housecoat, having not yet completed her toilet.

It was a blessing, she reflected later, that the stroke had not affected HJ's speech, so that he was able to drape his misfortune in folds of characteristic rhetoric. 'I have had a paralytic stroke in the most approved fashion,' he informed Theodora almost proudly, after Des Voeux had examined him. And to his friend Fanny Prothero, who called that day, and was admitted to his bedroom, he confided that as he fell to the ground he had heard a voice, not his own, say distinctly: *'So here it is at last, the distinguished thing!'*

The distinguished thing was certainly approaching, but was still some way off. Henry was sufficiently himself to dictate a cable to his nephew Harry in America, carefully phrased so as not to alarm: *'Had slight stroke this morning. No serious symptoms. Perfect care. Wrote Peg yesterday.'* But that night he had a second stroke. Des Voeux called in Sir James Mackenzie, who looked grave and recommended that professional nurses be hired. Mrs William James, the widow of Henry's elder brother, the mother of Peg and Harry, cabled to say she was coming by the first available ship. 'She shouldn't, she shouldn't,' Henry said, shaking his head, thinking with a shudder of prowling U-boats in the Atlantic – the horror of the *Lusitania* was still a fresh memory – but he did not try to prevent her. Meanwhile his secretary took command of the household, hiring nurses, giving the servants their instructions, answering enquiries from concerned friends, issuing bulletins, forbidding visits, discouraging even telephone calls because the ringing of the bell disturbed the patient's rest.

Theodora Bosanquet, Cheltenham Ladies' College and University College London, was fully adequate to the crisis – in a way, her whole life since 1907 had been a preparation for it. One day in August of that year, a young woman of twenty-seven, working in the London office of Miss Petheridge's Secretarial Bureau on some dull indexing task, she was astonished to hear a passage from Henry James's *The Ambassadors*, one of her favourite novels, being dictated to a typist at a nearby desk. *'The court was large and open comma . . . full of revelations comma . . . for our friend comma . . . of the habit of privacy comma . . . the peace of intervals comma . . . the dignity of distances and approaches semicolon . . . the house comma . . . to his restless sense comma . . . was in the high homely style of an elder day comma . . . and the ancient Paris that he was always looking for dash . . . sometimes intensely felt comma . . . sometimes more acutely missed dash . . . was in the immemorial polish of the wide comma—'*

'Lord above, how many more commas?' the typist complained. 'His bally sentences seem to go on for ever.'

'This one is only another three lines,' said her helper.

'Only!' exclaimed the typist. 'I lose track.'

Theodora, unable to contain her curiosity, went over to the young woman and questioned her. It transpired that she was a candidate for employment as Henry James's typist, the previous occupant of this post having just left him to get married. Apparently – astonishingly, given the unusual complexity of his syntax – he dictated his novels instead of writing them out in longhand, and the young typist was practising with passages chosen at random from *The Ambassadors*.

'I envy you,' said Theodora. 'I can't think of a more wonderful position.'

'Well you're welcome to it,' said the typist. 'Give me a nice straightforward business letter any day.'

Theodora couldn't believe her luck. 'You mean – I could apply instead of you?'

'I'd be glad to get out of it.'

'Honestly?'

'Honestly. You'd have to live in Rye, though. A dead-alive place by all accounts.'

'I wouldn't mind that.'

'Can you type?'

'No, but I could learn.'

'Well, learn on a Remington, then. It has to be a Remington.'

Miss Petheridge tried to discourage Theodora from applying for the job. 'You would do far better to stay here in London,' she said. 'There is no security in being employed by an author.' But Theodora did not place a high value on security. Her favourite passage in *The Ambassadors* was the one where the middle-aged hero, Lambert Strether, exhorted his young friend, little Bilham, at a Parisian garden party: *'Don't forget that you're young – blessedly young; be glad of it on the contrary and live up to it. Live all you can; it's a mistake not to. It doesn't so much matter what you do in particular, so long as you have your life. If you haven't had that what have you had?'* It seemed to Theodora that she could best apply this counsel to herself by working for the man who wrote it.

Accordingly she acquired the use of an office Remington and taught herself to type in time to be interviewed by Henry James.

He was too polite to test her competence or even enquire about her speed before offering her the post, but he did assure himself that she was familiar with the Remington machine. He had got used to the distinctive tick-tick of its keys over the years – indeed it seemed to have become an essential aid to composition. When the work was going well, and he was in full flow, a kind of rhythm developed between HJ's lucent utterance and Theodora's answering staccato on the keyboard, and she felt like a pianist accompanying some virtuoso singer. 'My Remington Princess' became one of his fond sobriquets for her.

Fond, but not flirtatious. In her habitual dark tailored suits and plain blouses there was something about Theodora that did not invite flirtation. She was handsome, with a slender, upright figure and classical, slightly androgynous features. Her hair, cut short at the back, was softly waved and brushed across her brow, shading large dark eyes that observed the world attentively without revealing much about her inner self. Her voice was pleasantly low in timbre, and she never raised it. She was without question a lady, who would have graced one of the great country houses Henry James liked to write about, but only marriage would have placed her on such a stage, and she was as celibate by nature as her employer. Her background was genteel but financially pinched. Offered the choice of a small dowry or a university education, she had opted unhesitatingly for the latter, and the responsibility of earning her own bread.

Never perhaps were a writer and his secretary so well matched. She was calm, quiet, collected, while he was volatile, loquacious, nervous. She sat still, in perfect repose, during the long pauses while, pacing up and down the Garden Room, or leaning on the mantelpiece with his head cradled in his hands, he racked his brains for *le mot juste*, and never, never, did she venture to suggest one herself. She admired his work this side of idolatry, and had her private reservations about the ripe late style, but she didn't dream of even hinting a criticism. Her loyalty and discretion were complete. Her only regret was that she had entered HJ's employ after his finest work was completed – it would have been such an honour to collaborate in the production of the great trilogy of *The Ambassadors*,

The Wings of the Dove, and *The Golden Bowl*. She had had to make do with the Prefaces to the ill-fated New York Edition of his Collected Novels and Tales, the memoirs of his childhood and youth, and other relatively minor works. Nevertheless, she considered herself privileged to share so intimately the creative life of such a distinguished author, even in his sunset years.

'I think perhaps, Miss Bosanquet, you should inform Mrs Wharton of my – ah – stricken state,' Henry murmurs, the day after his second stroke. Theodora doesn't tell him that she has already done so. There is a subplot to his illness of which he is unaware.

Back in October, shortly after his return from Rye, Edith Wharton telephoned from a hotel in London, having taken a short break from her philanthropic war work in France, which ranged from raising funds for ambulances to providing for Parisian *haute couture* seamstresses suddenly deprived of employment. Typically she had somehow managed to cross the Channel in wartime with her motor car and chauffeur, and offered to take Henry to see their mutual friend, Howard Sturgis, at Windsor. Henry always enjoyed reading her letters about her exploits in France, and in times of peace excursions in her powerful Panhard had been one of his favourite recreations, but he was not equal in his debilitated state to the full force of her formidable presence, which he had for many years characterised in such mock-heroic terms as 'the Whirling Princess', 'the Incomparable One', 'the Firebird' and 'the Angel of Devastation'. He thanked her but told her he was too ill to go out or even to receive a visit. When she then asked if she could borrow Theodora's secretarial services for a few hours, he could hardly refuse to grant the favour. After all, she had generously paid for someone to look after Minnie Kidd's ailing mother in Hastings in 1913, so that Kidd could continue to look after himself, and she had loaned her own manservant to him when Burgess Noakes went off to fight in the War a year later. Theodora, who had only glimpsed Edith Wharton in the past, usually driving up to or away from the front door of Lamb House in clouds of dust and exhaust smoke, acquiesced readily in the plan, being curious to meet the celebrated novelist and international socialite at closer quarters.

And close it was. Mrs Wharton received Theodora in her suite at Buckland's Hotel in Brook Street dressed in an elaborately embroidered pink negligee that exposed her bare, well-fleshed arms to advantage, and an *écru* lace cap trimmed with fur – an outfit, Theodora calculated, that would have exhausted her own clothing budget for the year. She wore a heavy perfume that Theodora found oppressive in the overheated room, its windows firmly shut, and sat half-reclined on a chaise longue, smoking a Turkish cigarette in a holder. To Theodora, sitting upright in the least threadbare of her tailored suits, with her hands clasped in her lap, Edith Wharton appeared half *grande dame* and half *grande courtisane*, and the rumoured irregularities in her private life seemed all too plausible. Mrs Wharton quickly admitted that she had no need of Theodora's secretarial services – that had been just a ruse to obtain a reliable report of Henry James's state of health. Theodora, though resistant to her efforts to charm, recognised that her concern for the author's welfare was genuine, and would be backed up with practical assistance if needed. So she gave a frank account of HJ's condition, and agreed to keep Mrs Wharton abreast of any developments. She reported occasionally on his state of health by letter, and on the fourth of December sent a cable to Paris with the information that Mr James had suffered two strokes but was recovering.

The next day Edith Wharton cables back, '*Can come if advisable*,' but Theodora deems this unnecessary. Already HJ is perky enough to question the appropriateness of the epithet 'paralytic' to his stroke, and to demand a thesaurus to look for alternatives. A few days later he expresses a wish to dictate some notes on his condition. Des Voeux decides this activity can do no harm, and might be beneficial, so the Remington is wheeled into the master bedroom like a piece of medical apparatus, and Theodora takes her accustomed place at its keyboard.

'I find the business of coming round about as important and glorious as any circumstance I have had occasion to record,' he dictates, 'by which I mean that I find them as damnable and as boring.' The epithet 'damnable' gives Theodora a tiny shock – it is strong for HJ in dictation mode – and she notes the slight lapse of grammatical number in 'them', but on the whole his grasp of syntax seems unimpaired, and his reflections, though paradoxical, are coherent. 'Such is my sketchy state of mind,' he concludes, 'but I feel sure I shall discover plenty of fresh worlds to conquer, even if I am to be cheated of the amusement of them.'

A few days later, however, he shows signs of mental confusion. He asks Theodora where he is, and when she gives him the address of 21 Carlyle Mansions, he says: 'How very curious, that's Lady Hyde's address too.' He has got it into his head that Burgess is to take him to visit Lady Hyde. He is running a temperature, and the doctors declare that he is now suffering embolic pneumonia caused by a clot on his lung. Looking at him as he lies asleep on his back in the dimly lit, curtained bedroom, breathing stertorously, with his mouth turned down at the corners and hollow cheeks sunk deeply into his dentureless jaws, it seems to Theodora that the aura of the Great Writer, the 'cher maître', as he permits his younger admirers to address him, has finally evaporated, and he is just a simple sick old man such as one might find in any hospital ward.

But to her surprise she is summoned the very next evening to take more dictation – copious dictation, not entirely coherent, but full of striking phrases and vivid images. 'On this occasion moreover that having been difficult to keep step, we hear of the march of history, what is remaining to that essence of tragedy the limp? We scarce avoid rolling with all these famished and frustrate women in the wayside dust . . . They pluck in their terror handfuls of plumes from the imperial eagle, and with no greater credit in consequence than that they face, keeping their equipoise, the awful bloody beak that he turns around upon them . . .'

'He's ravin',' Burgess Noakes reports to Joan and Minnie in the kitchen, having heard some of this declamatory utterance as he crept in and out of the sickroom to replace the jug of Mr James's favourite sweetened lemon and barley water. He shakes his head sadly. 'He thinks he's on a march somewhere.'

Joan Anderson tuts and wipes her eye. This is not a sign of real emotion – she suffers from a chronically weeping eye – but it seems an appropriate gesture. Minnie Kidd finds a reason to leave the room and pauses for a few moments in the corridor outside James's bedroom to listen. 'He's writing a letter to his brother and sister, now,' she says on her return. 'They're all dead, ain't they?'

'You shouldn't eavesdrop, Minnie,' Joan murmurs.

'I weren't!' she says defensively. 'No more 'n Burgess.'

Burgess however seems not to have heard Joan's reproach. 'Yes, all dead,' he says. 'The three brothers, William, Bob, and Wilky, and the sister, Alice.'

'Something about a palace, it was,' says Minnie.

Sitting round the kitchen table, the three servants silently contemplate the decay of the great mind that has funded their existence for so many years. But not for much longer. When Mr James dies they will all be unemployed, and what will become of them then? It doesn't seem decent to raise the question at this moment, so Minnie asks another.

'Did you ever read one of Mr James's books, Burgess?'

'No,' he says emphatically, then adds: 'Why, did you?'

'No, but . . .' Minnie's voice tails away.

'I had a look at one once,' says Joan. 'I couldn't make head nor tail of it.'

'Well, they weren't written for the likes of us,' says Burgess. 'Them books are Literature.'

To Theodora Bosanquet, plying the keys of the Remington in the master bedroom, it is clear that HJ is suffering from a delusion that he is Napoleon Bonaparte. He possesses a great many books about the history of the Napoleonic era, and she has often observed him browsing in them. In his hallucinatory state his brother William and sister Alice have evidently metamorphosed into the siblings of the Emperor, and he is dictating letters to them in his imperial persona – now about the progress of his campaigns (*'We see the beak sufficiently directed in that vindictive intention, during these days of cold grey Switzerland weather, on the huddled and hustled campaigns of the first omens of defeat'*), now with instructions for the decoration of the imperial palaces ('*Dear and most esteemed brother and sister, I call your attention to the precious enclosed transcripts of plans and designs for the decorations of certain apartments of the palaces here, of the Louvre and the Tuileries . . .*'). These elaborate fantasies are, in their way, impressive evidence of a still active imagination, like the last salvoes of a holed, sinking, but defiant battleship.

The next day Theodora comes into the big sitting room overlooking the river that serves as HJ's study as well as his main reception room and surprises Minnie standing beside the bookshelves, leafing through an open book, her feather duster lying neglected on a table. Minnie guiltily snaps the book shut and replaces it.

'What are you doing, Kidd?' Theodora asks.

'Oh, nothing Miss! I was just looking.' Minnie grabs her duster and whisks it over the shelves – not the books themselves, which only Burgess and the master himself are allowed to dust.

'Looking for what?'

Minnie blushes. 'Well, that story you mentioned, Miss, the one Mr James wrote. About the beast in the jungle.'

Theodora smiles. 'You wish to read it?'

'If you don't think Mr James would mind, Miss.'

'I don't think he would object, but . . .' Theodora regards the young woman thoughtfully. 'When did you leave school, Minnie?' She uses her first name to show the question is meant kindly.

'Fourteen, Miss. But I was always good at reading.'

'Very well, if you promise to take great care of the book—'

'Oh, I will, Miss!'

'And return it promptly . . . then you may borrow it.'

'Thank you, Miss.'

Theodora hesitates a moment between *The Better Sort*, the collection of eleven stories in which 'The Beast in the Jungle' first appeared in 1903, and Volume XVII of the New York Edition in which it was reprinted in 1908. She finally chooses the former, as less bulky and intimidating in appearance. Its scarlet cloth binding has faded with the years, though the gilt lettering is still bright. 'Here you are, then, Minnie.'

That night Minnie goes to bed early, taking the book with her. Instead of switching on the electric light she lights a candle on her bedside table, so that the other members of the household won't be able to tell from the illuminated slit under her door that she is awake. She opens the book and turns its pages reverently until she finds the story called 'The Beast in the Jungle'. She reads the first sentence.

What determined the speech that startled him in the course of their encounter scarcely matters, being probably but some words spoken by himself quite without intention – spoken as they lingered and slowly moved together after their renewal of acquaintance.

Minnie blinks and reads the sentence again. She still doesn't understand it. She knows the meaning of all the individual words but she can't make any sense of the way they are joined together. Can this really be the beginning of the story? She turns back a page to confirm that indeed it is. She holds the book closer to the candle-flame and reads the sentence again. Again she is completely baffled. Minnie is used to stories where you are told at the outset who is who – what the names of the heroine and the hero are, and where they live, and what they look like – before the story proper gets going. This sentence seems as if it comes from the middle of something. It doesn't tell you who 'him' is or who the other person is, or what was going on between them except to say, strangely, that it doesn't matter anyway.

Minnie thinks perhaps everything will become clearer in due course, so she reads on, but the deeper she gets into the story the thicker is the fog of her incomprehension. After a while the two main characters are given names, and there seems to be some possibility of their falling in love, but John Marcher is a cold stick and May Bartram an irritatingly reserved heroine. There is nothing about whether she is pretty or beautiful or what clothes she wears, and there are pages and pages of dense print in long intimidating paragraphs, about some meeting they had in the past, before they start speaking to each other in the story, and then it is hard to know what they are talking about because they keep interrupting each other and answering questions with more questions. Most puzzling of all is that there is no jungle, and no beast, except for one sentence: *'Something or other lay in wait for him, amid the twists and turns of the months and the years, like a crouching beast in the jungle.'* But what it is Minnie can't work out. She almost groans aloud at the frustrated effort to understand. The lines of print blur and waver in the candlelight. She yawns and rubs her eyes and pinches herself to stay awake. Then she peeps at the end of the story to see if it is a happy one. It is not. In the last sentence John Marcher flings himself on a tomb that is probably May Bartram's. That is enough for Minnie. She closes the book, blows out the candle and falls instantly asleep.

The next day Minnie returns the book to Theodora Bosanquet.

'Did you enjoy it?' Theodora asks.

'Well Miss, it's fine writing, I could tell that, but . . .'

'But?' Theodora's big brown eyes almost twinkle.

'Well, to be honest, it's a bit above me.'

'Yes, Mr James *is* a difficult writer on first acquaintance. He demands a lot of his readers. But the rewards are great.'

'Oh yes, I'm sure, Miss. But you need the education for it.'

'What did you find especially difficult to understand?' Theodora opens the book and leafs through it.

Minnie hesitates, tempted to reply: *'Everything!'* Instead she says: 'Well, I thought it was going to be about the jungle . . .'

'Ah. The beast in the jungle is just a metaphor. A symbol.'

'Oh.' Minnie looks blank.

'All his life Marcher has had a presentiment – a feeling – that something extraordinary and terrible is going to happen to him, which he compares to a wild animal waiting to spring on its prey.'

'Oh, I see.' And Minnie does begin to see.

'And he discusses with May what it might be – endlessly, obsessively, self-centredly, in meeting after meeting, year after year. Until she dies. And only then does he realise, too late, that she loved him.

He realises that nothing ever *is* going to happen to him because he is incapable of love.'

'Ah, so that's what it means,' Minnie murmurs, almost dreamily, her eyes unfocused.

Theodora finds the last page of the story and reads aloud: ' "She had lived – who could say now with what passion? – since she had loved him for himself; whereas he never had thought of her (ah, how it hugely glared at him) but in the chill of his egotism and the light of her use." You understand?'

'Yes. Thank you, Miss.'

The telephone shrills in the hall. They hear Burgess answer it, and a moment later he comes into the room.

'Mrs William James,' he announces. 'Telephoning from Liverpool. Her ship docked this morning.'

'Thank you, Noakes.' As she goes to take the call, Theodora reflects that the man seems to have no difficulty in answering the telephone. She can't help thinking that he often pretends to be deafer than he really is, but has no intention of challenging him on this point. One of the last letters HJ dictated to her before his stroke was to the Prime Minister's private secretary, asking if Burgess Noakes could be given a medical discharge from the army, and citing his deafness as a reason. Putting patriotic considerations aside, Theodora can only hope that the appeal succeeds, for Noakes's contribution to the care of HJ has been invaluable, and the two female servants, especially Kidd, have seemed much happier since he returned. There has been an acknowledgement of the letter but no further communication to date.

Mrs James arrives at Carlyle Mansions that evening. In her well-made but old-fashioned clothes of black satin and worsted, with her white hair drawn back above her ears and gathered in a knot at the back of her head, and a scrubbed complexion untouched by cosmetics, she might have time-travelled to shabby wartime London from the Victorian age, or its New England equivalent. She insists on seeing Henry straight away, though Theodora warns her that he may be confused – earlier that day he has been under the impression he is in Cork. 'Why

Cork?' Mrs James wonders aloud. 'He was there only once in his life, years ago.' Theodora leads her into the dimly lit bedroom and hangs back respectfully by the door. 'You may leave us, Miss Bosanquet,' Mrs James says in a tone that is more like an order than an invitation. Henry lies on his back with the coverlet pulled up to his chin and tucked under his arms. He has been freshly shaved in his sister-in-law's honour and his big oval head glimmers on the pillow like a gibbous moon haloed by cloud. The lid of one eye droops, half-shut. He raises a hand feebly and holds it out as she approaches the bed.

'Henry!'

'Alice!'

That she happened to have the same Christian name as her husband's sister was always a cause of confused reference in a family already burdened with several generations of Williams and Henrys. She bends and kisses him on the forehead, wondering if he knows which Alice she is. 'I don't dare to think of what you have come through to get here,' he says, a remark which implies that he does know, though 'here' might as well mean Cork as Chelsea. But he seems pleased to see her and holds her hand for some minutes, as if comforted by its touch. In fact, she has come through severe Atlantic storms as well as the threat of U-boats to get here, but nothing would have stopped her, for she promised William when he was dying that she would go to his brother when he was in the same extremity. She is sixty-six years of age, but stout in mind and body, and she has had a lifetime's experience of looking after the illness-prone Jameses. Before falling asleep in the guest bedroom that night she recalls that Henry stopped in Cork on his way back to England from attending his mother's last illness and funeral in 1882, so perhaps there is a connection between Cork and death in his disordered brain. Her husband, the great psychologist who coined the phrase 'stream of consciousness', would have been interested in this example of the association of ideas, and she wishes she could tell him about it.

Mrs James makes it clear the next day that she is taking over command of the household. This is her right, but there is a certain abrasiveness about her manner of doing so which is hurtful to Theodora. In fact Alice is somewhat paranoid about protecting the privacy and dignity of the family, and thinks Theodora has been presumptuous in acting as if she were one of them since Henry's stroke. She resents Theodora's occasional references to her employer as 'HJ' rather than 'Mr James', and particularly disapproves of her correspondence with the notorious Edith Wharton, which Theodora unwisely mentioned.

So Theodora is given to understand that her attendance in the flat is no longer required unless requested for secretarial duties. She considers this treatment unjust, but conceals her hurt feelings. She continues to call daily at the flat to enquire about HJ's health, and to see him if appropriate, observing increasing signs of strain in the household on these occasions. Mrs James annoys the nurses by interfering in their care of the patient, and she lacks an easy manner with the English servants. Meanwhile HJ's condition continues to decline, mentally and physically. He thinks he is in Cork again, or Dublin or Edinburgh or New York, and when assured that he is in London he accuses his attendants of being in a conspiracy to deceive him. There are intervals when he seems to acknowledge that he is suffering from delusions, but only to exchange one delusion for another.

'Will my madness affect the house, do you think?' he asks Mrs James one day, raising his head from the pillow and clutching her arm anxiously.

'Do you mean Lamb House, Henry?'

'No, no,' he says, shaking his head impatiently. 'The *house!* The *house!* If the gallery should find out . . .' He lets his head fall back with an expression of extreme apprehension on his face, and she realises that he imagines he is in a theatre.

A few days before Christmas Theodora calls when Mrs James is resting and no nurse is on duty, and takes the opportunity to look in on the patient. He is asleep, awkwardly splayed among cushions and pillows and disordered bedclothes, with his head lolling sideways like an abandoned puppet and his bare feet sticking out from under the blanket. His unshaven face is haggard and his feet are cold to the touch. She wonders, as she rearranges the bedclothes and covers his feet, whether he will live to see the New Year.

Christmas is a dismal feast that year for most people in Britain. It is the second one of the war, and its approach revives ironic memories of a confident phrase bandied about in August 1914. '"*It'll all be over by Christmas*" – remember that?' Burgess says to Minnie and Joan as they sit round the kitchen table. 'Some 'opes!' Every day he scans *The Times*, still being delivered to the flat even though Mr James is beyond taking any interest in it, for news of the war. The news is not encouraging. The Gallipoli campaign has come to an ignominious end with the withdrawal of the Allied forces – their smoothly executed evacuation is the only thing in the whole sorry business that has gone according to plan. On the Western Front the big autumn campaigns have stalled in the mud with hardly any significant gains of territory, and the exhausted armies are digging in for the winter and counting their casualties. Half a million British servicemen dead, missing and wounded since the War began, the Prime Minister said, replying to a question in Parliament. 'You were one of 'em, Burgess,' says Minnie. 'Aye, one of the lucky ones,' he says grimly. Food, though not yet rationed, is in short supply and expensive. Joan Anderson complains that she doesn't see how she is supposed to make a Christmas pudding without raisins, though she has been promised a goose for Christmas dinner by paying an outrageous premium to the poulterer.

As it happens they scarcely have time to enjoy their dinner. On Christmas Day the patient's condition takes a new and alarming turn: he becomes restless as well as confused and keeps trying to get out of bed. When they attempt to restrain him he grows angry and abusive. Boxing Day is worse. He insists on being moved into the sitting room, and once Burgess and Minnie get him there, half carrying, half dragging him with his arms draped round their shoulders, he keeps wanting to change his place from one chair to another. He is a heavy man and nearly dead weight. When Theodora calls in the evening she finds the nurse having hysterics in the passage, Noakes and Kidd prostrate in the kitchen, and Mrs James alone in a corner of the sitting room with signs of panic in her eyes. Mrs James complains that she asked Dr Des Voeux to give Henry enough morphine to sedate him, but he refused.

The following day, however, things improve. A couch with wheels fixed to its feet is delivered to the flat on the resourceful doctor's instructions, and by this means Henry is easily moved from the bedroom to the sitting room. Burgess pushes the couch up to the window so that he can look out at the boats and barges plying up and down the brown waters of the river. It is a view he has always loved and he seems to find it soothing, so it becomes a daily routine to move him to the window. He gazes out for hour after hour, silent and apparently quite content, with Burgess sitting quietly beside him, occasionally offering him a drink of lemon and barley water, or feeding him soup from a bowl – 'Just like a nurse,' Minnie reports to Joan Anderson. 'Fact 'e's more gentle with Mr James than them regular nurses, if you ask me.'

Minnie always liked Burgess, ever since she was taken on at Lamb House in 1905, but their relationship was different in those days. She was twenty-three and he claimed to be nineteen, but he looked much younger, because of his short stature and fresh, open, snub-nosed face, and he was still called the house-boy then, his job being to clean shoes, knives, doorsteps, windows, run errands and make himself generally useful. In the hierarchy of the servants he was under Mrs Paddington who was housekeeper then, and about equal with herself as parlourmaid, her own greater age and more mature appearance being balanced by his sex and longer service in the household. Their relationship was a bantering, teasing, competitive one at first, like elder sister and younger brother. But in the years that followed Mr James began to groom Burgess to be his man-servant – bought him suits of clothes, taught him how to shave him, how to choose and pack his clothes when he went away, gave him books to read to improve his mind, and relieved him of the more menial jobs around the house. Burgess became more polite in his speech and manners – especially when he was on duty – and Mr James became more and more dependent on him for managing the practicalities of life. When Mr James went to America in 1910, with his ailing brother and Mrs James, Burgess went with him, and when he came back months later he was a man of the world, correct and confident in everything he did, and somehow more handsome. He became in effect butler as well as valet, and the tacitly acknowledged head of the servants. Minnie admired him and strove always to impress him with her work, but she didn't realise she loved him until he went off to join the 5th Battalion of the Royal Sussex in August 1914.

Standing on the doorstep of Lamb House beside Mrs Anderson and watching Burgess walk away down the cobbled hill with Mr James, who was going to see him off at the station, it was suddenly borne in upon her that she might never see him again, and the thought was unbearable. At that moment Burgess turned and waved cheerily at them, and Minnie waved back but burst into tears and couldn't stop crying for the rest of the day, so that Mrs Anderson told her to get a grip on herself. While Burgess was away she wrote to him regularly, giving him the news of Rye and London and the household, and got back short, cheerful, grateful replies in which however there was never a trace of tender sentiment. He said she would be tickled to know that the other lads in his platoon thought he must have a sweetheart back home to be getting so many letters in such a nice round hand. When the news came, back in May, that he was wounded she nearly fainted, but when it appeared that he was not too badly hurt and had got leave to look after Mr James she was overjoyed, rehearsing in her mind the moment when he would walk through the door and she would throw her arms round the returning hero. But when the moment came Mr James was there, and Joan Anderson too, and Minnie had to be content with a handshake and a kiss on the cheek.

Looking after Mr James has certainly brought them closer together, especially since he had the strokes, and Burgess is always kind and appreciative towards her and tells her they make 'a good team', but he has never shown a sign of romantic interest. Is this, she wonders, because she is not pretty enough, or because she is older than him (though nobody could tell, now, to look at them), or because he thinks her greater height would make them look ridiculous as a couple (he made a joke to her once about such an ill-matched pair of lovers who they saw from the sitting-room window down on the Embankment)? Or is it because, like the man in Mr James's story, he simply hasn't noticed that she loves him?

In the late evening of New Year's Eve Mrs James summons the servants to the sitting room. She asks Burgess to make sure the nurse is in the master bedroom, and that the door of the sitting room is firmly shut. Then she tells them she was privately informed a few days ago that Mr James is going to be awarded the Order of Merit in the New Year's Honours List. It will be in *The Times* the next morning. Till then the information is confidential, and she has decided not to tell Mr James himself until it can be talked about openly, in case he should get over-excited. A very old friend of his, the writer Edmund Gosse, who knows about the award, has asked if he could have the privilege of telling Mr James the good news and he would be calling early tomorrow morning for that purpose.

'Excuse me, Mrs James,' says Burgess, after a pause. 'But this Order of Merit . . . Is it a medal, like?'

'I understand it's a very high honour, recommended by the Prime Minister to the King,' says Mrs James. At the word 'King' a little tremor of excitement passes through her audience. 'Something like a knighthood, but without the "Sir" attached,' she goes on, in a cool, almost off-hand tone of voice. Her own feelings about the news are ambivalent. As an American and a republican she regards all royal patronage with suspicion, and like most members of her family she deplored Henry's decision to exchange his American citizenship for British. On the other hand she cannot but take pride in what is obviously a very exceptional public recognition of her brother-in-law's achievements. Looking at the eager interested faces before her she allows herself a smile of tribal satisfaction. 'Mr Gosse told me it is actually *more* distinguished than a knighthood, because only twenty-four people can hold the Order of Merit at any one time.'

'Well, jolly good for Mr James, I say!' Burgess exclaims, grinning broadly, and Joan and Minnie murmur their agreement.

Back in the kitchen they excitedly discuss the news.

'I think she should have told him,' says Joan Anderson. 'Suppose he died tonight.'

'Oh, don't say it!' says Minnie.

'The old toff isn't going to pop off yet,' says Burgess. 'I just hope he can take it in, when they tell him tomorrow. Anyway, we ought to drink to his health, eh? What do you fancy, Mrs Anderson?'

Joan says she always enjoys a glass of port. Minnie, who seldom indulges in alcoholic drinks, thinks it safest to follow suit. Burgess goes to the pantry and brings back a bottle of vintage port, and scotch whisky for himself. 'We can see the New Year in at the same time,' he says.

Joan Anderson lays out some biscuits and cheese and pickle while Burgess pours the drinks. They sit round the table and raise their glasses as Burgess says: 'To Mr James, God bless him.' Minnie feels a warm glow spread through her whole body as she sips the heavy crimson wine. Relaxed by the whisky, Burgess reminisces about his years of service with Mr James, his experiences in America, and in the great country houses of England. Even the usually taciturn Joan Anderson becomes almost skittish. 'You didn't have a moustache in those days, Burgess,' she says after one anecdote. 'It suits you.' 'Aye,' he says, with a chuckle. 'When the battalion was marching from Calais to the front all ranks was ordered to grow moustaches. I reckon it was to make us look older – most of the lads was quite young, you see, years younger'n me. Some of 'em looked like school-boys. Well, I was finding the marching hard going, I don't mind telling you, what with my short legs, but I had no trouble growing a moustache in under a week. I out-moustached them all!' He chuckles.

'Your legs ain't so short, Burgess,' Minnie blurts out, and then blushes furiously.

He glances curiously at her. 'Well, there's advantages in being short in a trench,' he says. 'You're less likely to show your head over the top when you get up on the fire step.'

'So how was you wounded, then?' Minnie asks boldly.

'Well, that were a mortar bomb.' He mimes with his hand the steep trajectory of a mortar round, up high in the air and down again. 'You can't duck one of them if they get the range right. You can hear it coming in but you don't have time to move.'

He has never said so much about his war experiences before. Minnie is eager to hear more, but Burgess changes the subject. It is nearly midnight, and at his suggestion they creep into the sitting room (Mrs James has gone to bed, and the night nurse is dozing beside her patient in the master bedroom), turn out the lights and open the sash windows so that they will hear the clocks striking twelve. It takes a little while for their eyes to accommodate to the darkness. The gaslamps along Chelsea Embankment are dim because of the lighting restrictions, and the vessels moving up and down the river show only navigation lights. The silhouette of the Albert Bridge, downstream to their left, outlined with electric light bulbs in peacetime, is scarcely visible. At intervals the doors of the King's Head and Eight Bells pub on the corner of Cheyne Walk and Cheyne Row open and shut, expelling a gust of voices and piano music into the damp night air. Licensing hours have been extended according to tradition, in spite of official concern about the effect of excessive drinking on the war effort (according to *The Times*, the Royal Family have given up alcohol for the duration). Looking down at the little public garden that separates the entrance of Carlyle Mansions from the Embankment, Minnie sees pairs of lovers taking advantage of the darkness, embracing under the leafless trees. She moves closer to Burgess until she is brushing against him, willing him to put his arm around her waist, but he doesn't take advantage of the opportunity. The church clocks begin to chime midnight – from Chelsea behind their backs, from Battersea across the river, and faintly but distinctly in the background they hear the gong-like sound of Big Ben.

'Happy New Year, Joan!' says Burgess, and kisses her gallantly on the cheek. He turns to salute Minnie in the same manner, but she gives him a hug and angles her head to kiss him on the mouth, feeling the soft cushion of his moustache yield against her lips and his body stiffen in surprise.

'Happy New Year, Burgess,' she gasps, and hurries from the room.

Edmund Gosse, versatile man of letters, poet, critic, essayist, translator, recently retired Librarian to the House of Lords, who has known Henry James for thirty-five years, calls as arranged, a little after ten the next morning.

'Happy New Year, Kidd,' he says as she takes his hat and gloves in the hall, and helps him off with his grey overcoat. His suit is grey, matching his grey hair and drooping grey moustache. But for the bright blue eyes behind his steel-rimmed spectacles he might be an incarnation of the fog rising from the river outside.

'Thank you, sir. And the same to you, sir.'

'You know why I've come so early?'

'Oh yes! But I don't know as whether he'll understand you, sir,' Minnie says. 'He's very poorly this morning. Barely conscious, you might say.'

'That's a shame.'

Minnie shows him into the master bedroom. For the sake of James's lungs the curtains are drawn as insulation against the cold damp air outside, and a single shaded table lamp is the only illumination. It is so dark in the room that Gosse has almost to grope his way to the bedside. The author is lying on his back, breathing heavily, his eyes shut.

'Is he asleep?' Gosse whispers to Minnie. There is no nurse on duty today.

'Perhaps, sir. It's hard to tell sometimes.'

Gosse stoops over the recumbent form. 'Henry, this is Edmund – can you hear me?' he says, in a tone that he tries to make both quiet and penetrating. 'Great news. They've given you the O.M.' No change of expression on the sunken features indicates that the message has been received. 'Congratulations, my dear chap,' Gosse adds. The face remains impassive. Gosse looks at Minnie. Minnie shrugs. In the silence of the room they hear the foghorns lowing mournfully to each other on the river. A little dispirited by this anticlimax to his announcement Gosse exits quietly from the bedroom, while Minnie stays behind to adjust the bedclothes. As the door closes behind Gosse, the author opens his eyes and murmurs: 'Turn out the light, Kidd, and spare my blushes.'

Later in the day James shows more animation, as messages of congratulation pour into the flat, by telegram, telephone, and special delivery. Theodora Bosanquet calls to deliver her congratulations in person and shares the lift to the fourth floor with a boy from the telegraph office who has a great sheaf of telegrams for Flat 21 in his leather satchel. She helps Mrs James open the envelopes and read out the messages – for there is a temporary truce between the two ladies in the excitement of the hour. The names are a roll-call of Henry James's wide and distinguished acquaintance, especially in the world of letters: Rudyard Kipling, Thomas Hardy, George Bernard Shaw, J. M. Barrie, Hugh Walpole, Arnold Bennett, Max Beerbohm, Mrs Humphry Ward . . . The telegrams, letters and discarded envelopes litter the counterpane of James's bed. He sits up, propped by pillows, smiling benignly above the mound of paper like (it occurs to Theodora) a Buddha receiving the written petitions of his worshippers.

Not all the names receive a pleased nod of recognition. The name of H. G. Wells draws a frown – the wound inflicted by his *Boon*, a satirical *jeu d'esprit* published earlier that year, with its cruel caricature of HJ's late style (*'It is a magnificent but painful hippopotamus resolved at any cost, even at the cost of its dignity, upon picking up a pea which has got into a corner of its den'*), has not healed. Theodora is unsurprised, having typed HJ's hurt letters to the younger writer, whom he had previously counted a friend and admirer. But it is another name that provokes the strongest negative reaction, and the biggest surprise, when Theodora reads it out: *'Warmest congratulations on your much deserved honour. I am proud to have been the producer of Guy Domville, even though it was not a success. Sir George Alexander.'*

James's face darkens, his brow beetles, the sparse hairs on his head seem to bristle. He positively scowls. 'Alexander,' he says quite distinctly, 'is a shit.'

The two ladies glance at each other in dismay. Never, ever, has either of them heard Henry James utter this word, or anything remotely comparable in crude indecency. It is a measure of his mental deterioration that he should use it in their presence. In fact it is hard to believe that he has ever used it before in any company. Perhaps he overheard the word as he passed a group of rough men loitering at a street corner, or in the smoking room of some club less respectable than his own Reform, and, buried in his memory, it has risen to his lips unimpeded by the filter of his usual fastidious manners. Or perhaps it was a verbal slip, replacing some other intended word. Or perhaps he didn't utter it at all – perhaps they misheard him. The two ladies are just about to make a tacit contract to ignore the offending expletive, when he says: 'A treacherous shit.'

'Henry!' Mrs James exclaims. 'For shame! Such shocking language.'

Henry seems indifferent to the reproof. Theodora hastens to find some distraction from this unhappy interruption to the flow of good will. 'Here's another,' she says, ripping open an envelope. 'Let's see who it's from . . . Gerald Du Maurier! *"Heartiest congratulations, the Governor would have been delighted."*'

'Du Maurier's dead,' says Henry.

'No, no, Henry,' says Mrs James. 'That was your old friend, George Du Maurier. This is from his son, I presume.'

'Yes, Gerald, the actor,' Theodora joins in. '"*The Governor*" must mean his father.'

'They said it was matter around the heart,' says Henry. 'But it was Trilby that was the matter.'

'That was George Du Maurier, Henry,' says Mrs James. 'This message is from his son Gerald.'

'You remember him, Mr James,' says Theodora. 'We met him one day about a year ago in Fortnum and Mason, and you talked about old times in Hampstead when he was a boy. He was Christmas shopping with his little girl, Daphne.'

'I don't recall a Daphne,' he says. 'There was Trixy, and Sylvia, and May. And two boys, Guy and . . . and Gerald. Gerald became an actor.'

'Yes, yes,' says Mrs James. 'It is he who has sent you the telegram, Henry.'

'He was the original Captain Hook, if I am not mistaken,' says Henry.

'Very good!' Theodora claps her hands.

'Tick tock,' says Henry, with a strange leering grin. His drooping eyelid looks like a heavy wink.

'What does he mean?' says Mrs James.

'I believe it's an allusion to the crocodile in *Peter Pan*,' says Theodora.

'An awfully big adventure,' says Henry, and closes both his eyes.

'I think perhaps we should let him rest now,' says Mrs James.

In the hall, as Theodora is putting on her topcoat and her gloves preparatory to leaving, Mrs James says: 'I would be obliged, Miss Bosanquet, if you would forget that my brother-in-law ever uttered that word.'

'Of course, Mrs James. I will expunge it from my memory. He was not himself.'

'Quite so . . . But the telegram from the Alexander man was tactless. There was a very unpleasant episode at the first night of *Guy Domville*. Did you know?'

'Well, I have heard it spoken of,' says Theodora. 'We never discussed the matter.'

'Henry blamed Alexander for it. He wrote to William at the time, that they were the most horrible hours of his life. Those were his very words. *"The most horrible hours of my life."* I'm afraid I thought to myself, well Henry, if that's the worst thing you experience in life, you'll be lucky.'

'But it's hard for authors,' says Theodora. 'They have to put up with being criticised all the time. And when the criticism is especially rude or unfair, then . . .' She left the sentence unfinished.

'I know all about that,' says Mrs James. 'I was married to one.'

'It's strange how his memory comes and goes,' says Theodora, pulling on her sensible calfskin gloves. She notes a split seam on the left-hand one which needs to be repaired. 'The way he rattled off the names of all those Du Mauriers . . . I wonder what he meant by saying – about George Du Maurier – "Trilby was the matter".'

'I don't know, I'm sure,' says Mrs James. 'It was the most tremendous success in its day – in America, anyway. Henry was very attached to him, I believe, but William could never understand what he saw in the little man.'

Minnie approaches to open the front door for Theodora.

'You look pale, Kidd,' says Mrs James. 'Are you unwell?'

'Quite well, thank you, ma'am. I was up late last night.'

'It's probably all the excitement,' says Theodora with a smile. She extends her hand to Mrs James. 'Good afternoon, Mrs James. It's been a great day. Thank you for letting me share it.'

'Good afternoon, Miss Bosanquet,' says Mrs James, shaking her hand without warmth.

Minnie shuts the door behind Theodora.

'I am going to my room to rest, Kidd,' says Mrs James. 'I'm exhausted.'

'Yes, ma'am.'

'Ask Burgess to sit with Mr James. He seems to like to find Burgess there when he wakes up.'

'Yes, ma'am,' says Minnie.

PART TWO

I

IN the 1880s, if he was in town on a Sunday and the weather was dry, he would often walk from his rooms in Bolton Street, Piccadilly, or later from his more commodious *quatrième* in De Vere Gardens, South Kensington, up to the heights of Hampstead, to visit George Du Maurier. Their acquaintance had begun much earlier – indeed on Henry's side it had begun before they ever met, as he liked to explain to the Du Maurier children, who listened politely to his elucidation of this paradox. A mutual friend has shown him some of their father's illustrations in the magazine *Once a Week* as early as 1862, when he was a student at the Harvard Law School. He had been much taken with them, and followed with keen interest and appreciation the artist's subsequent progress, especially his drawings for *Punch*, in which the Du Maurier children often figured, sometimes identified by their real names. 'So you see, my dear Trixy,' (or my dear Guy, or my dear Sylvia, or whoever it was he happened to be addressing) he would say, 'I met you all in the pages of *Punch* – met you two-dimensionally as it were – long before I saw you in the, ah – in person. And on that – on that memorable – on that *auspicious* day, you were all just as I expected – though a little bit more grown up, of course. Only Chang looked exactly the same as in his pictures – and he still does, you know.' Chang was the family's giant St Bernard, who also made occasional appearances in Du Maurier's drawings.

'It's all right for Chang,' Gerald grumbled when it was his turn to receive this reminiscence. 'He didn't have to go to school and get ragged silly because somebody found a picture of him as a tiddler in skirts in an old copy of *Punch*.'

'Yes,' said Henry, smiling sympathetically through his beard, 'I can see that might be an embarrassment. Schoolboys are not the most sensitive – the most tactful . . . But when you grow up, Gerald, you will appreciate what a fine thing it is to be immortalised in the pages of *Punch*, even as – what was that delightful expression? A "tiddler in skirts".' Later in the day he identified the cartoon the boy was probably referring to, framed and hanging in the entrance hall of New Grove House, which was a kind of private gallery of the artist's work. Entitled 'Delicate Consideration', it depicted the Du Maurier children in the back garden, holding on to each other's waists, one behind the other in graduated order of height and senior-ity, and Trixy was explaining to Mamma: *'We're playing at railway trains. I'm the engine and Guy's a first class carriage and Sylvia's a second class carriage, and May's a third class carriage, and Gerald, he's a third class carriage too – that is, he's really only a* truck *you know, only you mustn't tell him so, as he would be offended.'*

Punch had always occupied a privileged place in Henry's conscious-ness. His mental images of England and the English were first formed by the creased and dog-eared back numbers he and William pored over as boys in New York. When he was taken to England for the first time since infancy, at the age of twelve, and looked about him, his eye had already been trained by the woodcuts of Leech. By the time he returned as a young man, *Punch*, its pictorial range now extended by Keene and Du Maurier, was his guide, his Baedeker and Bradshaw, for the interpretation and negotiation of English social life. Experience soon revealed its limitations for this purpose, but Du Maurier's cartoons – the drawings rather than the sometimes ponder-ous text beneath them – recorded a fine-grained satirical observa-tion of social behaviour that Henry found helpful and suggestive as, shifting his base restlessly between America and Europe in the 1870s, he developed his own 'international' fiction of manners. When he visualised his English characters, when he dressed them and had them sit down and stand up and walk about and converse in various public and domestic settings, his mental images were often in black and white, as if one of Du Maurier's tableaux had come to life. Du Maurier understood perfectly how dress and décor told you a person's class or caste, while their features and posture gave you their individual characters. It was this tension between conformity and individuality, expressed in line and shading, that was the secret of Du Maurier's art – and perhaps, Henry sometimes thought, of the man himself.

It wasn't until 1878, two years after he had decided irrevocably to make his literary career in London, that they actually met, at one of the notorious one hundred and seven evening engagements he accepted that winter. Henry was amused to discover that the draughtsman whose figures – especially his upper-class beauties and their escorts – seemed to be growing taller and taller by the week in the pages of *Punch*, was himself quite short and slight in stature. He held himself straight and squared his shoulders to make the most of his inches, and in every other respect he was a good-looking man, with delicately chiselled features, flared nostrils, and a mop of soft wavy hair that the balding Henry could only envy. He wore a wispy moustache and imperial that seemed to fit his name and profession. His natural expression in repose was rather melancholy, but in company he was always smiling and animated. The two men took to each other, on that and subsequent occasions when they met. Du Maurier was commissioned, at Henry's suggestion, to illustrate the magazine serialisation of *Washington Square* in 1880. The drawings were deemed disappointing by the publishers, and in truth by the novelist himself. But it had been a misconceived project – Du Maurier was out of his natural element with a story set in New York, which he had never seen. Henry felt partly responsible for the failure, and his anxiety to smooth the waters ruffled by this little contretemps only served to bring the two men closer together. He had long entertained the idea of writing an article for one of the magazines about Du Maurier's work, and asked if he might call on the artist to discuss it with him, a proposal that elicited a prompt invitation to New Grove House. After a very agreeable summer's day, spent looking through portfolios in the morning and rambling over the Heath in the afternoon, Henry was urged to call on any Sunday thereafter without formality. As the Du Mauriers lived so far out of town, they made themselves available to their friends in this way, and expected to feed them.

Sunday suited Henry very well for these excursions, a day when he could put his work aside without a guilty conscience, and the London streets were less crowded and noisy than on weekdays. It was a long walk, and entailed more walking later, but he needed the exercise to combat the effects of a sedentary occupation and a slightly alarming tendency to corpulence that manifested itself in early middle age. His route took him though Mayfair or Bayswater to Baker Street and St John's Wood. From the Swiss Cottage he mounted the long unremitting incline of Fitzjohn's Avenue, which had been almost a country road when he first trod it as a young man, but had since become hemmed with mostly hideous villas of raw red brick. It was always a pleasure to reach the quaint, crooked lanes of Hampstead village, and to thread one's way through them for the last few steep furlongs to New Grove House, which like so many things in England called 'new' was actually quite old – about a hundred years old.

The house had been rather clumsily extended halfway through this lifespan, and consequently had an odd, piebald appearance, half Georgian cream stucco and half Victorian brown brick. Its exterior was more pretentious than the interior warranted, and it possessed virtually no grounds – just a walled backyard with a patch of grass that hardly deserved the name of garden. The open, breezy expanses of the Heath, however, were only ten minutes' walk away. The great attraction of the house for Du Maurier was manifestly the large, light-saturated drawing room that he used as his studio. There was nothing selfish in this annexation because he liked to have his family around him as he worked. The children when they were young had romped and rolled around the floor under his feet as he stood at his drawing board, and thus found their way into his pictures. In the evenings after dinner Emma would read to him or play the piano as he put in a few more hours, smoking cigarette after cigarette. Visitors were received there. It was the social centre of the house.

Henry, having breakfasted well, and perhaps paused on his way for some light refreshment, would time his arrival at New Grove House for early afternoon, when it was Du Maurier's custom to take his Sunday constitutional on the Heath. Off they would go together, perhaps with some of the children, perhaps with another visitor, certainly with a dog – Chang, or his diminutive successor the terrier, Don – down the hill and on to the Heath, past the ponds, past the place where in summer the donkeys waited patiently to give rides to children, and then wander as their inclination, or the dog's wagging tail, took them, perhaps towards the Spaniards Road, where Du Maurier, in obedience to some superstitious private ritual, had to touch the last tree with his stick before turning home, or perhaps to Parliament Hill, where they would look down on the London plain, picking out the landmark buildings of Westminster and the City piercing the haze of coal smoke. Then, as their shadows lengthened, they returned to New Grove House for dinner, a classic English joint of beef or mutton which Emma ensured was big enough to feed casual visitors and which Du Maurier – always last to arrive in the dining room, announcing his approach with a distant fanfare on the piano – deftly carved at the head of the table. After the meal there would be conversation and music-making and parlour games in the studio-drawing-room. At about ten Henry would leave and Du Maurier invariably insisted on accompanying him. 'I'll see you on your way,' he would say, 'just to the top of Fitzjohn's,' and when they got to the Avenue, 'just a little further,' and usually he ended up keeping Henry company as far as the Swiss Cottage, and sometimes even on the Atlas omnibus to Baker Street (for he delighted like a child to ride on top of an omnibus) before turning back to climb the long hill home.

Their acquaintance began at a time when Henry's social and artistic horizons were rapidly expanding. His second novel, *The American*, had made an impression on both sides of the Atlantic in 1877, and the novella *Daisy Miller* was a palpable 'hit' in 1879. The appearance of *Washington Square* and *The Portrait of a Lady* a couple of years later consolidated his claim to be the coming man of the literary novel in the English-speaking world. His elegant, cosmopolitan essays appeared in the most prestigious reviews. Hostesses competed for his presence at their dinners and soirées. His diary was always full. Only by fleeing occasionally to France or Italy could he escape the relentless pressure of London social life. So, as he himself was aware, it was a cause of puzzlement and even jealousy on the part of some of his friends that he gave so much of his time to the Du Mauriers, who were neither rich nor 'smart' nor dazzlingly clever. Poor Emma was certainly none of those things, and aspired to be nothing more than a comely, caring wife and mother. Du Maurier himself was good for light repartee at a dinner table, or a musical evening at home, but he was not intellectual; indeed, he was something of a philistine in cultural matters, constantly sniping at the Aesthetes in his cartoons from the conservative ramparts of *Punch*. Henry knew all this, but didn't care. He liked Du Maurier, he liked his family, and he liked spending Sundays with them.

On that first visit to Hampstead, during the leisurely walk they took on the Heath after lunch, with only Chang for company, Du Maurier related to Henry the principal events of his life, and a very interesting story it was, with elements of mystery, romance, pathos, and a precarious triumph over adversity. The mystery was mainly to do with his origins and name. His paternal grandfather had been a French *gentilhomme verrier* – that is, as his grandson was at pains to point out, a gentleman with a glassblowing business, not a mere artisan. His name was Busson, but at some stage of his life he attached to it the name of Du Maurier, which belonged to an aristocratic estate to which he had a never-realised claim. He had to flee to England at the time of the Revolution to escape the guillotine, but returned to France after the defeat of Napoleon. His son Louis-Mathurin, George's father, met and married his English wife, Ellen Clarke, in Paris, though how her family came to be living there Henry never quite understood. George Du Maurier was brought up in the Parisian suburb of Passy, with frequent trips to visit relatives in England, and had happy memories of an idyllic early childhood. But Louis-Mathurin was an inventor and entrepreneur whose schemes never prospered, and he gradually frittered away his fortune. The development of a patent carbide lamp proved a particularly expensive and fruitless venture. He moved his operations to London, leaving his family in France for long periods, but had no better luck there.

'It was *maman* who held the family together,' said Du Maurier. 'She had the stronger character. My father was charming and had a delightful voice – he could have been an opera singer – but he was no scientist and no businessman. Unfortunately he tried to pass his own misconceived ambitions on to me. When I failed my *bachot* at the Sorbonne – I was plucked in Latin – he sent me to University College London to study chemistry. Can you imagine me as a chemist?'

'No,' said Henry truthfully.

'Well, my very first employment was testing samples for gold in a Cornish mine,' said Du Maurier. 'But it didn't last long. There was no gold. You could say it was a sign, that I would never make my fortune in commerce, any more than my father had. What I really wanted to be was an artist. I was always sketching, even as a child, on scraps of paper, on the backs of letters, in the margins of my school books . . . any blank white space was an irresistible invitation to fill it with figures and faces. When Father died, in London – he died in my arms, murmuring the words of a drinking song, I'm sorry to say – we returned to Paris, and my mother agreed that I should study art there. It was the best possible place to do so, at the time. I'm not sure it is any more, with these slapdash Impressionists setting the fashion, but in those days the English academies were stuffy, reactionary places. You had to spend three years drawing plaster casts before you were allowed to draw and paint from life. Three whole years! And even then there were all kinds of prudish restrictions. In Paris it was quite different – they had the *atelier* system. You enrolled at an established artist's studio – I went to Gleyre's – and joined a crowd of other young hopefuls grouped around the model, drawing and painting for all they were worth, day in and day out. On Fridays old Gleyre himself came in and criticised your work, but basically you learned by doing it, or you discovered you didn't have the stuff in you. There was rivalry, of course, and rough horseplay, and a fair amount of dissipation, but there was also tremendous comradeship. We were all poor as church mice, but wine was cheap and you could get a decent dinner for a franc. Some of the friends I met then made a name for themselves later – Tom Armstrong,

Jimmy Whistler . . . A few of us got together and rented a studio of our own on Rue Notre Dame des Champs where we could live cheaply and paint all the hours God gave us.'

'It sounds like *Scènes de la Vie de Bohème*,' Henry remarked.

'Exactly!' said Du Maurier – then seemed to want to qualify his endorsement. 'Murger exaggerated some things, of course. But he was pretty near the mark. Morals were loose in Montparnasse, it can't be denied. But I kept in mainly with English chums – and the odd American, like Jimmy Whistler. We had higher standards than the French, and took more exercise. They thought we were very eccentric, exercising with dumbbells or swinging on the trapeze when they would rather be lounging in a café and flirting with the barmaids.'

'The trapeze!' Henry exclaimed.

'Yes, we had one in the studio, hung from a beam in the ceiling . . . Anyway, after a year or so of this life, enjoyable as it was, I felt the need of a little more, what shall I say . . . discipline. So I enrolled in the Academy in Antwerp, which had a very fine reputation then. Alma-Tadema was a contemporary of mine there, and Felix Moscheles. At first all went swimmingly, and then . . . the great disaster happened. The worst thing that can happen to an artist – or the next to worst.'

'My dear fellow,' Henry said compassionately, grasping Du Maurier by the arm, and guiding him to a nearby bench, for the subject seemed too grave for an ambulant conversation. 'I believe I know what you refer to. Someone told me of your dreadful – your cruel misfortune.'

Du Maurier nodded gloomily. An awful shadow had come across his face as he relived the moment. Even Chang, noticing that the two men had sat down, loped back from a thicket he was investigating and lay at his master's feet, looking up at him with every appearance of sympathy. 'I was drawing from a model one day. I glanced up from my board – and suddenly the girl's head seemed to dwindle to the size of a walnut. I covered my left eye with my hand, and the head returned to normal size. Then I covered my right eye and realised that I'd lost the sight of the left one. It was a detached retina. An irreversible condition – and the eye doctor I consulted warned me that the same thing could happen to the other eye. You can imagine how cheerful I felt at that bit of news.'

'My dear fellow,' Henry murmured again.

Du Maurier took from his pocket a small enamel case in which he kept the rather disreputable-looking cigarettes that he rolled himself, extracted one, lit it with a safety match, and blew a plume of smoke into the air. 'I'll spare you the details of the next few years of my life, going from doctor to doctor, desperately anxious to preserve what sight I had as long as possible. I moved from Antwerp to Malines, from Malines to Düsseldorf, to be near the men who were most highly recommended. One of them nearly blinded me with his treatments. I tried to keep up my painting, but I was afraid to overstrain my good eye. I was idle a good deal of the time, I'm afraid, idle and depressed. There were times when I seriously contemplated suicide. The only thing that saved me was meeting Emma, by chance, in Düsseldorf, when she was on holiday there. I'd first met her years before in London, when she was only twelve, a schoolfriend of my sister's, but I'd been struck by her looks then. Now she was a blooming young woman. We fell in love – but it seemed a hopeless case. I had no money and no prospects. Then Tom Armstrong, bless him, paid me a visit in Düsseldorf and gave me some sound advice. "You'll never be a first-rate painter with only one eye, Du Maurier," he said, "but you could be a damn fine draughtsman in black and white, and there's money to be made in that line in England, with all the illustrated magazines we have now." He happened to have with him a copy of the *Punch Almanac*, and he showed it to me. That was in '59 or '60. It was full of fine things by Leech and Keene. I saw what could be done with the medium, and I thought I could learn to do it. So I went to London, bunked with Jimmy Whistler till I found a place of my own, and taught myself how to draw on a block. My one aim was to earn enough tin to marry on. Emma's parents were not keen to allow the engagement – understandably, I suppose – and to persuade them I foolishly undertook to save a thousand pounds before we married. I soon realised I had set myself an impossible task. After a while my prospective *beau-père* lowered the threshold to two hundred, but that was still a huge sum to a beginner like me. I peddled my wares from one editorial office to another, got some work from *Once a Week*—'

'Where I first saw it,' James interpolated.

'Yes, I did a good deal for them, mostly illustrations for the serials, but it wasn't very well paid, certainly not at first. I had my sights set on *Punch*, and a salaried position on the staff. I got my foot in the door, but for a long time no further. A few initials – decorative capital letters, you know – at fifteen shillings a go. One cartoon – not very well drawn, though I have a soft spot for it now. "The Photographer's Studio".'

'I remember it,' said Henry.

'Do you?' Du Maurier was gratified but surprised.

'I told you I followed you from the beginning,' said Henry. 'If I remember rightly, there's a rather overdressed, Jewish-looking photographer in his studio, and three young artists coming in through the door, smoking cigarettes, and he is telling them very pompously that they mustn't.'

'What a memory you have, James!' exclaimed Du Maurier, and proceeded to quote the caption, with appropriate accents: ' *"Please to remember, Gentlemen, that this is not a common Hartist's Studio." Dick Tinto and his friends, who are Common Artists, feel shut up by this little aristocratic distinction, which had not yet occurred to them.*' Du Maurier chuckled, enjoying his own joke. 'There was a lot of rot being talked then, of how photography would kill off the illustrator's trade, so there was some personal feeling behind it. Also I was always a friend of tobacco, you know. Or I should say it has always been a friend to me, from my miserable days as a chemistry student. Gerald says they should name a brand of cigarettes after me, I roll so many of them.'

Henry wondered privately whether the smoke in which his friend was so often wreathed might not be harmful to his one good eye. As if intuiting the unspoken thought, Du Maurier said: 'I've tried to give up, but I just can't work without the weed.'

'I resort to the occasional gasper, myself,' Henry confessed, 'when inspiration seems to fail.'

'Ah, but you're a very moderate man, James,' said Du Maurier, turning his head and regarding him with a smile.

'Am I?' he said, startled, and not altogether delighted by this characterisation: 'moderate' did not sound sufficiently different to his ear from 'dull'.

'As far as my observation goes, I've never met a man so moderate in all his appetites. You enjoy the good things of life, but never to excess. Food, drink, tobacco . . .' He left the sentence unfinished.

'I have immoderate ambition,' said Henry.

'Do you? For what?'

'I want to be the Anglo-American Balzac,' Henry said, and immediately added: 'Please don't tell anybody I told you that.'

'My dear, chap, mum's the word. But why not? It's a perfectly honourable ambition.'

'Because the literary world is full of journalists and gossip, and it would be sure to get into print somewhere and make me an object of ridicule.'

'You can depend on me, of course. But I envy you, James. You have an ambition and still a hope of achieving it. You *will* achieve it, I'm sure. Whereas I wanted to be a great painter . . .'

'You're a great illustrator, and that's no mean achievement. As I hope to demonstrate in my article.'

'You're very kind, very kind,' Du Maurier murmured shyly. 'Shall we move on? Or perhaps it's time to return home for tea.'

'By all means,' said Henry. The two men rose to their feet, and Chang, having perhaps heard the familiar syllable 'home', led them off in the right direction without a further hint from Du Maurier. 'But you haven't told me,' said Henry, as he fell into step beside him, 'how you came to be married and a pillar of *Punch*. Which came first?'

'Oh, marriage. Otherwise I should probably be dead long ago, or locked up in a lunatic asylum somewhere. You know that painting by Arthur Hughes, *The Long Engagement*? I believe it's in the Birmingham Municipal Gallery now.'

'I very rarely go to Birmingham,' said Henry, 'and then only to change trains on my way to somewhere else.'

'Well, you must have seen engravings of it. There's this chap lean-ing up against a tree in a rather autumnal-looking wood and his sweetheart is clasping his hand and trying to comfort him. He's I suppose in his thirties, but looks prematurely aged. He's grey and haggard with worry and frustration and has on his face an expres-sion of utter hopelessness. The long engagement is obviously killing him. That was exactly me, in those days. Eventually I had a kind of breakdown, physical and mental – dreadful stomach pains and headaches, periods of total apathy and sudden fits of weeping. I went to see a doctor – he said 'Get married, and take a holiday.' Easier said than done – but we did it: persuaded Emma's old man that we had enough to live on, even if it was short of the magic figure of two hundred, and that my prospects were sound. In fact of course they weren't, far from it, but as soon as he caved in my health began to improve, and I did some of my best work just before and after the wedding. I began to be noticed and talked about, I got more work accepted by *Punch* . . . and then I had a stroke of luck at last – though I couldn't call it that. Leech died.'

'Ah, yes,' said Henry, who imagined in a flash the mixed emotions of the young Du Maurier on hearing the news. 'And so there was a vacant seat at the *Punch* table.'

'It was the strangest, awkwardest thing,' said Du Maurier, 'because I first got acquainted with Leech in the few months immediately before his death. Before that I knew him only by his work – I admired it enormously, of course, but with the arrogance of youth I thought I could do better, and I envied him his secure position. Then in the summer of '64 I met him in person, quite by chance, in Whitby of all places. I'd just finished doing the illustrations for *Sylvia's Lovers*, which is set there, you know, and Emma and I decided to take a holiday in the place, Elizabeth Gaskell had made it seem so pretty. And it *is* – perfectly charming. We're going back next month, as it happens, for a family holiday. You should join us, James – Lowell will be there – he's quite devoted to the place.'

Henry had introduced James Russell Lowell, the versatile man of letters who was now the United States Ambassador in London, to Du Maurier a year or two ago, and they had since become great friends. 'Thank you for the suggestion,' Henry said. 'It's always a pleasure to see Lowell, but my plans for August are already settled. You were saying – about Leech . . . ?'

'Yes, we met him on that first visit to Whitby – he happened to be staying there at the same time, trying to improve his health. He was in a bad way, worn out with financial worry and overwork – his wife was a fool, who insisted on living in a style above their means – but I liked him immensely. We went for walks together. He was a wonderful raconteur. But it was obvious that he was a sick man, and I couldn't suppress the thought that if he were to peg out, it would be my great chance to get on to *Punch* and have a regular salary at last. There was no other artist on the staff who was likely to retire in the foreseeable future – Tenniel and Keene were still in the prime of life. It seemed despicable to be thinking such a thing, as if I were wishing the poor man dead—'

'No, no,' Henry murmured. 'Anyone would have had the same thought in your situation.'

'I suppose so,' Du Maurier sighed. 'We all step into dead men's shoes, whether we are aware of it or not. But I was painfully conscious. Poor Leech was hardly cold before the *Punch* board offered me his place – they needed someone urgently to work on the new *Almanac*, you see. I went to his funeral with that confidential information in my pocket. Imagine! It was a very emotional occasion – he was greatly loved, and it seemed like the end of an era. Millais broke down completely, poor old Mark Lemon the same. I shed some tears myself – but then I thought of the letter of appointment in my pocket and I had to struggle to stop myself grinning all over my face in the middle of the service! It was horrible.'

'But you lived happily ever after,' said Henry, smiling.

'I wouldn't go so far as to say that,' said Du Maurier. 'I had hopes of being made editor when Taylor died in 1880, but the job went to Frank Burnand. He's there for life. It's an ambition I'll never achieve.'

'I understand your disappointment,' said Henry, 'but I venture to say that more people associate *Punch* with the name of Du Maurier than with the name Burnand.'

'It's kind of you to say so, James,' said Du Maurier with a wan smile, 'but there's something else which makes my happiness less than perfect . . .'

'Oh?' Henry prompted, as Du Maurier fell silent.

'I live in perpetual fear of going blind. Not a day passes without the thought crossing my mind that my good eye might fail, as suddenly as the other one did years ago. And then all this' – he extended an arm to take in the undulant expanse of green grass and the surface of the ponds winking between the trees, the walkers and their gambolling dogs, the pastel-coloured summer dresses and parasols of the women, the white smocks and sailor-suits of the children, the young men in shirtsleeves tossing a cricket ball between them, the whole animated multicoloured urban pastoral spread out before them under a canopy of pale blue sky – 'all this would be snatched away from me for ever, and I would have to grope my way across the Heath in perpetual darkness, with the aid of a stick and Chang. I would never be able to draw again. My income would dry up immediately – God knows what would become of us. The children tease me about my economies, they complain because I work so many hours of the day, but they don't know what it is like to lack money. I do.' They walked on in silence for a while, Henry feeling slightly ashamed of his facile allusion to fairy tales, and Du Maurier evidently lost in melancholy reflections. *'Vivre, ce n'est pas gai,'* he said at length, glancing at Henry with a wry smile.

'My dear Du Maurier,' said Henry, 'I spoke idly. I find your – your – your plight deeply – indeed the whole history you have unfolded to me – deeply – inexpressibly – moving.'

Henry's appreciation of the precariousness of Du Maurier's happiness – living always with the knowledge that his flourishing artistic career and the comfortable family life at New Grove House depended utterly for their continuation on the fragile connection of nerve and membrane in a single eye – this was certainly one of the foundations of their friendship. It made 'little Du Maurier' (as he used to refer to him early in their acquaintance) something of a hero in Henry's eyes, and Du Maurier recognised and valued his esteem. In other respects they had much in common, and their differences were complementary. Both were expatriates, who felt occasional spasms of exasperation with aspects of the English society in which they had chosen to live, and viewed it with a certain irony sharpened by comparisons with life on the other side of the Channel. Du Maurier was by far the more thoroughly assimilated, and more anxious to affirm his Englishness, one amusing symptom of this being his insistence on speaking French, in which he was fluent, with a pronounced English accent; but an attachment to France and things French constituted a bond between the two men. Du Maurier was always harking back fondly to memories of his childhood in Passy, or his student days in the Latin Quarter, and Henry too was in a sense an exile from France as well as America: he had spent much time there, in boyhood, youth and adulthood, and had at one time seriously contemplated settling in Paris. He was still subject to fits of nostalgia for Parisian life – its elegance and sophistication, not to mention its cuisine (when he asked the maid at Bolton Street if the cook might fry the potatoes occasionally instead of always drearily boiling them, she replied: 'Ooh, I don't think so, sir – would that be *French* cooking, sir?'). One undeniable benefit of his father's eccentric plan of education for his two eldest sons, which had entailed dragging or packing them off to the Continent every few years, and which had made it so difficult for either of them to settle on a career, was that Henry had learned to speak French fluently and correctly, and was frequently complimented by the natives on this accomplishment. It was a pleasure to both himself and Du Maurier to sprinkle French words and phrases into a conversation as a kind of verbal condiment, without being thought precious or required by blank looks to supply a gloss on their own remarks.

Although Henry was ten years younger than Du Maurier, they might have been contemporaries as far as looks went, and in many ways Henry, with his bushy beard, balding pate and incipient paunch, appeared the older and more mature. Du Maurier always had a slightly boyish air about him, even when his hair began to turn grey, whereas Henry had cultivated a middle-aged persona as early in his life as he plausibly could. In literary matters a quasi-tutorial relationship developed between them. Du Maurier's enthusiasms were intense, but personal and narrow. He adored Thackeray, and had been swept away by Swinburne's heady rhythms and pagan sentiments. Otherwise, the availabilities of Mudie's circulating library largely dictated his reading. But he was very willing to broaden his knowledge under Henry's guidance, especially of contemporary French literature, and began to sample the work of writers like Flaubert, Daudet, De Maupassant, the Goncourts, and Zola, considered too daring by Mudie's and downright disgusting by the English press.

But it was the Du Mauriers' family life, rather than conversation about the comparative merits of French and English culture and society, that drew Henry back to Hampstead again and again. He was a bachelor, a 'confirmed bachelor' as the saying went. He had made up his mind in his early thirties that he would never marry, and stated as much with increasing firmness to his disappointed mother until her death in 1882, and to other relatives and friends who were constantly teasing or goading him on the subject. The reasons were complex and he did not care to probe them too deeply even in self-communing. It was enough to tell himself that his pursuit of literary greatness was incompatible with the obligations of marriage. He needed to be free, free to be selfish – that is to say, selflessly committed to his art. Free to travel, free to seek new experiences, and free, when his muse beckoned, to shut himself up for hours and days at a time to write, without bothering about the needs, emotional and economic, of a wife and children. Du Maurier, admittedly, seemed to manage the trick of being an artist and a paterfamilias simultaneously, but at a cost: a certain limitation of horizons, both physical and mental. He was chained to his drawing board most of the year, and when he took a break it was always a family holiday, with all the human complication and material impedimenta inseparable from such excursions, in Whitby or Folkestone or some Anglicised resort on the Normandy coast. He had never been to Italy, a deprivation that Henry could hardly imagine.

But by the same token Henry was able to enjoy vicariously,

especially in the early years of his association with the Du Mauriers when their children were not yet grown up, something of the warmth and innocent fun of domestic life which he had renounced for the sake of his art. It would have astonished his sophisticated London friends to see him at New Grove House of a Sunday evening, joining in boisterous games like Blind Man's Buff and Hunt the Thimble and Hide and Seek, performing forfeits and charades amid whoops of laughter, calling out 'Bravo! Encore!' when Du Maurier sang one of his favourite ditties in his pleasant tenor voice, 'A wight went walking up and down', Thackeray's ballad of Little Billee, or '*Mimi Pinson est une blonde*', and joining lustily in the chorus of '*Vin à quatre sous*':

> *Fi! de ces vins d'Espagne.*
> *Ils ne sont pas faits pour nous.*
> *C'est le vin à quatre sous*
> *Qui nous sert de champagne!*

Like all large families the Du Mauriers had their own private language of nicknames and sayings and allusions which Henry quickly learned. Beatrix, named after the heroine of *Henry Esmond*, was 'Trixy', Sylvia was known as the 'Tornado' because of her volatile temper, Marie Louise was abbreviated to 'May', while Du Maurier himself was 'Kiki' (derived from a Belgian nurse in infancy, who used to call him *manneken*), and he addressed Emma familiarly as 'Pem'. The children, who took their comfortable middle-class existence for granted, complained mildly about his parsimony and teased their mother for her lack of sophistication. 'Cup of tea' and 'hock bottle' were two favourite expressions in the family *argot*, meaning dull, conventional, suburban – 'Oh, that's so cup of tea, Mamma!' or 'Don't be so hock bottle, Papa.' They were a good-looking and high-spirited brood. Beatrix, the eldest, was a real beauty, who had only just 'come out' when Henry met her, and being squeezed into a broom cupboard with her during some boisterous game of Hide and Seek, pressed up against her sweet-smelling, gently yielding form in the dark, had been one of the more remarkable sensations in his experience, and one which helped him to understand the ecstasy that lovers apparently derived from embracing. He watched with fascination as she opened like a flower to the warmth of a developing social life.

Du Maurier himself was brazenly prejudiced in favour of beautiful women. He kept two plaster models of the Venus de Milo in the house – one on the mantelpiece of the studio-living-room, and another on a pedestal at the angle of the staircase – as icons of his devotion to the ideal female form. If Leech's girls were 'pretty', Du Maurier's were classically beautiful (and tall enough to have tucked the artist under their arms and walked off with him if they had been so inclined). He took unabashed pride in Trixy's looks, and was cruelly critical of the flaws in Sylvia's, though he was gracious enough to admit, as she grew out of adolescence, that she had become an unusually attractive young woman, with a bewitching, slightly crooked smile and huge, wide-spaced grey eyes.

Before long, when she was still only nineteen, Trixy met and became engaged to a tall, handsome and well set-up young man of business, Charles Hoyer Millar. They were married in the summer of 1884, and Henry, who attended the wedding, declared they were the best-looking bride and groom of the year. Privately he thought that Du Maurier's own idealising pen could not have drawn a handsomer couple. Beatrix was – for once the cliché could not be improved upon – radiant. As he watched her coming up the aisle of St George's, Hanover Square, on her father's arm, and returning on her husband's thirty minutes later, as he observed her laughing and talking with the guests at the reception afterwards, with Charles's strong possessive arm round her slim waist, so perfect in her youthful bloom, his novelist's imagination could not help speculating on how she would react to the initiation that shortly awaited her into the mystery of sex. He grew quite hot, and slightly ashamed of himself, picturing her lying in the bridal bed with the sheets drawn up to her chin, waiting with quickened breath for her husband to emerge from his dressing room, or perhaps rising from her knees after saying her prayers and coming towards him in her white night-dress, like a lamb to the slaughter, putting her arms round his neck and hiding her blushes in his shoulder. Emma, presumably, like the dutiful mother she was, would have talked to her daughter about 'that side' of marriage, but probably, Henry surmised from his knowledge of her timid and conventional nature, with so much embarrassed euphemism and indirection as to leave the girl little the wiser. The thought crossed his mind that Charles might be equally unprepared for matrimony, but there was a kind of virile self-confidence about him that made it seem unlikely. Henry did not suspect him of dissipation, but he thought it probable that a handsome young Englishman who had been to public school and 'varsity and holidayed abroad with other young men would have found occasion to lose his virginity. It was perhaps because he had never relinquished his own that the plight of respectable young girls, brought up in innocence and ignorance of the sexual life, especially in the puritanical, hypocritical societies of England and America, and then thrown abruptly into the sea of marriage to sink or swim, stirred Henry's imagination and sympathy so deeply.

He knew of course about the mechanics of procreative intercourse, and from illustrated works of erotica – Lord Houghton's collection at his country house had been particularly informative – he was acquainted with the variations and perversions which human ingenuity and depravity had added. But he found it impossible to imagine himself performing any of these acts, even the most elementary, with anyone; and he had never, even as a young man, positively desired to do so – not with Minny Temple, the New England cousin with whom, before her tragically early death, he had sometimes thought he was in love, nor, at the other end of the female spectrum, with the prostitutes who constantly importuned him in Piccadilly during his first years in London. One consolation of his increasing years – perhaps the only one – was that his innate lack of concupiscence would seem increasingly less remarkable to others.

In the end it was probably the insistent pressure of sexual activity and sexual obsession in French literary life that had driven him from Paris and determined him to make his home in England.

Flaubert, Maupassant, Daudet, and the rest – they all had love affairs and mistresses and frequented brothels, ruining their health in the process, and they were constantly pushing at the boundaries of decency in their writings. When it dawned on them that Henry had no carnal interest in women they sometimes assumed his taste must be for men or young boys, which Henry found still more offensive. The idea that one might be celibate and yet an authentic artist was clearly unthinkable to them. The hypocrisy of English society, where the true extent of adultery and vice was suppressed and denied in life and in literature, only surfacing in the occasional sensational court case, was in many ways odious and repugnant, but it provided useful cover for a bachelor novelist who was fascinated by the power of sexual attraction in human relations but unqualified and disinclined to represent the intimate details of such experience. He aimed in his fiction to steer, by means of subtle suggestion and eloquent ellipsis, a middle course between the shocking but adult explicitness of the French novel and the childish evasions and falsehoods of the Anglo-American variety. It was however necessary to this project that the novelist should know exactly what it was he was leaving out. Therefore, although he went along, in polite society, with the conventional English disapproval of 'vile' and 'beastly' French novels, he read a good many of them.

Between Trixy's engagement and marriage he read Maupassant's *Une Vie*, which had just been published in France to an uproar of controversy about its explicitness, especially its account of the innocent heroine's honeymoon – the brutal shock of her first experience of intercourse, her distressed endurance in succeeding days of her husband's goatish demands, and then her own first astonished sensation of sexual pleasure. One hot day, on a deserted, tree-covered hillside in Corsica, as the couple were drinking from a refreshing spring, the husband, Julien, began to fondle his bride, Jeanne, who in a moment of unwonted '*inspiration d'amour*' filled her mouth with the cool water and offered by gesture to transfer it to his mouth, '*lèvre à lèvre*'. The completion of this act aroused Julien's desire to a pitch that for the first time evoked an answering response in Jeanne. She pressed herself against him and pulled him down with her on to the ground, her breast heaving, her eyes moist, murmuring *'Julien, je t'aime!'* and submitted eagerly to be possessed there and then. *'Elle poussa un cri, frappée, comme de la foudre, par la sensation qu'elle appelait.'* Henry had heard that cry on occasion, through the thin walls of cheap hotel rooms, from behind bedroom doors as he carried his candle along the dark corridors of great country houses, from the shadows under the archways of bridges in Paris at night, without any clear mental images of what it signified. Now he knew. Maupassant could certainly write, however impure the subject matter. Henry read these pages with extreme attentiveness, but without physical arousal: the idea of transferring liquid from one mouth to another, even between lovers, struck him as disgusting.

He did not lend or recommend *Une Vie* to Du Maurier, feeling that it would be tactless to do so at this particular time, especially as the heroine's enjoyment of marital love was shortlived (the odious Julien was soon unfaithful to her). It was obvious that his friend was deeply affected by the imminent flight of his eldest daughter from the domestic nest, and had to make an effort not to fall into gloomy silence when other members of the family were excitedly discussing arrangements for the great day. When the great day actually came Du Maurier of course rose to it heroically – smiled at everyone, made a witty speech, and chided Emma for crying when the bride and groom made their departure. But when Henry called on him the following Sunday at New Grove House, he was like a man bereaved. They went off together for a walk on the Heath and ended up, as they invariably did, sitting on the bench they had occupied on the very first such occasion, when Du Maurier told him the story of his life. It was not situated on some conspicuous height, with a distracting view, but tucked into a byway fringed with Scotch pines, facing south and sheltered from the wind, a situation that invited the sharing of confidences. Henry had indeed dubbed it 'the Bench of Confidences'.

When he congratulated his friend on the splendid way the wedding had gone off, Du Maurier sighed and shook his head. It was not that he had anything to object to in Trixy's choice of partner. 'He's a fine, clean-cut, upstanding young man,' he said. 'I'm sure he loves her and will take care of her. But it's a wrench, you know, when the little girl you've been nourishing and tending and protecting for years is suddenly a woman, and doesn't want your protection any more.'

'I understand,' said Henry sympathetically. 'But that's life, my dear chap. How else would the race be renewed?'

'Yes, it's life,' said Du Maurier gloomily. *'Ce n'est pas gai.'* It was one of his favourite expressions.

'After all, you took Emma away from her father – and you told me yourself he put up quite a struggle.'

'That's true,' Du Maurier admitted. 'But I believe the old devil's motives were entirely selfish – and her mother's. He'd lost a lot of money, you know, and they were counting on Emma to look after them in their old age. They couldn't see much prospect of that if she married me.'

'Well, I daresay *your* mother shed a genuine tear when you married.'

'*Maman?*' Du Maurier was evidently amused at the thought. 'The old lady wasn't sentimental about such things. D'you know, when I was making myself ill with anxiety and frustration over our long engagement, she advised me to take a mistress – some little *grisette*, or the Cockney equivalent.'

'You mean – instead of marrying?' Henry was startled by this disclosure.

'No – while I was waiting to be married,' said Du Maurier, an idea which Henry found no less shocking. 'Of course I told her it was out of the question,' Du Maurier added quickly. 'I told her – which was perfectly true – that I had made a vow in my heart of total fidelity to Pem, on the day we were engaged.'

Henry had the sense, which he had experienced once or twice before, that his friend had inadvertently opened a cabinet drawer on contents slightly compromising to the owner, and quickly slammed it shut. A woman who could make such a cheerfully amoral suggestion to her son shattered all received notions of maternal love; and the vow Du Maurier referred to implied a less than chaste existence up to that point in his life – which wasn't perhaps altogether surprising in someone who had been an art student in the *Quartier Latin*, but not the kind of behaviour one would have inferred from the irreproachable respectability of domestic life at New Grove House. The two men maintained a thoughtful silence as Du Maurier lit a cigarette.

'Did you never think of marrying, James?' he asked at length.

'No, not really,' he replied. 'The only woman I might have married died young.'

Du Maurier looked at him with interest. 'Who was she?'

'My cousin, Minny. Minny Temple. She was a very remarkable person.'

'Beautiful?'

Henry smiled. 'I'm not sure whether she would have satisfied your – ah – exacting standards, Du Maurier. She was immensely attractive – vital – natural – almost boyish in looks, especially when she had her hair cut short because of illness. But it was for her ardent spirit that I loved her.'

'You were both in love?'

He shook his head. 'It was never declared, on either side. We were both very young – in our early twenties – and she had many admirers. It was just after the end of the Civil War, you know, and there were several young men in our New England circle with heroic tales to tell. I had been excluded – that is exempted – excused – from military service, because of an injury to my back, which is still a cross I bear – so I felt a little, ah, intimidated – put in the shade, one might say – by these, these – bronzed and battle-scarred veterans. In short, I hung back. I didn't assert myself. But I believe we were both aware that we had a special affinity, Minny and I. She had exceptional sensitivity – exceptional delicacy of feeling, and a – a – a—' Henry stretched out an arm and groped with his hand as if to pluck the phrase he wanted out of the air – 'a burning desire to do something great with her life.'

'Like Isabel Archer, in *The Portrait of a Lady*?'

'There *is* something of Minny in Isabel,' Henry admitted. 'She used to say that the remote possibility of the best thing was always better than a clear certainty of the second-best thing. She reminded

61

me of that maxim in a letter shortly before her death. I've never forgotten it. In a way it has been the guiding light of my literary career.'

'How did she die?'

'Consumption. At the age of twenty-five. I was in Europe at the time. I knew she was ill – but when the end came it was a great shock. We had been corresponding about the possibility of her coming to Italy – of our meeting in Rome. She said the mere thought of it made her "crazy" with excitement. But it was not to be.'

'How very sad,' said Du Maurier. 'And there has never been another woman for whom you could feel the same attachment?'

'No,' said Henry.

This story was almost true, and Henry almost believed it himself. He had certainly loved Minny Temple, but if he had been 'in love' with her, he would not have gone off to Europe when he did, or he would have made more determined efforts to bring her across the Atlantic to join him. In her last year of life she dropped some timid hints of more than cousinly feeling – *'You don't mind if I am a little affectionate, now that you are so far away, do you?'* – to which he did not rise; and in their correspondence he kept the prospect of a reunion in Rome dangling without ever taking the initiative to bring it about. When the news of her death reached him he had felt, therefore, as well as grief, a certain guilt, which he relieved by vowing to perpetuate her spirit in his work, especially in his heroines. The story he told George Du Maurier, and others, of young love cruelly nipped in the bud by fate, both explained and sanctified his celibate dedication to his art.

2

HENRY said nothing to Du Maurier about Constance Fenimore Woolson, in recent years the nearest thing in his life to what was vulgarly termed a 'lady friend'. He could talk freely about Minny Temple because she was safely dead, but while they were alive Henry liked to keep his friends in watertight compartments, sometimes singly, sometimes in groups, so that information about himself should not leak from one to another. Writing fiction, however artful, was inevitably to some degree an exposure of the author's own self, his own soul, and the fewer facts about one's private life that one's friends and the general public had in their possession, by the light of which to make comparisons and inferences, the better. Very few people in Henry's large acquaintance were aware of his quite intimate relationship with Constance Fenimore Woolson.

She was the grandniece of Fenimore Cooper, that great, if (as he now seemed) quaintly archaic pioneer of the native American novel, creator of the much-loved *Leatherstocking Tales* and their frontiersman hero, Natty Bumppo. Constance had inherited her ancestor's literary talent, but applied it to the domestic and sentimental aspects of life, in sketches and stories set in Ohio and the post-bellum South which were published with increasing frequency in the 1870s, in the same quality American magazines to which Henry contributed. In 1879 *Harper's* began serialising a novel called *Anne* which was reputed to be exceptionally popular with the magazine's readers. At about the same time she published a highly complimentary article about Henry's work in the *Atlantic*. So he knew very well who she was when they met for the first time in Florence in the spring of 1880, and, as he told her, the letter of introduction which she presented, from Minny Temple's sister, Henrietta, was hardly necessary.

He discovered later that Miss Woolson had been carrying this letter about with her for months, vainly seeking an opportunity to use it. Making her first trip to Europe the previous December, with her sister Clara and the latter's daughter Clare, she had gone initially to London, hoping to meet Henry there, but learned that he had left the city to spend Christmas in Paris. When she crossed the Channel to France in the New Year, he had moved on to Italy. But she had finally caught up with him at a time and place propitious to the development of a friendship. After literature, she told him, her greatest enjoyment had been from music, but she was getting sadly deaf, and as this source of pleasure inexorably diminished she aimed to compensate by learning to appreciate the visual arts, with which she had had little previous acquaintance. As he intended to stay in Florence for some weeks, he offered himself as her guide to the artistic treasures of the historic city. She accepted gratefully and with undisguised delight.

He had come to Florence from Naples, where he had looked up Paul Zhukovski, a young aristocratic Russian expatriate whom he had got to know in Paris in the mid-'seventies, a would-be artist, a dilettante, a friend of Turgenev and a passionate admirer of the composer Richard Wagner. He and Zhukovski had in fact become very close at that time, going for long walks together, and spending hours talking about art and literature in the young Russian's studio apartment, cluttered with treasures and curios he had collected in his cosmopolitan wanderings. Henry looked forward eagerly to their reunion at Posilippo, just outside Naples, where Zhukovski had taken a villa. He had settled there to be near Wagner, who was spending a year at the Villa Ungri with his wife, surrounded by an entourage of Russian and German admirers and hangers-on to whom Henry was quickly introduced. The atmosphere of decadence and vice that permeated this little court shocked Henry, and he stiffened in resistance to it with the strength of a conscience partly formed in puritan New England. There were men who painted themselves, and women who made lewd jokes; couples fondled each other openly in company, and sometimes they were of the same sex. When Zhukovski, at the end of a bibulous evening, attempted to kiss Henry on the mouth, he fled the place and never returned.

It had not occurred to him in Paris that Zhukovski might be a

Uranist, and he wondered anxiously, in retrospect, whether there had been anything in his own conduct there which could have encouraged such a supposition about himself. To be sure, he would sometimes link arms with the young Russian when they went for their long walks, or clasp him by the shoulder while making some particularly impassioned point in conversation, but this was surely no more than normal behaviour between young men who felt a strong affinity of interests and enjoyed each other's company. It had never crossed his mind that their mutual attraction might turn morbid, and lead to unnatural and forbidden acts. Clearly whatever latent vice there had been in Zhukovski's character had been brought out by his exposure to the unwholesome atmosphere of the Villa Ungri. Sitting in the first-class carriage of his train from Naples to Florence, gazing through the window at fields green with burgeoning crops, orchards and olive groves brilliant with blossom, and the slow procession of picturesque hill towns and villages in the middle distance, Henry reviewed the past and acquitted himself of any indiscreet or misleading behaviour.

Meeting Constance Fenimore Woolson shortly afterwards could not have been more timely. To be kind to her and, up to a safe point, gallant, was a way of confirming his sense of his own normality without making any emotional commitment. It was an ideal arrangement. Miss Woolson was very anxious to learn, and he was very willing to teach. She had the benefit of his superior knowledge of Italy and Italian art; he had a personable, cultivated, and impeccably respectable female companion. Henry showed her frescos, paintings and sculptures by the Italian masters and strove to educate her taste, which remained at times stubbornly provincial, but which she defended with spirit. She admitted, for instance, to a difficulty in appreciating the nude.

'It offends your American notions of decency?' he asked.

'No, I'm not offended. I'm not a prude, I hope,' she said. 'But I'm not sufficiently familiar with the undraped human form to know when representations of it are beautiful and when they are not.'

'Not even the *Birth of Venus* in the Uffizi?' Botticelli was one of his favourite painters.

'Well, I see that she is beautiful, of course, but her nakedness is . . . distracting. I think she would be just as beautiful wearing a robe. Perhaps more so.'

'People are not usually born wearing robes, I believe,' he said sardonically.

'Well, for that matter, they are not usually born fully grown,' she retorted.

Henry had no ready answer to this riposte. 'The only way to remedy your condition is to look at more pictures,' he said.

His own aesthetic approach to the nude had been formed by an experience in early youth. One of the several careers his brother William had essayed and abandoned was that of artist. When Henry returned from a spell of study in Germany in 1860, and rejoined the family in Newport, Rhode Island, William was studying there under the painter William Hunt, and Henry, having nothing better to do, and driven by the competitiveness which had always characterised relations between the two brothers, occupied himself by drawing the plaster casts stored on the ground floor of Hunt's studio. One day, bored and dissatisfied with his efforts to copy Michelangelo's *The Captive*, he wandered upstairs to the studio proper and found William and another student drawing their cousin, Gus Barker, who was visiting the family at the time, and had volunteered for the task. Gus was standing on a dais, completely naked, in the attitude of a discus thrower. He grinned briefly at Henry, without relaxing his posture. Henry had never seen a completely naked adult human being before. In the bright northern light of the studio the young man's white, muscular limbs, and the proud heavy mass of his genitals, much bigger than Henry's own, or any he had seen on statues in art galleries, made an unforgettable impression. He watched his brother for a while, marvelling at the assurance and dispassion with which he reproduced the outline of his cousin's loins in charcoal, and he knew that he himself could never do it. The image of the naked Gus haunted him for days afterwards, with disturbing effects that were physical as well as mental. To be an artist, clearly, you had to have the courage to break the taboo on seeing another's nakedness, the detachment to contemplate it calmly, and the skill to release the abstract, ideal beauty that was concealed within it. He gave Miss Woolson the benefit of this theory in their discussions of the nude, without relating the personal experience on which it was based.

She was forty, just a few years older than Henry, but tended to exaggerate the age difference between them in the way she jocularly referred to herself as 'an old maid', or described her relationship to him as 'a kind of literary aunt'. At first he thought this was a strategy to reduce the risk of any perceived indecorum in their going about together, but later he wondered if it might not also be a way of reassuring him that she wasn't, as they said, 'after' him. She was capable of such sensitivity, and such subtlety, and his appreciation of these qualities was enhanced rather than diminished by his suspicion that, beneath her calm, spinsterly exterior there was a heart that beat a little faster when he was near. She was not beautiful, which was all to the good as regards not encouraging gossip, but neither was she plain. She had pleasing, regular features, smooth plump cheeks, and glossy dark brown hair drawn back above the ears and braided behind. Her womanly figure was always clothed with unostentatious good taste, and she showed remarkable stamina for walking and sightseeing. Her deafness was a slight impediment to easy conversation, but she appreciated the clarity of Henry's diction all the more. He enjoyed her company, and spent some hours with her almost every day.

He had of course read her article about himself in the *Atlantic*, with its gratifying opening statement, 'Mr James always offers an intellectual treat to appreciative readers,' and even if she had been unnecessarily emphatic in denying him 'the genuine story-telling gift', the general tenor of her remarks was both positive and discriminating. He had read some of her own work, and although it was limited by a typically feminine concentration on the themes of love and marriage, he found it full of happy touches, acute observation of people and places, and the marks of a genuine artistic integrity. She favoured tales of heroic renunciation and self-sacrifice by women in matters of the heart, and if there was sometimes a sense of strain in the emotional conflicts she contrived for her heroines, this was infinitely preferable to the trivial obstacles and facile resolutions of the usual 'love story'. In short, she was on the side of the angels – that is to say *his* side –

in the great aesthetic war in which Henry considered himself to be engaged: the effort to make truth to life, to life as experienced on the pulses and in the consciousnesses of individual human beings, the main criterion of value in the English and American novel, as it was in the best French and Russian fiction. Constance (within a few weeks they were on first-name terms) was much more confident of her taste in literature than in art and Henry developed a great respect for her critical judgement. When it was time for him to return to England, he expressed a sincere hope that they would meet again.

A few months later he was startled to read, in the pages of the *Atlantic*, a short story by Constance called 'A Florentine Experiment' that was plainly inspired by their perambulations of the churches and galleries of Florence. In this piece a young American woman called Margaret Stowe, with a coiffure closely resembling her creator's and a similar dry wit, met in Florence a fellow expatriate called Trafford Morgan who was the same age as Henry and had the same superior knowledge of Italian art. As he escorted her around the artistic sites of Florence, they developed a half-contentious, half-flirtatious relationship, in which each at different times pretended to be 'experimentally' paying attention to the other in order to overcome a disappointment in love, when in fact they were all the time really in love with each other. In a climactic scene, set rather effectively in the shadows of the Duomo's interior on a damp autumn day, they confessed their real feelings and formed a permanent attachment. Henry read this story with some alarm, recognising not only aspects of himself and Constance in the characters, but whole sentences from their conversations. But as time passed, and nobody in his acquaintance seemed to connect the tale with himself (he had covered his tracks very skilfully, making little or no reference to Constance in his letters from Florence), he felt easier, and even allowed himself to admire the author's skilful blending of fact and fiction. However, when he returned to Italy the following January he based himself in Venice rather than Rome, where Constance, after much wandering around Europe, had temporarily settled, and where, he knew, she eagerly awaited their reunion. He held off for some months, partly to avoid distraction from his work on

The Portrait of a Lady, and partly to punish Constance a little for her cheek in writing 'A Florentine Experiment'. But in early May he relented and went to Rome.

Constance was living alone in a fourth-floor apartment with exclusive use of a glazed *loggia* on the roof which she referred to as her 'sky-parlour'. In this sunny retreat, adorned with potted plants and shaded by trailing vines, she gave him tea and listened sympathetically to his anxieties about the progress of his novel. He did not show her any part of his manuscript, but he told her enough about the story to explain his doubts: was he giving too much importance to Madame Merle at the beginning? Would his readers 'see' the full devious depths of Gilbert Osmond's character? She reassured him, making deft reference to his success with comparable characters and situations in earlier stories. Henry had other female acquaintances who claimed to hold his work in high esteem, but none who had Constance's understanding of what was involved in the creative process. He asked what she was working on herself.

'I'm revising *Anne* for the book publication.'

'Ah, a delightful occupation,' Henry said. 'Creation is always such an agonising effort, but revision is pure pleasure. If only one could revise without having to write first!'

'Well, it's something you can do even when you're depressed,' said Constance, smiling. 'It has that to be said for it.'

'Are you depressed, then?' Henry enquired, with concern.

'I have been,' she said. She confessed to being prone to periods of deep depression. It was in the hope of overcoming this affliction that she was experimenting with an expatriate life in Europe, but wherever she settled it seemed to catch up with her sooner or later.

'I sympathise,' Henry said.

'You suffer yourself?'

'Of course. It's the occupational disease of artists. We're always striving to imagine and think what has not been thought before, and so always risking defeat and disappointment.'

'But isn't it temperamental too?'

'Yes, I'm afraid so,' he sighed. 'And probably inherited. My whole family are connoisseurs of melancholia – apart from my mother. It's something that runs in the Jameses, evidently. My father found relief in the teaching of Swedenborg, but none of his offspring has found it answered.'

In spite of this exchange of confidences, neither of them made any reference to 'A Florentine Experiment' that afternoon, or on the two or three other occasions when they met during his short stay in Rome. He could feel the pressure of Constance's curiosity, about whether he had read the story and what he made of it, like a palpable presence in the air between them, but she evidently intuited that he would have fled from Rome if she had openly questioned him about it.

On the day before his arranged departure, they visited the Colosseum, which inevitably evoked memories of *Daisy Miller* – 'Your masterpiece, I think,' Constance said, adding hastily, 'to date.'

'Well, it's certainly my most popular work – but I made very little money out of it. It was pirated in America, you know – they sold twenty thousand copies, and I didn't get a sou.'

'But that's shocking!' Constance exclaimed.

'I do feel bitter about it,' said Henry. 'But it was my own fault. I forgot to secure the American copyright until it was too late.'

They were sitting in the shady side of the arena, on one of the crumbling terraces, looking down at the dusty oval which had so often been soaked in blood in the infamous past, and where Daisy Miller, recklessly defying decorum and common sense, had walked at midnight with her Italian escort, observed by the jealous and disapproving Winterbourne, and fatally contracted malaria.

'Poor Daisy,' Constance sighed. 'Why didn't Winterbourne marry her?'

'It would have been a much less interesting story. Your own tales are not notable for glib happy endings of that sort.'

'I know,' said Constance.

'Winterbourne is not the marrying kind,' said Henry.

'Yes, you can tell that from his name,' said Constance.

★ ★ ★

They did not meet for another two years, during which Henry made two trips to America, and suffered the double blow of losing both his parents, his mother dying at the beginning of 1882, and his father in December of the same year. Meanwhile Constance roved restlessly around Italy, Germany and Switzerland, writing a new novel and soaking up the historical and artistic heritage of Europe. They did not meet, but they corresponded. Detained in America by family obligations, Henry wrote to Constance begging for her news. He was, as she shrewdly observed, homesick for Europe. She obliged with long, stylishly written, gently teasing epistles, full of praise and encouragement for his literary projects. *The Portrait of a Lady* she pronounced a masterpiece – more ambitious and therefore greater than *Daisy Miller* – and Isabel Archer was a triumph of insight into a particular type of imaginative, idealising girl doomed to be unhappy.

She only put a foot wrong once in this correspondence, when she made reference to the success of her own novel, *Anne*. It had been so popular as a serial that the publishers, Harper, had voluntarily doubled her fee and promised her a generous royalty on the forthcoming book even though this had been explicitly excluded from the original contract. Henry thought she was glancing at the comparatively modest sales of *The Portrait*, and made a wry comment to this effect in his next letter, but it was evident from her prompt reply that she was innocent of any such intention. 'Of course you understood that what was a great success to me, would be nothing to you,' she wrote, 'and even if a story of mine should have a large "popular" sale (which I do not expect) that could not alter the fact that the utmost of my best work cannot touch the hem of your first or poorest. My work is coarse besides yours. Of entirely another grade. The two should not be mentioned on the same day.' The near-blasphemous extravagance but obvious sincerity of this tribute suffused Henry, as he read it, with a creamy satisfaction that was almost physical.

Constance, or 'Constanza' as he sometimes apostrophised her, by association with the country where they had first met, complained with some justice that her letters were far longer and more comprehensive than the condensed and allusive reports of his doings, scrawled in a large hand on small sheets of notepaper, which she received in return; and that he was forever holding out the vague prospect of their meeting again without doing anything to bring it about. When she mentioned that she was wondering whether to return to America, and he replied that he would like to talk it over with her against an Italian church wall, she commented tartly, 'there has never been but that one short time (three years ago − in Florence) when you seemed disposed for that sort of thing. How many times have I seen you, in the long months that make up three years? I don't complain, for there is no reason in the world why I should expect to see you; only don't put in these decorative sentences about "Italian Church walls".' Henry blushed a little when he read this reproof: she had caught him indulging in a bit of sentimental rhetoric which he had no intention of acting out. The only reason why she might 'expect' to see him would be if he were in love with her, and he was not. But was she in love with him? When she asked apropos of the three long novels he planned to write, 'why not give us a woman for whom we can feel a real love? Perhaps let someone love her very much; but at any rate let *her* love, and let us see that she does' − was this a coded message about herself and her feelings for him? He went back to 'A Florentine Experiment' and read it more carefully. When Trafford Morgan first proposed to Margaret, she turned on him with scorn: *'With the deeply-rooted egotism of a man you believe that I love you, you have believed it from the beginning. It was because I knew this that I allowed the experiment to go on: to make you stand convicted of your dense and vast mistake.'* But this devastating rejection turned out later to be a lie, or at least a self-deception. Did Constance truly consider him to be a selfish egotist, or was thinking it the only way she could control her feelings for him? The application of the story to their relationship was deeply ambiguous, but equally uncomfortable whichever way one interpreted it.

When Constance announced that she was moving to London in the autumn of 1883, Henry's first reaction was panic, fearing that she was coming in pursuit of him. But although she took lodgings very near his own in Bolton Street, she quickly made it clear that she did not wish to embarrass him. She seemed perfectly happy to see him alone, discreetly, when it suited him, while she occupied herself in the intervals with her literary work and the exploration of London, retracing the topography of favourite novels by Dickens and Thackeray. He relaxed, and began to enjoy her company again. They were seen occasionally together at the theatre, but as far as Henry's other friends were concerned Constance, if they were aware of her existence at all, was someone on the rim of his large circle of acquaintance. He encouraged this view by the way he referred to her conversationally as 'an old maid', 'an excellent little woman', whose company he valued for the sake of her intelligence and good sense. He began to address her familiarly as 'Fenimore', which had the effect of de-feminising her and stressing her literary credentials. It helped this social performance that her hearing had deteriorated further and she was now obliged to use an ear-trumpet in the theatre: who could suspect Henry of carrying on an intrigue with a lady through an ear-trumpet? Not that he *was* carrying on an intrigue, but their unchaperoned meetings and excursions might have excited comment if they had been observed. When Fenimore stayed in Salisbury for a period he visited her there and they went to see Stonehenge together, in a carriage that was nearly blown over by the gale-force autumn wind, dining cosily afterwards on a Michaelmas goose at her lodgings in the Cathedral Close. When he went to a hotel in Dover for a few weeks in August to write, away from the distractions of London, Fenimore took rooms in the same town for the same purpose. They went for walks along the white cliffs in the intervals of work. Nothing amorous or improper happened on this and similar occasions. Their relationship was one of platonic companionship and informed conversation about subjects of common interest. Nevertheless Henry enjoyed the spice of secrecy and concealment that was inseparable from these meetings. He felt something of the excitement and sense of risk that he imagined must attend real assignations, and stored up the experience for future literary use.

* * *

The only person who had any idea of the extent of Henry's association with Fenimore was his sister Alice. The baby of the family, five years younger than Henry, she had been subject to devastating prostrations and long periods of invalidism from the age of seventeen. Her impressive catalogue of symptoms – facial neuralgia, stomach pains, paralysis of the legs, palpitations, fainting fits and hysterics – had baffled members of the American medical profession, who were unable to find anything organically wrong with her; so in 1884 she came to England to see if she would fare any better there. It was clear to Henry that she could hardly fare worse. After the death of their mother she had rallied remarkably, apparently finding fulfilment, and unsuspected reserves of energy, in looking after her widowed father; but when the old man died in turn less than a year later – a peaceful, almost self-willed death – Alice collapsed again. William, now deeply absorbed in his academic career at Harvard, and with a wife and young family to attend to, had scant time to give to Alice. In any case Henry suspected that William's domestic happiness, much as she rejoiced in it publicly, was painful for Alice to contemplate at close quarters – hadn't her near-suicidal depression of '78 coincided with his engagement to another Alice? With her parents and one brother dead (Wilky, after a short, unhappy post-war life, had succumbed to heart disease in 1883), with her beloved oldest brother married, and her youngest, Bob, struggling with massive problems of his own (he was unhappily married, and an alcoholic who periodically committed himself to an asylum), there was nothing for her in Boston. It would do her good to get away from a place associated with so many painful emotions and experiences for six months. Her friend Katharine Loring had an ailing sister, Louisa, whom she proposed to take to Europe for her health late in 1884, and was ready to escort Alice to England at the same time.

Henry met them at the Liverpool docks on a grey drizzling November day, with a hired maidservant at his side. The voyage had not been at all rough, but Alice had spent most of it prostrated in her cabin, and had to be carried ashore by two sailors. Henry was shocked at the sight, and had a premonition that his sister would never return to America. She had to be put to bed directly in an hotel, and stayed there for two days before she was fit to make the railway journey to London, where Henry took lodgings for her in Clarges Street, just round the corner from his own rooms, while Katharine Loring went on to Bournemouth with Louisa. Henry was able to see Alice frequently, sometimes twice a day, for brief chats in the interstices of his literary and social commitments. He entertained her with accounts of what he had been doing, the parties he had been to and the plays he had attended. Alice was a shrewd and observant woman, who had always been possessive about her brothers' affections, and suspicious of other women's designs upon them. It did not take her long to notice how often the name of 'Miss Woolson' occurred in Henry's accounts of his doings, or that he sometimes referred to her as 'Fenimore'. She teased and chided him on the subject.

'Are you interested in this woman, Henry?'

'She interests me, yes. Her views of literature are remarkably perceptive.'

'You know what I mean, Henry. Do you have intentions towards her?'

'Do you mean matrimonial ones? Certainly not.'

'I think she has them towards you.'

'Fenimore understands perfectly the nature of our friendship. It is based on a common interest in books and writing.'

'I wonder you have the patience to read her dreary stories,' said Alice petulantly.

Her jealousy was so transparent that he was able to tease her in turn, and make light of the matter. As Alice led a sequestered life, rarely venturing from her lodgings, there was little danger of her enouraging gossip in London, though he could not prevent her from dropping dark hints in her letters to William. Fenimore was of course aware of Alice's presence in London, and inferred, from Henry's discouragement of any proposal that she should call on her, Alice's hostility to herself. So there was Henry, shuttling between two women, both living within a mile of each other in the heart of London, both with a keen interest in himself, who never met and relied entirely on him for information about each other. If it hadn't been so close to home, he sometimes thought he might have made a story out of the situation. It was perhaps because Fenimore too found it slightly absurd that she withdrew from London and took lodgings in Leamington Spa for the summer of '85, though her ostensible reason was to explore Warwickshire.

Alice's health, meanwhile, did not improve. The English doctors frowned and poked and examined; they diagnosed 'suppressed gout' and 'an abnormally sensitive nervous system'; they prescribed pills and potions, electric shocks and saltwater baths. Nothing had any effect. She became a chronic invalid, confined to her rooms, and for much of the time to her bed. She was sincerely grateful to Henry for his attentiveness, especially when Katharine Loring was away looking after her sister. 'Don't you resent having a helpless woman dumped on your shoulders, like the Old Man of the Sea?' she asked him once, and he replied, quite truthfully, that he didn't mind in the least. Unlike most of her friends and relatives, Henry did not find Alice's hypochondria either exasperating or tragic; he found it interesting. It seemed to him that she cultivated her ill-health as he cultivated his art. It had become her vocation, her *raison d'être*, and in a way an instrument of her will. He could not but observe, for instance, that whenever Katharine Loring came back from nursing her sister, Alice had a collapse and took to her bed, thus ensuring that Katharine would stay on to look after her. Although Henry took a solicitous interest in Alice's experiments with different medical practitioners, and reported them conscientiously in letters to William, at heart he never expected any of them to succeed. He never supposed she would 'get better', and did not distress himself with vain hopes on that score. He did his duty by her, he visited her and saw that she was well looked after, but otherwise got on with his life as before. Fenimore returned to London in the winter, and they resumed their occasional outings to theatres, museums, and art galleries. She was no longer disturbed by paintings of the nude, and was able to contemplate Edward Burne-Jones's chastely stripped maidens with equanimity, though she had some reservations about the purity of Alma-Tadema's imagination, which Henry privately shared.

* * *

For some time Henry had been thinking of looking for more spacious and comfortable accommodation for himself. His rooms in Bolton Street were conveniently situated, but they were rather dark and poky, especially in the winter months, and afforded only an oblique glimpse of the Park from the front windows. In the New Year he took the plunge, and a lease, on a fourth-floor flat in a new mansion block in South Kensington. It was a handsome symmetrical mass of pale ochre London brick, with stone facings, bay windows and delicately fashioned wrought-iron balconies, situated halfway down De Vere Gardens, a quiet, broad cul-de-sac off Kensington Gore. The address sounded a note of distinction which pleased him and the accommodation offered a huge improvement in amenities. He took Fenimore to see the flat in February, when it was still being furnished and decorated according to his instructions, choosing a Saturday afternoon when the workmen would be gone. He called for her at her lodgings in Sloane Street and they walked to De Vere Gardens.

'Won't you find the stairs rather trying, living on the fourth floor?' she said as he pointed up to his balcony from the street.

'Ah, wait and see,' he said, twinkling.

'An elevator!' she exclaimed when they arrived.

'Only they call it a lift,' Henry observed, swishing open the latticed metal door, and ushering her into the little oak-panelled cubicle. Lifts in private residences were still something of a novelty in England.

The flat was spacious and many-windowed. Light flooded into it even on a grey London February day. Exulting in the pride of ownership he led her from room to room, their feet echoing on the polished wooden floors (the carpets and rugs had not yet been delivered by Barker's). 'This is the drawing room, but I shall use it as a study – I had the bookshelves fitted specially . . . shall use this sitting room for receiving visitors . . . the dining room, nicely proportioned, don't you think? . . . master bedroom . . . guest bedroom . . . kitchen and servants' quarters.'

Fenimore blinked a little at this last. 'You're going to have servants living in?'

'A butler and cook-housekeeper. I've hired an admirable couple, a Mr and Mrs Smith. He was in service to an earl in his previous employment.'

'My, Henry!' Fenimore exclaimed. 'You've certainly gone up in the world – metaphorically as well as literally.'

He smiled complacently and led her back to the drawing room, where he opened the French windows and led her out on to the small balcony. 'It's an elegant street, don't you think? Rather Parisian, I feel. And if you lean out a little' – he suited the action to the word and pointed down the street to his left – 'you can see Kensington Gardens and Kensington Palace beyond. 'I'm going to get myself a dog and take him for walks in the park.'

'It's a wonderful apartment,' Fenimore said. 'I congratulate you, Henry.'

'And will be even more wonderful when fully furnished,' he said. 'You must dine with me as soon as I've settled in. I have hopes – high hopes – of Mrs Smith's cooking. At any rate it must be a great improvement on Bolton Street. It – ah – could not possibly be worse.' He chuckled, and ushered her back into the drawing room.

'And when will that be?' Fenimore enquired.

'I plan to move in around the middle of March,' he said, closing the French windows.

'Ah, I'm afraid I shall be gone by then,' she said.

'Gone?' He almost whirled round in his surprise.

'Yes, I'm going back to Florence.'

'But why?'

'Surely I don't need to persuade *you* of the attractions of Florence?' she said with a smile.

'No, but . . .' He hung fire.

'I've had my fill of the English countryside and the diversions of London. So what is there to detain me here?'

Henry could not answer her. If he said, 'Myself,' there was no knowing what direction the conversation might take. As if sensing his embarrassment, Fenimore relieved him of the burden of replying. 'One of the advantages of being a free woman, with an income of my own, and without ties, is that I can please myself where I live.'

'Of course,' he said, with a little acquiescent inclination of his head. She spoke with justifiable pride: she had done well out of the royalties on *Anne* – Henry had heard reports of American sales in tens of thousands, though she had tactfully abstained from telling him the figures herself – and she had a new novel in the press. 'But I shall miss you,' he thought it safe to add.

'Will you, Henry?' Fenimore said. 'I think not. I never knew a man with so many friends.'

'But very few of them understand what it is to be a writer and an artist – as you do.'

'We can discuss those things by letter, as before,' she said. She turned aside to examine the Lincrusta wallpaper, and ran a gloved finger over the raised pattern – because the flat was unheated, they had kept on their outdoor clothes. 'This is nice,' she murmured.

'I'm told it's the latest fashion,' he said. 'Did I tell you, the *Atlantic* has asked me to write a retrospective article about your work?'

Even though her head was half turned away from him, he saw Fenimore's smooth white cheek suffused with a blush. 'No,' she said, 'you didn't.' Henry knew very well that he hadn't mentioned the proposal to her before, because until that moment he hadn't made up his mind whether or not to accept it.

'And will you do it?' she asked, still examining the wallpaper closely.

'Yes – once I've finished with *The Princess*,' he said, referring to his inordinately long novel, *The Princess Casamassima*, currently being serialised in the *Atlantic*. He couldn't quite have explained, had there been a witness present who enquired, why he had committed himself to writing the article, and almost at once he regretted doing so. Was it to demonstrate his esteem for Fenimore as a writer, or an attempt to make her feel guilty about deserting him? If the latter, the gambit was singularly unsuccessful.

'Oh!' she exclaimed, turning round to face him. 'Then I'm very glad I'm leaving London. To go around with you, conscious all the time that you were reading my work and sitting in judgement on it, would be intolerable.'

'I don't promise not to follow you to Florence, however,' he said. 'The very sound of the word "Florence" in grimy foggy London makes me – makes me long for its sunwashed walls, and shady walks in the Cascine.'

'Of course I should be very glad to see you there. But what would Alice say?' She smiled as she put this question, but there was a challenge in her calm, unblinking gaze.

'Nothing but what would be perfectly fitting and amiable,' said Henry suavely.

By the time Fenimore left for Florence, Henry was so preoccupied with the innumerable practical problems of moving house that he scarcely registered her departure; and then in April, just as he began to draw breath and seek society again, a welcome new source of company arose: the Du Mauriers moved into London for a longish spell. A gregarious man, who loved dinners and parties, and was the recipient of numerous invitations, George Du Maurier had long chafed at the inconvenience of living so far out of London when attending evening engagements. To hire a cab was devilishly expensive, as he frequently complained, for the drivers charged a substantial premium to climb Fitzjohn's Avenue or Haverstock Hill. There was only one local cab available, and he often found himself competing for its services with a friend, Samuel Jealous, editor of the *Hampstead and Highgate Express*. Sometimes they shared it, and made a joke of this economy by telling the driver to announce 'Sir Hampstead Landau's Carriage' when at the end of the evening he called to collect them at their respective venues in his rickety conveyance. The jest concealed a continuing sense of dissatisfaction and frustration. Du Maurier didn't want to give up New Grove House, or deny his family the healthy air of Hampstead, so he had the happy idea of letting their home for three months of the year while he rented a furnished house in Bayswater. He and Emma were then free to accept as many invitations as they liked for a period. The experiment proved so successful that he resolved to make a regular habit of it in future. Henry was a frequent caller at 27 Gloucester Gardens, and they would take evening strolls together through the streets of Bayswater.

That summer Guy de Maupassant made a visit to London, and Henry, who had known him in Paris, arranged a dinner at Greenwich in his honour to which he invited Du Maurier along with Edmund Gosse and others. Du Maurier was flattered to be included in this distinguished literary gathering, while Henry was glad to have at least one guest capable of conversing easily in French (although Gosse was official translator to the Board of Trade, his spoken French was appalling). The evening went off extremely well, partly no doubt because it was a private, all-male occasion. A few days earlier, Henry had lunched with Maupassant at a fashionable London restaurant, and the Frenchman had embarrassed him by trying to enlist his help in picking up a woman seated alone at a table on the opposite side of the dining room.

'Go and ask her if she would like to join us, Henri,' Maupassant said. (Mercifully they were both speaking French.)

'I couldn't possibly, Guy,' said Henry. 'I don't know who she is.'

'Well, send her a note by the waiter. Tell her we would like to make her acquaintance.'

'Certainly not.'

'I would do it myself, but my English is not good enough.'

'You simply cannot do such things here, Guy,' Henry protested. 'It's impossible.'

'Why not?' Maupassant demanded, helping himself to more wine, to the distress of the hovering waiter who considered this operation to be his duty. 'She is available, without doubt. Why else is she dining alone in a public restaurant?'

'There is a new species of respectable but emancipated ladies in this country who are laying claim to some of the traditional prerogatives of men. I daresay she is one such.'

Maupassant snorted derisively. 'I want a woman,' he grumbled. 'Not an emancipated one, just an ordinary woman, as long as she has a pretty face and a nice arse. I haven't had one since I got to London.'

Henry was relieved to get him out of the restaurant without creating a scene. It confirmed all his prejudices about the morals of French writers. How right he had been to flee Paris!

After meeting Maupassant at Greenwich, Du Maurier took a particular interest in the French writer's work, and began to look out for his books. The following March he wrote to Henry: 'Have you read "Une Vie" by Maupassant – It beguiled a rainy day in Brighton – certain forbidden things are treated with a wonderful skill, simulating naïveté – there is a honeymoon scene in a wood in Corsica, which is either charming or revolting – I blush to say I found it the former.'

Henry received this letter in Venice. He had been in Italy ever since early December, when he felt an irrepressible urge to skip the damp chill of the English winter and the ponderous festivities of the English Christmas, and join Fenimore in Florence. He was exhausted by his labours on *The Princess Casamassima*, and somewhat dejected by its cool reception when it was published in book form at the end of October. Du Maurier praised it to the skies – 'long as it is, there is not a line too much,' he wrote to Henry after receiving an inscribed copy. But the reviewers were less tolerant of the book's length, and Kiki's opinion, though welcome, was a flimsy counterweight in the critical balance – he was, after all, an amateur in the field of literature. Henry hankered for Fenimore's moral support, and wrote to ask for her help in finding accommodation in Florence. As it happened, she had leased but not yet occupied some rooms in the Casa Brichieri in the picturesque hill village of Bellosguardo just outside the city, and offered them to Henry while she remained in her accommodation in the Villa Castellani next door until the New Year. The villa belonged to their mutual friends, the Bootts, who had moved down into Florence for the winter, so Henry and Fenimore enjoyed each other's company undisturbed. It seemed only sensible to dine together in the evenings at the same table in one or other of their respective apartments. As he had hoped, she heaped discriminating praise on *The Princess*, and smoothed his slightly ruffled authorial wings. The weather was mild, the views enchanting. When Fenimore had to occupy her rooms in the Casa, Henry moved down the hill into Florence and took his place on the social carousel of the city's expatriate community, but he continued to see her frequently. He was minded to extend his stay in Italy, and arranged for Alice to occupy his flat for a few months, for her own greater comfort, and to justify the expense of paying the Smiths their wages. Alice enjoyed the amenities of De Vere Gardens, though harbouring suspicions of Smith's drinking habits and Henry's motives for staying abroad. 'Henry is gallivanting on the continent with a *she-novelist*,' she wrote to William, who transmitted the words gleefully to his brother.

Henry thought it prudent to withdraw from Florence for a time, partly to discourage such gossip, and partly because of a little contretemps with Fenimore. His article for the *Atlantic*, simply entitled 'Miss Woolson', was about to come out and he had left a galley proof with her as they parted one evening. When they met the next day by arrangement for a walk in the Boboli Gardens, she seemed subdued, even morose. He thought it was perhaps the rather sombre trees and shrubs of the garden, and their excessively geometrical arrangement, that was having this effect, which he had observed before in visitors, until they seated themselves on a bench looking down the alley of cypresses, and she returned the galleys to him with frigid thanks.

'I fear you are displeased with the article, Fenimore,' he said.

'No, no,' she said, unconvincingly. 'I'm sure you are right.'

'Right about what?'

'The modest extent of my achievement.'

'But I praise your work very highly!' Henry protested.

'Do you? Let me see it again.' Fenimore took the article back from him and scanned it rapidly. 'You say that *Anne* – which is the novel for which I'm best known – is my worst.'

'Not "worst".' Henry demurred. 'I think my words were, "*least happily composed*".'

'And that *East Angels* is my best,' she continued. This was her most recent book, published the previous year.

'I believe it is,' he said. 'By far the best.'

'And then you say, "*and if her talent is capable, in another novel, of making an advance equal to that represented by this work in relation to its predecessors, she will have made a substantial contribution to our new literature of fiction."* It seems to me, when I do the calculation in that sentence, that I still have a long way to go before my work will amount to anything.'

Henry was disconcerted and discomfited, taken quite by surprise, and as usual in such circumstances his speech became somewhat disjointed. 'My dear Fenimore – you misunderstand – the last thing in the world I wished to – I was of course invoking – I was measuring you against the very highest – the very greatest writers – the giants – Balzac – well, perhaps not – but George Sand – George Eliot – the Brontë sisters . . .'

Fenimore listened impassively to his protestations, and then suddenly laughed in his face. 'Henry, you are priceless,' she said. Her good humour returned at once, but Henry found this incomprehensible remark the most disconcerting part of the whole conversation. The next day he accepted a standing invitation to pay an extended visit to his friend Mrs Bronson in Venice.

This wealthy New England socialite occupied the Casa Alvisi on the Grand Canal just opposite the Salute, and her hospitality in these imposing quarters, especially to celebrities in literature and the arts, was legendary. Henry's visit was, however, a disappointment to him. Venice, which he had enjoyed so intensely in the winter and early spring of 1881, was cooler this year, and wetter. One day it even snowed, a spectacular transformation of the city – the dome of the Salute helmeted with a white crust, the black prows of the gondolas scything through flurries of snowflakes – but shortlived. A grey mistiness returned. His apartment was in an annexe at the back of the Casa, rather dark and dank, overlooking a gloomy minor canal. Knowing that Robert Browning had occupied it in the recent past rendered it no more inviting. Henry felt himself becoming depressed, and wrote to Du Maurier, coaxing him to bring Emma to Venice for a holiday. Kiki's company and amusing conversation would cheer him up, he felt, and he would enjoy acting as their *corriere*, showing off his familiarity with the treasures of Venice. To this end he somewhat exaggerated the charms of its present aspect in his letter.

'The weather glows – the lagoon twinkles, and the old marble-fronted palaces look hungry for you,' he wrote. Du Maurier sent back a long, chatty, ruefully envious reply. 'Florence – Venice – to me these words are just magical – But I do not see much chance of my seeing what they represent. Yours seems a delightful existence enough – to winter in such places with a delightful occupation that depends on no skill of hand or eye, precarious organ!' Nevertheless, he sounded in good spirits. He had let New Grove House again for a few months, and taken a house in Bayswater Terrace, setting up his drawing board by the window of the front parlour, where the shifting urban scene afforded constant diversion and inspiration. He had seen a good deal of 'poor old Millais' and they took long walks together '*bras dessus bras dessous*' – and there was a minute sketch of the two men arm in arm squeezed between the lines of script. He asked if Henry had heard the story about the bishop who called on Mrs Gladstone. '*Mrs G: Oh, Bishop, the country's going to the dogs. Bishop: Ah – trust me – there's One above who orders all things for the best. Mrs G: Yes, he'll be down directly.*' Reading this, Henry laughed out loud for the first time in days, and wished more keenly than ever that his friend could join him in Venice. But clearly Kiki felt too burdened with financial anxieties and family responsibilities to move out of working range of the *Punch* offices. He reported that they had spent Christmas and the New Year at Brighton, where he read a lot of French novels, notably *Une Vie*.

Henry stayed on in Venice for a couple of months without much enjoying himself. He suspected that he had developed jaundice and, distrusting the local doctors, sought the advice of the American physician William Baldwin who served the expatriate community in Florence, sending him urine samples, carefully wrapped, through the post, marked 'a.m.' and 'p.m.'. He wrote a rather self-pitying report of himself to Fenimore, and she generously suggested that he return to Florence, mentioning that there were rooms available in the Casa Brichieri. He took her advice and began to feel better as soon as he arrived. The view from the Casa's windows, of the clustered roofs, domes and towers of the city, bisected by the tawny Arno, was a tonic in itself; so was the Tuscan sunshine. Neither he nor Fenimore made any further reference to 'Miss Woolson'. They resumed their pleasant writerly companionship, now under the same roof.

He began work on a story based on an anecdote he had heard in January, about an American bookman who had discovered that Clare Claremont, Byron's mistress and Shelley's sister-in-law, now an old lady, was living with her niece in Florence, in possession of priceless Byron–Shelley letters. The man had plotted to lay his hands on them by infiltrating the household as a lodger, with interesting consequences. Henry transposed the setting from Florence to Venice, and made the author of the coveted letters a fictitious American poet called Jeffrey Aspern. The work went well, for the subject gripped his imagination. He was able to evoke the obsessive biographical curiosity of his American protagonist because on occasion he had felt it himself, about Byron and George Sand and other writers. But the more he worked on his story the more conscious he became of the essential depravity of this urge to uncover the secrets of dead authors, to possess their private thoughts and deeds, and to publish them to the world. It was hateful to think of his own papers being rifled by strangers after his death.

In early May he found it necessary to return to Venice to make more notes on the setting of his story, and then it would be time to go back to London. He and Fenimore took a last walk in the Cascine beside the Arno, now in the growing heat a viscous yellowy-green, flowing slowly between its banks like olive oil. 'You will write, of course, when you have time, and tell me how your work goes,' she said.

'Of course,' he replied. 'And I trust you will do the same. You know how I value our correspondence. But – may I make a suggestion?'

'What is it?'

'That in future we burn each other's letters after reading them.'

She stopped on the footpath and stared at him. 'Whatever for? Are they so very compromising? Are you afraid they may be read out in court at some future date?'

He grinned uneasily. 'Don't be absurd, Fenimore, of course not.

They're not in the least compromising. But they are . . . private. I hate the idea of people reading them after we are dead.'

'Dead! What a morbid thought.'

'And not only reading them, but publishing them, and making money out of them. It's the way things are going in this dreadful Americanised age of ours. There is no privacy, no decency any more. Journalists, interviewers, biographers – they're parasites, locusts, they strip every leaf. The art we lavish – the pains we take – to create imaginary worlds – is wasted on them. They care only for trivial fact. I feel it is our duty to deny them, to defeat them. When we are dead, when we can no longer defend our privacy, they will move in with their antennae twitching, their mandibles gnashing. Let them find nothing – only scorched earth. Ashes.'

Fenimore moved on, in meditative silence. 'I can see you feel deeply about this, Henry,' she said at length.

'I do.'

'And you have prepared this speech to persuade me.'

'I admit it.'

'May I ask if you've made a similar compact with any of your other correspondents?'

'No. There's no one else to whom I've unburdened my hopes, ambitions, doubts as I have to you.' Fenimore blushed, perceptibly gratified by this confession. 'Of course,' he added, pressing his advantage, 'if you don't agree, I won't stop writing to you. But my letters will not be as spontaneous, as unfettered, as they have been in the past.'

'Very well, I agree,' she said with a sigh.

When Henry got back to London he read through all Fenimore's letters and then destroyed them. To his annoyance he was unable to find the one in which she had said that the best of her work was not worthy to touch the hem of his poorest, for he would have liked to bathe himself in its delicious, self-abasing praise once more. He must have lost it or left it behind in Boston.

He kept the letter from Du Maurier which he had received in

Venice, but never responded to its comments on Maupassant's *Une Vie*. He always privately associated that novel with Beatrix Millar, though wild horses would not have dragged the admission, or an explanation, from him. Soon after she was married, her husband had carried her off to America and Canada, where his City firm had offices, and they were absent for nearly a year, but Henry saw them both frequently after his return from Italy, for they were regular visitors to New Grove House on Sundays, with their young son Geoffrey. The marriage, as far as one could judge from external appearances, was evidently a much happier one than poor Jeanne's in Maupassant's tale. Motherhood had brought Trixy's beauty to ripe perfection, and young Geoffrey was the image of the curly-haired cherub in the 'Bubbles' advertisements for Pears soap. In due course she produced a second son, called Guy after his uncle, and Henry was asked to be a godfather. He accepted the duty with pleasure, though warning the parents that his associations with the Church were of the loosest. 'My religious upbringing was – what shall I call it – pewless,' he told them. 'My father was converted to the teachings of Swedenborg when I was but six months old.'

'What do Swedenborgians believe, sir?' Charles Millar asked him earnestly.

'My dear boy, what do they *not* believe?' Henry answered with a sigh. William had just edited and published, as an act of filial piety, the *Literary Remains* of Henry James Sr., a handsomely bound and printed volume that had been met with a resounding silence by the public at large. Reading it (or, to be accurate, reading in it) had reminded Henry of the fantastical foundationless ideas to the elucidation of which his father had dedicated his considerable intellect for most of his life. There was nothing quite so sad, to Henry's mind, as a book plainly doomed to count its readers on the fingers of one hand.

Du Maurier in contrast had hardly any beliefs at all. 'I think I was a born sceptic,' he told Henry when they were seated one day on the Bench of Confidences. He had been brought up as a Protestant, since his father was of Huguenot ancestry, and his mother's family Anglican, but their attitude to religion was more pragmatic than dogmatic. 'My brother Eugene was baptised in a Catholic church to please an aristocratic friend of the family he was named for. I think they would have made him a Hindoo if it would have improved his prospects.' Du Maurier laughed a little shamefacedly at his own joke. 'No, that's not fair – they were Christians of a kind, but not devout. My father had a loathing of priests and pastors – '*les corbeaux*' he used to call them because of their black cassocks. He and *Maman* seldom went to church. They taught me to say my prayers – but even as a young boy I couldn't see the point of praying. If God was so wonderful, why did he need me to tell him so? And what was the point of asking him for favours, since if he existed he knew what I wanted already?'

'You were a remarkably precocious little atheist,' Henry remarked.

'No, I was never an atheist,' said Du Maurier. 'I'm what Huxley calls an "agnostic" – a very useful word. I don't know whether there is a Supreme Being, but if there is I'm sure He – or rather It – doesn't resemble the irritable old man with a long white beard one was taught to fear in childhood, or his humourless son.'

Henry tittered at this satirical description of the godhead. 'Does Emma know about these views of yours?' he enquired.

'She knows, but we don't discuss them. It would upset her – she's a conventional soul, the dear girl. I'd privately renounced, the Christian religion before we fell in love.'

'Was there a particular moment when you ceased to believe or was it a gradual process?' Henry asked.

'Both, in a way. But the crisis came when I lost the sight of my eye, and feared to lose the other,' Du Maurier said. 'I was in despair. For once I was tempted to turn to prayer. I was living in Malines at the time – I'd gone there to consult a specialist who didn't seem to be doing me much good. I don't know if you've ever been there? No? Well, it's a town full of churches – I've never been to a place that has so many for its size. Most of them – all the nice old ones anyway – are Roman, but one day when I was feeling particularly blue I passed a Lutheran church, and went in and knelt there and tried to pray, without much success, or relief. After a while a minister came in and noticed me. When I got up to leave he engaged me in conversation, and I explained my plight. He questioned me closely about the circumstances in which I lost the sight of my eye. As you know, I was painting from the life at the time, a young girl. He asked me if the model was nude. 'I think his term was "unclothed". I said yes. He said: "Then perhaps God has punished you for that." '

'Good heavens!' Henry exclaimed. 'What a monstrous thing to say!'

'Wasn't it jolly of him? His theory was that God had blinded me in one eye for painting a subject likely to arouse lust – my own and other people's – through the organ of sight, and that my best hope of preserving my good eye was to renounce such art for ever.'

Henry was reminded of the day long ago when he entered Hunt's studio in Newport to find Gus Barker posing nude – poor Gus, who three years later was shot dead by a Confederate guerrilla on the Rappahannock River – and his own emotions on that occasion, but he said nothing of this to Du Maurier. 'Outrageous,' he murmured. 'And cruel.'

'Yes, I sometimes think cruelty is the only real sin,' said Du Maurier. 'I told him I couldn't believe in a God capable of such petty spitefulness, and that I intended to return to the life class at the next opportunity. In fact I'd given up serious drawing and painting to rest my eye, but it made a good exit line as I stalked out of the church. He yelled after me: "Put not the Lord thy God to the test!" And I admit there were moments in the days following when I felt a certain . . . superstitious anxiety. How would I feel, I wondered, if I lost the sight of the other eye? After giving the matter a lot of thought I came to the conclusion that it would just be my bad luck. The causes of my weak sight were purely physical, and nobody's fault. Things are as they are for perfectly natural reasons that sooner or later science will explain – has already explained to a large extent. That was my final parting with religion. And what about you, Henry?' he concluded. 'Where do you stand?'

'Ah, that would take a long time to tell,' said Henry. 'In brief – like you, I'm a sceptic when it comes to doctrine. But I must admit to a kind of emotional attraction to the Roman Church – emotional and aesthetic. I adore Italian painting from Giotto and Botticelli to

– oh, Tintoretto, Titian . . . those old masters *humanise* the biblical legends in a way I find immensely moving. And I think I take a gloomier view of human nature than you do, Kiki. I believe there is such a thing as evil – original sin if you like – and that perhaps humanity needs religion as a bulwark against it. And I rather envy the Romans their rituals and symbolism – the sung masses, the votive candles, the anointing of the sick . . .'

'You wouldn't convert, though, would you?' Du Maurier enquired, almost anxiously.

'No, no fear of that,' Henry said with a smile. 'Consciousness is my religion, human consciousness. Refining it, intensifying it – and preserving it.'

The infant Guy Millar was baptised in Hampstead parish church by Canon Ainger, a neighbour of Du Maurier's who was his regular walking companion on the Heath on weekdays. Since Ainger was otherwise occupied on Sundays it was the first occasion on which Henry met this gentleman, though he had heard a lot about him. Like Du Maurier he was small in stature, with strikingly white hair, and a slightly theatrical manner (he had in fact acted in some of Charles Dickens's celebrated amateur productions). To Henry nothing better illustrated the comfortable tolerance of the Church of England towards diversity of belief than the friendship of these two men. Ainger was a learned churchman of orthodox Low Church views, and a popular preacher at the Temple, where he held the position of Reader. He must have been aware that Du Maurier never went to church apart from family weddings, christenings and funerals, but it seemed to make no difference to their mutual regard, which was based on common secular enthusiasms – for walking, music, amusing conversation and convivial society. Henry had been rather apprehensive that his qualifications for godparenthood would be put to the test by Ainger before the christening, or at the reception afterwards at New Grove House, but Du Maurier had reassured him. 'Ainger's far too sensible a chap to bring up religion on an occasion like this,' he said mischievously. 'Anyway, there's another godfather who's certainly been confirmed, so you needn't worry.' This turned out to be Edward Warren, a young architect who had been at school with Charles Millar. He was a pupil of Bodley's and a disciple of William Morris. Henry liked him and his pretty fiancée exceedingly and immediately struck up a friendship with them which proved enduring.

Friends! Friends! Henry was always making new ones. They looped round each other like needlework stitches and he felt himself to be at the centre of an ever-expanding tapestry of relationships the maintenance of which, either by social contact or correspondence, absorbed a frightening amount of his time. But he depended on friends for human interest and input, for the stimulus of other minds, for the occasional anecdote that might be the 'germ' of a new piece of fiction, and, in his bachelor state, as an antidote to loneliness. About this time he made another: Jules Jusserand, *chargé d'affaires* at the French Embassy, a dapper, diminutive man, even smaller than Du Maurier and Ainger, but a highly cultivated scholar and critic, equally well versed in French and English literature. Henry introduced him to Du Maurier, who promptly issued him with an open invitation for Sundays. Henceforward Henry often enjoyed Jusserand's company on the long walk from Kensington to Hampstead and back, and the level of conversation at New Grove House rose several notches on the scale of educated reference – indeed rather too high for the younger members of the Du Maurier family. The Sunday afternoon walks became more sedate and adult excursions, usually composed of Henry, Du Maurier, Jusserand and, towering over the other three, Charles Millar. They would walk and converse in pairs, Henry with Du Maurier and Charles with Jusserand on the outward leg, to the flagpole or the Spaniards Road, and then Du Maurier and his son-in-law would change places for the return journey. Henry usually did most of the talking on the way back, to the polite and deferential Charles, but on the way out he mainly listened, as Du Maurier entertained him with a stream of jokes, anecdotes and stories, some of them autobiographical, some fantastic. It was on one such walk that Du Maurier first mentioned to Henry his idea for a story later known to the world as *Trilby* – he could never be sure when exactly it was, for he took little notice at the time. But the second occasion on which Du Maurier spoke of it made an impression, and Henry wrote a lengthy note about it in his journal on the following day, March 25th, 1889.

3

BY the end of the 1880s Henry had become increasingly anxious about the progress of his career as a novelist – or rather, about its lack of progress. At the beginning of the decade he had set himself an ambitious programme, to write three major novels which would build on the achievement of *The Portrait of a Lady* and establish him as the rightful successor to the great English novelists of the previous generation – Dickens, Thackeray, George Eliot (to cast one's eyes no lower down the slopes of Parnassus) – whose work, for all its merits, was beginning to look increasingly old-fashioned in form and content. The first stage of this endeavour, *The Bostonians*, had excited very little interest, apart from complaints emanating from Boston that he had irreverently portrayed a well-known local bluestocking, Miss Peabody, in the character of Miss Birdseye (and so he had, though he denied it in correspondence with William). Henry was in fact not entirely satisfied with this novel himself. The subject – a young girl torn between the attractions of a reactionary but virile Southern male admirer and a dominating New England feminist soul-mate – was a good one, but he was ready to admit that the treatment was too expository in manner and dawdling in pace. He had more invested – more time and effort, and greater hopes – in his next major work, *The Princess Casamassima*, a panoramic social novel on a Dickensian or Balzacian scale, crowded with characters from all classes and walks of life from aristocracy to anarchists. He researched the background to this story with the dedication of a French naturalist – even visiting the dismal Millbank Prison to ensure the authenticity of a scene in which the youthful hero was taken to see his incarcerated mother. The novel was nearly 200,000 words long and ran for over a year in the *Atlantic*. He was well paid for it by the magazine, but there was an almost audible sigh of relief from the other side of the ocean when they received the final instalment. More disturbingly, the sales of the published book were deeply disappointing and it failed to earn out its advance. Taking stock of his life in the New Year of 1888, Henry wrote to his American friend and fellow author William Dean Howells: 'I have entered upon evil days – but this is for your most private ear. I am staggering a good deal under the mysterious and (to me) inexplicable injury wrought – apparently – upon my situation by my last two novels, from which I expected so much and derived so little.'

By 'situation' he meant his finances as well as his literary status, for he depended on his authorial earnings to support the gentlemanly way of life to which he had become accustomed. To the leasing and running costs of the spacious modern apartment in Kensington, with its establishment of servants, he had to add the cost of frequent travelling in England and occasional sorties abroad, tailors' and bootmakers' bills, subscriptions to clubs and societies, book purchases, and many other expenses. But his financial anxiety was more than a matter of practical accounting; it also touched his personal pride. He had always secretly hoped that he might become wealthy as well as famous by his writing. It was not because he lusted for gold as such, or for the luxuries that it might buy – yachts and carriages and diamond cravat pins had no attractions for him. It was because to make significant amounts of money *and* to advance the art of fiction – to transfix this double target with a single arrow – was the only way for a novelist to impress the materialistic nineteenth century. Dickens and George Eliot had managed it. Why not HJ?

There was a hereditary factor in this ambition. His grandfather, William James, who had emigrated from Bailieborough, County Cavan, almost a hundred years ago, arriving in Albany, New York State, with hardly more than two coins to chink together in his pocket, rapidly accumulated an immense fortune through a series of shrewd business ventures in dry goods, tobacco, transportation and real estate, and was worth three million dollars when he died, one of the two or three richest men in America. Henry's father had inherited (after a legal struggle, for he had been excluded from the will) a share of the estate worth $10,000 a year, enough to support himself and his family in comfort without further exertion on his part, and to leave his offspring well provided for when he departed this life. Yet by the time that sad event occurred the money had been mostly frittered away in injudicious investments and periodically settling the debts of his two youngest sons, Wilky and Bob. After the Civil War they had embarked on an idealistic venture to run a plantation in Florida with freed slaves as workers, but it proved a hopeless commercial failure. Neither of the brothers subsequently distinguished himself in any other branch of business, and Wilky had died young, a bitter and disappointed man. William, after years of vacillation, seemed at last to be carving out a successful academic career for himself at Harvard, but it was unlikely to make him rich, even if he finally managed to finish the *Principles of Psychology* on which he had been labouring for a decade. None of the Jameses was poor, but none of them was entirely free from financial anxiety either. The father's estate, divided between his five children, did not constitute significant wealth, and Henry made over his own share to Alice to ensure her financial security. This generous decision was also an act of faith in his future as a professional author. It was shocking to reflect on how far the family fortunes had declined from the level achieved by Grandfather James. To reverse this decline by the work of his pen, to count his readers and his royalties in tens of thousands, while maintaining the highest artistic standards, was Henry's dream. But as the years passed the prospects of realising it appeared fainter and fainter.

Not that it was getting more difficult for novelists to become rich – quite the contrary – but they were the wrong ones. There was Rider Haggard, for instance, whose bloody and preposterous *She* sold 40,000 copies in 1887, the year of its first publication, while Robert Louis Stevenson, whose tales of adventure were infinitely superior, had to be content with much more modest sales (though they were considerably better than Henry's, without doubt). Henry, who had befriended Louis in Bournemouth the previous summer when he took Alice to the resort for a holiday, and loved the man as much as he admired his work, wrote to him: 'the fortieth thousand on the title page of my *She* moves me to a holy indignation.

It isn't nice that anything so vulgarly brutal should be the thing that succeeds most with the English of today.' But it was even more mortifying when one's literary friends had an undeserved success.

Among his large acquaintance was Mary Ward, a niece of Matthew Arnold and the wife of Humphry Ward, a former Oxford don who was a critic and leader-writer for *The Times*. Henry was a frequent visitor to their house in Russell Square, and in due course became a friend and literary counsellor to Mary. She was an earnest, intelligent woman of moderately progressive views, with ambitions to write fiction. In 1884 she had published *Miss Bretherton*, a short, slight novel about the life of an actress which was actually inspired by a visit to the theatre with Henry to see the celebrated American actress, Mary Anderson. The novel was commendable as a first effort, and kindly received, but sold few copies. Mary Ward had some difficulty in finding a publisher for her next attempt, a long novel about the travails of an Anglican clergyman who lost his faith and sought a new vocation in serving the poor. When *Robert Elsmere* finally appeared, early in 1888, the first reviews were cool and few in number, but the novel's themes of embattled belief and honest doubt, of social injustice and philanthropic idealism, evidently touched a nerve among educated readers, who began eagerly to recommend it to each other. Mudie's re-ordered the novel in bulk. Mr Gladstone himself was moved to write an immensely long article about it in the May issue of *The Nineteenth Century*, entitled 'Robert Elsmere and the Battle for Belief', describing it as 'brilliant but pernicious', which gave a huge further boost to sales. It was the book everyone who dined out in London that season *had* to read and it went through impression after impression. Henry read his inscribed copy amid this hysteria with total bewilderment. How could people fail to see that, well-intentioned and edifying as it was, and interesting as the social and theological questions it touched on were, in terms of fictional form *Robert Elsmere* was creakingly antiquated? The point of view from which the story was told shifted abruptly as narrative expediency dictated, with no concern for consistency or intensity of effect; the characters debated the issues in long set speeches that bore very little resemblance to natural utterance; the descriptive passages were heavy with cliché; and the plot flagrantly served the purposes of ideological debate. Of course the book was not entirely without merit – fortunately so, because he was obliged to write a congratulatory letter to its author, and he was aware that a few vague complimentary lines would not suffice. Mrs Humphry Ward (thus she styled herself in print) would expect a detailed critique from her mentor. He put off this duty so long that he had to apologise profusely for the delay, and make up for it by the unctuousness of his praise, leaving only the tiniest loopholes through which his artistic conscience might wriggle. 'The hold you keep of your hero is I think very remarkable and especially in relation to the *kind* of hold you constantly attempt to make it,' he wrote, 'and much as you tell about him you never kill him with it: though perhaps one fears a little sometimes that he may suffer a sunstroke from the high, oblique light of your admiration for him.' He was confident that the triumphant authoress would not detect any implied criticism in the word 'attempt' or any irony in 'sunstroke'. She wrote back to thank him for his generous words, mentioning casually that her publishers were about to bring out a six-shilling one-volume edition of her novel and were predicting a total sale of thirty thousand copies by the end of the year. Henry had recently published *The Aspern Papers* in a volume with two other tales. Macmillan had printed just 850 copies and had no plans to reprint.

The Aspern Papers was, Henry thought, one of the best things he had ever done, and he had written other short pieces of late which had similarly satisfied him – in particular a wickedly ironic story called 'The Lesson of the Master', about a gifted novelist who had sacrificed his artistic integrity to *'the idols of the market; money and luxury and "the world"; placing one's children and dressing one's wife; everything that drives one to the short and easy way'*. Having made this confession and given this warning to a worshipping young protégé, the novelist cynically betrayed him in a narrative twist of which Henry was particularly proud. These stories were first-class, Henry had no doubt of that, but collections of short tales didn't 'sell' and they didn't make an impression. It was the novel, of which Mary

Ward's lumbering three-decker was such a dispiriting example, that counted in the literary marketplace.

In that year he began writing the latest of his own efforts on this scale, *The Tragic Muse*, a novel about politics and the theatre, similar in form and social scope to *The Princess*. It was not his original intention that it should be as long as its predecessor, but it grew and grew in his hands like some towering vessel on a potter's wheel. He worked tremendously hard on the book, conscious of how much depended on it, but he didn't really enjoy the effort, and some small inner voice told him, though he tried to be deaf to it, that *The Tragic Muse* wasn't going to be any more successful than *The Princess*. Although, dipping at random into his bulky manuscript, he couldn't find fault with any particular passage or scene, he sensed that it lacked the intangible force that made a reader reluctant to put a book down and eager to pick it up again. This was a dismal admission to make, even silently, to himself, in the watches of the night. Was it possibly true, as Fenimore had said in her article, that he lacked 'the true story-telling ability'? The loyal *Atlantic* began serialising *The Tragic Muse* in January 1889, and Henry, who was writing the final chapters, waited in vain for some encouraging word from the editors about the response of its readers. Meanwhile his English publisher, Macmillan, was offering a much reduced advance against royalties on the new book.

'In fact – to be candid with you – in the strictest confidence – he offers just seventy pounds,' said Henry.

'Seventy pounds! Why *Punch* has been known to pay that for a single drawing,' said Du Maurier.

They were strolling through the residential streets off Porchester Square on a surprisingly balmy evening at the end of March. Henry had been invited to dine *en famille* with the Du Mauriers at the house they were currently renting in Bayswater. He had arrived early, and the meal was a little delayed by some kitchen crisis, so Henry suggested they should take the air, since it was so pleasant. The streets were quiet, with few cabs or carriages about. It was the twilight hour that most flattered London. The gaslamps were coming on, throwing the shadows of the leafless plane trees on to the pavement, and here and there in the gardens an early flowering cherry tree made a pink splash against the brick walls.

'Seventy pounds for *The Tragic Muse* is an insult,' said Du Maurier.

'I know, but what can I do?' said Henry. 'Macmillan lost money on *The Bostonians* and *The Princess*. I can't really blame him. The fact is my books don't sell.'

'Your publisher must take some of the blame for that. Does he advertise them?'

'Not much.'

'There you are! Take Rider Haggard, for example—'

'I would rather not,' said Henry.

Du Maurier laughed. 'I know what you mean! But why is he so successful? He has a clever publisher – Cassell, isn't it? You remember when they brought out *King Solomon's Mines*?'

'Happily I was abroad at the time.'

'It was his first book, of course – he was completely unknown. Cassell's men plastered the whole of London the night before with posters, saying *"KING SOLOMON'S MINES – THE MOST AMAZING BOOK EVER WRITTEN"*. People woke up the next morning and saw these posters everywhere as they went to work. Of course they were curious to find out more. It worked like magic.'

'I don't think it would work for me,' said Henry James. 'In any case I detest the idea of selling books as if they were brands of soap.'

'Of course, I wasn't suggesting anything as vulgar as that . . .' said Du Maurier.

'Now if Mr Gladstone were to write a review of *The Tragic Muse*, that might do the trick,' said Henry with a rueful smile. 'It did for my friend Mary Ward. But I don't think it's likely.'

'*Robert Elsmere*?' Du Maurier made a face. 'We got the first volume from Mudie's. Neither Emma nor I could be bothered to read the other two. She can't *write*, Henry, not like you.'

'It's very kind of you to say so, my dear Kiki, and I won't pretend to disagree with you. But the fact is that the demand for my work is diminishing. It's a frightening prospect – I tell you this in confidence, you understand,' he repeated, clasping Du Maurier's arm to impress the earnestness of his sentiments. 'It's been weighing on my mind of late, and I have to tell somebody.'

'Your time will come, Henry,' Du Maurier said.

'I feel it's running out. I find it more and more difficult to think up plots.'

'Do you? My head's full of plots! I just wish I had your skill with words to tell 'em.'

'Well, if you have any to spare . . .' Henry said jokingly.

'Why don't you use that story I told you a year or so ago?' said Du Maurier. 'About the young girl and the mesmerist?'

'The young girl and the mesmerist? I'm ashamed to say, Kiki, I've forgotten the details,' said Henry. 'Remind me.'

'Well, there's this girl, a young servant girl, who has an unusually beautiful voice, but no ear at all for music – she's tone deaf . . .' A faint memory of the story came back to Henry as Du Maurier summarised it. The girl became a famous *chanteuse* on the Continent under the tutelage of a little foreign Jew, a musician. She was sought out by a young impoverished artist who had known her as the good-looking but stupid daughter of his landlady, and was intrigued and baffled by her success. He heard the girl perform and was overwhelmed by the beauty of her singing. 'In fact he begins to fall in love with her,' said Du Maurier. 'But then he discovers that the Jew is a mesmerist and the girl can only perform when she's under his influence. When the Jew suddenly dies, in the middle of a performance, she becomes totally ordinary again – sings like a crow. I'm not sure how the story should end.'

'It's a very interesting idea,' said Henry. 'Where did you get it from?'

'Oh, I made it up one day when I was daydreaming. Years ago – when I was saving up to be married. I sent it in to a magazine, but they didn't publish it and somehow the manuscript was lost. You're welcome to try and make something of it, Henry.'

'You're very generous, my dear Kiki, but . . . I don't know if it's quite my line.' Henry thought for a few minutes in silence as they paced the level pavement. From an open window came the sound of a man singing in German to a piano accompaniment.

'Ah!' said Du Maurier, stopping and lifting his hand. 'Schubert's "Serenade".'

They stood under the window and listened until the song came to an end. Du Maurier applauded enthusiastically, and after a moment two startled faces, a young man's and a young woman's, appeared at the window embrasure. 'Bravo!' cried Du Maurier. The couple smiled, waved and withdrew, pleased, amused and embarrassed all at once.

'I could never identify a tune like that,' said Henry as they resumed their walk.

'Oh, it's one of my favourite pieces,' Du Maurier said.

'No matter. You could recognise a hundred others, I know. And that's the difficulty, you see – I mean as regards your generous offer. I haven't the musical knowledge that would be essential to write that story.'

'Nonsense! I could help you with the musical details.'

'Why don't you write it yourself?' Henry said.

'Are you serious?'

'You told me you started a novel once.'

'Yes, and never finished it.'

'A novel is a big undertaking – a daunting task – as I know all too well. But a short story . . . The captions to your drawings show you have an ear for dialogue.'

'You're very kind, Henry. I must admit that I've sometimes thought of taking up the pen again – I mean an author's pen. But I'm afraid of failure. I don't know whether I have the gift in me.'

'Well, you'll never find out unless you try,' said Henry.

Their conversation turned to other topics and family news for the remainder of their walk, and over dinner. Sylvia had been courted for some time by a promising young barrister called Arthur Llewelyn Davies, and the announcement of their engagement was imminent. Du Maurier liked the young man, who was handsome, athletic and industrious, having put himself through 'varsity at no expense to his father by winning scholarships and prizes, though Emma suspected him of having an awkward temper. They had just received a letter from Guy, now an army officer serving with the

Royal Fusiliers in India, describing a Christmas entertainment he had produced, to great acclaim, for the troops in barracks. As a boy Guy had always been a prime mover behind the burlesque playlets that were a feature of family life at New Grove House. 'And now, you see, it's turning out to be an advantage in his military career,' said Du Maurier proudly. 'His young brother, however, seems to have no talent for anything *except* theatricals.' Gerald would be leaving Harrow in a year or two and Du Maurier was at a loss what to do with him.

No more was said between them that evening about the story of the singer and the mesmerist, but as he walked home across the Park after dinner, Henry turned it over in his mind and found it more and more intriguing. The next morning he wrote down a summary, with some embellishments of his own, in his notebook. What interested him was the relationship between the girl and her disreputable mentor, as an illustration of the genuine artist's unique power. 'She had had the glorious voice, but no talent – he had had the sacred fire, the rare musical organization, and had played into her and through her,' Henry wrote. He rather regretted, now, that he had encouraged Du Maurier to try writing the story. In spite of his want of musical knowledge, he thought he might like one day to see what he could make of it himself.

They next met a week or two later, at one of the Gosses' Sunday afternoons, at their house overlooking the Regent's Park Canal. Kiki came up to him as soon as he entered the crowded drawing room, holding a cup of tea in one hand and waving a cigarette in the other, beaming all over his face. 'Henry! Congratulate me. I've written forty pages already – or rather Emma has written them. I dictated them.'

'You've started writing your story, then?' said Henry. He felt a little pang of disappointment at this news, which he managed to disguise with a smile.

'Yes,' said Du Maurier. 'But not the one I told you.'

'Not about the young girl singer and the Jewish mesmerist?'

'No, another subject entirely . . . Something I've been turning over in my mind for a long time, but never had the confidence to begin. What you said the other day gave me the impetus. After you left, I sat up half the night making notes. It's going to be quite long – a novel, not a story.'

'Well, I'm very pleased,' said Henry, sincerely.

'I can't wait to show you some of it. But it's too early yet.'

'I should be delighted. Whenever you choose.'

'You must be quite honest,' said Du Maurier. 'I want you to tell me if I'm making a complete ass of myself.'

In Henry's experience, when apprentice writers showed him their work and asked him to be quite honest, honesty was usually the last thing they wanted, and if they were friends the situation could be delicate. He had learned to temper criticism with words of praise and encouragement, but he was incapable of utterly perjuring himself on matters of literary value. He therefore awaited his first sight of Du Maurier's work in progress with a certain anxiety. In fact it wasn't a sight but a hearing that he obtained first: Du Maurier read the opening chapter to him and Jusserand, one Sunday evening in May at New Grove House, after the family had given up their Bayswater tenancy and returned to Hampstead. Henry was relieved and pleasantly surprised by this sample of the novel, which was entitled *Peter Ibbetson*. It took the form of a memoir by the eponymous hero, who appeared to have composed it in prison for reasons not immediately divulged. Like his creator, Peter Ibbetson had a French father and English mother, and had been brought up on the outskirts of Paris; the opening section was indeed little more than an affectionately nostalgic evocation of Du Maurier's own happy childhood in Passy. Henry did not as a rule approve of the pseudo-autobiography as a fictional form. An 'I' narrator might serve very well for a short story or tale, but in the long haul of the novel it was apt to encourage diffuseness and irrelevance. For a beginner, however, it had its advantages as a narrative method, solving many potential problems by simple elimination, and it lent itself to Du Maurier's lyrical celebration of a child's loves, hopes and fears, the adult man's effort to recover a lost world of impressions. A phrase occurred, '*to ache with the pangs of happy remembrance*', which epitomised the mood of the whole thing. It was done with considerable charm and delicacy, and no dissembling was required on Henry's part, when the reading was concluded, to congratulate the author and urge him to continue with the good work. Jusserand added his commendations and vouched for the authenticity of the French local colour.

Du Maurier was delighted with this reception. Henry could tell that he was hugely excited by the project and eager to go on with it. It was a second lease of artistic life, and all the more welcome because his sight was giving him great concern. He wore tinted spectacles most of the time now, with lenses of such a dark blue that they were all but opaque and gave him the disconcerting appearance of someone who was really blind, especially when he had a walking stick in his hand. The vision of his good eye was deteriorating, and this was affecting the quality of his draughtsmanship, for he was obliged to use a broader, coarser etching technique than in the past. He was seriously concerned about how long he could continue to work as an artist under this handicap, and the possibility of adopting another medium, not so dependent on the fine co-ordination of hand and eye, was enormously cheering. It was to save his sight that he had decided to dictate his story to Emma instead of writing it out himself. Henry was intrigued by their account of this process: apparently she scribbled down his words as he fluently uttered them, sitting at ease in his armchair in the studio, smoking cigarette after cigarette, and she made a fair copy later for him to read and revise. Henry rather envied Kiki this comparatively effortless method of composition, and said so.

'Well then, Henry,' said Du Maurier with a smile, 'you must get yourself a devoted little wife, like Emma, with a nice neat hand.'

'Ah, it's too late for that, I'm afraid,' he replied. 'Besides, I would drive the poor woman to distraction with my protracted gropings for *le mot juste*.'

'Well, of course I don't hope to achieve such a fine polish on my style as yours,' Du Maurier said humbly.

'No, no, my dear fellow, I meant no such imputation,' said Henry. 'You have a natural unforced eloquence which I envy. *Continue, mon bon!*'

In the following months Du Maurier read to him further chapters of the novel which made a less favourable impression. The story took a somewhat melodramatic turn. The young hero was orphaned and adopted by a relative, Colonel Ibbetson, who brought him up to be an English gentleman but turned out to be himself a cad. (Henry guessed it would be revealed in due course that it was for killing or injuring this man that Peter was imprisoned.) Peter became an architect, and fell hopelessly in love with a beautiful young duchess who proved to be his childhood sweetheart. Whereas the early chapters had had a naïve but genuine truthfulness to life about them, the rest of the novel seemed to be drifting more and more towards the fatal shore of romance. There was also a little too much philosophising by the hero, who shared his creator's prejudices against orthodox religion. But Henry did not feel it was his duty to cast cold water on the author's hopes. There came a point when he said to his friend: 'Don't show me any more. You must find your own way now. Let me read it when it is published – for it surely will be.' This was said partly to excuse himself from giving further time and attention to Du Maurier's novel, for he was preoccupied with an exciting new project of his own – to become a playwright.

4

HE had always been fascinated by the theatre. As young children in New York he and William were frequently taken to pantomimes, circuses and similar entertainments by their parents, who were themselves regular playgoers. One of his earliest and most vivid memories was of his mother and father going off one winter's evening from the house on Fourteenth Street to see a celebrated actress of the time, Charlotte Cushman, in *Henry VIII*, leaving himself and his brother, aged about seven and eight respectively, to do their preparation for the next day's lessons, and his father bursting into the room about an hour later, snatching up William, and rushing off with him (insofar as a man with a wooden leg, the legacy of an accident in youth, could rush) back to the theatre. The first Act had been such a sublime experience that Henry Sr. was determined his eldest son should see the rest of the performance, and had dashed home in a cab in the first interval to abduct him for that purpose. Henry, deemed too young to appreciate Shakespeare, was left alone in the lamplight with his books, bitterly resenting the deprivation. His father tried to make up for it subsequently with excursions to classic and modern plays on Broadway, but there was a sense in which no performance, in boyhood or adulthood, in New York or Paris or London, ever quite rose to the dramatic heights Henry imputed to that fabulous unseen production of *Henry VIII*. It haunted his imagination for ever after as a kind of Platonic ideal of theatrical ecstasy, which every visit to actual theatres was a vain effort to realise. During his years in Paris he frequented the *Comédie Française* and familiarised himself with the repertoire of Scribe, Sardou and Dennery. He was a regular theatregoer in London, though its usual fare of broadly acted melodramas and farces was much inferior, in his opinion, to the productions of the Parisian stage. Indeed, it seemed to him that the English nation's besetting sin of Philistinism was nowhere more apparent than in its drama. He went night after night to sit in the stalls in the faint hope of being gripped or enchanted, and invariably returned home disappointed, sometimes before the play was over.

He happened to be in Paris, in December 1888, gratefully renewing his acquaintance with its more sophisticated style of dramatic entertainment, when he received a letter from an English actor-manager, Edward Compton, inviting him to adapt his early novel, *The American*, for the Compton Comedy Company. His first instinct was to decline. The jaunty name of the company was not promising, and he had accepted a similar proposal some ten years before, to adapt *Daisy Miller* for the New York stage, which had come to nothing. He had published the unperformed play and resolved not to waste any more time on such ventures. But on reflection he wrote a cautiously encouraging reply to Compton, and after his return to England made some enquiries of and about him, the answers to which were reassuring. Compton had a good reputation as both an actor and a manager. The repertoire of his company consisted mainly of classic English comedies by Shakespeare, Garrick, Goldsmith and the like, which they toured round the country week by week. Compton wished to enhance this programme with a new play by a prestigious writer, and to bring the production into London if it prospered. He believed that a dramatic adaptation of *The American* would fit the bill and offer rewarding parts for himself and his wife, Virginia Bateman Compton, the leading actress of the company.

The more Henry thought about this proposal – and he thought about it a good deal, sometimes when his mind should have been focused on the final chapters of *The Tragic Muse* – the more it attracted him. By May 1889 he had agreed in principle to write the play. More than that, he had privately determined to write several plays – half a dozen – a dozen – whatever it took to conquer the English stage. For all its vulgarity and aesthetic crudity, it was for an author the shortest road to fame and fortune – if, of course, one were successful. But why shouldn't he succeed? He believed he had thoroughly assimilated the craft of skilful playmaking through years of attendance at the fountainhead of the *Française*, and – heaven knew – he had sat among English audiences long enough to know what would 'go' with them. Compton's proposal, which he had almost dismissed out of hand, now seemed providential, offering a solution to the professional crisis he had confessed to Du Maurier during their walk around the environs of Porchester Square on that mild March evening a year before. Cushioned by moneybags fat with playhouse royalties, he need no longer haggle with publishers over their paltry advances, or bewail the paucity of discriminating readers able to appreciate his novels. With the proceeds of his commercially successful plays he would buy himself the space and time to write real literature without having to worry about its marketability. It was an extra enticement that, even if the playwriting side of this projected double career entailed some compromises with popular taste, it would not be in itself soulless drudgery. It might even be fun. The prospect of getting involved in the practicalities of putting on a play, of meeting actors, attending rehearsals, and consulting about costumes and sets, produced an undeniable tingle of pleasurable anticipation. And then, the excitement of seeing one's work performed in front of an audience, to hear their laughter and applause . . . At this juncture of his thoughts he was prone to lapse into a kind of daydream, bathed in a golden glow of footlights, in which he himself, immaculate in evening dress, was pulled half-resisting from the wings of a stage amid resounding cries of 'Author! Author!' from the auditorium, and took bow after blushing bow.

He already knew that he must compress and divide the action of his novel into three or four acts, with strong curtain lines; that he must exaggerate the brash 'Americanness' of his hero for the amusement of the English; and that he must contrive a happy ending to the story. In his novel the rich, self-made American Christopher Newman, an innocent abroad in Paris, was at first permitted to pay court to the beautiful young widow, the Comtesse Claire de Cintré, by her aristocratic relatives, the Bellegardes, and then snobbishly coldshouldered by them. Fate put into his hands the means of disgracing the Bellegardes or, by the threat of exposure, compelling them to allow Claire to marry him, but in a gesture of revulsion against European cynicism and corruption, Newman renounced both love and revenge and returned to his native land, while the Comtesse retired to a convent. Henry did not need Edward Compton to tell him that such a bleak conclusion would not do for a final 'note' on which to send English theatregoers home in their cabs and omnibuses and suburban trains – though Compton told him so anyway, tactfully but unequivocally, in the course of their correspondence.

For various reasons – other pressing commitments on Henry's part and a dilatoriness on Compton's that he would come to recognise as an occupational vice common to all theatrical producers – seven months passed before he actually got down to the task of adaptation. In the meantime he told nobody about his grand plan except Fenimore, who approved it; and even when he finally began writing the play, early in 1890, he told only Alice and her companion Katharine Loring, and then in the strictest confidence. Later he let William into the secret, but again with elaborate, almost Masonic, adjurations to preserve it. He feared failure as much as he lusted for success in this new field of endeavour, for only success would justify his setting aside the fine-pointed pen of the novelist to take up the cruder instrument of the playwright. It would be especially humiliating if the project were reported in the newspapers, but in the end never reached the stage at all, as had happened with *Daisy Miller*. He therefore postponed as long as possible telling his literary friends – even George Du Maurier – about his dramatisation of *The American*, or, as he had re-titled it, *The Californian*.

The work went well. He had sent drafts of the first two acts to Compton by February, and the third and fourth by April. The manager's responses were encouragingly positive, though tantalisingly brief and unspecific. Curiously (as it seemed to Henry) they had never met face to face up to this point. Compton always seemed to be in some provincial town or city, moving on to another with his company week by week; and whenever he happened to be in London, Henry was invariably out of town. But eventually, early in May, they made an appointment to meet in De Vere Gardens.

* * *

He awaited Compton in his large light study overlooking the street, leafing through the drafts of the play to refresh his memory. Tosca, the handsome dachshund bitch curled up at his feet, pricked her ears and barked, sensing the arrival of the visitor, and moments later Smith opened the door to announce: 'Mr Edward Compton and Master Compton.' Smith pronounced these names with the slightly exaggerated sonority he had learned in the earl's service, a tone that always reminded Henry of a stage butler. Perhaps for the same reason Edward Compton seemed unsurprised and unintimidated by the performance. It was Henry who was surprised, and somewhat disconcerted, by the presence of the young boy, an alert, goodlooking lad aged about seven or eight, dressed in a white sailor suit, standing beside his father with a blue leather-bound book in his hand. He was also taken aback by Compton's physical appearance. A handsome, clean-shaven man in his mid-thirties, with a noble profile and a fine upright figure, he was as bald as an egg.

'I beg your pardon, Mr James,' said Compton, after they had shaken hands. 'As you see, I've taken the liberty of bringing my son with me.' He looked fondly at the boy, who was already making friends with Tosca. 'I remember what a thrill it was to me, when I was his age, to be introduced to Thackeray by *my* father – not far from here as it happens, we were walking by Kensington Gardens – and what a pleasure it was to recall that meeting in later years. I couldn't find it in me to deny him a similar privilege.'

'Of course, of course – he's most welcome!' Henry murmured, delighted by the implied compliment, though flustered by the social challenge presented by the boy. 'But how will he divert himself while we discuss our business?'

'He's under strict instructions to sit still and not interrupt,' said Edward Compton. 'But if you would be so kind as to sign his birthday book first . . .'

'Certainly, with the greatest of pleasure,' said Henry, taking the book from the boy's outstretched hand. He read the title embossed in gold on the cover. '*The Tennyson Birthday Book*. Very good. And what is your name, young man?'

'Edward Montague Compton Mackenzie,' said the boy, very clearly.

'A fine name! But how is it . . . ?' Henry wrinkled his brow in puzzlement, leaving the question unfinished.

Compton laughed. 'My own name is really Mackenzie, as was my father's. He dropped it when he went on the stage, because his Scottish relatives disapproved of the profession, and I followed suit. We usually call this young fellow "Monty".'

'I see . . . and what must I write in this fine volume, Monty?'

'Your name, if you please, sir,' said the boy. 'Under your own birthday.'

'Well, that is April the fifteenth,' said Henry, leafing through the book, which was designed like a desk diary, with a quotation from Tennyson for every day. ' "*Gorgonized me from head to foot / With a stony British stare*" – *Maud*,' he read aloud. 'Hmm. A somewhat abrasive motto for my birthday – though I know that stare. Do you know what "gorgonized" means, Monty?'

The boy blushed. 'No, sir.'

'You know about the Gorgon, Monty,' his father prompted.

'Oh the *Gorgon*,' said the boy. 'He was a monster who turned you to stone if he looked at you.'

'Very Good! Excellent!' said Henry, impressed. 'Though I believe the creature was female.' He carried the book over to his standing desk, and wrote his name with a flourish in the appropriate place. The boy watched this operation with great curiosity.

'Do you always write standing up?' he asked.

'Monty!' his father cautioned, evidently fearing the question was impertinent.

'No,' Henry laughed. 'Sometimes I writing sitting at that desk over there' – he gestured to the desk by the window covered with drafts of the play – 'and sometimes I write lying down.' He led the boy and his father over to the chaise longue, attached to which was a small lectern on a swinging arm, and demonstrated how this apparatus worked. 'I suffer from a back, you see,' he said to Compton in explanation, 'and must change my posture from time to time.'

'Very ingenious,' said Compton, admiring the swinging lectern.

'And do you hope to follow in your father's and grandfather's footsteps, Monty?' Henry asked. The boy looked blank.

'Mr James means, do you want to be an actor when you grow up,' Compton explained. 'Actually, we think he might turn out to be a writer,' he said to Henry. 'He always has his head in a book.'

'Indeed! Then we must find you one to read now.'

Finding books for his guests to read while he was otherwise engaged was a task Henry took very seriously, aiming always for a perfect match of reader, text, and context. 'I'm afraid I don't have very much in the way of juvenile literature,' he said running his eyes anxiously along the shelves of books, pulling out an occasional volume and then replacing it with a sigh and a shake of the head. 'Andrew Lang's fairy tales are somewhat insipid I always think . . . Robert Louis Stevenson is perhaps a little advanced . . .'

'Stevenson will do admirably, Mr James,' said Compton, a little impatiently. 'I don't want to take up too much of your valuable time, and we have a play to discuss.'

'Yes, yes, of course,' said Henry, and gave young Monty *Treasure Island* to read, while they got down to business.

'I have read your fourth act,' said Compton, pulling the draft from his coat pocket.

'And approve of it, I trust?' said Henry.

'It is well written, but somewhat depressing.'

'Depressing! But it has a happy ending! The hero gets his bride.'

'Only in the last two lines. Up till then the tone is bleak and forbidding, more like a tragedy than a comedy – we *are* the Compton Comedy Company remember. The death of the brother, Valentin, casts a pall.'

They discussed this point for some time. Henry strenuously defended the death of Valentin from wounds received in a duel. The duel, with its antiquated and essentially hollow notion of 'honour', was a dramatic embodiment of the ethical difference between Europe and the New World, and the moving reconciliation of Valentin with his opponent before he expired prepared for the ultimate union of hero and heroine. Henry felt he had already sufficiently compromised the spirit of the original novel by allowing them to marry. Compton, evidently a pragmatic man, capitulated.

'Very well, but do what you can to lift the audience's spirits a bit sooner,' he said.

They went over the earlier acts and Compton made numerous suggestions for possible improvements, most of which Henry felt he could accept.

'Well, that seems to be it,' said Compton, squaring up the scattered sheets. 'I look forward to receiving a complete text – as soon as you can. Oh – one more thing: I don't care for your new title.'

'Dear me! I thought that by making Newman a Californian – as you will remember, he's from the South in the novel – I would license myself to make his manners a little rougher, and thus more amusing in the Parisian setting,' Henry explained.

'Move him to California by all means,' said Compton, 'but keep the original title. A lot of people will come to see the play because they've read the book.'

'Really? How curious. I thought that might be a deterrent,' said Henry. Privately he had wished to suggest that the play was a new piece of work by giving it a new title, but he accepted the manager's judgement.

'Excellent,' said Compton. '"*The American*, by Henry James". It will look well on the billboards.'

'Does this mean then – am I to understand – that you are definitely going to . . .' Henry scarcely dared complete the question for fear of a negative or ambiguous answer. '*Do* it?' he finally breathed.

'Of course. Didn't I make that clear?'

'Not entirely . . . I'm delighted to hear it.'

'I'm in correspondence with your agent about terms. I'm sure there will be no difficulty.'

Henry had lately put his literary affairs in the hands of Charles Wolcott Balestier, an amiable and energetic young American who had taken up the relatively new profession of literary agent in London. Henry liked and trusted him and was delighted to have the sordid business of financial negotiations taken off his hands. 'When? And where?' were his next questions.

'We'll give the first performance at the Southport Winter Gardens, in January,' was the answer.

Henry's euphoria suffered a certain deflation. 'Not till next year?'

'We'll need all that time. There's much to be done with a new play – you'll see.'

'And why Southport? I'm not sure I even know where it is.'

'It's a seaside resort near Liverpool. A very nice place. A lot of well-off, theatregoing people live there.'

'A long way from London.'

'All the better.' Compton shot Henry a shrewd, appraising glance. 'I take it that you're interested in making money out of this play, Mr James?'

'I blush to say,' he replied, 'that it is my prime motive for venturing into this field of endeavour.'

'Well, the only way you'll make any money to speak of is with a good London run. When we tour the provinces, we spend a week in each place and put on a different play every night – so we'll only do *The American* once a week. Seat prices being what they are in the provinces, you're not going to make a fortune out of that, even if we get good houses. But in London, with stalls at half a guinea, it's a different story. A successful play could earn you a hundred pounds a week, in royalties. More.'

'Really?' Henry's eyes widened. 'So, if it ran for, say six months . . .'

'You would earn two or three thousand. Then if a play really takes, the word travels, and you get productions in America, Australia, all over. Henry Arthur Jones earned ten thousand in one year from his last play.'

'Good heavens!' Henry could almost hear the chink of sovereigns being counted in some windowless backstage office.

'But don't count your chickens before they're hatched,' said Compton, as if reading his thoughts. 'London audiences are hard to please, and the competition is fierce. That's why I want to work on this play in the provinces – give it a good airing on tour – see how it goes with audiences – get everything right before we bring it to London. You understand me?'

'I do, and am much obliged to you for the explanation,' said Henry.

'Southport is a good place to start. As a matter of fact the Winter Gardens was the very first venue the company played. It's always been a lucky house for me. Theatre folk are somewhat superstitious about such things. Have you any other questions, Mr James, before I go?'

Henry had another question, but didn't quite know how to put it. Compton however, perceived the import of his involuntary upward glance.

'Yes,' he said, smiling. 'I shall wear a toupee for the part of Newman.'

'I presumed so,' said Henry, but he was relieved to hear it.

Henry heard the story of Compton's premature baldness a few months later from the stage manager and prompter of the C.C.C., who had been with the company from its foundation, and a very dramatic story it was. A decade or more ago, Compton was engaged to be married to an actress with whom he had worked professionally for several years. On a trip to Paris to buy her trousseau, however, she collapsed suddenly after drinking a glass of iced milk, and died in his arms. The shock was so great that he lost all his hair, and it never grew again. He decided that his future as an actor must be in costume drama, in which he could easily disguise his baldness with wigs, and consequently formed a company dedicated to performing classics of English comedy, using for this purpose some money left to him by his deceased fiancée. In due course he met and married another actress, Virginia Bateman, the mother of young Monty, and the Compton Comedy Company became a popular and highly regarded institution of English provincial theatre. *The American*, therefore, was a bold venture for Compton: not only would it be his first attempt at mounting a London production, but it would also be his first performance for many years in a modern play, wearing a toupee rather than a wig.

This story of cruel heartbreak and resourceful recovery moved Henry much as George Du Maurier's courageous adjustment to his partial blindness had affected him. It epitomised the 'romance of the theatre' which had fascinated him since he was a child, had brought him night after night to sit in the stalls, and had finally drawn him to the other side of the footlights. But there was precious little that was romantic about the day-to-day life of a touring company as Henry observed it, and increasingly shared it, after *The American* went into rehearsal in the autumn of 1890. It was a hard life, rehearsing by day in gloomy and often chilly theatres, performing a different play every night, Monday to Saturday, sleeping and eating in lodgings that afforded varying degrees of comfort, and travelling on to the next venue each Sunday on slow cross-country trains with poor connections. The actors did this for forty-six weeks of the year, with only Holy Week, when all the theatres were closed, and a four-week summer break, in which to rest.

Henry's initiation into this world came in September, when he went to Sheffield, where the company was performing its current repertory at the Theatre Royal, to read his finished play to the assembled actors. Compton was at the station to meet him and conduct him to his hotel. Henry had never been to Sheffield before, knowing it only as a name stamped on cutlery, and was surprised to find how extensive it was, a city of grey stone and rusting iron, sprawled over the Yorkshire hills in the slanting late afternoon sunshine, with soot-blackened steeples, fuming factory chimneys, noisy bustling streets – and a theatre. The next morning he sat on its stage on a hard upright chair, with his back to the darkened auditorium, and the cast, similarly seated, facing him in a semicircle, and read the play straight through, with only brief pauses between the acts. He threw himself energetically into the task, drawing on such histrionic skills as he had acquired in the charades at New Grove House, and similar party games in his New England youth. He knew it was important to enthuse the actors with the parts they would be playing, and it was also an invaluable opportunity to indicate how his lines should be spoken, for he was by no means confident of Compton's American accent, or the other actors' ability to impersonate French aristocrats. He had no idea what the protocol was on such an occasion, or what kind of response to expect from his little audience. They seemed to enjoy the first act, smiling and laughing aloud on occasion, but as the play went on they grew silent. The play itself of course became more sombre as it progressed, and that was no doubt the reason. When he finished, exhausted and hoarse from the effort, there was a patter of applause, and polite smiles and murmured thankyous from the actors, but they jumped up from their seats and disappeared with disconcerting speed.

'Where has everybody gone?' Henry wondered aloud as Compton helped him on with his overcoat.

'They have gone for their dinners,' said Compton, 'and I think we should go for ours. Mrs Compton is waiting for us.' Mrs Compton, who was to play Claire Cintré, had excused herself from attending the reading as she was already thoroughly familiar with the play from the various drafts Henry had sent. The manager led Henry out of the theatre and they walked side by side along the London Road.

'The road to London – a good omen,' Henry quipped.

'I hope so,' said Compton expressionlessly.

Henry waited for further comment, but none was forthcoming. 'So, what is your first – what is your immediate impression, my dear Compton?' he asked.

'The play is too long,' said the manager.

'Too long?' Henry exclaimed, genuinely surprised. 'You didn't say so when we met in May.'

'You have added a great deal since then,' said Compton grimly, striding on.

'Well, perhaps a line here and there . . .' said Henry.

'Much more than that. I told you the play should occupy two hours and three quarters, including the entr'actes.' Compton took out his fob watch from under the lapels of his topcoat, and examined it. 'You started reading at eleven o'clock this morning. You finished at about three. That's four hours.'

'But I read all the stage directions as well,' he pleaded in mitigation.

'Those actions have to be performed. It all takes time. Add the entr'actes, and if we begin this play at seven, it will be nearly midnight before the final curtain comes down. Quite impossible.'

'But what is to be done?' Henry cried.

'We must cut it,' said Compton.

Henry came to an abrupt stop in the middle of the pavement under the shock of this suggestion. He had laboured for weeks, weighing and polishing every line like a jeweller with his gems, to create a seamless glittering necklace of words. The idea of this beautiful artefact being hacked into an abbreviated form was like the plunge of a sharp instrument into his own flesh. '*Cut* it? How?'

'With a blue pencil.' Compton grinned, somewhat heartlessly Henry thought. 'There was never a play written that didn't benefit from cutting. My wife is very good at it.'

There commenced a very painful period of two months during which Henry was gradually compelled by the polite but implacable Comptons to surrender about a quarter of his precious lines. The process was carried on mainly by letter and telegram. Henry's expenditure on telegrams rose alarmingly, and threatened to consume a significant proportion of the advance of £250 that Balestier had negotiated for him. This medium of communication, though undoubtedly convenient, always confronted Henry with an agonising conflict between considerations of economy on the one hand and literary elegance on the other. Straining to reconcile these two desiderata he produced telegraphic communications that had at times something of the quality of a Japanese haiku, like: 'WILL ALIGHT PRECIPITATELY AT 5.38 FROM THE DELIBERATE 1.50. HENRY JAMES.' When professional matters were involved the thought of economising on the length of the message, sacrificing nuances of meaning to save a coin or two, did not even arise; and it often cost him a hundred telegraphed words to defend the retention of a single phrase in his play, which in the end he was obliged, more often than not, to discard. It was a miserable and frustrating business, but he persevered, reminding himself all the while that this was how he was going to liberate himself from the chains of financial anxiety. An added spur was continuing evidence that he would never achieve such a happy state through his prose fiction. *The Tragic Muse* had been published as a book that spring. Though he had called Macmillan's bluff and secured an advance of £250 by threatening to take it elsewhere, the sales were disappointing, and by November it was clear that the publisher was likely to make another loss. In the same month, for the first time in his life, Henry had a short story rejected, and by the *Atlantic* of all periodicals, which had been his reliable patron for so long. He soon placed 'The Pupil' elsewhere, but the experience was like a chill breath on the back of his neck. He resumed work on cutting *The American* with renewed determination. And there was after all a kind of grim satisfaction to be obtained from wrestling successfully with the arbitrary constraints of theatrical convention and the stubborn prejudices of actor-managers. To pare down one's dramatic material sufficiently to squeeze it into the rigid frame of performance-time insisted on by Compton, without actually killing it in the process, was a not negligible feat.

He went down to Portsmouth in November, where the company had set up shop for the week, for a run-through of the revised play, and was rather pleasantly surprised by how well it flowed, and how little the scars of the last two months' brutal cutting showed. The quality of the acting, especially in the minor roles, gave him some concern, and he spent at least an hour giving notes to the cast and getting them to repeat certain lines and scenes with more expression; but it was a bitterly cold day and the actors were obliged to wear their outdoor clothes in the unheated theatre, which inhibited their style. As Mrs Compton disarmingly remarked, it was hard to play a love scene with a dewdrop perpetually forming at the end of one's nose. Henry's opinion of this lady had steadily risen, and not only because she had intelligent and appreciative things to say about *The Tragic Muse*, a copy of which he had presented to her husband (though for his part he gave no sign of having opened it). Henry recognised the patience and good humour she had shown in their debates about the 'cuts', and her portrayal of Claire Cintré was taking shape very pleasingly. Compton himself was so far something of a disappointment, but it was impossible to draw attention to his lapses in front of the rest of the cast. Henry therefore went back with the Comptons to their lodgings and spent another two hours with the actor in private, going over every line of his role for expression, intonation, and accent (his hold on the American 'a' was particularly shaky).

He wrote to William on his return to London: 'The authorship (in any sense worthy of the name) of a play only *begins* when it is written, and I see that one's creation of it doesn't terminate until one has gone with it every inch of the way to the rise of the curtain on the first night.' He was to discover that it didn't even terminate then, but for the moment he could not, as far as *The American* was concerned, think beyond the premiere, now only a few weeks off, to which he looked forward with a mixture of excitement and apprehension. Meanwhile he had already begun writing a second play, provisionally called *Mrs Vibert*, and had conceived the idea for a third.

On the afternoon of Saturday the 3rd of January 1891, with only hours to go before the first public performance of *The American*, Henry paced up and down his sitting room in the Prince of Wales Hotel, Southport, belching and breaking wind intermittently. He had declined Compton's invitation to share the dinner the manager always took punctually at three o'clock when he was performing in the evening, and ordered a cold collation in his room, but perhaps this had been a mistake. A hot meal would have been more calming to bowels churning with anxiety. He summoned the waiter to remove the soiled dishes, and sat down at the table to write some letters – rather like a soldier, it occurred to him, on the eve of a battle which he might not survive. He wrote to Du Maurier and to Gosse, thanking them for their kind messages wishing him success, and saying that he counted on them 'to spend this evening in fasting, silence, and supplication'. He wrote to William, congratulating him on the safe arrival of his third son, drawing a parallel with the imminent birth of his own dramatic first-born, and describing himself as 'in a state of abject lonely fear'. He wrote to a French friend: ' *"Je fais du Théâtre – je suis tombé bien bas – priez pour moi."* ' None of these letters would reach their recipients before his fate was decided, but composing such humorous hyperboles afforded him some relief from the real stress he was suffering.

The dress rehearsal of the previous day had confirmed his opinion that the play would stand or fall by its intrinsic qualities, for the acting was mostly pedestrian and the stage settings minimal (though it was an undoubted enhancement to see Compton with a toupee covering his bald pate at last, and a moustache on his upper lip for good measure). Henry had tried to watch the play as if it were the work of another hand, and it seemed to him that it *did* hang together and move along at an exemplary pace. But it was hard to judge with only a thin scattering of auditors, mostly employees of the theatre and their relations, in the cavernous theatre. All fifteen hundred seats were sold for tonight, and he would have to sit among the occupants and register their verdict. One of them would be William Archer, the influential critic of *The World*, who had written to Henry welcoming the prospect of a new play by a distinguished man of letters, and announcing his intention of attending the premiere. Henry was both flattered and alarmed by this message. Archer had something of a mission to raise the literary standards of the English stage, an aim with which Henry had every sympathy, but he was a fervent supporter of Ibsen, about whom Henry had reservations, and he could be a harsh critic of work that displeased him. Henry had replied, stressing the limitations of the provincial production and recommending him to wait for the London one that it was hoped would follow, but Archer declined to be put off.

To kill time Henry put on his overcoat and went out to post his letters himself, instead of giving them to the hotel reception desk, where he paused however to bespeak a late supper for himself, the Comptons, and Balestier, who was on his way from London by train. The meal would be either a celebration or a wake. After calling at the Post Office, he strolled along the marine promenade. There were few people about on this cold winter afternoon. The tide was out, far, far out, and the sun, largely obscured by cloud, was setting over the flat wet sand and an almost invisible sea. An inordinately long skeletal pier stretched from the shore towards the horizon, as if it had set off to bridge the Irish Sea and lost heart.

It seemed absurd that he, Henry James, the 'distinguished man of letters', the cosmopolitan author equally at home in London, Paris, Rome and New York, should have fetched up here in the middle of winter, in this flat and featureless provincial resort, on the very rim of civilisation as it seemed, anxiously to await the determination of his fate as an aspirant playwright. At the thought he gave a loud, barking guffaw of self-mocking laughter, which caused a gentleman passing by to look at him sharply and disapprovingly, obviously under the impression that he was drunk.

Henry went on to the theatre. The man in the little cubby hole by the stage door recognised him. 'There's nobody in from the company, Mr James. They're all having a rest this afternoon.'

'I know,' said Henry. 'Thank you. I merely wish to reassure myself about some details of the set.'

He mooned around the stage for some time, fiddling with the props for the first scene, 'A Parisian Parlour', by the dim illumination of a single gaslight, and adjusting the placing of the chairs by an inch or two. The curtain was down for some reason. On an impulse he parted the two flaps, stepped out in front of the curtain, and looked into the enormous maw of the dark, empty auditorium. He waited a few moments till his eyes accommodated to the gloom and he was quite sure he was alone. Then, gravely and deliberately, he practised a bow.

If it was an act of hubris, it went unpunished. A few hours later he stood in the same spot, dazzled by footlights, bowing with the applause of fifteen hundred spectators roaring in his ears. The ovation was loud and long – long enough to warrant three bows. The beaming Compton, who had already taken several himself, seized Henry's hand in both of his own and shook it vigorously. His lips formed the word 'Congratulations!' Then the curtain came down for the last time, and the applause died away into a buzz of animated conversation as the audience filed out of the theatre.

Compton turned to the actors. 'Well done, ladies and gentlemen,' he said.

'Yes, indeed, you were all wonderful. Wonderful!' Henry seconded, going round shaking their hands. He had a special word of thanks for Mrs Compton, whose hand he kissed in homage. The actors dispersed to their dressing rooms with pleased smiles. Henry and Compton followed them into the wings. 'It seemed to go very well,' Henry said, with affected casualness.

'Well? It was a triumph.'

'Do you really think so?'

'Absolutely.'

'You were magnificent, my dear Compton,' Henry said, and he spoke sincerely. The manager's performance had been a revelation. Nothing he had seen in rehearsal had prepared him for its passion and energy.

'Having an audience makes all the difference.'

'Indeed it does,' said Henry. Being part of it that evening, watching his own play through its ears and eyes, had been an extraordinary experience, as if the big black maw of the auditorium which he had looked into that afternoon had swallowed him and, like Jonah in the whale, he was both part of this great live breathing creature and yet distinct from it. He felt every tremor and vibration of its reaction to the spectacle on the stage, he registered the strength of every collective laugh and chuckle, and measured the intensity of every silence at moments of dramatic tension, while himself remaining strangely detached, unmoved and unamused by the familiar material. It was such a novel sensation that at first he distrusted the evidence of success. In the interval at the end of the first act he hastened backstage and buttonholed Compton in the wings. 'In heaven's name,' he said, 'tell me. Is it *going*?' 'Going? Rather!' had been the reassuring reply. 'You could hear a pin drop.' And to judge by the reception at the end, the other three acts had 'gone' just as well.

Balestier came up, his fresh eager face nodding enthusiastically atop his long, thin, wandlike frame, and wrung Henry's hand. 'Congratulations, my dear chap, we have a hit on our hands,' he said.

'Do you really think so?' Henry said.

'Ask this man,' Balestier said, nodding at Compton.

'I've already told him,' said Compton. 'And it will be even better by the time we get to London.'

Henry left them talking, and hastened back to the hotel to order champagne to be served with the supper. He floated along the street in a kind of bubble of euphoria, which survived a slightly prickly encounter shortly afterwards with William Archer. He was surprised, while supervising the laying of the table in his sitting room at the hotel, to receive the critic's card, but invited him to come up. He struck Henry as surprisingly young, somewhat resembling a Nonconformist minister in appearance and manners.

'I see you are preparing for a party,' he said, looking rather disapprovingly at the champagne bottles cooling in ice buckets. 'I will not detain you long. I thought I would give you the benefit of my first impressions of your play. I could not find an opportune moment at the theatre.'

'It's very kind of you,' said Henry politely, though he would willingly have postponed the pleasure. 'Indeed it's excessively kind of you to have made a pilgrimage all the way up here to see my apprentice effort.'

This modest description of his piece did not elicit the emphatic protest Henry expected. 'For a first play it has much to commend it,' Archer said evenly. 'But there are certain imperfections to which I feel I should draw your attention.'

Archer proceeded to make some detailed criticisms of the play's construction, which Henry hardly had the patience to follow. There would be a time for tinkering and polishing later. Now he wanted to gorge on his success. 'You will grant, I think, that the play was very well received tonight,' he said, with a touch of asperity.

'Indeed. But it is the kind of play that goes better in the provinces than in London,' said Archer. Shortly after delivering this opinion, he took his leave.

Henry's spirits were slightly dashed by the encounter, but soon afterwards the Comptons and Balestier arrived in buoyant mood, and after a glass or two of champagne the bubble of euphoria enclosed him again. When he told them about Archer's pernickety criticisms of the play, and his apparent indifference to its ecstatic reception, mimicking the young man's somewhat pedantic and humourless manner, they howled with laugher. The trouble with Archer, Balestier remarked, was that having appointed himself keeper of the English theatre's conscience, he thought everyone should ask his permission and advice before writing a play. They ate their supper with leisurely relish as they reviewed the many high points of the evening, like soldiers lolling in their tent, reliving a victorious battle. It was nearly two o'clock in the morning when the happy party broke up. Before he retired to bed, Henry drafted a telegram to be sent to Alice first thing the next morning, as he had promised. For once, a not strictly grammatical stream of words and phrases seemed rhetorically justified. He wrote:'UNQUALIFIED TRIUMPHANT MAGNIFICENT SUCCESS UNIVERSAL CONGRATULATIONS GREAT OVATION FOR AUTHOR GREAT FUTURE FOR PLAY COMPTONS RADIANT AND HIS ACTING ADMIRABLE WRITING HENRY.' It summed up his feelings about the evening perfectly.

The next day the company had to move on to Wolverhampton, where they were due to perform at the Grand for the following six days. Henry shared their journey which, it being a Sunday, was slow and uncomfortable, with long waits for connections at Liverpool and Crewe, where the refreshment rooms were closed by Sabbatarian decree and only bleak, unheated waiting rooms afforded shelter. The trains seemed to stop at every little station, and there were seldom attendants available to remove and replace the footwarmers in the carriages. The high spirits of the author and the manager survived these trials, however, and they exchanged warm farewells when the company alighted at Wolverhampton. Henry stayed on the train until its termination at Birmingham, where he stayed the night at the Midland Hotel. He was going on to visit Fenimore in Cheltenham the next day.

Fenimore had returned to England the previous summer after months of restless movement. Her old enemy depression had returned to plague her, and her usual remedy was a change of scene, or several changes in succession. In the autumn of 1889 she was in England, then in France, and in the following winter and spring she made an adventurous tour of Greece and Egypt with her sister, which she wrote up in lively articles in *Harper's*. Henry particularly enjoyed her lyrical descriptions of Corfu, and a humorous account of being rescued from a crowd of ferocious brigand-like porters on the quayside at Patras by an imperturbable German hotelier. She did not return to Florence at the conclusion of these travels, claiming that she had grown weary of its inward-looking, gossipy, expatriate community. Instead she settled in Cheltenham. Why Cheltenham? She couldn't give much of an explanation, except that it was a pleasant spa town with an abundance of convenient lodgings. Going back to Leamington Spa was out of the question, because Alice James was living there with Katharine Loring, having moved out of De Vere Gardens after Henry returned from his long sojourn in Italy. When asked about her choice of Leamington as a location Alice gave the absurdly trivial reason that she had heard of lodgings there from which one could hear the music of a band that played daily on a corner of the Parade. Henry privately thought it had something to do with the fact that Alice knew Fenimore had lived in Leamington for a time, and hoped somehow to learn more about her by retracing her steps. The motives of these two women, who circled his existence like moons, showing him at most only half of their selves, were never entirely clear, but Alice continued to be both fascinated by and jealous of the unseen Fenimore. Once when William had arrived in England without warning they travelled down to Leamington together and Henry went ahead to prepare Alice for William's visit. 'I must tell you something,' he began. 'You're not going to be *married*?' she shrieked. Henry did not need to ask whom she thought he might be about to marry.

One thing the two women seemed to have in common, apart from an interest in himself, was a liking for the English institution of lodgings, where unmarried ladies could have their meals served in the privacy of their own rooms; on the Continent one either ate at a public table, or had to take a house and employ one's own servants. Not long after Fenimore settled in Cheltenham, however, Alice left Leamington. Her health seriously deteriorated in the summer of 1890, and in the autumn she and Katharine moved back to London, taking rooms in a hotel in Kensington, to be near Henry and medical specialists. Alice and Katharine were now locked in a relationship that, it was obvious to Henry, would only end with Alice's death. If there was in Katharine's dedication something more than pure altruism, an emotional investment of a kind he had written about in *The Bostonians*, Henry was not disposed to comment or criticise. He gave daily thanks that his sister had such a devoted carer who relieved him of what would otherwise have been a crushing responsibility. His function was mainly to cheer Alice's spirits with news of the great world and his own doings in it.

One unexpected bonus of his plunge into the unfamiliar and murky waters of the theatre was that it had proved a source of inexhaustible interest and diversion for his sister. She had been the first, enthusiastic, reader of the complete text of *The American*, and had followed every phase of the play's progress to production with eager attention, empathising with his volatile hopes and anxieties. As promised in his telegram, he had written a longish letter to her and Katharine before leaving Southport giving details of the triumphant premiere, the first instalment of a fuller account to come when he returned to London. This was done partly to counter any jealousy Alice might feel that Fenimore should be the first to receive his verbal account of the event. He was aware of the risk, but he had made the arrangement with Fenimore nevertheless, feeling that, if the play were to fail, she would be the person best qualified to dress his wounded self-esteem. That service, happily, was not required, but there was another that he had in mind.

Fenimore occupied a pleasant set of rooms in a terrace of Regency town houses that looked on to the Parade and its shops from behind a double screen of trees. Henry had visited her there before on a couple of occasions, staying conveniently in a 'bed and breakfast' establishment next door. She was standing by the window of her sitting room when the maidservant of the house showed him in.

'Congratulations,' she said with a smile.

Henry gaped at her. 'How did you know?'

'I have been watching out for you,' she said, smiling. 'When I saw you striding along the pavement, there was such a bounce in your step, and such serenity in your expression, I knew the play must have been a success.'

'It was a triumph,' he said, and told her the whole story. Only the maidservant knocking on the door to bring in fresh coals brought his narrative to a conclusion. He strolled to the window and looked out as Fenimore instructed the girl about serving their luncheon.

'An admirable situation, Fenimore,' he said, when they were alone again. 'Quiet, but not too quiet.'

'It does well enough,' she said, with a shrug, 'but I'm getting bored with Cheltenham.'

'You do "use up" places at a rate,' he gently teased her.

'I've become a nomad,' she said. 'I don't belong anywhere in Europe, but I've been away from home too long to go back.'

'Well, I'm in much the same condition,' he said. 'I like to think it is conducive to literary creation.'

'It has been for you, Henry, but I find writing more and more difficult.'

'It seems to me you still produce a good deal for the magazines,' he said.

'Yes, but my new novel drags.' Fenimore had published one novel since *East Angels*, called *Jupiter Lights*, in 1889. It had not been the advance in achievement that Henry had hoped for in his 'Miss Woolson' article. Both were aware of this, and the unspoken thought created an awkward silence between them.

'So you are well and truly launched on a new career,' she said.

'Well, one mustn't, as the admirable Compton says, count one's chickens, but I'm hopeful, genuinely hopeful. I've already written a second play – in fact – if it would not be too much of an imposition – if I might read it to you – a part of it – while I'm here . . . ? I would greatly value your opinion.'

'Of course, I should feel privileged,' she said.

They took a walk after lunch, through the Pittville estate to the huge neoclassical Pump Room at the summit of the park, and imbibed a little of the brackish-tasting water under its echoing dome. Then, with dusk falling, they returned to her cosy sitting room, drew the curtains, seated themselves in easy chairs on either side of the fire, and Henry read the whole of his play, *Mrs Vibert*. The plot was very loosely based on a tale by a tolerably obscure French writer, Henri Rivière, which he had read in *La Revue des Deux Mondes* twenty-five years ago, and had transferred to an English country house setting. The young hero was in love with his father's ward, an heiress. The father's former mistress, Mrs Vibert, turned up unexpectedly with their grown-up illegitimate son, and a villainous tutor, in tow. Mrs Vibert tried to attach the ward to her son, and the tutor sought to exploit the situation through blackmail. In the end his bluff was called by a morally reborn Mrs Vibert and all ended happily. It was a comedy. Fenimore listened, frowning with concentration. She used her ear trumpet, angling her head to enhance its effectiveness. At the end she pronounced the play 'very striking'.

'You didn't laugh very much,' he said.

'I laughed inwardly,' said Fenimore. 'I didn't want to miss anything. You write beautiful dialogue, Henry.'

'Thank you, Fenimore.'

'If only people spoke in such perfectly formed sentences in real life,' she sighed. Henry observed her closely to see if any irony was intended, but Fenimore's expression was transparently sincere.

5

HAVING drunk the heady wine of theatrical success in Southport, Henry could not bear to be separated from his play for more than a few days at a time as it began its tour of the Midlands. He saw it at Wolverhampton, at Leamington, and at Stratford-on-Avon, where he was recognised in the audience and prevailed upon to go up on to the stage and take a bow, an action that already seemed as natural to him as a cardinal holding out his ring to be kissed. On each visit he conferred with Compton about improving the play by small adjustments to the text and the actor's performances, and he stayed on at Leamington to rehearse some revised scenes. It was hard to contemplate with patience the long interval that would elapse before *The American* in its improved form would be presented in London. September was the earliest possible date, because the company was committed to tour the provinces until July.

He no longer bothered to conceal from his friends his involvement in the theatre, though he affected to despise it as a 'base occupation', forced upon him by financial need. The truth was that he was thoroughly engrossed by the new medium, fascinated by the challenges it presented to authorial ingenuity, and seduced by vague visions of the glory as well as the gold he hoped to obtain from it. In February he started yet another play, his fourth, and confided to William in a letter: 'Now that I have tasted blood, *c'est une rage* (of determination to *do*, and triumph, on my part), for I feel at last as if I had found my *real* form, which I am capable of carrying far, and for which the pale little art of fiction, as I have practised it, has been for me but a limited and restricted substitute.' On reading the letter through before sealing the envelope, the sentiment seemed somewhat extreme, but he let it stand. It expressed his current mood.

Shortly afterwards Compton communicated some news which threatened to upset their plans: Mrs Compton was with child, and would have to retire temporarily from the stage at the end of the provincial tour. This was a great blow, and one that in the past would have plunged Henry into helpless despondency. Instead he immediately began to apply his brain to the finding of a substitute, and some cunning unsentimental part of it (the 'organ' of theatrical management no doubt) told him that there might be an opportunity here to enhance the play's prospects by employing an actress with a little more glamour than the worthy Mrs Compton. He had lately seen Ibsen's *Hedda Gabler*, in Gosse's translation (a very bad one according to the rival Ibsenite, William Archer), and he had been deeply impressed by a young American actress called Elizabeth Robins in the title role. He was not alone – Archer wrote in *The World* that 'Sarah Bernhardt could not have done it better'. He was seized with the idea of casting her as Claire Cintré, took Compton to see her at a matinee, and won his agreement. He then wrote a subtly flattering letter to Miss Robins, arranged a meeting between her and Compton, and was rewarded with her acceptance of the part in April. The prospect of having a rising 'star' performing in his play strengthened his faith in its future.

That an American actress would be playing his French heroine and an English actor his American hero didn't bother him in the least. In the theatre, as in all art, successful illusion was produced by a professional mastery of the appropriate technique, not by amateurish authenticity. A nice illustration of this principle was an anecdote George Du Maurier had told him recently, about a genteel couple, down on their luck, who had come to him on the recommendation of Frith seeking employment as models. They had been reduced to that expedient, lacking any qualification or skill other than impeccable manners. 'They knew that I do a lot of pictures of people in good society,' said Du Maurier, 'and they offered themselves as the real thing. I gave them a trial, but they were completely hopeless – stiff as pokers. My little Cockney model Jessie, who works as a barmaid of an evening, can make herself look far more convincing as a society hostess welcoming a guest than Mrs Harrington will ever manage in a month of Sundays.' Henry made a note of the anecdote for future use as the kernel of a short story, but for the time being all his energies were focused on playwriting. In the same month that Elizabeth Robins agreed to perform in *The American*, he had another piece of encouraging news. Some time ago he had read his play *Mrs Vibert* to the actress Geneviève Ward, who had passed it to the well-known manager John Hare, who after weeks of silence wrote to say that he considered it 'a masterpiece of dramatic construction' and would be happy to undertake a London production as soon as he was free of current commitments. This was just the additional vote of confidence in his dramatic powers that Henry needed. It seemed to him that his grand plan to conquer the English stage was proceeding very satisfactorily.

Only Alice's declining health threw a shadow over the beginning of summer. By this time she and Katharine were living in a little house that Henry had found for them in Argyll Road, Kensington, not far from De Vere Gardens. 'A very nice house to be ill in,' he described it to William in a letter, but it seemed now that it would have to serve as a house to die in. A lump in her breast had been causing her pain, and at the end of May they called in a specialist, Sir Andrew Clark, who informed Alice that she had a cancerous tumour which was incurable by surgery or any other means. It was only a matter of time, he said – months rather than years – and the only thing that could be done for her now was to ease her pain as much as possible with morphia. Curiously – or perhaps, on reflection, not so curiously – this sentence of death seemed to improve Alice's spirits. All her life she had suffered from illnesses that could not be diagnosed except as the product of her own hypersensitive nervous system, and had been so wretched that on at least one occasion she had seriously contemplated suicide. Now at last she really was undeniably, irrefutably, mortally ill. The fact, and her knowledge of it, gave her a kind of authority which she had never had before. No one could argue with a tumour. She prepared herself for death with considerable courage and a sometimes disconcertingly dark sense of humour. 'I am working away at getting dead,' she would say, 'to relieve Katharine and Henry of their burden.' Her only reason

133

for wishing to prolong her life was to share the excitement of the London opening of *The American*, and she admitted to a regret that Henry had not started his dramatic career earlier, so that she might perhaps have been carried to the theatre and wheeled into the stalls in a bath chair to see it. He did his best to keep her up to date with the preparations, and one day brought her a sample of the cloth from which one of Elizabeth Robins's dresses was to be made, which he had chosen himself.

Compton had taken a lease on the Opera Comique, a largely subterranean theatre at the Aldwych end of the Strand, for the London debut of his company. Henry thought the name unfortunate, and the site unattractive, but the theatre had been recently refurbished and boasted 'the latest sanitary arrangements', a feature by which Compton set great store. Rehearsals took place there throughout September, punctiliously attended by Henry. 'You don't have to come *every* day, you know, James,' Compton assured him, but if he stayed away for a day or two the actors were apt to let their accents slip or introduce unauthorised bits of 'business'. In any case, it was useless to stay at home and pretend to work. His thoughts were always with the play. Compton sometimes seemed impatient with his comments and interruptions, but the actors bore them goodhumouredly. He had endeared himself to them by providing refreshments. Shocked to discover that they were expected to rehearse from ten in the morning to four in the afternoon without sustenance, and feeling not a little peckish himself on these occasions, he arranged for Mrs Smith to prepare daily a hamper of sandwiches and other cold victuals which her husband delivered to the theatre at noon, and from which Henry invited the actors to help themselves when they were 'off'. Miss Robins remarked that it was the first time in her experience that a playwright had thought of feeding his company.

She was an interesting and intelligent young woman, very different from the usual run of actresses. She was delighted when he told her that *Hedda Gabler* had finally converted him to Ibsen and convinced him that the Norwegian was a truly great playwright, for she had produced the play in partnership with another actress, and they hoped to form a company to put on more plays by Ibsen and other major European dramatists. She had come from America partly to distance herself from a tragic personal history: her husband, also an actor, had drowned himself in the Charles River in a suit of theatrical armour, a piece of symbolic action that Ibsen himself might have invented. Henry sympathised with her cultural ambitions and missionary spirit, and succumbed to her personal charm and the hypnotic effect of her huge eyes of crystalline blue. As an actress she was exceptionally quick to grasp the dramatic point of every scene and line, and magnetised one's attention as soon as she began to move or speak. Henry's only worry was that she was perhaps trying too hard to make the most of her relatively modest part, investing the essentially passive and pathetic character of Claire Cintré with Hedda Gabler's intense and independent spirit. 'Well, *you* chose her,' Compton said rather brusquely, when Henry confided this thought to him. 'That's the kind of actress she is. I can't ask her to change her performance now.' The play was due to open in a week's time, on September 26th.

Henry began to feel again all the nervous doubts of the prelude to the first night at Southport. 'Will it "go", my dear Compton?' he asked at the end of the first dress rehearsal. 'Shall we conquer London, do you think?' Compton was still in his costume, the chief feature of which was a coat of startling design, made of brown velveteen with light blue facings and enormous mother-of-pearl buttons, evidently the costumier's idea of an American millionaire's usual attire, which made Henry wish he had taken as much interest in the male actors' costumes as in the ladies' dresses. 'I'll tell you in four weeks' time,' said the always down-to-earth manager. 'There are two things you need to succeed in London. Good reviews and good word of mouth. Ideally you want both, but sometimes you can pull off the trick with one. With neither, you're sunk.' There had been only a couple of reviews of the Southport production, neither of them a reliable augury: a neutral one from Archer, kind to the playwright but reserving judgement on the play, and a complimentary but stupid one in the local paper.

* * *

The reception of the play at its London first night was auspicious: warm applause at the end, and calls of 'Author! Author!' to which Henry responded, contenting himself with a single deep dignified bow, standing alone in front of the curtain. The knowledge that so many friends and admirers were in the audience – Fenimore, George and Emma Du Maurier, the Gosses, John Singer Sargent and George Meredith, among many others – made the ovation especially sweet. It was also pleasing to know that celebrities from the world of the theatre were present – the playwright Arthur Pinero, for instance, the American impresario John Augustin Daly, and Geneviève Ward, who was to take the title role in Hare's promised but postponed production of *Mrs Vibert*. Most gratifying of all was the presence of William, who had crossed the Atlantic, typically at short notice, primarily to see his ailing sister, but also to share his brother's big night. He came trailing clouds of glory himself, for his monumental *Principles of Psychology*, which had finally appeared the year before, was gathering plaudits from all over the world. All their lives the two brothers had been rivals for the attention, first of their family, then of the public at large. But now all competitiveness was suspended in a sincere enjoyment of each other's success.

Henry had arranged a supper party at De Vere Gardens for William, the Comptons, Miss Robins, their mutual friend Mrs Hugh Bell and her husband, Balestier, and the Du Mauriers. He had decided after some hesitation not to invite Fenimore, because it would have revealed the closeness of their friendship too obviously, and would have entailed inviting her dull sister, who was visiting her; but he managed to speak to her alone in the second entr'acte while the sister was otherwise engaged. She was bright-eyed with the excitement and glamour of the occasion, and commented on the dazzling appearance of the ladies. 'I've never seen so much expensive jewellery all at once – or, I have to admit, so much bosom,' she said. Her own bosom was as usual covered up to the throat, but her long dress of dove grey with a little black velvet tippet was elegant, and he complimented her on it, to her obvious pleasure. She congratulated him on the play, which she had seen in Cheltenham on its provincial tour. 'I enjoyed it then,' she said, 'but it is immensely improved. I can understand why you've become so immersed in the theatrical world, Henry. It must be quite intoxicating to know that *you* are responsible for all this.' She gestured with a gloved hand to take in the glittering, chattering throng under the chandelier in the foyer, eating their ices, smoking their cigarettes and fanning themselves with their programmes.

'It's not so intoxicating at a morning rehearsal in a dark unheated theatre in Sheffield or Portsmouth, I assure you,' he said, putting his mouth close to her ear trumpet, for the noise in the enclosed space was tremendous. Even so, he was not sure she had heard him.

'I have thought lately of trying my own hand at drama,' she said. 'Perhaps we might collaborate on a play together one day.'

'That is an intriguing idea,' he said politely, and changed the subject. 'How are your new lodgings?' Fenimore had recently moved to Oxford, which she claimed to find much more congenial than Cheltenham, but there was a difficulty in finding long-term accommodation in the city, and she had changed her address twice already.

'Very comfortable, thank you. My landlady's husband is the steward of Exeter College, so I get dishes from the college kitchens. Those dons look after themselves very well, I must say.' Whether it was due to the ambience of Oxford or the quality of the food diverted to her from Exeter's high table, Fenimore seemed in uncommonly good spirits.

'Who was that lively little woman you were talking to, with the ear trumpet?' William asked him afterwards, as they were driving in a four-wheeler to De Vere Gardens, and when Henry told him he said: 'Really? The famous "she-novelist"? I would have liked to shake her hand.' Henry felt a pang of regret that he hadn't invited her to supper, but it was soon forgotten in the high spirits of the party. Mrs Smith excelled herself with a lobster salad, and Smith served the wine with majestic aplomb, in spite of having imbibed a good deal of it, Henry suspected, while waiting for him and his guests to arrive. William made a speech ending with a toast to 'Henry, and his brilliant play'.

★ ★ ★

The professional critics, alas, did not share William's opinion. The reviews were not exactly bad, Compton said, but they were not good either. To Henry they seemed awful, terrible, cruel. He was particularly wounded by suggestions that his play was too melo-dramatic in its serious parts and too broad in its comic parts, for these were precisely the faults of which he himself accused most English drama. 'Is it conceivable that the play satisfied the author of the novel?' asked *The Academy*, and the question stung. William Archer's notice, to Henry's surprise, was one of the most favourable. He saw in the play 'the touch of the born playwright', but his comment on 'neat and charming dialogue which is grateful to the ear even when it does not ring dramatically true' was a double-edged compliment. Nearly all the critics remarked on Compton's unfortunate coat, and at times they seemed to be reviewing the coat rather than the play. 'Why the outer man of Christopher Newman should be clothed in a garment of chocolate faced with sky-blue remains a mystery known only to himself and his tailor,' commented one, while another marvelled at the 'mother-of-pearl buttons as large as cheese plates'. Compton's performance was rated as no more than adequate, and Elizabeth Robins seemed at times, said one critic, to be acting in another play, perhaps one by Mr Ibsen.

The reviews, clearly, were not going to make the play a success, and the hopes invested in it therefore depended on what Compton called 'word of mouth'. For several weeks they watched the modest box office receipts, looking in vain for signs of an upturn. Henry quipped to Alice that he had two invalids on his hands, herself and his play, but the joke concealed a sombre presentiment of failure. There was a brief rally in the play's fortunes when the Prince of Wales expressed a desire to see it in October, and Henry, all dignity thrown to the winds, scrabbled around to 'dress' the house with distinguished friends for the occasion. Young Master Compton was allowed to attend this performance as a special treat, and Henry found him with his father when he went backstage afterwards. Monty had grown considerably since Henry had last seen him, and was dressed smartly in a navy-blue Norfolk jacket and matching trousers. Henry asked him if he had enjoyed the play.

'Oh yes, sir, very much,' said the boy. 'But I think it was a shame that the lady's brother had to die. It made me sad.'

'I told you so,' Compton said to Henry with grim satisfaction. 'Monty is a very good judge of a play.'

'Well, we can't change the ending now,' said Henry with some asperity. He suspected Compton of having prejudiced his son against the last act in advance.

'How did His Royal Highness seem to be enjoying it?' Compton asked.

'I don't know,' Henry confessed. 'I didn't think it would be polite to stare at the Royal Box.'

The publicity generated by the Prince's visit improved box office takings for a week or so, but they slumped again in November. When Compton told Henry that he had no alternative but to take the play off, he could not reasonably resist the decision. The run finished on December 3rd, after seventy performances. Henry had not earned out his advance, and if he had bothered to tot up the expenses he had incurred in connection with the play from the beginning − the telegrams, copyist's fees, railway fares, hotel bills, hampers and supper parties − he would probably have found himself out of pocket, but he hadn't the heart to do the calculation.

Compton had lost considerably more money by the venture, and to add to his woes the play he hurried into production to plug the gap in his programme, an adaptation of Longfellow's *The Courtship of Miles Standish*, was a complete 'flop', as they said on Broadway, and closed after only a week. Compton phlegmatically accepted his failure to establish himself in London, terminated his lease of the Opera Comique, and prepared to return to touring the provinces in the New Year. For what it was worth − not very much in terms of money − he proposed to continue performing *The American* in repertory. The verdict pronounced by William Archer in Southport had proved true: it was a play more likely to succeed in the provinces than in London. How vain and foolish the extravagant hopes and dreams of that first night now seemed!

As if to reinforce the point, fate had one more cruel blow to inflict. On December 11th Henry received the shocking news that

Wolcott Balestier, who had been so closely associated with the fortunes of *The American*, had died suddenly of typhoid blood poisoning while visiting Dresden. He was only thirty years of age. Henry made the long journey to attend the funeral in Dresden a few days later. He wept, standing beside Balestier's widowed mother and sisters, as the coffin was lowered into the muddy grave. It seemed incredible, and irreconcilable with any notion of a benign Providence, that such a promising young life should have been snuffed out by an action as trivial as drinking a cup of contaminated water – probably in London, before his departure for Germany. But the tears were for himself too. Balestier had been more than an efficient agent; in their brief association he had become a friend, almost like a son or young brother, a source of energy and encouragement and a staff to lean on in times of trouble. Henry could not imagine that he would find a substitute.

As the mourners moved away from the graveside, Balestier's sister Caroline, a petite, intense young woman, who had bravely controlled her grief throughout the obsequies, whispered that she wished him to share with her one of the ornate black-and-silver coaches that were to carry them back to a reception. In the deeply upholstered privacy of this conveyance, she astounded Henry by telling him that she was engaged to be married to another of Balestier's clients, Rudyard Kipling, and even more by asking him if he would 'give her away' at the wedding in place of her brother. 'Wolcott had such a high regard for you,' she said earnestly. 'He looked up to you as a kind of father. I can think of no one more appropriate.' In the highly emotional circumstances Henry could find no way decently to decline the office, but he did not look forward to performing it, even though Caroline assured him the wedding would be a small private ceremony. He had read Kipling's short stories and poems about India, army and empire, and admired their force and originality, as everyone had. Kipling's 'boom', especially since he returned to England from India in 1889, had been phenomenal, but its literary foundations were real. He was not another Rider Haggard – he was in a different category altogether. Every new book confirmed it, and he was still under thirty! As Du Maurier had said of him in a letter, 'the little beast is Titanic'. But there *was* something beastly about the man and his work, a coarse streak of masculine arrogance that Henry found alien. If Rudyard Kipling was the British reading public's idea of a great writer, then clearly it was not one that HJ would ever be able to satisfy. He had no wish to become personally intimate with this young lion, and the prospect of acting as a kind of pseudo-father-in-law to him was full of potential embarrassment.

During the past year Henry had spent fewer Sundays with Du Maurier than previously, partly because the long walk up to Hampstead seemed less inviting now that Jusserand, who had been promoted and posted to Copenhagen, was no longer able to bear him company, and partly because of the pressure of theatre business, which occupied so much of his time that he needed his Sabbaths to catch up with correspondence and other work. He and Kiki continued to meet regularly at social gatherings in London and exchanged letters in the intervals – they commiserated at length with each other over the death of Lowell, far away on the other side of the Atlantic, in August – but Henry was guiltily conscious of having neglected him a little in the second half of the year. The guilt derived from a secret relief at having the excuse of his involvement in *The American* to avoid a long private conversation about *Peter Ibbetson*, which was serialised in *Harper's* between June and December with illustrations by Du Maurier himself, and published as a book about halfway through this period. The long first section about the hero's childhood stood up well on reacquaintance, but the further Henry read into the part of the novel which was new to him, the more his earlier misgivings were confirmed. For a while the narrative simply rambled, as the author, ill-concealed behind the mask of the narrator, obviously wondered what to do next. *'On reading and re-reading these past pages I find that I have been unpardonably egotistic, unconscionably prolix and diffuse,'* Peter admitted; and 'Yes, yes, my dear fellow, I'm afraid you have,' Henry murmured as he read these words. Then the story took a sudden swerve into the supernatural. Peter, incarcerated in a prison for the criminally insane (for having murdered his villainous stepfather), and his beloved, the Duchess of Towers, were able miraculously to communicate and share a kind of life together by a technique of 'dreaming true'. This allowed them to travel back in time to their idyllic childhood and observe their young selves, and also to inhabit as adults a virtual world of their own choice, travelling effortlessly around Europe, and moving from, say, a gallery in the Louvre to a box at La Scala as the mood took them. After pages of this sort of whimsy, the Duchess was killed in the real world, nobly saving a child from a railway accident, but returned to the hero in dream to cheer him with a mystical-evolutionary vision of the future of humanity and life after death: *'Ever thus may a little live spark of your own individual consciousness be handed down mildly incandescent to your remotest posterity.'* It was all excruciatingly embarrassing and for Henry painfully reminiscent of his father's Swedenborgianism. Why was it that apparently sensible people who rejected orthodox religion on rational grounds invariably constructed something infinitely less plausible in its place? From a literary point of view Du Maurier's fatal error was not to have made the element of the uncanny ambiguous, with some possibility of a natural, materialistic explanation of the 'true dreaming'. One had either to take it seriously or to leave it, and any intelligent reader would do the latter. He wondered briefly if he could have prevented this mistake by taking a more sustained interest in the novel's development, but recalled that Du Maurier had complained bitterly about the interference of Harper's editors while the book was in production. Like many beginners in the art of fiction, he combined modest claims for his work with a certain obstinacy in defending his execution of it.

Henry of course kept his opinion to himself, and sent Du Maurier vague but warm messages of congratulation by letter as the serialisation proceeded and the book began to circulate. It helped that reviewers were on the whole lenient in their comments on Du Maurier's first attempt at fiction, and that most of his other friends were apparently genuinely impressed by it. They had never suspected the artist had it in him to write a full-length novel, and that he had illustrated it himself was an additional source of pleasure to its readers. Sales were modest, but respectable, though this was not a matter of crucial concern to Du Maurier, since he had taken a flat fee of £1,000 for the copyright, rather than a smaller sum as an advance against royalties. He preferred cash in the hand to the uncertain prospect of future gain, and it was not, Henry conceded, though he disapproved in principle, a bad bargain for a first novel.

Du Maurier seemed more than ever anxious about money these days, and to supplement his income further he engaged to do a lecture tour in the winter and spring of 1891–2, which would take him to eighteen venues in England and Scotland. His subject – he gave the same lecture in each place – was 'The Artists of *Punch*', principally Leech and Keene, illustrated with sixteen lantern slides. Henry received an amusing account by letter of his first engagement, at the Wolverhampton Literary and Scientific Society on 12th November, whither he was accompanied by the faithful Emma. 'When we saw the hall & were told that it would be quite full, we both turned pale and dissembled – When we were told that the audience would thoroughly appreciate every *joke & hit* of a famous *Punch artist*, we reflected that there wasn't a single joke in the whole lecture, and dissembled again – when we traipsed up and down the street of the most unbeautiful town in an east wind and thought of what was before us, a deadly chill, a wave of terror swept over us . . .' It reminded Henry of his own first night at Southport, and seemed to have ended similarly with a reassuring ovation. Indeed he saw a parallel between Du Maurier's journeys to far-flung lecture halls, and the slow progress of *The American* around the provincial theatre circuit that was about to recommence.

'We are both old troupers now, you and I, Kiki,' he said, putting a fraternal hand on Du Maurier's shoulder, 'compelled to learn new tricks and perform them wherever an audience can be found.' It was a fine but very cold Sunday just before Christmas, and Henry had made the effort to walk up to Hampstead and take Du Maurier out for his constitutional on the Heath, according to custom. They were alone, apart from the terrier Don, who nosed about on the frost-hardened ground looking frustrated at the scarcity of interesting smells. It was too cold to sit on their favourite bench – cold enough for people to be skating on the ponds. Watching them, Du Maurier recalled an occasion long ago when a dog fell through the ice on the Whitestone Pond and got into difficulties, and he had plunged into the icy water to rescue the creature. 'The grateful owner tried to tip me half-a-crown, and when I shook my head he raised it to five shillings, upon which I'm afraid I was rather short with him. *"I beg your pardon,"* he said, *"I didn't realise you were a gentleman."'* Henry laughed, though he had heard the story before – it was something of a family legend. It was hard to imagine Du Maurier acting so heroically now, he looked so frail, with his stick and dark glasses.

'You must be careful not to overstrain yourself with all this lecturing, Kiki,' Henry said. 'It sounds like a terribly gruelling programme.'

'Emma goes with me everywhere, and looks after me,' said Du Maurier. 'She makes sure the beds in the hotels are aired and warms my nightshirts at the fire, bless her. Anyway, I need the tin. My sight is getting worse. I've had to give up drawing altogether these past few weeks.'

'My dear fellow,' Henry murmured sympathetically.

'Gerald will be leaving Harrow soon, and we've decided to make him a solicitor. That will cost money. *He* won't be paying his way by winning bursaries and scholarships like his future brother-in-law, you can rely on that. And Sylvia's wedding will be another expense next year.'

'Is the law Gerald's choice?' Henry asked.

Du Maurier gave a rueful laugh. 'Not likely! He wants to be an actor, but his mother won't hear of it. I'm not in favour myself, for that matter.'

'I understand your reservations,' said Henry. 'But I have to say that the Comptons are thoroughly respectable people, and so are most of the other English actors I have met – unlike the French ones. The French are cleverer and more amusing, but quite impossible to know socially. If Gerald has the gift – and I recall some family entertainments when he showed distinct promise – then perhaps . . .' Henry shrugged to imply that Du Maurier should reconsider his opposition.

'Oh, he has the gift all right,' said Du Maurier. 'I remember once, he couldn't have been more than twelve or thirteen, he dressed up in some men's clothes – you know I keep a hamper of clothes at home for my models – he put on a wig and false beard and spectacles, and pretended to be a stranger who called asking me for a loan. It was ten minutes before I twigged! Of course, with my poor eyesight, it wasn't so difficult to fool me, but even so . . .' Du Maurier laughed reminiscently. 'The little devil. He was good at taking you off, too, Henry.'

'Me?' said Henry, disconcerted. 'And how did he do that, pray?'

'Well, you know you have a rather distinctive way of speaking, especially when you're animated. Gerald had it off to a T.'

'Did he, indeed?' said Henry, rather stiffly.

'I'm afraid you're offended,' said Du Maurier anxiously.

'Not at all,' said Henry, though he was a little. 'But I am curious to know – what features – that is to say – what were the distinctive characteristics – the idiosyncrasies of vocabulary or syntax – to the "T"s – not that I profess to understand precisely what a T is in this, this . . .' He felt himself momentarily in danger of losing the thread of his sentence, but triumphantly caught it by the tail: '. . . to the Ts of which your – your precocious offspring so remarkably approximated?'

'Like that, Henry,' said Du Maurier, laughing. 'He did you exactly like that.'

Henry had to smile himself, but at dinner that evening he kept a wary eye on Gerald, who was at home for the Christmas holidays, and contributed less than usual himself to the conversation.

He did not see Du Maurier again for two or three months. A wave of illness – not his own, fortunately, but other people's – seemed to engulf him in the New Year. There was an influenza epidemic in London, to which the Smiths succumbed, and for a week or so he had to dine at his club and at other times forage pathetically for himself in the kitchen at De Vere Gardens. Carrie Balestier's mother and sister were both stricken, and absent from her marriage to Kipling in consequence, though this was not a cause of real regret, since it made the wedding an even smaller, briefer and more restrained affair than had been planned, and he was able to perform his function, pay his respects, and promptly depart, without the demonstrations of bonhomie usually expected on such occasions. Fenimore wrote to say that she was suffering terribly from headache and earache, apparently the result of trying out 'false ear-drums' recommended by her doctor to improve her hearing. Not surprisingly, this experience had cast her into depression again. And of course there was always Alice, sinking slowly but inevitably towards death.

He called almost daily, but it was stressful to sit at her bedside and hold her hand and see her wan worn face smiling bravely up at him from the pillow, knowing she was in pain and being helpless to relieve it. The sainted Katharine was the guardian of the morphia that made Alice's suffering just tolerable. 'She knows I would give her as much as she wants, even if its effect should be to curtail her life,' Katharine confided in him one day, 'but she has made the decision to live her death by degrees, to the very end.' Henry admired his sister's courage, but wondered at it too. He did not think he would want to extend his own life in the same circumstances. It was like being present at some poignant, unbearably drawn-out final act in a tragedy, and he could not conceal from himself that he longed for the curtain to come down, to release them all from the tension. He tried to distract himself with work, developing ideas for plays, sending out drafts and scenarios to likely managers, and writing short stories and articles while he waited for their always dilatory responses. He had resolved to write no more fulllength novels while he was trying to establish himself as a playwright.

Henry was surprised to receive a letter from Du Maurier in February telling him that *he* had started another novel, dictating it to Emma as before. He had assumed that his friend was one of those people who had one novel 'in him', and having got it out of his system would be content; but the modest success of *Peter Ibbetson* had evidently encouraged him to try again. The subject was the story he had once offered to Henry, about the young girl who could only sing under hypnotism, '*la chanteuse magnétisée*' as Du Maurier referred to her in his letter. This was written entirely in French, appropriately enough, because he had decided to set the story in Paris, thirty-odd years ago, drawing on his memories of being an art student in the Latin Quarter. He claimed to be enjoying the writing '*énormément*' and in a postscript scribbled on the back of the envelope hinted at a certain raciness in the material: '*Nouveau roman n'est pas pour les petites filles.*' Henry had not given any thought to writing the story himself for years, but now that the possibility was closed for ever he felt a perverse and childish pang of deprivation. Du Maurier of course had no inkling that this narrative 'germ', as Henry liked to call the starting point of a work of fiction, had been buried in the dark humus of his notebook, awaiting the day when it would be transplanted to the foolscap sheets of his writing pad. The only way he could rid himself of futile regret for the lost opportunity was by resolving instantly to make use of another idea that Du Maurier had given him, the anecdote of the genteel couple who had come to him looking for work as models, and failed abysmally to imitate their own type. The story came easily, and he finished it in little more than a week. He called it 'The Real Thing', and sent it to the magazine *Black and White*, whose editor accepted it promptly for publication in April.

If only putting on plays were so quick and simple! Hare, who had accepted *Mrs Vibert* with such gratifying praise nearly a year ago, had procrastinated and prevaricated ever since, even though Henry had revised the play, now retitled *Tenants*, in accordance with his suggestions. Henry was beginning to lose faith in him. Meanwhile Compton had failed to rise to the bait of scenarios and draft first acts for two other comedies he had offered him in recent months. This lack of enthusiasm was perhaps understandable given the commercial failure of *The American*, but Henry now believed that that project had been doomed from the start. It had been a mistake to subject a complex and subtle novel to the inevitable compressions and compromises of theatrical adaptation. Those who knew the novel were dissatisfied with the play and those who didn't were puzzled by elements in the story which could not be properly developed for lack of time. Henry was convinced that he would only conquer the English stage with an idea that was conceived as a play from the beginning.

He now went to the theatre no longer as a disinterested consumer of more or less pleasurable experiences, but as a sharp-eyed, tight-lipped professional, looking out for likely actors and producers, studying the dramaturgical tricks of successful playwrights, and measuring himself against other newcomers to the field. An occasion of special interest was the first night of Oscar Wilde's *Lady Windermere's Fan*, at the St James's Theatre. Henry had no great liking for Wilde either as a man or as a writer. Ten years ago, when one of his private visits to America coincided with one of Wilde's grand lecture tours, and encouraged by a reported remark of Wilde's to the effect that no contemporary English novelist could hold a candle to James and Howells, he had called on him at his hotel in Washington, only to be disgusted by Wilde's manners. Wilde patronised him, capped his remarks with silly epigrams, dropped the names of people with whom Henry was much better acquainted than himself, and generally behaved in a vain and exhibitionist manner. Henry also felt there was something leering and unwholesome about Wilde's person and personality, a whiff of the moral decadence he had encountered in a more flagrant form when he visited Zhukovski in Naples. Henceforward he had kept his distance from Wilde, whose *détermination à épater les bourgeois* in his life as in his writings more and more confirmed the wisdom of this decision. London society hummed with rumours of his neglect of his wife in favour of dubious male companions.

There was no question, however, that the man was clever, as *Lady Windermere's Fan* demonstrated. The plot was not substantial or credible enough to bear a moment's serious consideration, but it was all so wittily managed, with such an abundance of amusing *mots*, batted back and forth across the stage like so many shuttlecocks, that one scarcely noticed. Certainly the first-night audience didn't. How they laughed! And how they clapped at the end. Needless to say, Wilde was not backward in responding to the calls of 'Author! Author!' With a green carnation in the lapel of his evening dress, and holding a cigarette in one mauve-gloved hand, he gave a long speech, concluding: 'The actors have given us a *charming* rendering of a *delightful* play, and your appreciation has been *most* intelligent. I congratulate you on the *great* success of your performance, which persuades me that you think *almost* as highly of the play as I do myself.' Although a typical provocation, and received as such with much laughter, these immodest sentiments were, Henry reflected, quite sincere and largely true. He certainly agreed with Wilde about the performances. George Alexander, the actor-manager responsible for mounting the play, had been particularly good as Lord Windermere. He had been a popular *jeune premier* in Henry Irving's company, specialising in romantic costume roles which displayed his handsome looks to advantage, but had since shown himself to be, as Oscar might have said, more than just a pair of pretty legs. A couple of years ago, at the age of only thirty-two, he had set himself up as a manager, taken a lease on the St James's Theatre, installed electric lighting and refurbished the seating, and began to put on new plays which had commercial appeal and suitable leading roles for himself, but were not devoid of artistic merit. So far he had been very successful. Henry was impressed by the meticulous care that had obviously gone into every aspect of his latest production, and made a mental note of Alexander as a potential producer of his own work.

Alice died on March 5th. Before she lapsed into a coma, she dictated a cable to Henry to send to William: 'Tenderest love to all. Farewell. Am going soon. Alice.' Later Henry applied his writerly gifts to fill out those spare, poignant words with the dense specificity of the event. 'Towards the end, for about an hour, the breathing became a constant sort of smothered whistle in the lung,' he wrote in a letter to William. 'The pulse flickered and went, ceased and revived a little again, and then with all perceptible action of the heart, altogether ceased to be sensible before the breathing ceased. At three o'clock a blessed change took place – she seemed to sleep – I mean to breathe – without effort, gently, peacefully and naturally, like a child. This lasted an hour, till the respirations, still distinct, paused, intermitted, and became rarer – at the last for seven or eight minutes, only one a minute, by the watch.' Henry paused in his task. Some might think so minute an observation of his sister's dying was almost callous, but William, the scientist, would understand and appreciate the effort to be truthful and exact. Nevertheless he decided to put in a little more human feeling. 'Her face then seemed in a strange, dim, touching way, to become clearer. I went to the window to let in a little more of the afternoon light (it was a bright, kind, soundless Sunday), and when I came back to the bed she had drawn her last breath.' He read the paragraph through again, struck out the cliché 'last breath', and substituted 'the breath that was not succeeded by another'.

For some weeks subsequently he was preoccupied with making arrangements and writing letters connected with Alice's death. She had asked to be cremated, a typically unconventional choice, necessitating a railway journey to the crematorium at Woking, but one that seemed appropriate to the small number of mourners – just himself, Katharine, and Alice's devoted nurse, Annie Richards – and the experience quite converted him to this funerary method. Everything was simple, seemly and dignified. It was a cold, sleety day, and he was glad to be taking his sister's ashes back to London, for eventual translation to their parents' grave in America, rather than leaving her remains to moulder in the dank earth of what had always been for her a foreign country.

Then there was Alice's will to be read and administered. She had divided her estate equally between Henry, William and Katharine, passing over Bob on the grounds that he had married into a rich family and had less need than his brothers. Henry predicted trouble from this exclusion – quite correctly as it turned out. Bob, who hated his financial dependence on his father-in-law, vigorously protested, and was only pacified when Henry offered to give him $5,000 of his own share.

'You are very generous,' Katharine said to Henry when she heard of his gesture.

'For some reason the Jameses always squabble over wills – I find it very distressing,' Henry replied, pretending his motive was to bring the dispute to a swift conclusion. In fact he was seeking to expiate a certain measure of transferred guilt about Bob and his dead brother Wilky – transferred from their father, and going back to the Civil War. Henry James Sr. had discouraged his two eldest sons from volunteering for the war at the outset, and given them every support in claiming medical exemption, on the grounds that no cause, however honourable, was worth dying for before a young man had had a chance to taste what life – especially love and marriage – could offer. But with typical inconsistency he seemed to change his mind after a year or two, and urged his two younger sons to volunteer when they were hardly more than boys – Wilky at seventeen and Bob, who lied about his age, at sixteen. Both of them had seen action, and behaved with great courage. Both had been wounded, and Wilky had nearly died – one of the stretcher-bearers carrying him from the field of battle had had his head blown off by an exploding shell. They were, in short, heroes, by whom Henry felt humbled, and almost shamed, at the time. Yet their subsequent lives, personal and professional, had been one long, doleful tale of failure, disappointment, and broken health. The traumatic experience of war had, it seemed, permanently incapacitated them for life in peace, and eventually brought Wilky's to a premature conclusion, while he himself and William, who had lived in ignoble safety as students throughout the conflict, had prospered and achieved distinction in their respective fields. To give Bob a substantial proportion of his share of Alice's estate hardly compensated for this inequality of fortune, but it eased Henry's conscience somewhat. He did not ask or expect William, who had four children to look after, to do the same, nor did his brother offer to do so.

William, however, agreed happily with Henry that Alice's bequest to Katharine, treating her on an equal footing with her brothers, was entirely right and proper, considering the care and devotion she had received from her friend over many years. But Henry was surprised to read in the will that Alice also bequeathed her journal to Katharine. He hadn't been previously aware that she kept a journal, and the information set off a small reaction of alarm in his mind at such a private document passing out of the control of the family.

'She began it about three years ago, when we moved to Leamington,' Katharine told him. 'Lately, when she was too weak to write, she used to dictate her thoughts to me, so I feel as if I had a share in them. It will certainly be my most precious relic of her.' When Henry hinted that he would be interested to read the journal, Katharine was uncooperative. 'Alice told me she would like to have it type-copied, so I'm sure she wanted it to be read, eventually,' she said. 'But I feel it's too soon to show it to anyone, even to you, Henry. And, to be honest, it's so precious to me I couldn't bear to let it out of my possession, even for a few hours. When it's been copied, then of course you and William may read it.'

Another intriguing piece of information he obtained from the same source was that in the last week or so of her life Alice had asked Katharine to read her a story of Fenimore's called 'Dorothy', recently published in *Harper's*. 'She thought very highly of it,' said Katharine. 'I'm glad to say that we finished it shortly before she died.' Henry naturally read the story himself at the first opportunity. It was a typical product of Fenimore's pen, an artfully angled glance at the mysteries and vagaries of women's emotional lives, a comedy of manners from which a sentimental tragedy unexpectedly emerged. Henry immediately recognised the principal setting as a lightly fictionalised version of the Villa Castellani at Bellosguardo, with its glorious views and dizzying balconies, where a group of American expatriates variously flirted and yearned. Dorothy, an attractive, Daisy Millerish young American girl, surprised everyone by marrying the rich but middle-aged Mackenzie. When he died suddenly, not long afterwards, it was assumed she would make a second, more brilliant and more romantic marriage, but in the event she died herself, apparently of grief. The appeal of the story for Alice was presumably the value it placed upon death as an idea, or aspiration, inexplicable to the common herd. In Fenimore's work it took its place in a long series of fictions about women who showed their nobility of character by renouncing the prospect of ordinary worldly happiness.

He paid a visit to Fenimore in Oxford not long afterwards, and looked forward to telling her of Alice's admiration for her story. She would be surprised and pleased, and it would provide a convenient excuse for avoiding discussion of more complicated emotions connected with Alice's death. He blurted out his discovery almost as soon as Fenimore had greeted him in her little parlour in Beaumont Street, and was disconcerted when she coolly replied:

'Yes, I know.'

'You know? How?'

'Your sister sent me a message, just before she died, through Miss Loring,' said Fenimore. 'That was part of it.'

Henry could barely restrain himself from rudely asking what the other part consisted of. He had not been aware that they were in contact by correspondence, and said as much.

'We were not,' said Fenimore. 'But of course we were aware of each other's existence, through our common intercourse with you. I knew that she was jealous of me – I mean of the time you spend with me – not that it is so very much.' Fenimore blushed a little at this, and turned her head to glance out of the window at a rag-and-bone merchant's horse and cart grinding past in the street, its driver uttering a hoarse, unintelligible cry to attract attention. 'But I understood how she felt, given her unfortunate circumstances. I bore her no grudge. But I think, as her end grew near, she felt a wish for – not reconciliation, for we had never quarrelled – but you know what I mean.'

'I think so,' said Henry, though he was still puzzled, and felt that Fenimore was keeping something back about Alice's message. She eyed him in a thoughtful, but slightly abstracted way, as their conversation shifted to more banal topics: the tranquillity of the college precincts in the Easter vacation, the riches of the Bodleian where she had been fortunate enough to secure a reader's ticket, the splendid singing of the choir in Christ Church Cathedral on Sundays which she could appreciate even with her impaired hearing.

'Tell me about the beastly false ear-drums,' he said. 'They sound like instruments of torture.'

That, apparently, was exactly what they felt like. She said it was like having two sharp instruments permanently embedded in one's ears. She kept them in for two weeks until she could bear the pain no more, but when she took them out the headaches and ear-aches continued for a month.

'Did they improve your hearing, while you had them in?' he asked.

'Not in the least.'

'Then why did you persevere, my dear Fenimore?'

'I hoped they might work if I got used to them,' she said. 'I would do almost anything, suffer almost anything, to hear again as I used to.'

The day was fine and they went out for a walk. Beaumont Street, just off St Giles, was conveniently situated for exploring the streets and alleys and quadrangles of the time-worn, studious city. They spent a pleasant half-hour browsing in Blackwell's excellent bookshop, surreptitiously checking its stocks of their own books, as authors do. Henry was pleased to see several copies of *The Lesson of the Master*, the title of his latest collection of short stories, on the 'Recently Published' table.

'That's a horrid story, Henry,' Fenimore said later, when he mentioned this observation at dinner. They were dining at the Randolph Hotel, where he was staying the night. 'Clever, but horrid. It's a libel against women.'

'Nonsense, Fenimore, it's no such thing,' Henry protested. 'I admit Mrs St George is something of a tyrant. But you might just as well call the story a libel against men. Consider the treachery with which St George steals the girl from his young protégé after his wife dies.'

'But he has been corrupted by his wife's materialism. And the girl is just as bad in the end. It's no use protesting, Henry, the moral of the story is clear: women are only interested in feathering their own nests and are consequently the enemies of art.'

'You exaggerate, my dear Fenimore,' Henry said with a smile which he hoped was disarming. 'But I think you will admit that there may be a conflict of interests between – not women and art – but *marriage* and art.'

Fenimore flushed slightly, and chewed her cutlet in silence for a few moments. 'Do you advocate free love, then, as a *modus vivendi* for the artist?' she enquired ironically.

'Of course not, Fenimore, you know how I hate all such, such – bohemian sordidness,' said Henry, growing a little excited in spite of himself. 'And of course I don't deny that there are successful artists who have been happily – many more who have been *un*happily no doubt – but even so – yes, some have been happily married. My friend Du Maurier, for instance – but who knows what more he might have achieved without the constant worry of looking after his growing family? Now it's driving him to write novels, which is not his *métier* at all.'

'Marriage does not *necessarily* entail having children,' Fenimore said, laying down her knife and fork. Her ear trumpet lay beside her plate like another, specialised piece of cutlery, but she had not needed to use it in the hushed, high-ceilinged dining room.

'No, but that is its usual consequence – and principal purpose, if we are to believe the Prayer Book,' said Henry forcing another smile. Fenimore, he worked out by a rapid calculation, must be over fifty now, well past normal childbearing age. Was she nurturing some dream of a marriage of true minds rather than bodies, the two of them working away in separate studies, and meeting for companionable meals and strolls, as they had done at Bellosguardo? It had worked well there, but the very attraction of that arrangement had been its provisionality, its open-endedness and amenability to sudden closure. Marriage would be inevitably a surrender of one's freedom. And then again, even in mature years there should be, if not desire, then some physical tenderness in a marriage. Fenimore was a comely woman for her age. He admired her neat figure and the quiet good taste with which she clothed it, he liked to look upon her smooth round cheeks, still surprisingly unblemished by wrinkles, her wide, calm grey-blue eyes, the slightly amused set of her lips in repose, as if she were biting the lower one, the well-fleshed throat with its invariable velvet choker. He enjoyed her company. But he had not the slightest inclination to reach out and touch her, let alone to put his arms round her and kiss her on the lips, let alone . . . He pursued this train of thought no further. A slightly embarrassed silence fell on the table, which Fenimore broke.

'Tell me about your plays, Henry.'

'Alas, there is nothing new to report. Theatrical managers are the most dilatory, vacillating, fickle race of men I have ever encountered.'

'You may remember,' Fenimore said timidly, 'we spoke once of collaborating on a play together.'

'Yes, indeed,' he replied. He had anticipated that this subject would arise during his visit, and had his answer ready. 'But I wouldn't dream of embroiling you in the wretched and demoralising business until I am much better established in it myself.'

'That is thoughtful of you,' she said, but she looked disappointed.

Henry could not conceive of collaborating with anyone in writing prose fiction – it was too private and personal a process; but there was, inevitably, a collaborative element in the staging of every play which made sharing the compositional process in this form not entirely unthinkable. He had however no intention of getting involved in such an experiment until he had seen his current dramatic projects through to completion and run out of ideas for new ones. Meanwhile, there was no harm in being vaguely encouraging to poor Fenimore. 'We will speak of it again when I can feel confident of actually getting our work produced,' he said.

'Very well, Henry,' she said, brightening perceptibly at the word 'our'.

'A prospect that seems very distant at present,' he cautioned. But he was not sure she heard him correctly.

'Good,' she said.

6

BY the late spring he felt the need of a long break from London and duty. The exacting business of administering Alice's estate was concluded, and his theatrical ships were apparently becalmed at sea, far from port. There was nothing to detain him in England, and he yearned unspeakably for Italy. He made arrangements to join the French writer Paul Bourget and his young American wife in Siena, and to stay afterwards with another friend, Mrs 'Jack' Gardner, well-known hostess and patron of the arts, in her rented palazzo in Venice. It was a signal advantage of being a bachelor with a large circle of friends that one could make such plans at relatively short notice, and the development of the railroad system in Europe had made it absurdly easy to carry them out. One boarded a train at Victoria or Waterloo station and two or three days later alighted in some warm historic southern city, a journey that at the beginning of the century would have taken weeks by coach and diligence. The drawback of such progress in transportation was of course that too many people took advantage of it, leading to the plague of English and American tourists now infesting all the most interesting and picturesque places in Europe, but he hoped to avoid the worst of the hordes by going to Italy in the months of June and July, traditionally regarded as too hot for the comfort of Anglo-Saxons.

Just before he departed he attended Du Maurier's lecture on *Punch* artists, which finally reached the capital, after its long circuit of provincial venues, in late May. The Prince's Hall in Piccadilly was not as full as might have been hoped, for the Season was in full swing and Society's mantelpieces groaned under the weight of invitations, but a number of Du Maurier's friends besides Henry turned up loyally for the occasion. They were asked to sit on the stage behind the speaker as a 'platform party', an exposure to public gaze that Henry did not welcome, but submitted to for his friend's sake.

Alma-Tadema was in the chair, a rather comical circumstance, since the two men looked so alike that they were frequently mistaken for each other. (When congratulated in error for Alma-Tadema's paintings by enthusiastic ladies Du Maurier would sometimes imitate his colleague's thick Flemish accent and say, clasping their hands, 'Tank you zo much, gom to me on my Chewsdays' – or so he claimed, adding: 'I often wonder if they go.')

Du Maurier had given his lecture so many times by now that he knew it by heart, and seldom needed to do more than glance at the text which he had had printed in an eighteen-point typeface so that he could read it easily. He was plainly bored with it, and delivered it without any ornament of gesture or intonation, yet somehow he managed to avoid the consequence that might have been expected, of boring his audience. There was something so palpably honest and decent and modest about the man that one's heart went out to him, and if there was nothing intellectually incisive about his discourse – the only crumb of aesthetic nourishment Henry carried away from it was the statement, *'It must be remembered that there are no such things as lines in nature'* – nevertheless he did succeed in evoking the individual qualities of his great precursors, Leech and Keene, simply by the play of his own personal knowledge over their characters and their work. With Du Maurier everything was personal, and more often than not rosily tinted with a lyrical nostalgia that was never sickly because it was palpably sincere. It was what had made the first part of *Peter Ibbetson* so charming. It was a real gift – not enough to carry a whole novel, but certainly a whole lecture.

Afterwards Henry had supper with him and Emma – poor Emma, how many times had she listened to that lecture? But she claimed she never tired of it. She was looking a little pale and worn, having only recently recovered from a frightening episode of family illness, of which Henry now received the full story. In April Trixy had succumbed to typhoid fever while on a visit to the Isle of Wight, and Emma had gone to Shanklin to nurse her, only to fall ill with blood-poisoning herself, so that mother and daughter were ill in bed in adjoining rooms, while Du Maurier was unable to fly to their assistance because of his lecturing commitments. Henry, who still harboured a special fondness for Trixy, and had had a particular dread of typhoid ever since Balestier's death, listened to this saga with sympathetic concern. Then he asked how the new novel was progressing. In contrast to his eagerness to solicit early opinions of *Peter Ibbetson*, Du Maurier had kept this second effort very much to himself so far.

'Pretty well, I think,' said Du Maurier modestly.

'It's wonderful,' Emma enthused. 'I'm always longing to find out what will happen in the next chapter.'

'Ah, well, you're biased, my dear,' said Du Maurier fondly. 'We must wait and see what the people at Harper think.'

'Do you have a title for it yet?' Henry asked.

'Yes, it's called *Trilby*,' said Du Maurier. 'That's the name of the heroine.'

'"Trilby",' Henry repeated. 'Is it her first name or her second name?'

'Her first name. "Trilby O'Ferrall".'

'She's Irish?'

'Scottish. The child of two rather disreputable Scottish parents, but born and brought up in Paris. Not that she was brought up in any proper sense. Her father was a drunkard, and her mother not much better.'

'She's orphaned at fifteen, poor thing, and left to look after her infant brother,' Emma elaborated. 'So she works as an artist's model.'

'"Trilby",' Henry said again, musingly, rolling the syllables on his tongue as if to suck the flavours of association from the name. As a title it was certainly more euphonious and memorable than *Peter Ibbetson* (he was never confident about where to put the *e* and the *o* in the surname when he wrote it down). 'I seem to have heard it before, but not as a girl's name.'

'I came across it in a French fairy tale, when I was a boy,' said Du Maurier. 'Trilby was the name of the fairy, but the story for some reason was set in Scotland. Whether the name is French or Scottish I have no idea, but it caught my fancy, and stuck in my memory. It seemed appropriate for my *chanteuse*.'

'I remember now!' Henry exclaimed. 'It was the name of Eugénie Guérin's pet dog!'

'Was it, by Jove?' said Du Maurier, laughing. 'Fortunately not many of my readers will have your knowledge of French literature, Henry.' Superstitiously he touched the wood of the table. 'If I'm lucky enough to *have* any readers, that is.'

Henry enjoyed his Italian holiday. Siena was delightful, not yet 'discovered' by as many tourists as Florence or Rome, while crowded, *vaporetto*-ridden Venice still offered sanctuary and treasures and incomparable views to the discriminating visitor, especially if he had the good fortune to reside in a palazzo on the Grand Canal, with a gondola always at hand to waft him to some unfrequented church or unspoiled island in the lagoon. From Venice he went to Lausanne, where William, who was on sabbatical leave from Harvard, was spending the summer with Alice and their four children, two of them infants whom Henry had not seen before, while young Harry and Peggy had grown considerably since he had dandled them on his knee on his last visit to America. He was disconcerted by William's departure on a walking tour not long after his arrival – there had been some misunderstanding about plans – and cut short his visit after ten days, which was however quite long enough for doing duty as genial uncle, and for Switzerland too, for that matter. He had never quite been able to see the point of Switzerland. He returned to London, with only a brief pause in Paris, in the middle of August. In his luggage was the complete draft of a play called *Mrs Jasper*, which he had written in the course of his travels.

This was a light-hearted comedy of manners, verging on farce, loosely based on one of his own short stories, but set in England instead of the original Italy. The plot turned on the efforts of an unscrupulous mother to compromise a young man into marrying her daughter. The eponymous heroine, a young widow, at first gave her support to this plan, then recoiled against it and tried to help the young man to extricate himself from his engagement, only to fall in love with him herself and he with her. There were a great

many other flirtations, jealousies, unrequited loves, and misunder-
standings among the characters, which kept them in a constant
flurry of exits and entrances, pursuing or hiding from one another,
and there was a good deal of business with a photographic camera
in the first act, which Henry thought would be a novelty. He saw
the piece as a pure entertainment that would beguile the audience
by the adroitness with which it juggled the balls of an admittedly
exiguous plot. It would of course require actors endowed with
comic *élan* and immaculate timing, and a charismatic actress in the
title role.

The one he had in mind was Ada Rehan, an Irish-American
actress who was the star of the productions of Augustin Daly, himself
an interesting theatrical phenomenon. Having made his reputation
as a producer on Broadway, he had in recent years brought his
company to London for several highly successful seasons at the
Lyceum. He had been bold enough to include in his varied repertory productions of Shakespeare's *The Taming of the Shrew* and *As
You Like It*, in versions closer than usual to the original texts, which
had been rapturously received, with special appreciation of Ada
Rehan's performances as Katherina and Rosalind. The venerable
Poet Laureate, Alfred Lord Tennyson, had been so ravished that he
had offered Daly his verse play about Robin Hood, *The Foresters*,
on the understanding that Miss Rehan would play the part of Maid
Marion, and a production was reported to be in preparation, with
music commissioned from Arthur Sullivan.

Henry had met Miss Rehan the previous autumn, just before the
premiere of *The American*, and on that occasion she passed him a
message from Daly, inviting him to submit a play with a good part
for herself. The proposal was all the more enticing inasmuch as Daly
had just announced that he intended to build a new theatre in
Leicester Square as a permanent London home for his company,
while continuing his operations in New York, thus opening up the
prospect of having one's work produced on both sides of the Atlantic
by the same management. Henry had invited Daly to the first night
of *The American*, and sent him two outlines for plays which failed
to elicit any response. Now, however, he thought he had something

that might appeal to both manager and actress. He wrote to Miss Rehan asking if he might read the play to her, and she agreed readily, suggesting that it might take place one afternoon at the home of their mutual friends, Mr and Mrs Barrington, where they had first met.

This couple were very happy to make their drawing room available for the reading, to play the part of an audience, and to provide tea between the acts. Ada Rehan was a little late, perhaps by design, for she obviously liked to 'make an entrance'. She was an actress from the toes of her delicately fashioned shoes to the top of her elaborately coiffed hair, and smiled and fluttered her eyelashes and gestured expressively as she apologised for her lateness. She was tall and beautiful, and possessed of what one critic had called 'a velvet voice'. When she had finished her little performance she subsided into the upright armchair prepared for her and assumed an attitude of studied attentiveness, while Henry sat on a similar chair facing her and read his play, and the Barringtons listened from the comfortable depths of a sofa. Miss Rehan did not laugh quite as much as he might have wished, and certainly not as much as the Barringtons, but he had a sense that she was smiling a good deal, and when he had finished she said: 'Well, that was lovely. Thank you very much, Mr James.'

The Barringtons added their plaudits, and then discreetly withdrew to allow author and actress to confer privately.

'So – do you think it would "go"?' he asked.

'I don't see why not,' she said.

'And can you see yourself as Mrs Jasper? I must say that I believe you would be quite perfect.'

'Yes. Yes, I think I can,' she said, to his delight. 'The part has great possibilities. I'm not sure I followed all the intricacies of the plot—'

'No, I understand – but of course in performance—'

'Yes, in performance I'm sure it would all become clear. I can't answer for Augustin, of course, but let's send him the play and see what he thinks of it.'

Henry would have liked a more detailed discussion of his work, but she was already picking up her belongings preparatory for her departure. It seemed that she was late for another appointment. She undertook, however, to pass the play to Daly personally with her own commendation, and Henry walked home with a spring in his step.

A week or so later, he received a brief letter from the producer saying that the play had pleased him but not satisfied him, and offering to elaborate further in a meeting. Henry took this to be a rejection, but an encouraging one, and thought it was worth accepting the invitation. A few days later he called on Daly by arrangement at his office in Shaftesbury Avenue. The producer, a well-built man of about fifty, with a long, handsome, slightly melancholy Irish face, and dark centre-parted hair strikingly combined with a pale grey moustache, received him with American informality in waistcoat and shirtsleeves, and offered him whisky to drink at three o'clock in the afternoon, which Henry politely declined. Daly had the plans of his new theatre spread out on his desk, and took pleasure in showing them to Henry and boasting about all the latest scene-shifting and lighting facilities it would have, and the splendour of its public spaces. When they got down to discussing *Mrs Jasper*, it seemed to be not the inquest on a dramatic corpse that he had expected, but a consultation about remedial surgery. Daly had a number of criticisms and suggestions to make, most of which Henry accepted, especially the importance of building up the Ada Rehan part and contriving that she should have the last line at the end of each act. He agreed to write another draft of the play incorporating these notes and to resubmit it.

He hastened home and commenced the task the same day, while the ideas were all clear in his head. Within a few weeks the work was completed, and Henry sent off the revised play to Daly, who had gone back to New York to supervise his season there. Very soon he received a brief letter from the manager to say that he accepted the play and offered a flat rate of $25 per performance. Henry was overjoyed. The only snag was that the production would have to wait for the completion of the new theatre in London, since Daly wanted it to be an ornament of his first season there. However, he held out the prospect of producing it first in New York in the meantime.

Then an all too familiar inertia seemed to overtake the project. Henry heard nothing from Daly for weeks. He tried to contain his impatience, and distracted himself meanwhile by once again grooming that old warhorse, *The American*. Compton had signalled from the provinces that the fourth act continued to have a lowering effect on audiences, and made a suggestion for rewriting it that would allow Claire Cintré's brother Valentin to survive the duel. Henry didn't care for the clumsy emendation Compton proposed, but his busy brain couldn't leave the matter alone, and he soon saw a more satisfactory way to achieve the same effect.

He dashed off an enthusiastic letter to Compton promising a speedy delivery of the new act, but the task proved more complicated and time-consuming than he had anticipated, necessitating numerous small alterations of the three previous acts to make them consistent with the rewritten fourth, and much consultation by letter and telegram between himself and the Comptons as the drafts passed to and fro between London and whatever provincial outpost they had pitched their tent in. It was necessary to borrow and return the prompt-book at intervals because this was the only reliable text of the whole play, and to have the new scenes copied again and again, as they went through various drafts, and whenever he sent one of these to the Comptons he felt driven to accompany it with a detailed explanation of the dramatic reason for every change, and equally detailed notes on how the new lines should be delivered. Henry thought his boots must be wearing a perceptible trail in the pavement between De Vere Mansions and the West Kensington Post Office.

He knew that by any rational criteria this expenditure of effort was absurd. However much he improved *The American* there was no prospect that it would ever have another chance on the London stage; and if Compton decided to drop it from his provincial repertoire he himself would lose little income or glory in consequence. Yet he could not bear to let it sink into the oblivion of failed plays as long as there was a possibility of keeping it afloat. It was, after all, to date, still the only one of his dramatic works that had been professionally staged, and he had hopes of one day persuading Compton to take on another. So he slaved away on *The American*, stitching and unstitching and restitching its speeches, until he had done as much, he told Compton, 'as flesh and blood could bear'. In mid-November he went down to Bath, where the C.C.C. was occupying the charming Theatre Royal, to deliver the fully revised play in person. The Comptons pronounced themselves delighted with the new fourth act, but a try-out in Bristol revealed some further problems which necessitated more adjustments, more cuts and more new speeches, which he worked on in the last week of November, in a London choked with a sooty 'pea soup' fog that hung in the streets like a sinister miasma and, even on the fourth floor of De Vere Mansions, required lamps to be lit all day.

Just before he was finally, finally finished with *The American* he heard again from Daly, who wanted more cuts and revisions of *Mrs Jasper* and asked if he could supply an amusing piece of verse in rhyming couplets for Ada Rehan to recite at the end of the play, *à la* Restoration comedy. Henry, who had not written a line of verse since youth, was dismayed by this suggestion, but, perceiving in these demands that the New York production must be imminent, gamely composed a pretty, genial, graceful speech in rhythmical prose for the purpose, and dealt expeditiously with the other points raised by the manager. He sent off the revised script and waited in suspense for several weeks, only to learn eventually that a New York production was not after all feasible, and the London one was held up by delays in the building of Daly's Theatre (for that, rather vaingloriously, was what it was to be called) caused by the national strike of bricklayers. It seemed, however, that the revised play was to the manager's satisfaction, since there was no word to the contrary. About Hare's plans for *Mrs Vibert* he no longer bothered to enquire, for he felt demeaned by the endless sequence of excuses, empty promises, and transparent prevarications that such enquiries inevitably elicited. So the year drew towards its close, with his plan to make his fortune as a playwright still more of a dream than a reality.

Meanwhile Du Maurier was having better luck in his effort to establish himself as a novelist, as Henry learned from a letter received at the beginning of December. He had dined with Harper's Clarence McIlvaine who told him that they liked *Trilby*, and wanted to publish it on both sides of the Atlantic subject to certain excisions of controversial matter, 'anticlerical tirades and so forth'. Du Maurier had been shown some of the readers' reports and quoted one of them: '*a decided advance upon* Peter Ibbetson – *a beautiful piece of work, full of faults, but full also of that illuminated something that soars above criticism – it is so large, so human, so searching that it will appeal to a great multitude.*' Harper were offering the same terms as before, but Du Maurier was hopeful of getting them to cough up more for the 'illuminated something'. A postscript in French jokingly described the kind of illumination to be expected: '*Lampions anticléricaux. Spécialité d'éclairage moral. Nudité – chasteté &c. &c. voir "Trilby".*' Henry felt just the tiniest prick of jealousy – no publisher's reader had ever greeted his own work so effusively – but immediately dismissed it as ignoble and indeed absurd. He wrote back quickly with his congratulations: 'Brava Trilby – bravo Harper, & Harper's Readers & Harper's McIlvaine & bravi tutti! I rejoice with all my heart in the big verdict.' He was quite curious to read the novel now, but Du Maurier was apparently in no hurry to publish. He secured a fee of £2,000 for the copyright of the new book, twice as much as for his first, undertook to illustrate it himself, and was given a year to do the necessary drawings and to revise his text.

7

1893 began inauspiciously for Henry with an attack of gout, his first experience of this painful affliction, possibly brought on by drinking in the New Year with tumblers of hot punch at a gathering of friends at Gosse's house. Gosse was always lavish with liquor on such occasions, compensating no doubt for the austere abstinence of his puritanical upbringing. Immobilised in the flat he wrote to his friend, only half in jest, 'I feel it is the beginning of the end.' He would be fifty in April. He had, even by the most wildly optimistic estimates, fewer years left than he had lived, and he was oppressed by the consciousness of unfulfilled ambitions, declining vitality and diminishing reserves of time. He felt he was in danger of losing his identity as a writer, falling into a void between a fading reputation as a novelist and a still elusive one as a dramatist. If he could only attain the latter he felt sure he would have the strength and the confidence to revive the former. Meanwhile he was tormented by the spectacle of other writers – Kipling, Wilde, Thomas Hardy, for instance, not to mention Mrs Humphry Ward – getting the kind of attention and praise that he felt was *his* due; felt, but could not openly admit even to his closest friends without appearing pathetically weak and envious. Instead he put these complicated misgivings and yearnings into a short story that he called 'The Middle Years'.

The hero, Dencombe, was a novelist whose work, produced slowly and with immense pains, was respected but not widely appreciated, and now, in middle age, he had an illness which threatened to cut short his hopes of achieving greatness. *'This was the pang that had been sharpest during the last few years – the sense of ebbing time, of shrinking opportunity . . . he had done all he should ever do, and yet hadn't done what he wanted.'* This dismal thought occurred to the listless Dencombe as he sat on a bench facing the sea at Bournemouth, balancing on his knee a package just received from his publisher, which he knew contained a copy of his latest – and almost certainly last – novel. Having summoned up the energy to remove the book from its wrapping, and after dipping into it with a flicker of revived self-esteem, he recognised by its cover another copy of the same book in the hand of a young man escorting two ladies, one old and one young, along the cliffside path. He also recognised the people, for they were staying in the same hotel as himself. The young man, Doctor Hugh, turned out to have obtained an early copy of Dencombe's novel because he was passionately devoted to his work. *'Chance had brought the weary man of letters face to face with the greatest admirer in the new generation of whom it was supposable he might boast.'* Dr Hugh henceforth dedicated himself to caring for, and perhaps curing, the sick author, who *'soaring again a little on the weak wings of convalescence and still haunted by that happy notion of an organised rescue, found another strain of eloquence to plead the cause of a certain splendid "late manner," the very citadel, as it would prove, of his reputation, the stronghold into which his real treasure would be gathered'.* This was a recurring daydream of Henry's own, to be fulfilled when he had put himself above all concern with vulgar notions of 'success' as a novelist by demonstrably achieving it as a dramatist, but one he did not wish to reveal too obviously. Decorum in the ordinary as well as the literary sense of the term required that the fictitious author should be denied this happy consummation. Dencombe must die at the end of the story, in his middle years, his life's work incomplete. Imagining himself in this plight Henry summoned up a deathbed speech of such poignancy and eloquence that it brought tears to his own eyes as he penned it: *' "A second chance – that's the delusion. There never was to be but one. We work in the dark – we do what we can – we give what we have. Our doubt is our passion and our passion is our task. The rest is the madness of art." '* He was not quite sure himself exactly what the last two sentences meant; like the speeches of Hamlet or Lear they contained more than any prosaic paraphrase could express. If he were to die tomorrow, he would be happy to have them inscribed on his tombstone.

To intensify what was at stake in the story he decided that Dr Hugh's devotion to the author would cause him to alienate the old lady, his patroness, and thus lose the chance of marrying the young one, her companion. Reading the story over, it struck Henry that Fenimore would say he was once again opposing women to art, or marriage to art – and she would be right: the evidence was undeniably there on the last page, as the Doctor declared that he sacrificed his attachment to the young woman willingly, and assured the dying novelist of his literary achievement: ' *"You're a great success!" said Doctor Hugh, putting into his young voice the ring of a marriage bell.*' Henry thought about deleting or replacing the ironic hymeneal trope, but let it stand. Fenimore would feel both angry and vindicated when she read it, but it was just as well that she should be under no illusions as to his real feelings. About some things they communicated more honestly through their fictions than in their conversations.

There were several analogues to the figure of Dr Hugh in Henry's life now – clever and charming young men, usually American expatriates as it happened, who applied the balm of private admiration to the wounds inflicted by public neglect. Poor Balestier had been one such. William Morton Fullerton, a handsome and highly intelligent journalist who came from Boston to London in 1890 and quickly secured a position on *The Times*, had helped to fill the gap in Henry's life which Balestier left, and so had Henry Harland, a talented writer and a publisher of vision, who moved from America to England at about the same time, joining John Lane at The Bodley Head as an editor. Then there was Jonathan Sturges, a victim of polio bravely borne, fortunately provided with a substantial private income which he supplemented with journalism, *belles lettres* and translations, including a collection of Maupassant's stories initiated and completed with Henry's support. He was conscious that none of these young men conformed to the approved Anglo-Saxon pattern of hearty masculinity, though they diverged from it in different ways and for different reasons: Sturges on account of his physical affliction, poor fellow, Fullerton because he seemed to be attracted equally by male and female beauty, and Harland (who was married) because of his interest in what used to be known as aestheticism and was now beginning to be called, as *la fin du siècle* drew nearer, the Decadence. All three, in fact, were friends of Oscar Wilde, the presiding spirit of this movement in the arts as far as England was concerned.

Although Henry kept his distance from Wilde, and the aura of sexual scandal that he carried with him everywhere, this did not affect his relations with the three young men, which were affectionate but of course entirely proper. The upsetting experience with Zhukovski in Naples, which had in a sense precipitated his intimacy with Fenimore, belonged to his own younger self. Now, having reached the calm waters of middle age, having survived all the perils and problems, the vague longings and physical disturbances, associated with sex in early manhood, Henry felt quite safe in cultivating the friendship of sympathetic young men. Old comrades like Du Maurier and Gosse were of course inestimably precious; but after all one took their support for granted, and their praise of one's work with a pinch of salt. There was nothing quite so sweet to injured merit as the tribute of an intelligent and gifted young man, the deference of disciple to master. Morton Fullerton even carried his homage to the extreme of imitating Henry's own style in writing to him, incorporating whole phrases from a published article into one of his own letters, for which Henry thought it prudent to administer a mild slap of reproof. One could, after all, have too much of a good thing.

The letter had come from Paris, where Fullerton had been posted at the beginning of the year to work at the *Times* bureau. Henry missed the young man's company and conversation, and it was partly in order to enjoy them again that he went to Paris in the middle of March, for an extended visit. He stayed at his favourite hotel, the Westminster, in the Rue de la Paix, just off the Place Vendôme. The gout was still troubling him, but he managed to hobble around the boulevards to meet Morton at the cafés and restaurants he had 'discovered'. Henry Harland also happened to be in Paris at the same time, and they had a convivial dinner at which the young man eagerly explained his plans to publish a new high-quality literary periodical that would be more like a book than a magazine – indeed it was to be called *The Yellow Book* – designed to challenge and transform the stuffy Philistine world of English letters. It would publish the best work of the younger generation of writers who took their cue from recent developments in French literature, and be illustrated by a dazzling new artistic genius called Aubrey Beardsley;

but Harland was anxious to solicit contributions from Henry to give the publication what he called 'copper-bottomed literary quality'. Henry had seen some of Aubrey Beardsley's black-and-white illustrations, which were about as remote from Du Maurier's in style and content as could be conceived, and was not sure his own work would sit comfortably with the young artist's between the same covers; but he gave a cautious welcome to Harland's invitation and promised to think about a suitable contribution to *The Yellow Book* when it was nearer to making its debut. 'Anything from you would be wonderful,' Harland said. 'And it can be as long as you like.' That was certainly an incentive, for Henry's stories had a way of quickly expanding beyond the limits previously agreed with magazine editors. He had just emerged from a heroic struggle to keep 'The Middle Years' under the six-thousand-word limit insisted upon by the implacable editor of *Lippincott's*, where it was to appear in May.

While he was in Paris he heard from Gosse of the death of John Addington Symonds, a figure of considerable and longstanding interest to Henry, in the contemplation of whose life he was able to define and clarify his own position regarding the delicate question of affectionate relationships between men. Symonds had first impinged on his consciousness in the 1870s as the author of a multi-volumed study of the Italian Renaissance which he greatly admired, as he admired subsequent works of scholarship and criticism from the same cultivated pen. Symonds, who suffered from tuberculosis, lived with his wife and children in Switzerland, making frequent visits to Italy, and Henry had met him only once, in London in the late 'seventies; but some years later he sent him in *hommage* one of his essays on Venice, and received a graciously complimentary reply. According to Gosse, who was much closer to Symonds, he was unhappily married to a severely puritanical wife who deeply disapproved of the tenor of her husband's work, which she regarded as pagan, hyper-aesthetic and tolerant of immorality. Henry made a note of this *donnée*, and later worked it up into a dark little story, 'The Author of *Beltraffio*', one of his first tales of literary life, in which a novelist's wife so loathed her husband's work-in-progress that she allowed their son to die rather than let him grow up and read it. (More grist to Fenimore's mill, Henry had to concede, as he recalled this story.) It was set in England and of course contained no recognisable portrait of Symonds, though the Italianate title of the fictitious author's novel was a clue to a few knowing readers. Henry left the precise nature of the scandalous content of 'Beltraffio' obscure and ambiguous – indeed, he didn't find it necessary even to know himself what it was. In due course, however, it became clear that Symonds was by temperament, and probably in practice, a Uranist, or, to use a term that had just begun to circulate, homo-sexual, and this was the real cause of incompatibility between him and his wife. Only a few months before his death Gosse had sent Henry a copy of a privately printed booklet by Symonds called *A Problem in Modern Ethics* which was nothing less than a plea for the toleration of phys-ical love between men, citing the precedent of such relationships between mature citizens and youths in Plato's Athens to argue that they were not incompatible with the highest kind of civilisation. Henry found the Athenian or Platonic model of mentor and ephebe an appealing one for his own relations with his young admirers, but only up to a point that stopped well short of the grossly physical. A hug or embrace between friends, on greeting or parting, was of course perfectly natural, and he deplored the frigid Anglo-Saxon prejudice against such demonstrations of affection – or love, why not call it love? – between men. But something fastidious in him recoiled from any thought of intimate sexual contact involving nakedness, the groping and interlocking of private parts, and the spending of seed. Admittedly (though he would only admit it to himself, in his most secret self-communings) he found it easier to picture himself thus engaged with a beautiful youth than with a beautiful maiden, but that only strengthened his resistance to any possible temptation to act out such disturbing fantasies. If there were men attracted to other men who found it impossible to detach love from sensuality then let them indulge the latter in private, and not seek the permission and approval of society, or challenge society by flaunting their deviance – that was Henry's considered opinion. Society could only openly endorse the normal sexual instinct that was inextricably linked to procreation, the great life force that carried the race forward into the future. Henry regarded Symonds's printed apologia as a reckless act which might have damaging consequences for himself and his friends, and he thought Gosse (a dear chap, but his name always irresistibly suggested 'goose' and 'gossip') imprudent to circulate it. He returned his copy as quickly as he could, with a carefully worded letter that disguised his real feelings behind a mask of urbane, amused detachment. It was perhaps just as well for poor Symonds that he had died, even at the early age of fifty-three, before he pulled down the full weight of society's disapproval upon his head.

Henry had brought with him to Paris an idea for a new play which he began to work on in the intervals between meeting his friends, visiting galleries, going to the theatre, and other diversions. It was based on an anecdote he had heard in Venice the previous summer, about a member of an old Venetian family who had become, or was about to become, a monk, but was snatched out of his convent and virtually forced to marry because he was the last surviving male in the family and it would otherwise become extinct. He decided to set the action of his play in late eighteenth-century England, in one of the pockets of Old Catholic gentry who quietly practised their faith in those pre-emancipation days, and he had Edward Compton very much in mind as producer and leading actor. A period piece, with a big part that called for wearing a full wig, should appeal to him much more than the ideas for modern comedies Henry had vainly offered him over the past year or so. He alerted Compton to the fact that a new play was in gestation before he left London. The manager was impatient to learn more, but Henry wanted to get a first act written before he exposed his subject for consideration, having an intuition that in bald summary it might not immediately recommend itself. Personally he was delighted with it, and sent the Comptons what he hoped were enticing little notes of his progress while he kept them waiting. During the laborious revision of *The American* he had acquired the services of a copyist in competent possession of a Remington typewriter (by his reckoning one of the few unambiguously beneficial contributions of America to civilisation) and he was now wedded to this method of copying and circulating dramatic manuscripts; but sending his handwritten drafts from Paris to Miss Gregory in Hampstead, getting them back again for correction – and inevitable, irresistible, emendation – and returning them once more for further retyping, all took up time. He had several times to postpone sending the promised first act to the Comptons.

It began with the hero, Guy Domville, tutor to the son of an attractive young widow, Mrs Peverel (a role that would be just the ticket for Mrs Compton), preparing to depart the very next day for the Benedictine monastery at Douai, to fulfil a longstanding vocation to the priesthood. Mrs Peverel was in love with Guy but had concealed her feelings out of piety to their shared religion, while he had an utterly chaste regard for her which, it was subtly conveyed, might in different circumstances have ripened into something else. Guy's friend Frank Humber, quite unaware of Mrs Peverel's feelings, was pressing his suit on her himself. Though recognising that he would make a good husband and stepfather for her son, she was emotionally incapable of giving her consent until Guy had irrevocably gone, and asked Frank to wait till the evening for her answer. Frank asked Guy to plead his cause, and Guy agreed – why should he not? Then a relative of Guy's, Lord Devenish, in whose name the suggestion of 'devilish' appropriately lurked, arrived with the news that Guy's dissolute cousin had died suddenly without legitimate issue, and that he had inherited the family estate. Devenish brought a message from Mrs Domville (not Guy's mother, who was dead, but a widowed senior member of the family, and Devenish's mistress) that it was Guy's duty to marry and ensure the continuation of the line. After much agonising Guy was persuaded by Mrs Peverel, who saw an opportunity providentially opening up for herself, that this obligation should indeed have priority over his religious vocation, and he prepared to leave immediately with Devenish to take up his inheritance. When Frank asked Mrs Peverel for her answer she rejected him, and he bitterly inferred that she must be in love with Guy. Guy, however, knowing of his friend's attachment to Mrs Peverel, could not allow his own feelings for her to develop in his new-found liberty. The first act ended with Devenish informing the dismayed Mrs Peverel that Mary, the daughter of Mrs Domville by her first marriage, would be the perfect match for Guy – 'a bride in a thousand – a Catholic, a beauty, and a fortune'.

Henry had in mind a second act, set some months later at Mrs Domville's home on the eve of Guy's wedding to Mary, in the course of which Guy would discover that she was in fact Devenish's daughter, and had been manipulated by him into the match for his own gain, and had another, honourable lover, a naval lieutenant, with whom Guy would help her to elope. Then there would be a third act in which, by means Henry had not yet determined, Guy would recognise his true feelings for Mrs Peverel, and hers for him, but, unable to contemplate hurting his friend Frank, and generally disillusioned with the materialism and corruption he had encountered in secular society, would renounce the possibility of marriage, commend Frank to Mrs Peverel, and depart to take up his religious vocation after all. It was Henry's intention however to submit the first act to Compton with only the outline of what was to follow.

At last it was ready. Personally he considered that it was easily the best thing he had done so far as a dramatic author: the delicate web of moral scruple and tender feeling that connected the principal characters (the blackguard Devenish excepted) stretching and tightening under the pressure of circumstance, produced a seamless succession of poignant personal dilemmas that would surely hold any audience enthralled, and offer wonderful opportunities for actors. On the 16th April he wrote to Compton to announce the dispatch of the first act under separate cover to Hartlepool, the C.C.C.'s current base, adding that he hoped it would arrive by p.m. the next day rather than the morning of the following one, 'as I shall like to think of you and Mrs Compton conning it together, after the performance, by the quiet midnight lamp'.

It was a grievous blow, after conjuring up this cosy picture, to receive a letter from Compton a few days later expressing disappointment with the first act, and misgivings about what might follow it. He was unhappy with a play that put so much emphasis on the moral problems and religious beliefs of Roman Catholics, with which ordinary British theatregoers would find it difficult to sympathise, and he feared, from the few hints that Henry had given, that he was bent upon an ending even unhappier than the first version of *The American*. Henry replied immediately and at length, defending his choice of subject, concluding: 'Above all I thought it *dramatic*. I accept of course completely your statement that, for your purposes (which are the only purposes in question), I am in error. It's sufficient that you don't *like* the subject – we will drop it on the spot.'

This pained but dignified communication had the effect, gratifying as far as it went, of making Compton withdraw or moderate his criticisms in a prompt reply. It had certainly not been his intention to reject the play outright at this stage, and he was eager to see the next two acts as soon as Henry was able to show them to him. But he did earnestly advise him to bear in mind the prime importance of giving a happy ending to the story, with the union of Guy and Mrs Peverel. Their correspondence continued for several weeks, during which time Henry moved on from Paris to Lucerne, to join up with William and his family, whose sabbatical year in Europe was drawing to a close. He saw no point in showing Compton any more of the play as long as they differed so fundamentally on the question of the ending. 'The ending you express a dread of *is* the only ending I ever dreamed of giving the play,' he declared. To make Guy abandon his vocation in order to marry Mrs Peverel would be 'not only no subject at all, but a very ugly and displeasing (as well as flat and undramatic) substitute for one'. Compton however remained stubbornly unconvinced. Henry resolved to continue to work on the play by his own lights in the hope that it would find a sympathetic home one day; meanwhile he kept Compton sweet by offering him another idea, this time for a comedy set in Monte Carlo.

Henry's vigorous defence of the envisaged ending of the play was not wholly based on the considerations of dramatic form and good taste that he advanced to Compton. He felt an intense personal identification with his hero, seeing in Guy's final, heroic renunciation of love and marriage in favour of the religious life a parallel to his own celibate dedication to the vocation of authorship. Perhaps into the character of Mrs Peverel he put a little of Fenimore's: her pathos, her wistfulness, her undeclared but always implied yearning to be loved. Fenimore was very much on his mind at this time, for she was leaving England once again, and going to make her home in Venice. She had been talking of this plan for ages, complaining that the grey skies and chilly winters of England made her more susceptible to depression, and that of all the places in the world she had visited Venice was the one which most satisfied her senses and soothed her spirit. She had put off the move, and submitted to one more English winter, in order to complete the novel, *Horace Chase*, on which she had been labouring for several years. Now that it was finished, and running as a serial in *Harper's*, there was nothing to detain her. She wrote to Henry to say she had given notice to her landlady and begun 'packing'. The portentous weight of that word was not lost on him. The assembling and filling of trunks that preceded all Fenimore's major migrations was a complex and protracted business, which she conducted as seriously and methodically as the quartermaster general of an army. If she was 'packing', then her decision was certainly irrevocable.

Not that he wished her to revoke it, or had any right to try and persuade her to do so. He certainly couldn't quarrel with her choice of location. Venice was to him, too, the most charming city in the world, and he had even toyed with the idea of acquiring a *pied-à-terre* there to retreat to when the filth and fogs of London, the press of people (and the people of the press!) became too much to bear. But, as always in his relations with Fenimore, he had ambivalent feelings about her move. When she was present, he was oppressed by an obscure sense of responsibility for her happiness which he could not possibly fulfil, but when she was absent he missed her. He certainly felt that it was not right, it was not seemly, that she should be quitting England in his own absence, without a valedictory meeting. He therefore arranged to coincide with her in Paris for a few days in the middle of May, where she could break her journey to Italy, and he his journey back to London from Switzerland.

* * *

They did not stay in the same hotel. Fenimore pretended that the Westminster was far too grand and expensive for her, but Henry knew that she knew that it would embarrass him to be sleeping under the same roof as herself, taking his key from the same desk in public view, and he was grateful for her tact. She arrived in Paris a day ahead of him and left word at the Westminster of her accommodation in a more modest establishment not far away in the Rue des Capucines. He arrived on the Geneva express in the late evening, and waited upon her the next morning. He thought she looked pale and drawn, her usually plump smooth cheeks faintly wrinkled like apples that have been stored too long. When he asked about her health she said she had found her 'packing' more than usually exhausting, and then, staying in London for a week after leaving Oxford, she had had an uncomfortable session with a dentist, and caught a bad cold.

'Paris will revive you,' Henry said. 'Paris at this time of year is a sovereign tonic.'

'Meeting you here revives me already, Henry,' she said, smiling.

He offered his arm and they walked out into the street. Almost at once they were in the Place Vendôme, with its elegant façades and huge central column surmounted by the statue of Napoleon. 'The statue is a replica, you know,' Henry observed, 'the Commune tore down the original in 1871.' They walked round the massive monument, admiring the bronze bas-relief of heroic battle scenes that wound its way from the bottom to the top.

'It's like Trajan's column in Rome,' she said. 'Do you remember we saw it together in, what was it, 'eighty-one?'

'Yes indeed. This was of course built in explicit imitation of Trajan's column. The metal came from twelve hundred cannon captured at Austerlitz,' he said.

'Goodness, Henry, you're a walking guidebook.'

'I have a special interest in this place,' he said. 'Seeing it is my earliest memory.'

'How early?' she said.

'I was less than two years old.'

'Impossible, Henry, you must have dreamed it.'

'No, from a very early age I had a mental image – a recurring vivid mental image – of myself in a moving carriage, sitting on my aunt Kate's knee – in long clothes – facing Mother and Father, and seeing through the window a tall column decorated with the shapes of human figures. They brought me here – my parents – in 1844, on their first visit to Europe. There was no such column in any other city I was taken to in infancy. I was ten years old when I next visited Paris. It must have been that first occasion that I remembered.'

'Well, it's very remarkable,' said Fenimore.

'I've been fascinated by Napoleon ever since I traced the memory,' said Henry. 'Shall we walk on?'

They strolled down the Rue de la Paix and the Rue de Castiglione, paused for coffee and a pastry in the pâtisserie on the corner, crossed the Rue de Rivoli into the Jardin des Tuileries, and made their way along the neat gravelled paths to the Louvre. It was one of several walks they took in the days that followed – happily Henry's gout had disappeared, and Fenimore was always a stalwart walker. He was right: the capital was at its beguiling best. The weather was mild, the breezes soft. The sun glinted on the gold statues, crosses, and weathercocks surmounting the pale grey buildings, on the foaming wakes of pleasure boats cruising on the Seine, on the plate glass windows of the *grands magasins*, and on the jingling harness of the carriage horses trotting along the broad boulevards. The chestnut trees in the avenues were in glorious leaf and blossom, the parterres in the parks flamed with colour. There was a controversial exhibition of the *Salon des Indépendants* and an excellent *Misanthrope* at the Comédie Française.

For a few days Henry, unusually for him, wrote nothing, not even a letter, but gave himself up to pleasure and entertaining Fenimore. She was grateful and appreciative, commending everything he suggested and arranged, and she began to look better, with more colour in her cheeks and more spring in her step. But he sensed a deep underlying melancholy which lay still and undisturbed by all these distractions, like a pool in some dark underground cavern. She didn't seem elated by reports that the serialisation of her new novel was being well received in America. She was revising the text for book publication and begged Henry to wait to read it in that form.

She claimed that it would be her last novel – that she couldn't face the effort of writing another, and hadn't any new ideas anyway.

'Venice will give you ideas,' said Henry encouragingly.

'I doubt it. What is there left to say? All the best writers have browsed over the place and nibbled it clean – yourself included.' At the most she might manage to produce a story or two. 'I see my output dwindling into silence,' she said, and then with a smile: 'Unless of course we were to write that play together.'

'Alas!' he sighed. 'I'm no further forward in my theatrical endeavours than when I last spoke to you.' And he told her the whole saga of his latest dealings with Compton.

'Still, you *have* written another play, Henry—'

'Partly written—'

'I'm sure that sooner or later you will succeed,' she said earnestly.

The last service he was able to perform for her was to see her off from the Gare de Lyon on the next stage of her journey, a day before he himself was due to depart. The great caravan of trunks and packing cases had gone on ahead to Venice, but she still had a formidable number of bags and boxes and valises, the transportation of which from hotel to cab to train he supervised. Having seen them safely stowed in the guard's van, he returned to Fenimore, who was standing on the platform next to the open door of the *wagon lit.*

'Rest assured, your luggage will be well looked after,' he said to her. 'I tipped the guard and asked him to give it his particular attention.'

'Thank you, Henry.' She looked at him fondly. 'You're a good man.'

Henry was slightly flustered by the compliment. 'Really, Fenimore, such a – such an ordinary courtesy does not deserve so – so—'

'I don't mean just the luggage,' she said. 'You've been most kind, most attentive all through these last few days. I'm very grateful.'

'It was a pleasure, my dear Fenimore.'

'I hate goodbyes,' she said.

The station was all steam and smoke and diffused light, like one of the extreme Impressionist paintings that they had seen the day before. He commented on this for want of something else to say, but the platform was clamorous with sounds – exhalations of steam, bells, whistles, shouts, curses, and even, somewhere in the distance, a band – and Fenimore did not appear to hear him. She did not have her ear trumpet to hand.

'When shall I see you again?' she said.

'I don't know – perhaps in the autumn. I like to see something of Italy every year if I can manage it,' he said. 'And Venice is always an attraction.'

'What?' She cupped her ear.

He raised his voice. 'I said, Venice is always an attraction. In fact I've often thought of getting a little place there myself—'

'Have you really?' Fenimore's face lit up.

'Just a couple of rooms, you know, something very cheap!'

'I'll look out for something suitable.'

'Well, it's just an idea – a dream—' Henry was already regretting that he had mentioned it.

'Then we could write our play together.'

'Yes, indeed – but first, you know – I must have a success first, on my own account.'

A railway official standing nearby blew a piercing blast on his whistle. Doors began to slam all along the train. *'Montez, madame, s'il vous plaît!'* the man said to Fenimore.

'Goodbye, Henry,' she said, extending her hand. 'Till we meet again in Venice.'

'Yes indeed.' He took her hand and, being in Paris, raised it gallantly to his lips, but to his surprise and some alarm, she drew him into a kind of flurried embrace and kissed him briefly on the cheek, burying her face in his beard, before climbing into the train. The official slammed the door shut behind her and he saw her appear at the window of the corridor, walking towards him, waving and timidly smiling, but receding as the train slowly drew out of the station. He stood with his hat in his hand, waving with the other, until the last carriage was out of sight. Then he put on his hat, and, taking out a pocket handkerchief, wiped his bearded cheek. He turned and walked towards the *Sortie* sign, with a certain sense of relief, and the agreeable consciousness of having a day left in Paris to do as he pleased. He might call at the *Times* Bureau and see if Morton Fullerton was free to dine with him.

8

NEAR the top of the heap of mail that awaited him at De Vere Gardens on his return from Paris was an invitation to the premiere of a new play by Arthur Pinero, entitled *The Second Mrs Tanqueray*, at the St James's Theatre. Henry went to it with an interest quickened by already knowing something about the production through the involvement of his friend Elizabeth Robins. It was apparently a daring, 'Ibsenish' piece, about a woman with a past which finally caught up with her, destroying her happiness and her marriage. Pinero and George Alexander had wanted to cast a little-known but highly promising young actress called Mrs Patrick Campbell as the heroine, but she was contracted to another management, so Elizabeth Robins had been offered and accepted the part. At the last possible moment, however, Mrs Campbell became available, and Miss Robins, being appealed to, very generously yielded to her. Henry felt she had been badly treated, though Elizabeth Robins denied it. But the price of her generosity rapidly became evident at the first night. The mercurial, desperate and doomed Paula Tanqueray was a great role, and allowed Mrs Patrick Campbell, ably supported by Alexander as her devoted husband, to demonstrate that she was a great actress. The audience was spellbound; their applause at the end rapturous. Henry had never been in a theatre before when the sense of a 'success' was so palpable – almost physical, like a powerful aroma carried from some banquet of delicious food. He inhaled it hungrily; it renewed his appetite to sate himself on such a feast. How he envied Pinero taking his bow at the end of the play, bow after bow! How he pitied poor Elizabeth Robins to whom he spoke in the entr'acte, valiantly praising her rival's performance, and whom he glimpsed hurrying away from the theatre at the end, anxious, no doubt, to avoid any more such tests of her self-control.

It was no surprise that *The Second Mrs Tanqueray* was widely acclaimed by the critics and that 'House Full' notices soon appeared outside the St James's Theatre. What particularly impressed Henry was that Pinero and Alexander between them had achieved popular success with a play that challenged its audience with an uncompromisingly 'unhappy' ending – indeed, a tragic one. Tanqueray knew his wife had a disreputable past when he married her, but believed she could be redeemed by his love, only to discover that the prejudices of society and the conflicts in the woman's own character undid his good intentions and drove her to suicide in the end. Coming so soon after the success of *Lady Windermere's Fan, Mrs Tanqueray* further enhanced Alexander's reputation as an actor-manager. He seemed to have a golden touch – what might it not do for Henry's plays, especially the one he had been working on most recently?

Accordingly he wrote to Alexander requesting a meeting, to which the manager responded promptly and positively, saying that he was always looking for new plays by good writers. They met in his office at the St James's, in King Street. It was the only theatre in this exclusive part of London, and somewhat removed from the main entertainment district, but it was an area that Henry knew well and felt at home in. The London Library was just round the corner in St James's Square, and his club, the Reform, was only a few minutes' walk away in Pall Mall. The theatre had an elegant Georgian façade with a pillared portico and a balcony above it where patrons could take the air on warm evenings between the acts. Pausing on the pavement to look up at the building before he went inside, Henry was struck by how much more suitable and congenial a home it would make for his dramatic work than the underground Opera Comique at the seedier end of the Strand, and the very name – his patron saint – was auspicious. He sprang up the steps and pushed through the polished swing doors more eager than ever to secure Alexander's interest.

In the event the meeting went exceedingly well. Henry did not exactly warm to the young actor-manager, but he was favourably impressed by him. He had the air of someone who knew exactly what he wanted, and what needed to be done to attain it. The whole theatre had the atmosphere of an extremely well-run ship whose captain was respected and a little feared by the crew. His office was in immaculate order; only the large mirror on one wall seemed a little incongruous and hinted at an element of personal vanity in the occupant. But he was undoubtedly a very handsome man, with a strong assertive chin and a fine head of naturally wavy hair, who might be forgiven for an occassional complacent glance at his own reflection. He received Henry dressed in a perfectly tailored pale grey suit with trousers pressed to a knife-edge in the latest fashion, shook his hand, and pulled up a chair for him with grave courtesy. 'I'm at your disposal for three-quarters of an hour, Mr James,' he said.

Henry described three items in his current portfolio of half-written plays and scenarios, chosen because they all had commanding roles for a leading actor; but he particularly 'pushed' the play about Guy Domville, at present provisionally entitled *The Hero*, and to his delight it was this one that seemed most to take Alexander's fancy. Henry undertook to send drafts or scenarios of all three plays for his consideration, but privately he decided to give priority to *The Hero*. For this purpose he withdrew to a hotel in Ramsgate for several weeks in June and July, and gave up the use of his flat to William and Alice, who wanted to spend some time in London on their own before they collected their children from Switzerland and finally returned to America. He chose Ramsgate because it was cheap but also because it was such a notoriously Cockney seaside resort that he was sure he wouldn't run into anybody he knew, and thus be distracted from his task. He derived some amusement from the contrast between its cheerful crowds sucking their rock candy and eating their cockles and mussels and dropping their aitches with carefree abandon, and the refined historical drama on which he was engaged.

Early in July he sent Alexander a revised version of his first act, together with detailed scenarios of the second and third. Admitting that 'my dénouement does not belong to the class of ending conventionally termed happy', he artfully invoked the precedent of Alexander's current success: 'Mrs Tanqueray seems to me to have performed the very valuable service of showing that the poor dear old British public can rise to a dénouement that isn't a mere dab of rose-colour.' He sent Alexander at the same time brief scenarios for the two other plays, but to his delight Alexander plumped unhesitatingly for *The Hero*. It was, he said, in his letter of acceptance, 'the most beautiful poetical play produced in this country since *Olivia*'. He evidently didn't know, or had forgotten, that Henry had himself reviewed *Olivia*, a feeble adaptation of Goldsmith's *The Vicar of Wakefield* by W. G. Wills, less than favourably on its first presentation in 1878. The comparison took some of the savour from Alexander's tribute, but this was obviously sincere and very gratifying. When it came to agreeing terms Alexander drove a hard bargain, offering a basic £5 per performance and setting a ceiling of £2,000 on royalties, but Henry was again impressed by the manager's fair and unambiguous dealing. The only slight shadow over this new and exciting partnership was the prospect – yet again – of delay. Not only had *Mrs Tanqueray* settled into what was obviously going to be a very long run at the St James's, but Alexander now admitted that he had in principle agreed to put on a new play by Henry Arthur Jones immediately after it. Alexander hinted that he was doubtful if Jones's play would be ready in time, and Henry, selfishly hoping he would be proved right, worked hard to finish *Guy Domville* (as they had now agreed to call it) so that it would be available to go into production the moment it was decided that *Mrs Tanqueray* must close.

Meanwhile Daly's long-becalmed production of *Mrs Jasper* hove in sight. His new theatre had opened in late June with a revival of the popular *Shrew*, but the plays that followed had not gone down well with either the critics or the public. The melodrama *The Hunchback* was perceived as too old, the French comedy *Love in Tandem* too frivolous and the farce *Dollars and Sense* too broad to be worthy of Ada Rehan's talents. When Henry came up from Ramsgate in August to consult about sets and costumes, the manager seemed less confident and expansive than at their first meeting, and complained about the clannishness and conservatism of the London theatregoing public. 'Every house has its little flock of patrons, who go like sheep to see every darned thing that's put on in it,' he said, sucking on a savagely chewed cigar. 'When we played at the Lyceum, the same people who went to Irving's shows came to ours. But they won't come to 'em now we're in a brand-new theatre. It's the damnedest thing.' He planned to open *Mrs Jasper* in the late autumn, by which time Daly's Theatre should have attracted a following. He had a model of the stage set to show Henry, and some designs for costumes. It was a long time since Henry had worked on the play, and he was impatient for rehearsals to begin so that he could, as it were, roll up his sleeves and get to grips with it again.

With two new plays accepted for production in the near future by two leading London managements, Henry felt he was on the brink of really making his mark on the theatrical scene, yet after so many disappointments he was well aware of how fragile this happy state of affairs really was – like a house of cards which one must touch only with extreme caution and bated breath. He restrained himself with difficulty from pressing his managers for dates and decisions in case this should have the effect of turning them, however illogically, against his darling projects. More than ever he hoped for financial rewards from this source, for his income from writing had sunk to an alarmingly low level. He had published only one new piece of work so far that year, 'The Middle Years', and the sales of his books – those that were still in print – were depressing in the extreme. 'Tell it not in Samoa – or at least not in Tahiti; but I don't sell ten copies,' he wrote to Louis Stevenson, and he was hardly exaggerating. It was fortunate that the American rents he had donated to Alice on the death of their father had reverted to him under her will, together with the untouched capital that had accumulated while she held them, otherwise he might have been seriously embarrassed.

It was partly for reasons of economy that he decided not to go to Italy that autumn, as he had vaguely hinted to Fenimore that he might, and partly because he felt uncomfortable under the pressure of her expectation that he would join her in Venice. In mid-July he received a letter from their mutual friend Mrs Curtis, a long-term Venetian resident who was helping Fenimore look for permanent quarters, and, having heard from her that Henry too was seeking a *pied-à-terre* in the city, now offered her services in that regard. He wrote back immediately to say that he must have given Miss Woolson a wrong impression of the seriousness of his intention, that it was really only a daydream that he indulged in from time to time, but had no practical prospect of realising. He trusted Mrs Curtis to convey the gist of this message to Fenimore. He also mentioned in his letter that he hoped to visit Italy in the winter but had learned from experience not to make hard-and-fast plans. This too was designed for Fenimore's ear.

With Italy indefinitely postponed, Henry felt he needed – and deserved – some more modest holiday after the completion and delivery of *Guy Domville*, and therefore accepted a suggestion of Du Maurier's that he should join him and his family in their beloved Whitby in September. He had done this once before, in '87, when Lowell was also staying there, and had gone up again two years later, when Lowell alone was the attraction, the Du Mauriers having deserted it that summer for Dieppe. He had found it difficult on those occasions fully to share his friends' enthusiasm for the place, and without the inducement of their company would hardly have lingered for long. He felt this ambivalence again on revisiting Whitby. It was undoubtedly historic and picturesque, but its climate and topography were a constant challenge to visitors. Seen at a distance, on a sunny day, from high up on the moors, the huddled red and brown buildings of the port, the graceful skeletal ruins of the abbey on the grassy clifftop above, and the long arms of the harbour stretching out into the blue, white-capped waves, one grasping a lighthouse like a candle in its fist, made a delightful picture. But bitterly cold winds blew off the North Sea on to this rugged stretch of Yorkshire coast even in September, and the town was built along a river estuary in a deep and narrow valley, so that any attempt to get out of it entailed stiff climbs up pitiless gradients.

Admittedly the Du Maurier family, or tribe, as he felt inclined to call them, for they were so many now – sons-in-law and grand-children as well as children – seemed to thrive on the regimen of a British seaside holiday in this bracing setting. They bathed in the freezing sea off the beach that ran north-westwards from the harbour, and played cricket on the sand at low tide. They rowed up the river Esk, pulling their boat over the shallow dam, and climbed up precipitous paths to picnic beside the waterfall at Cock Mill. These pursuits and excursions were familiar to Henry, and to a large percentage of the British population, from the pictorial adventures of the 'Brown Family', a thinly disguised version of the Du Mauriers, which appeared regularly in the pages of *Punch*. But somehow the drawings didn't convey the chill of the winds or the steepness of the inclines. Perhaps the former disadvantage might have been less apparent earlier in the season, in July or August, but Du Maurier, with typical thrift, took his holidays in September, when rates were lower. Admittedly he needed to rent a house of some considerable size to accommodate his extended family and their servants – Trixy and Charles were there this year with their three boys, and Sylvia and Arthur with their firstborn, George, named after his grandfather. Henry politely declined the offer of a bed in St Hilda's Crescent, where one always seemed to be crunching sand and seashells under one's feet, and people were perpetually running up and down the stairs and slamming the doors and calling out for each other – his godson Guy as lustily as anyone. Instead he took Lowell's old rooms in a cottage down by the harbour, near the drawbridge that spanned the narrow entrance to the broader estuary. It revived pleasant memories of his friend to watch, as Lowell had loved to watch, the drawbridge being raised to let the big ships glide through with barely a yard to spare on each side.

Living independently, he was able to dodge some of the more strenuous expeditions of the Du Mauriers, and also to decoy Kiki himself away from them. It seemed to Henry that his friend was in danger of overstraining himself in the effort to keep up the Whitby family traditions. Nevertheless he agreed to join Kiki on one of his favourite walks, along the clifftop path to the little fishing port of Staithes. Although it was a good ten miles, it was mostly level going once you had climbed out of Whitby, and they arranged to have a pony and trap meet them in Staithes to drive them home.

It was a beautiful, sunny morning. 'One might almost say it's warm,' Henry remarked, as they strode along the cliffs towards Sandsend, passing the farmhouse said to be the model for the heroine's abode in *Sylvia's Lovers*.

Du Maurier, well aware of Henry's reservations about the North Yorkshire climate, smiled. 'The weather has been very kind to us this September,' he said. 'I can't remember a better one.'

He was in good spirits, not only because of the weather, but also at having finally finished the illustrations for *Trilby*. 'It's been a terrible sweat,' he said. 'There are a hundred and twenty-one of them.'

'A hundred and twenty-one!' Henry was astonished. 'I hope Harper's people appreciate your effort.'

'Oh yes, they're very appreciative. They're a bit nervous about the text, but they're very happy with the pictures.'

'Why are they nervous about the text?'

'Well, as I think you know, my heroine is not as pure as the proverbial.'

'Proverbial?'

'The driven snow. I mean, she is *really* – she's pure of heart – essentially innocent, essentially good. But not *virgo intacta*.'

'Ah,' said Henry. 'The readers of *Harper's* won't like that – especially the American ones.'

'That's what they're afraid of. But how could she be? The girl's an orphan, struggling to make a living as a model in the *Quartier Latin*, in the eighteen-fifties. She has no family or friends to look after her. She sits for the figure – *pour l'ensemble*. Girls like that simply weren't respectable. I know – I was there!'

'I believe you,' said Henry. 'But truth to life has never been an adequate excuse in the eyes of Mrs Grundy. I'm amazed that *Harper's* is prepared to risk her disapproval. What happens to your heroine? I mean apart from acquiring and losing her marvellous singing voice?'

'You'll have to wait and see,' said Du Maurier, with a grin. 'The serial starts in January.'

'And will there be a picture of Trilby sitting for the figure, *pour l'tout ensemble*?' Henry asked.

Du Maurier threw back his head and laughed. 'Not likely!' he said. 'The most you will see of her in that line are her bare feet.'

They reached Staithes in the early afternoon. For such a small, remote place, squeezed into a narrow ravine that dropped abruptly from the moor to the sea, and overshadowed on one side by Boulby Cliff, the highest point on the whole of the East Coast according to Du Maurier, it seemed remarkably busy and thriving. As they descended the steep, twisting, cobbled main street they had constantly to step aside and press themselves against the walls of the cottages to allow the passage of horse-drawn carts taking the day's catch to the rail-head above, or clattering down the hill unladen on their way back. With appetites sharpened by the fresh air and exercise they repaired immediately to the Cod and Lobster inn for what Henry called an 'eponymous dinner' (provoking blank looks from the landlady, who took their order in plain English from Du Maurier) washed down with good Yorkshire ale.

Perhaps the ale was unusually strong, for Du Maurier was particularly loquacious over the meal. He reverted to the subject of his dealings with Harper. It seemed that *Trilby* contained a passage of authorial polemic in favour of nudity, which the publishers wanted to cut out.

'I have a theory, you see, Henry, that if only our climate allowed it, we should be much happier going around without clothes. There is nothing inherently shameful or indecent about the human body.'

'The weather in North Yorkshire certainly precludes the experiment,' said Henry, as he cracked open a lobster claw. 'But even in Samoa – where I understand from Louis Stevenson the natives make do with very little raiment – even there I don't think I would care to meet my friends in a state of nature. Most of us are simply not beautiful enough.'

'Ah, but that's because we neglect our bodies. And we neglect them because we cover them up with layers of cloth – and in the case of women, distort their natural shapes with whalebone and bustles and lacing and suchlike. Now if we saw each other habitually in a state of nature, as you call it, as a matter of course, we should take pains to exercise and diet to *make* our bodies strong and healthy and attractive.'

'What about those who are irredeemably ugly or misshapen?' Henry objected.

'They wouldn't reproduce, because nobody would marry them,' said Du Maurier triumphantly, evidently seeing this as a knockdown argument. 'By Darwin's law of natural selection we would – in the course of a few generations – eliminate ugliness from the human race. We would also get rid of all the sniggering smut and furtive lust that surrounds the mere mention of the human body in polite society, and corrupts relations between men and women.'

'An interesting theory, if somewhat utopian,' Henry murmured, privately amused that the skinny, diminutive Du Maurier was so passionately commited to this cause.

'That's why the nude in art is so important,' said Du Maurier. 'It holds up the *beau idéal* of the human body, for our contemplation and emulation. But it can't be done without models, like my Trilby, taking off their clothes. And since exposing one's body to the opposite sex is simply not done in our society, the poor model is automatically cast beyond the pale. It's not surprising that most of them are no better than they should be – at least they weren't in Paris, when I was young.'

'Do you still paint or draw from life?' Henry ventured to ask.

Du Maurier smiled. 'No, Emma wouldn't approve. Anyway, I have no need to, in the kind of work I do. Though Sambourne wouldn't agree – you know Sammy, don't you?'

'I've met him a few times,' said Henry. Edward Linely Sambourne was one of the staff artists on *Punch*, specialising in political cartoons, but also contributing drawings of social life, often featuring pretty young women.

'He had no proper art training, you know, so he uses photographs when he's drawing figures, and copies them. He photographs the models naked, and then with their clothes on. He claims he needs to know the position of the limbs under the clothing to make the pose convincing.'

'And what does Mrs Sambourne have to say about that?' Henry asked, amused. 'Or is he not married?'

'Oh, he's married all right,' said Du Maurier, 'but amazingly she doesn't seem to mind a bit. I can't think she's seen many of his pictures, though. He showed me some of them once, and, well, frankly . . .' Du Maurier glanced around the room and lowered his voice – 'frankly, a lot of them are the sort of thing you might pick up in a shady print-shop in Paris. Girls larking about stark naked . . . or even worse – with just stockings on, or a hat or a mask, lolling about on sofas, showing their . . . well, showing everything. He has thousands of these pictures.'

'Thousands!'

'Yes. He belongs to the Camera Club in Charing Cross Road, where you can rent a studio and hire models by the hour. I can't help feeling there's something a bit "off" about it. There's no doubt some of the models are really beautiful. But some are not, and of course they've all got hair.'

'Hair?' Henry was puzzled.

'Pubic hair. It creates a pornographic effect.'

'But Kiki,' Henry objected, 'if we all went around naked as you advocate, we should have to get used to that feature of the human anatomy.'

'Yes, but since we don't, it's distasteful. Artists don't depict pubic hair – true artists, I mean.' He was evidently a little bothered by the imputation of inconsistency, for he added musingly: 'Anyway, women could always learn to shave – like men, but in a different place.'

Henry burst out laughing, and Du Maurier, who had not intended to make a joke, smiled sheepishly.

Afterwards they lounged about on the quayside, watching the men mending their nets and loading them into the long narrow open boats in preparation for the night's fishing, and wandered up and down the crooked alleys and peered into sheds for gutting and smoking and salting fish, and gave pennies to the shoeless children who stared at them from the doorways of cottages. It was all rather too overwhelmingly smoky and smelly and fishy for Henry's taste, but Du Maurier loved it, and kept taking out the little tablet of drawing paper he kept in his pocket, and sketching in pencil the outline of something that caught his attention, a boat or a building or a bonnet – for the women of Staithes wore a very distinctive article of that kind. He wanted to stay on until the evening to watch from the end of the long harbour wall the flotilla of boats going out to sea for the night's fishing, and Henry indulged him. It was indeed a moving sight, so frail the craft seemed, setting sail towards the coming darkness under the ominous bulging brow of the great cliff. Then, after a warming dram at the inn, they made their rendezvous with the bespoke pony and trap, and returned to Whitby in this conveyance, much pleased with their outing. In Henry's case, however, the agreeable mood was abruptly dissipated by something that was waiting for him when he got back to his lodgings: a message from Daly to say that the opening of *Mrs Jasper* had been postponed once more, until January.

Frustrating as this news was, it did give Henry an excuse for cutting short his holiday and returning to London – namely, to investigate the cause of delay – for he felt he had enjoyed enough of the delights of Whitby and environs for the time being. Du Maurier commiserated when he explained the situation the next day. 'It's a shocking way to treat a writer of your distinction,' he said. 'But, as I keep telling Gerald, theatre people are totally unreliable. You simply can't trust them. Not that it makes any difference. He's dead set on becoming an actor. I was hoping you would have a word with him, Henry, when he comes up here next weekend.'

The plan to make Gerald into a solicitor had been abandoned long ago. Instead he had gone into 'business', working for a shipping company, but he spent all his spare time in amateur theatricals and concert parties, sometimes with his sister May, and was beginning to make a name for himself and get written up in the newspapers.

'I'm afraid you must resign yourself, Kiki,' said Henry. 'It's a strange, compulsive business, the urge to make plays. To act in them, or write 'em, or produce 'em. It's no use appealing to reason. If Gerald really – I mean *really* wants to be an actor – nothing on earth is going to stop him.'

He was of course speaking for himself as much as for Gerald.

★ ★ ★

On his return to London he sought an early interview with Daly. The manager told him frankly that his theatre had still not yet found its feet, or its audience. Tennyson's *The Foresters* was in rehearsal, due to open at the beginning of October, and Daly was plainly worried that it might fail. 'There's no real interest, no advance take to speak of,' he said. 'Tennyson's a dead lion as far as the public's concerned.' He didn't think it would be a good idea to follow it with a new play by a comparatively untried playwright. Accordingly he had decided to hold back *Mrs Jasper* until after Christmas and to push a reliable classic, *The School for Scandal*, which had served him well for many years, into the gap. Henry accepted this decision without argument. He had no wish to see his play exposed to a public scrutiny rendered sceptical in advance by the company's sorry record. Failure in the theatre was contagious. So he possessed his soul in patience, though, as he wrote to William, he longed 'for the reality, the ingenuity, and the combined amusement and disgust of rehearsals'.

Daly's apprehensions about *The Foresters* proved well-founded. It was enjoyed by the first-night audience and kindly reviewed by the critics, but was a commercial failure – the house was reputedly 'papered' for every performance. Henry reflected with some complacency that, at this rate, Daly would soon be counting on *Mrs Jasper* to rescue his season and his reputation, so would put maximum effort into making it succeed. This motivation was certainly apparent, but manifested itself in an unwelcome form in the manager's next communication, at the end of October. He had reread *Mrs Jasper*, and considered that it was still too long. He asked for further cuts and revisions. Henry wearily agreed to go over it one more time, but after six days reported 'utter failure'. It was not possible, he believed, to remove anything substantial without 'detriment to elementary clearness – to the rigid logic of the action and the successive definite steps of the story'. He offered to consider any specific cuts Daly himself might propose, but the manager did not take up this invitation. He did however ask for a 'snappier title'. Henry made one or two suggestions, which the manager rejected. In a mood of barely controlled exasperation Henry sent him a list of sixty-four alternatives titles: *The Rescue*, *The Reprieve*, *The Remedy*,

The Release, The Response, Comfort, Compassion, Contrivance, Compunction
. . . the list covered a whole sheet of paper in three columns. Daly,
who seemed impervious to irony, rejected them all because they did
not draw attention to Ada Rehan's role – as, of course, the original
title had. Eventually they agreed on *Mrs Jasper's Way*.

Silence fell again. Towards the end of November he grew restive:
if the play was to be mounted in January, rehearsals would have to
start soon. Meeting Ada Rehan at a party one Sunday evening, he
made this point to her and was disconcerted when she casually
replied that she believed there were to be one or two readings of
the play at the theatre in the coming week. When he said he had
not been given notice of them, she looked embarrassed and said
that no doubt it was because the times had not yet been fixed. It
was impossible to continue the conversation further in the presence
of others, and soon afterwards she left the party without their
exchanging further words. Henry waited in vain for a message from
Daly until the following Saturday morning.

He was having his breakfast when Smith appeared at the threshold of the dining room with the first delivery of post on a silver
salver. 'Will you read your letters in here, sir, or shall I leave them
on your desk in the study?' he asked.

'Bring them here, Smith. Thank you.'

Smith laid the mail on the table beside him and withdrew.
Recognising Daly's handwriting on one of the envelopes, Henry
plucked it from the sheaf and tore it open. Inside was a curt note
saying that there had been two readings of the play at the theatre
that week which had revealed major problems, and that Daly proposed
to hold another reading with the full cast on the following Wednesday
morning so that Henry could see for himself what they were.
'Basically,' Daly concluded, 'it lacks story.'

Henry had consumed only one of his customary three coddled
eggs. He pushed aside the dish containing the remainder, and support-
ing his head in his hands he groaned aloud. After all this time, after
the play had been unconditionally accepted and an agreement drawn
up, after so many revisions and deletions and fine adjustments to
dialogue and stage directions, to be told after all that '*it lacked story*'!

How in the name of God was he supposed to put more story into it at this time of day? At first he was devastated; then he grew angry. Clearly Daly, rattled by the string of failures in his famous 'season', had lost his nerve, and his faith in *Mrs Jasper's Way*, to the extent of forgetting his own once favourable opinion of it. What most angered Henry was the sly going behind his back, trying out the play with the actors before Henry had had a chance to introduce it to them himself and describe the nature of the roles they were to play.

He went to the reading on the following Wednesday morning determined to rectify this injustice – to take the company by the scruff of its neck and make them see how the thing should be done – only to find himself completely outmanoeuvred. The actors were already gathered on stage, in a silent and wary semicircle, with their playbooks in their hands, when James arrived. Even Ada Rehan only flashed him a brief, wan smile as Daly performed perfunctory introductions, naming the actors one by one. She looked pale and drawn. Then, just as Henry was taking out his notes to address the cast, Daly suggested he should take a seat in the pit.

'Shouldn't I say a few words first?' Henry asked.

'I don't think that's necessary, Mr James,' said Daly. 'We've been through the play a couple of times already, as I told you.' He glanced at his pocket watch. 'I think we'd better get on. Are you ready, ladies and gentlemen?' With a stiff nod, that he hoped expressed dignified resentment, Henry vacated the stage, and went down the steps at the side into the auditorium.

Daly began reading out the stage directions. ' "*An old-fashioned lawn or small pleasance, in a slightly neglected or deserted condition, on a height or slope, commanding, in the distance, across a valley, a little winding, shining river—*" ' He stopped in mid-sentence. 'I guess I needn't read out all this scene-setting. You've all got the picture. So, Sir Montagu and Mrs Wigmore, please.' And the actors playing these parts began to read them in a stammering monotone, like children 'called on' in the classroom, with heads lowered and eyes bent on their playbooks. Those who followed did no better. They rushed at their lines and gabbled them as if they couldn't wait to get to the end of the speeches. They stumbled over the syntax, and put emphases in the wrong place, or left them out entirely. Above all they utterly failed to convey any sense that they found the story they were presenting remotely interesting or amusing or believable. It was without doubt the worst presentation of a playwright's words by professional performers that Henry had ever witnessed. Even Ada Rehan seemed to lose all her vivacity and sense of timing. Her pallor became deathly, her features positively haggard, as the ghastly travesty proceeded. She was a good enough actress to know what was happening and to feel some shame at her own involvement.

What was happening of course, as Henry grasped after only ten minutes, was that a trap had been set for him. Daly had designed the reading to be as bad as possible because he had already decided, for his own sordid financial reasons, which were themselves the consequence of his managerial incompetence, to cancel the production of *Mrs Jasper's Way* as being too risky a venture, and he hoped to get Henry to agree by demonstrating that the play was sure to fail. It would not have been necessary for him explicitly to instruct his actors to perform the piece badly. It would have been enough to deny them any advice or direction on how to perform it well, to suggest by sneers and sighs at the earlier readings the hopelessness of the case, and above all to keep the author at a distance.

Henry sat through the proceedings with a stony, impassive countenance, though inwardly he fumed with rage. He mentally rehearsed what he would say to Daly at the end, so that he would not lose his composure. The end came mercifully soon, because they did the whole play at breakneck speed, without intervals. Ada Rehan came to the front of the stage and stumbled through the little epilogue he had written specially for her, shot him one agonised glance, as from a soul in torment, and fled into the wings, rapidly followed by the rest of the cast. Daly sauntered to the side of the stage, and came heavily down the steps into the auditorium. Henry rose from his seat at the front of the stalls, buttoned up his overcoat, and waited for him.

'Well, Mr James?' said Daly. 'What d'you think?'

Henry paused for a moment before giving his answer. 'I shall take some hours to become perfectly clear to myself as to the reflections which this occasion – taken in conjunction with your note of Saturday – causes me to make. And then I will write to you. Good day.' Without waiting to see the effect of this speech on Daly's countenance, he turned on his heel and walked out of the theatre.

That evening he wrote a letter to Daly, to be posted on the morrow, saying that he would have been glad to have been informed at an earlier moment of the year during which his play had been in the manager's hands that it was fundamentally unsuited to his purpose – 'Your few words of Saturday so definitely express, in spite of their brevity, or perhaps by reason of the same, the sudden collapse of your own interest in it, that I withdraw it from your theatre without delay and beg you to send me back the MS. For myself – I cannot for a moment profess that the scene I witnessed on your stage yesterday threw any light on the character of the play.'

Daly promptly returned the manuscript with a letter in which he defended his conduct, adducing his expenditure on set designs and costumes in the summer (which must have cost him all of twelve guineas) as evidence of commitment to the play. He concluded: 'it was you who offered me the play in the first place, and it is you who now request its return. I am satisfied to accept your word as compliment to my judgement now as then.' This haughty response provoked Henry into another much longer letter, detailing the entire history of their dealings over the play to show that nothing in them had prepared him for the fundamental objection to it that Daly had made at the last possible moment. But this letter was written more for his own satisfaction and relief rather than in any hope of making Daly contrite or even embarrassed. The man, as he told Elizabeth Robins, was a cad.

His friendship with this young lady had developed steadily over the past year or two. He had helped her with advice on plays by Ibsen and Dumas *fils* and other foreign writers that she and her partner were thinking of producing, while she in turn gladly submitted to having his work-in-progress read to her, and gave him the benefit of her professional opinion. Of all his friends, she was the one best qualified by experience to sympathise with his ill-treatment by

Daly. She was the first person he informed of the reading *débâcle*, in a brief note written the very same day, and he called on her not long afterwards in her flat in Manchester Square at the top of seventy concrete stairs, and kept her up until one in the morning, pouring out his bitter sense of betrayal. 'Daly must be laughing up his sleeve,' he said. 'Because he has won – he has got me to withdraw my play, so he can pretend it was my own choice. I could have forced him to make the first move. I could have made *him* cancel the production.'

'No, you made the right decision,' said Miss Robins. 'Once a producer has lost faith in a play it's doomed. You've had a lucky escape.'

'A lucky escape?' Henry couldn't see any luck at all in his situation.

'I mean, suppose you had somehow forced him, or persuaded him, to go through with it, and done all the revisions he demanded – rewriting it after every rehearsal, right up to the first night – it *still* wouldn't have worked, not if he and the actors didn't believe in it. I know – I've been through that kind of horror myself.' She shuddered expressively.

'Somehow I can't draw much consolation from that thought,' said Henry. 'The experience of last Wednesday was so painful it blots out all hypothetical horrors.'

'Perhaps some other management might be interested,' Miss Robins suggested.

'No, no, I've finished with this play. Daly has spoiled it for me for ever,' Henry said gloomily. 'The idea of trying to find another producer for it fills me with nausea. I must go,' he added, seeing her stifle a yawn.

'Well, it *is* getting late,' she said, rising to her feet. 'But you're not going to give up the theatre in disgust, I hope?'

'No,' he said. And then, after a meditative pause, he added: 'I'll give it one more year.'

The thought calmed him, and became his mantra in the days and weeks that followed. One more year. The fact that a calendar year was coming to an end and a new one would soon begin, lent a satisfying logic to his resolution. He was in no mood for Christmas festivities, and declined the several invitations he received, spending the holiday contentedly alone at De Vere Gardens, reading, catching up on correspondence, and simply musing, with Tosca lying voluptuously on his lap, stroking her gleaming coat. He dressed for Christmas dinner, even though he was alone, and was served by Smith with proper ceremony, but ate the meal with a book propped up in front of him. A blessed quiet reigned in the street below his window. On Boxing Day he took Tosca for a walk in the Park and watched the horse-riders on Rotten Row and the swimmers taking their traditional dip in the Serpentine, without meeting or seeing anyone he knew. Sitting by the fire that evening he sketched out an idea for a play, a dark melodrama that he provisionally called *The Promise*. It would involve, for the first time in his work, a murder – the murder of a child. He quite shocked himself with the evil deed his imagination had conjured up, but as always the mere confirmation that one was capable of generating a new idea was enormously cheering.

On the 29th he wrote to William and Alice, saying: 'I have passed no more selfishly complacent Christmas, in the cheerful void left by the almost universal social flight to the country.' Towards the end of his long letter he gave an account of the collapse of the production of *Mrs Jasper's Way*, presenting himself as relieved to have severed all connection with the cad, Daly. 'It was none the less for a while a lively disgust and disappointment,' he admitted, '– a waste of patient and ingenious labour and a sacrifice of coin much counted on. But *à la guerre comme à la guerre*. I mean to wage this war ferociously for one year more – 1894 – and then (unless the victory and the spoils have by that time become more proportionate than hitherto to the humiliations and vulgarities and disgusts, all the dishonour and chronic insult incurred) to "chuck" the whole intolerable experiment and return to more elevated and more independent courses.'

One more year.

PART THREE

I

'ONE more year.' He had not forgotten making that bargain with fate at the end of 1893, but in the event he had been obliged to wait slightly longer – till the fifth day of 1895 – to discover whether or not he would succeed as a playwright. He had underestimated (though he should have known better, given what he had already experienced) the chronic delays, the endemic frustrations, the multiplicity of unforeseen obstacles, that seemingly attended every theatrical venture. The whole of 1894 had passed with *Guy Domville* still waiting impatiently in the wings of the St James's to 'come on', as *Mrs Tanqueray* ended its long run only to be succeeded by the almost equally extended run of Jones's *The Masqueraders*. The success of *that* play had been all the more frustrating for being unforeseen – though he suspected Alexander of having misled him about its prospects in order to secure his option on *Guy Domville*. Theatre people, managers anyway, were blithely and chronically mendacious about such matters – they simply told you whatever they thought you wanted to hear, and whatever it suited their interest to have you believe, at any given moment. If Alexander had been perfectly frank in the summer of 1893 when they had their first meetings, and had told him that in all probability he would not be able to put on *Guy Domville* for another eighteen months, he might very well have decided to take it elsewhere. Not that that would necessarily have been to his advantage, for he would merely have encountered another set of delays, frustrations, and obstacles from a different source. At least Alexander was an efficient and hard-working producer. It was not his fault that he had gone down with German measles just after *The Masqueraders* closed, so that rehearsals for *Guy Domville* had to be postponed for three weeks. If it hadn't been for that unlucky circumstance the play in which all his hopes of dramatic glory were now invested would have been put to the test just inside the stipulated calendar year. But now, at last, the waiting was a matter of hours.

How many hours he could not precisely calculate. He had heard a distant clock strike the half, but of which hour? It might be three, or four, or five. It could hardly be only half past two, since he had not gone to bed until past midnight (Alexander had called for a second, late dress rehearsal) and he felt as if he had had at least a few hours' sleep; but he sensed that it could not yet be past six o'clock – the silence in the street outside was too profound. The pitch darkness of his curtained bedroom gave no clue – that would last until well after seven o'clock in the depths of a London winter. He could of course fumble for a match and look at his watch, lying on the bedside table where he always left it on retiring, but in truth he didn't really want to know the time. If it was only a quarter past three or four he would be depressed by the thought of how many hours he had to get through before Smith rapped on the door and brought him his hot water. He felt wide awake. It was going to be a long vigil – that was already evident. It would last right up till the moment the curtain rose that evening at the St James's – no, longer than that, because he had no intention of sitting and suffering in the theatre while his fate was decided.

The original plan, concocted with Gosse, had been to spend the evening in the saloon bar of some quiet public house in the vicinity, where his friend, hurrying out in the entr'actes, might give him brief bulletins of how the play was going; but on reflection this seemed a bad idea. He envisaged himself sitting alone in a corner of the pub over a pint of ale, watching the hands slowly move round the face of the clock over the bar, speculating futilely about the progress of the play, but unable to think of anything else. It would be unendurable. Accordingly he had written to Gosse that afternoon, cancelling their arrangement and saying that he had decided to fill the time by watching somebody else's play. He had it in mind to see Oscar Wilde's *An Ideal Husband*, which had just opened at the Haymarket. *The Times* had given it a favourable review, but not *too* favourable. Their critic shared, even if he expressed it more mildly, his own opinion that Wilde's dramatic art consisted wholly of giving tired theatrical devices a superficial gloss of wit. What was it he had said? *'Mr Wilde's passion is to adorn the commonplace with epigrams.'* Something like that. But it sounded as if the piece was diverting enough to serve his purpose, which was simple distraction. When it ended, or before if necessary, he would stroll over to the St James's in time to watch from the wings the cast take their curtain calls, and if the reception warranted it, to take a bow himself. That would be at about eleven. God in heaven! He still had almost an entire day to get through before his suspense would be relieved, for better or worse.

The distant clock struck the three-quarters.

'One more year.' Where had it gone? What, creatively, had he achieved in it? Nothing, certainly, in the dramatic line, except the usual excruciating business of cutting and trimming *Guy Domville* as it went through rehearsals. He had sent a scenario of *The Promise* to Compton, thinking that the part of the hero would appeal to him, but Compton had rejected it so promptly and emphatically, recoiling in such horror from the subject, that he was discouraged from trying it on anyone else. Perhaps one day he might turn it into a novella. His earlier proposal to Compton of the Monte Carlo comedy had also come to nothing: after an absurdly long-drawn-out correspondence it became evident that there was nothing about the plot that Compton positively liked and that his suggested changes amounted to a prescription for writing an entirely different play. What a waste of time! He had conceived no fresh ideas for plays since then which had progressed further than the pages of his notebook.

And what had he published in the past year? A couple of stories in *The Yellow Book*, and *Theatricals*, which was nothing but a sad testament to frustrated ambition, consisting of two plays, *Tenants* (originally *Mrs Vibert*) and *Disengaged* (originally *Mrs Jasper*), which in spite of all his efforts had failed to reach the stage. Although he had prefaced this volume with an elaborately humble authorial Note, admitting that it commemorated practical failure, and pleading only for indulgence in the compensatory idea of 'virtual' performance in the reader's mind, he had nourished secret hopes that reviewers might take his part against the producers who had at first encouraged and then turned against his work – lamenting that the theatregoing public had been denied the pleasure of seeing the plays, and even calling for new efforts to stage them. Vain hopes! The reviews had ranged from tepid to icy, and neither Hare nor Daly would have been caused a moment's discomfort by any of them. It was an extra source of chagrin that Daly's fortunes had taken a turn for the better immediately after his procured abortion – one could really call it no less – of *Mrs Jasper*. The production of *Twelfth Night* he had mounted in its place last January had been a huge hit, and Daly's Theatre had subsequently gone from strength to strength.

So, two tales and one book of plays – was that all he had to show for 1894? There was the little article puffing Du Maurier's *Trilby* in *Harper's Weekly* – but to recall that piece was to recall the state in which he wrote it: still reeling in shock from Fenimore's death, struggling to finish it and send it off to the magazine before he journeyed to Italy to deal with the aftermath of the ghastly tragedy.

He groaned softly, turned over on to his stomach and buried his face in the pillow. The last thing he wanted to think about was poor Fenimore – now he would never get back to sleep. But the creative dearth on which he had been brooding had surely been caused in part by her death. It had taken him nearly a year to get over it, if indeed he had yet done so. It seemed that he hadn't, for already a sickening recollection of the emotions with which he had received the dreadful news, in ever more devastating instalments, was rising irrepressibly in his consciousness like waves of nausea from the pit of the stomach. First, shock and disbelief at receiving, late in January, a cable from Fenimore's sister Clara Benedict in New York, curtly informing him of her death without further explanation, and asking if he could go to Venice immediately. Then bewilderment, as cables from other parties arrived to say that the funeral was to be in Rome – but still without a word about the cause of death. Then, on the very day that he arranged his journey to Rome – immediately after he returned home from Thomas Cook's, in fact – the horror with which he read the Venetian newspaper cutting, sent by a friend, which stated that Fenimore had fallen, or thrown herself, from her bedroom window on the second floor of the Casa Semitecolo in the early hours of Wednesday, January 24th.

He was instantly stricken with the certain belief that she had taken her own life, and it was so reported in the English newspapers in the following days. But there was an element of ambiguity about the circumstances which Fenimore's sister and other relatives understandably clutched at. She had been ill, and confined to bed for some days before the fatal event, and the family's explanation was that she had fallen accidentally from the window in the delirium of fever. He would have liked to believe this, but he was too well acquainted with Fenimore's character, her chronic sadness, her proneness to crippling depressions, that dark grotto of melancholy hidden deep inside her outwardly composed social self, to doubt that her death was suicidal. Of course it was likely that illness had precipitated the dreadful act – he seized on this circumstance as eagerly as the family – but it hadn't caused it. His theory, which he broadcast among mutual friends and acquaintances in a flurry of correspondence, was that she had suffered a sudden fit of madness or dementia, brought on by feverish illness, in which her chronically depressive temperament became momentarily self-destructive. It was in short an act committed, 'while the balance of the mind was disturbed', to use the forensic formula, but of course no less tragic for that. He was in a state of near-collapse at the horror and pity of it, and cancelled his journey to Rome, unable to face the ordeal of attending the funeral. He offered instead to go later to Venice to help Clara Benedict deal with Fenimore's effects. And how much later it turned out to be . . .

All through February and most of March he had waited in London for Clara Benedict and her daughter to cross the Atlantic, in a state of growing anxiety and suspense about what might be found in the sealed rooms of the Casa Semitecolo, and especially in the sealed box mentioned by Fenimore's cousin, Grace Carter. It was Grace Carter, happening to be in Europe at the time, who had been first on the scene of the fatality, and reported that Fenimore had recently given instructions that in the event of her death the apartment was to be sealed by the American consul to await the arrival of her next-of-kin, and had expressed a wish to be buried in the Protestant cemetery in Rome, because she hated the gloomy island cemetery of

Venice. It seemed that Fenimore had greatly exaggerated the seriousness of her indisposition, or so her doctor and secretarial assistant had believed, and fallen into what they regarded as a morbid habit of brooding on the subject of death. There was of course another possible explanation for her behaviour, the contemplation of which made him deeply uneasy – namely that she had all along been coolly and deliberately planning to kill herself, while pretending that her mind was disturbed by sickness. The word 'sealed' which recurred in these communications, suggestive of portentous secrets awaiting discovery, made him uneasy. Although he had no doubt that Fenimore had taken her own life, and was sufficiently devastated by that tragic fact, what he really dreaded was finding some evidence that she had done it on account of *him*. The correctness of his intuition on the first count had been confirmed as soon as he saw, from inside the apartment, the window from which Fenimore had fallen – there was no way an adult, however feverish, could fall out of it accidentally – but the second possibility had proved much more difficult to determine, and still remained hauntingly ambiguous.

Oh God! Must he go over it all again in his mind, tread once more this *via dolorosa* of memories? Beginning with his slightly shaming manoeuvres to ensure that he would be one of the little party who broke the seal on the door of Fenimore's apartment – travelling to Genoa to meet the Benedicts off their boat from New York, seeing them on to the train to Rome to pay their respects to Fenimore's grave, and proceeding to Venice to secure accommodation for them there. He himself took Fenimore's old rooms at the Casa Biondetti where she had stayed temporarily before moving into the nearby Casa Semitecolo, in the vain hope that inhabiting the space she had occupied would somehow help him retrospectively to inhabit her mind. He haunted the precincts of the Semitecolo for days, squinting from jetties at its worn faded façade, wondering if the fact that it faced north across the Grand Canal, and was seldom warmed by the rays of the sun, had contributed to Fenimore's final, lethal depression, and staring up from the Ramo Barbaro, the dark, narrow, smelly alley to the rear of the house, at the window from which Fenimore had pitched herself on to the hard paving stones below. It was one of the penalties of possessing a novelist's imagination that he had all too vivid and visceral a sense of the poor woman's last moments – the rush through the air, the blinding pain of impact, the semi-consciousness of the distraught soul struggling to free itself from the broken body. The newspaper reports said that the two men who came across her crumpled form in the dark alleyway, shortly after one a.m., thought at first it was a bundle of whitish clothing or bed linen that lay before them, and it was only when one of them poked it with his walking stick, and they heard a faint moan, that they realised it was a human being and raised the alarm. Poked her with a stick! Reliving the moment *in situ* he had run from the Ramo Barbaro to the nearest side canal, and vomited into the water. She had been carried into the house and laid on her bed, but lapsed into a coma and was dead before dawn broke.

The violence of her death, however, lent credibility to his theory that it happened in a moment of temporary madness. Surely nobody in their right mind would coolly choose such a terrifying and painful end? Or one so shocking and distressing to family and friends? When Alice had her second serious breakdown, in the late 'seventies, and asked their father if she was wrong to feel tempted by suicide, the old man had serenely replied that he could see no objection to her taking her own life providing she did it 'in a perfectly gentle way in order not to distress her friends' (friends of course in the old, now almost obsolete, sense of close relations). He had thought this wickedly callous of his father when he first heard of it from William, though it had the desired effect of making Alice furiously determined to live. But if Fenimore had taken a considered decision to end her life she would have agreed with Henry James Sr.'s pragmatic counsel, and chosen some means less distressing to herself and those who loved her than defenestration. What means? Well, drowning for instance – that would have been easy enough to accomplish, and to disguise as an accident, in watery Venice.

But that train of thought summoned up what was possibly the most unwelcome memory of all those attached to Fenimore's demise – the expedition to dispose of her clothes in the lagoon. He tried to suppress it, but it bobbed up again immediately, like the air-filled dresses themselves. It had seemed such a good idea at the time – the Benedicts had certainly welcomed it as an imaginative solution to a delicate problem. Having already filled twenty-seven trunks and boxes with Fenimore's effects – 'packing' seemed to be a family obsession – they did not really want to ship her clothes as well back to America, but to burn them would risk setting the old chimneys of the Semitecolo alight, to dispose of them as rubbish would be degrading, and to give them away would invite the risk of encountering one day a double or ghost of Fenimore on some canal path or bridge. Why not, then, sink them in the waters of the lagoon that she loved so much, and had written about so eloquently in the last pages of her notebook? It was agreed; and one evening (dull and misty, not the glorious golden Turneresque sunset he had hoped for) he took a gondola piled with dresses well out into the lagoon and, under the puzzled and somewhat scandalised gaze of Tito, Fenimore's faithful gondolier, began to pitch them overboard. Of course, in retrospect, he should have attached weights to the clothes, but he hadn't thought it would be necessary; he had pleased himself with a vision of the waterlogged dresses gracefully subsiding beneath the waters of the lagoon. Instead of which, buoyed up by the air trapped inside their voluminous folds, they floated on the surface, surrounding the gondola like swollen corpses, like so many drowned Fenimores. It was a spectacle at once macabre and farcical, and he felt acutely the humiliation and folly of his own part in it. Fearing that some passing vessel might be drawn to investigate, he ordered Tito to use his oar to thrust the items of clothing down into the depths of the sea, a task of some difficulty, for the velvets and silks clung to the blade as if mutely appealing for rescue, and he was obliged to seize a boathook himself to assist the man. What he had conceived as a tender and poetic farewell to his friend had turned into a grotesque masque suggestive of a guilty conscience striving to hide the traces of a crime.

And of course it was no use denying that he had felt a degree of guilt, or at least responsibility, for Fenimore's death, which still lingered to disturb his thoughts at vulnerable times like this, but was especially acute in those weeks in Venice when he called daily at the Casa Semitecolo and spent hours at a time helping the Benedicts go through Fenimore's books and the 'sealed box' containing her papers, deciding what should be preserved and what should be burned. He lived in dread of finding a suicide note saying in effect, *'I am going to kill myself because Henry James doesn't love me.'* He found no such document of course; nor did he find the letter that Alice had written to Fenimore just before she died, though he searched diligently for it. He had an intuition that Alice, on her deathbed, had made some generous impulsive womanly gesture towards her old unseen rival – writing at last to commit him to her care, saying that Fenimore was the only woman she could imagine Henry marrying, the only woman he should marry, the only woman who had earned the right to be his wife, and that her own spirit would rest easy in eternity if they were united. If his 'hunch', as they called it in America, were correct, that would have raised Fenimore's hopes to a pitch which might have made his subsequent failure to realise them too much to bear. But he found no trace of the letter, nor any intimate letters from himself. She had evidently been punctilious in carrying out their agreement to destroy their correspondence, for only a few brief recent letters, mostly banal communications about his planned visit to Venice, had survived. Those he destroyed: a suspicion that his repeated postponement of this visit might have contributed to her depression continued to trouble him.

The discovery that most disturbed him, however, was a passage in her notebook, apparently an idea for a story: *'imagine a man born without a heart. He is good, at least not cruel; not debauched, well-conducted; but he has no heart.'* Was it himself she was thinking of? It wasn't true of course that he had no heart, but was that the impression he gave? Her words had chimed with something Flaubert had said to him, back in the 'seventies, at one of those Sunday gatherings of writers in his fifth-floor eyrie in the Faubourg St Honoré, calmly reporting a devastating accusation of his mother's, without attempting to deny its truth. *'Your mania for sentences has dried up your heart,'* Mme Flaubert had written to her son. Even then, and even though the words were directed at another man, he had felt a little internal qualm of apprehension that they might one day be levelled at himself, for he shared Flaubert's mania for sentences,

sentences that were perfectly balanced, intricately constructed, subtly cadenced, and as densely packed with meaning as a nut with meat. Did such an obsession dry up one's heart? Was that the inevitable price one had to pay for artistic achievement? He sometimes feared that it was. *'Not cruel; not debauched, well-conducted.'* Flaubert, of course, *had* been debauched, and capable of cruelty to women. But at least he had known passion. While he himself had always been ... well-conducted. It was as if Fenimore had left a message for him to find after her death, saying in effect: you have not fully lived. Recalling the moment when he read the note in her neat copperplate hand, he felt a dark abyss of depression and despair opening up beneath him.

The clock began to chime the hour. Grateful for the distraction, he strained his ears to count the strokes. One ... two ... three ... four. Silence returned. Four o'clock. Four more hours to pass till Smith knocked at his door. Sixteen till the curtain rose on *Guy Domville*, Act One. *'The Garden at Porches'*. To try to stem the tide of gloomy thoughts he silently recited the stage directions, which he knew by heart: *'The garden of an old house in the West of England; the portion directly behind the house, away from the public approach. Towards the centre a flat old-fashioned stone slab, on a pedestal, formed like a table and constituting a sun-dial. Close to it is a garden seat. On the right a low wooden gate, leading to another part of the grounds. On the left a high garden wall with a green door. A portion of the house is visible at the back, with a doorway, a porch and a short flight of steps.'* It was a pretty set. He had nothing to complain of in the physical presentation of his play. The scenery and the costumes were of a high standard and had looked impressive at the dress rehearsals under the St James's electric lighting. With the possible exception of W. G. Elliott in the part of Lord Devenish, the acting was unexceptionable, and at times much better than that. Marion Terry, if not quite the equal of her sister Ellen, was subtle and touching in the difficult part of Mrs Peverel, which required her to express emotion while for the most part struggling to disguise it. The little bit of business she had developed lately, just before the curtain drop at the end of Act One, going across to the pillar of the porch and laying her face against it, lost in thought, was quite exquisite. And Alexander was capable of communicating the real anguish of the hero's divided loyalties when he forgot to be concerned about presenting his handsome head and tightly breeched legs in the most becoming attitudes. As a director of other actors he was excellent. The rehearsals had proceeded in a calm and orderly fashion, without the tantrums and sulks that had occasionally disturbed the productions of *The American*. It was a pity, a great pity, that he himself had been rendered speechless by laryngitis at the first read-through, so that he was unable to address the cast and guide them on the right paths to the interpretation of their characters, but instead had to sit in a silent agony of frustration as Alexander performed this task. He had done his best to make up for the manager's predictable bluntings and blurrings of the finer points of the text by interventions at subsequent rehearsals. And as for the text itself – how he had laboured to reduce its length, in obedience to Alexander's immitigable demands, without losing vital elements of dramatic substance. Every word that remained had survived several fine-combings designed to identify and eliminate any conceivable redundancy, however trivial. The thing had been sweated and strained and bled until there was not a surplus syllable in it. In short, everyone concerned in the production had given of their professional best. So why was he so nervous? Because, however careful the preparation, you could never be sure whether a play would 'go' until you put it in front of an audience.

He turned over on to his back and joined his hands on his stomach in the attitude of a sculpted figure on top of an old cathedral tomb. There was no statue on Fenimore's tomb, just a plain cross. He had finally visited it in May, having fled from Venice when the crowds of tourists became unbearable. It had been a soothing experience after all, and he wished he had not postponed the pilgrimage for so long. He had always loved the Protestant Cemetery, shaded by cypresses, its modest graves contrasting with the great pagan pyramid of Caius Cestius close by. Shelley and Trelawney were laid to rest there, and Keats under his poignant despairing epitaph, *'Here lies one whose name was writ in water.'* There was no epitaph on Fenimore's tombstone, just the bare name, *'Constance Fenimore Woolson'*, with the date, '1894', a reticence that would have pleased her, as would the ivy and violets growing in profusion over the fine white marble.

Fenimore again. It seemed that he was not going to be able to stop thinking of her during this long wakeful night, so he might as well spare himself the effort to do so. If it were true that he had no heart, or only one desiccated by the mania for sentences, would he have been so disturbed by her death, or have spent so many hours brooding on it? He had needlessly distressed himself by taking the words in the notebook so personally. But the idea of a man who was born without a heart – a good man, well-conducted, who however lacked some vital faculty of feeling – was an interesting one. Suppose the man sensed there was something missing in himself – suppose he spent his entire life waiting for something to happen to him, something very important though he didn't know what it would be, and confided this vague but obsessive expectation to a woman friend, only to discover, when she died, that what he lacked was the capacity to recognise and return the love the woman was all the time offering him. He might do something with that idea. Not immediately, not perhaps for years, but he would write Fenimore's story for her one day. The idea gave him a kind of peace and satisfaction, and he felt himself at last growing drowsy.

The next thing he was aware of was the rap of Smith's knuckles on the bedroom door.

'Eight o'clock, Mr James,' came the muffled summons.

'Thank you, Smith,' he mumbled in reply.

A few moments later Smith entered with a steaming jug in his hand, which he placed on the washstand. Then he went to the window and drew the curtains, revealing a view of roofs and chimney-pots and a strip of dull grey sky. 'A cold morning, sir,' he remarked, 'with a nipping wind. But only to be expected in January.'

'As long as it doesn't snow,' he replied. A heavy snowfall could keep half the first-night audience away.

Smith evidently followed his train of thought. 'It did say in yesterday's newspaper there might be a few flurries, but nothing to cause anxiety.' He knelt under the mantelpiece and applied a match to the gas fire, which ignited with a pop. 'Shall I run your bath, sir?'

'Yes, thank you, Smith.'

'And your usual attire for a Saturday in town? The soft black jacket and grey worsteds?'

'Yes, thank you.'

When the man had left the room and closed the door behind him, Henry got out of bed and emptied his bladder copiously into the chamber pot. As he returned it to the commode he felt, as always, a slight twinge of guilt at giving the housemaid the task of emptying it, but he was too lazy to put on his dressing gown and slippers and shuffle down the corridor to the w.c., and then back again to the bedroom to shave and then out again to the bathroom to bathe. He took off the little black silk cap that he wore in bed, and his pyjama jacket, shivering a little, for the gas fire had not yet warmed the air in the room. He poured water into the handbasin, washed and dried his face, and then, with a little shaving soap, a freshly honed razor and a pair of gentleman's scissors, shaved his cheeks and trimmed his beard. He took particular care with this operation, bearing in mind the evening to come. His was never a neatly shaped beard, like De Maupassant's imperial, for instance, or flowing and patriarchal, like William's, but bushy, flecked with grey, and blunt in outline. Someone had said once that it reminded him of a soldier's beard, or a sea-captain's, and he had not been displeased. Sometimes he thought of shaving it off, but now that the top of his head was almost entirely bald he felt he needed more than ever the compensatory mass of hair around his jaw; and besides he liked the slight air of mystery a beard created, the way it screened revealing facial expressions.

He put on his dressing gown and slippers and proceeded to the steam-filled bathroom. Tutored by long experience Smith had run a bath of precisely the right temperature, allowing time for the water to cool by some degrees while he was shaving. He lay back luxuriously in the hot water, his belly protruding from the surface like a small pink island. He had abandoned all hope of reducing it — however much walking he did made no difference, and even a course of instruction in fencing had failed to have any effect. It was, like

his baldness, like the gout, a sign of the body's inevitable degener-
ation. Du Maurier had left *that* out of account – the sagging dugs
and pendulous paunches of the elderly – in his utopian vision of a
world returned to prelapsarian nudity which he had expounded in
the Staithes pub. The corresponding passage in *Trilby* had been cut
from the magazine serial but restored in the book.

It had made little difference to the astonishing success of *Trilby*
in both forms of publication. Apparently *Harper's* had never published
a serial which generated such a huge demand for the magazine –
only Fenimore's *Anne* had come anywhere near it in this respect,
they told Du Maurier – and a hundred thousand copies of the book
had been sold in America since it was published last fall. *A hundred
thousand!* Sales in England had been slower at first, but the novel
was already in its seventh impression. Poor Du Maurier had reason
to regret having sold the copyright for a mere two thousand pounds,
but Harper had lately done the decent thing and promised to pay
him a royalty from the beginning of this year, so he wouldn't be
'poor' Du Maurier for much longer. Osgood McIlvaine had
announced a forthcoming six-shilling illustrated edition for which
the demand would be immense; and there was a stage adaptation
in preparation in America which would no doubt pour more gold
into Du Maurier's cupped hands.

He stirred the water moodily with his foot, sending ripples across
the surface that plashed against the slopes of his belly. He was
reminded of an epigram of Wilde's, in that essay 'The Soul of Man
under Socialism' in the *Fortnightly*, something like: '*Anyone can sympathise with a friend's failure, but it takes a truly exceptional nature to rejoice
in a friend's success.*' As so often, Wilde's cynical wit had enabled him
to put his finger on an uncomfortable truth. Of course he was glad
that Kiki's money worries were well and truly over, and the fame
and adulation lavished by Fortune on the author of *Trilby* could not
have happened to a more decent and deserving man. Nevertheless
he couldn't deny – though he hoped he disguised it from others –
that there were ironies in the situation which tasted bitter in contemplation. It was more than likely that Du Maurier, at only his second
attempt at writing a novel, had already sold more copies of it than

he himself had sold of his entire literary output to date. And this with a story once offered to himself, *gratis* – that was the most ironic twist in the whole affair, though of course nothing he himself might have done with the *donnée* would have tickled the public's palate in the same way. Why Du Maurier's treatment had tickled it to such an unprecedented degree remained, however, a mystery. Du Maurier, to do him credit, seemed mystified himself – mystified, and somewhat intimidated by the celebrity he had acquired in consequence.

He would be at the theatre tonight, he and Emma, applauding with all his might at the end, and no doubt calling out 'Author! Author!' along with many other friends and supporters, but perhaps with more sincere good will than any other. Du Maurier probably did have the 'exceptional nature'. If *Guy Domville* was a triumph, he would genuinely rejoice at his friend's success. That was a chastening thought, one that should make him ashamed of the hollowness of his own congratulations on the success of *Trilby*. The hollowness, he trusted, was known only to himself. *Basta!* Enough of this sour self-examination. He sat up in the bath with a sudden movement that sent a tidal wave slopping over the rim onto the linoleum floor, seized the loofah and began to scrub his back with the zeal of a medieval flagellant.

There was a letter from Du Maurier in the first delivery of mail, which Smith brought to the breakfast table, wishing him the best of fortune for the first night – 'I believe actors have a superstitious aversion to wishing each other good luck on these occasions,' he wrote, 'but the prohibition surely doesn't apply to authors.' There were letters from many other friends and well-wishers: Gosse (who acknowledged the change of plan for the evening), Elizabeth Robins, Mrs Hugh Bell, Mary Ward, Henry Harland, Jonathan Sturges and Morton Fullerton. There was, touchingly, a letter from Minnie Bourget in Paris, who had heard about the play from an American friend, a Mrs Edith Wharton, who claimed to be an admirer and sent, vicariously, her own good wishes. The correspondents who were not abroad would be in the theatre that evening, along with other friends and acquaintances, nearly all names to conjure with. There would be a whole academy of well-known artists, besides Du Maurier: Sir Edward Burne-Jones, Sir Frederick Leighton, George Frederick Watts, John Singer Sargent . . . When Alexander had seen the list drawn up by the box office manager, of seats specially requested or gratefully accepted by these well-known personages, he had allowed himself a low whistle of awe and admiration. 'Upon my word, Henry,' he said (they were on 'Henry' and 'Alec' terms by this time), 'upon my word, this is going to be the most distinguished first-night audience the West End has seen in years.' He didn't know whether to feel elated at the likelihood of their sympathetic attention or alarmed at the prospect of being collectively judged by them.

The delivery of *The Times* was annoyingly late, as it often was on a Saturday, but Smith brought it to the table as he was concluding his breakfast with a second slice of toast and marmalade and a third cup of coffee. He opened it at once and searched eagerly in the advertisement columns for the announcement of *Guy Domville*. There it was: 'St James's Theatre: Production of *Too Happy By Half*, one act comedy by Julian Field; and *Guy Domville* by Henry James, 7.40.' Was that all? His play tersely mentioned as if it were a mere appendage to Field's paltry curtain-raiser? He felt himself flushing with indignation at the insult and already wondering how to visit retribution on the offender, whoever it was, when his eye caught another, much longer advertisement in the next column: 'St James's Theatre. Mr George Alexander Sole Lessee and Manager. Tonight and Every Evening at 8.20. *Guy Domville*, a play in three Acts, by Henry James.' And there followed the complete cast list, and the scene-settings of the three acts, concluding with a brief mention of Field's farce. His anger subsided. He read carefully through the advertisement for a second time without finding any errors, and then ran his eye idly further down the column. The 372nd performance of *The New Boy* was announced. 'What a capital farce' – *Daily Telegraph*. 'Roars of laughter' – *The Times*. What might he read here next week about *Guy Domville*? 'A play of exquisite sensibility and profound human insight.' 'A drama of rare intelligence and poetic eloquence.' 'A masterpiece of dramatic construction.' He almost blushed at his own childish vanity, but what author in the world had never indulged in such fantasies? His eye travelled further down the column: 'Haymarket Theatre. A new and original play of modern life called *An Ideal Husband*, by Oscar Wilde.' He would walk to the Haymarket later and purchase a ticket – it would help to pass the time, and he could lunch afterwards at the Reform.

'Shall I clear the table, sir?'

He gave a start, not having been aware that Smith had re-entered the room. 'Yes, yes, please do. Thank you, Smith.' He rose, gathered up his letters and took them, with *The Times*, into his study. He hoped for some sensation in his bowels that might presage an evacuation, but was not rewarded.

He sat in an armchair and browsed through the newspaper without finding anything that held his attention for more than a few moments. There seemed to be rumbles of imminent trouble in Eastern Europe – when were there not? There was a situation in Armenia and a crisis in Newfoundland. The Japanese had seized Port Arthur from the Chinese, who had captured a few Japanese soldiers, chopped them up and carried the pieces about on sticks, and the enraged Japanese had retaliated by massacring five thousand Chinese. How very horrible – but so remote, it was hard to feel any emotion. The 'Police' column contained stories infinitely more trivial but of greater human interest. At Marylebone magistrate's court a well-dressed woman was charged with stealing umbrellas from two ladies while they were occupied in confessionals in Roman Catholic churches in the West End. At Clerkenwell, Ernest Henry Peckham, 33, clerk, was charged with indecent behaviour in St Paul's Rd, on Thursday evening. Evidence given by two young girls. Peckham a prominent member of his church (Congregational). Sentenced to three months' hard labour. Alas poor Peckham! His life was ruined. There was correspondence on the Drink Question, and on proposed changes in the rules of Billiards. There were advertisements for new books. *A Dark Interlude*. By Richard Dowling. *The Worst Woman in London* by F. C. Phillips. *Mrs Jervis: a romance of the Indian Hills* by B. M. Croker. He had never heard of any of these authors before – but then a familiar name leapt from the page and smote his heart with a pang of grief: '*My First Book* by Robert Louis Stevenson and 21 famous authors. With Prefatory story by Jerome K. Jerome.' Poor Louis! Dead at forty-six in Samoa, and it was apparently not the bronchial disease that had dogged him all his life, and driven him to the South Seas in search of a benign climate, that had killed him, but a brain haemorrhage, which might have happened to anyone, anywhere. The news had reached England in the first week of rehearsals for *Guy Domville*, so he had not had the leisure to mourn him properly, and chance reminders like this advertisement cut sharply. What was Louis' first book? he wondered. *Travels with a Donkey*? And who were the other twenty-one famous authors? He could have contributed a pretty piece himself, about *A Passionate Pilgrim and other tales*, but he had not been invited, presumably because insufficiently famous.

There was a tap on the door and Mrs Smith came in, as she usually did at this hour, to receive her instructions and discuss house-keeping matters. He did not detain her long.

'I shall lunch at my club, Mrs Smith. And as you know, I'll be out this evening, and having a late supper. Perhaps you would be good enough to provide a light meal at about six, to get me through the evening.'

'Something like a welsh rarebit?' Mrs Smith suggested. 'With a rasher of bacon?'

'Exactly.'

'And shall I leave a sandwich in the kitchen, for when you come in tonight?'

'I don't think that will be necessary. I shall be eating very late.' Not feeling equal to the task of hosting a party at home, as on the first night of *The American*, he had arranged to give the Alexanders and the rest of the cast supper at a restaurant in Duke Street after the performance.

'Very well, sir. And the lunch party tomorrow?'

'Oh yes, thank you for reminding me. Four gentlemen will be coming.' He ran through the guest list: Julian Sturgis, an old Boston friend who was visiting England, Philip Burne-Jones (Sir Edward's son), the novelist William Norris, and Gosse. As well as wishing to repay some debts of hospitality, he thought it might be interesting to hold an inquest on the production with some sympathetic friends after the dust of the first night had settled. He had thought about inviting Du Maurier, but decided it would not be fair to put him to the trouble of a second journey from Hampstead in two days.

'I thought perhaps roast lamb?' Mrs Smith prompted. 'With plaice fillets for the fish course. And apple charlotte for pudding.'

'Admirable.'

He signed some orders for groceries from the Stores, and handed them back to her.

'Thank you, Mr James.' Mrs Smith put her notepad and pencil away in her apron pocket, but hesitated as she turned to leave. 'And may I – may we both wish you the very best of luck tonight?'

'Thank you, Mrs Smith,' he said, blushing for some reason. 'You are most kind. Most kind. I haven't forgotten about the tickets.' He had promised to get them seats for the play on their next night off.

'Thank you, sir.'

After Mrs Smith had left the room, he went to the window and stared out in a preoccupied, unfocused way. Something in his recent thoughts was pricking his conscience. The real reason why he hadn't invited Du Maurier to lunch tomorrow was not the fear of inconveniencing him, but because if he were one of the company they would be sure to talk more about *Trilby* than *Guy Domville*. An ignoble motive, but he might as well admit it to himself. He went to the round table on which books recently read, or half-read, or waiting to be read, were piled, and took the three blue-bound volumes of *Trilby*, inscribed to himself by the author, to his desk by the window. He had developed a habit of picking them up and leafing through them from time to time to see if he could in this way surprise the work into yielding up the mystery of its astonishing popularity. Tucked inside the cover of the first volume were some loose papers which he took out and unfolded: a couple of pages cut from *Harper's Weekly*, 14th April 1894, containing his article on *Trilby*, then being serialised in Harper's monthly magazine, and a letter from Du Maurier thanking him for it. The publishers had asked him if he would review the first four instalments of the serial, and he had agreed, partly as a favour to an old friend, partly because he was intensely curious to read the novel. They had sent him a copy of the complete text, but asked him not to 'give away' the future development of the story. In fact, the early chapters, set in the Latin Quarter of mid-century Paris, among impoverished artists, art-students and models, were by far the best part of the whole, and he had been able to praise them with a clear conscience, though choosing his words carefully. Du Maurier had written 'to thank you for all the beautiful things about me you so beautifully expressed in Harper's Weekly – I feel almost vain enough to wish that you were not my friend and had written it all the same just as it is.'

Happily Du Maurier had failed to detect any note of reservation in his concluding tribute to the novel's narrative style, *'a style so talked and smoked, so drawn, so danced, so played, so whistled and sung, that it never occurs to us even to ask ourselves whether it is written'*. If you *did* ask yourself you would have to say it wasn't written very well. But as a stream of nostalgic reminiscence and anecdote, full of local colour, diversified with snatches of song and lines of poetry and dialogue in several different registers of French and English – polite, colloquial, dialect, literary, parodic, and 'broken' – it was irresistible to any reader sympathetically disposed towards the subject matter, brushing aside critical quibbles and scruples with its carnivalesque energy and *élan*. He had to admire Du Maurier's boldness in leaving much of the French dialogue untranslated. He would wager that very few of the masses who had read the story, especially in America, would have been sufficiently competent in the language to construe these passages, yet none as far as he was aware had complained. Perhaps they felt flattered by being assumed to understand the French. Perhaps they were amused by the effort to guess what it meant. Or perhaps its impenetrability strengthened the illusion of being transported to an exotic and unfamiliar time and place. There was, after all, little risk of losing a thread of the story on this account, because the story was so very simple.

There were the three young British aspirant painters, 'the Three Musketeers of the brush', the giant Yorkshireman Taffy, the bearded Scot known as the Laird, and the English hero, Little Billee, whose nickname, like so much else in the book, derived from Thackeray.

There was Trilby, the beautiful, natural, generous-hearted and usually barefoot young model whom they all in their different ways loved; and there was Svengali, the Jewish musical genius of mixed German and Polish origin, who recognised the unusual quality of Trilby's voice and realised he could overcome her tone-deafness by hypnotism and thus make his own fortune. Little Billee was in love with Trilby but was shocked to discover her one day in an *atelier* full of students sitting for the figure, *pour l'ensemble* (or as she said herself, 'sitting for the altogether'), and he ran away, but relented and was reconciled to her, and she agreed to marry him, but when his scandalised mother appealed to her she nobly gave him up and disappeared, later to be rescued from destitution by Svengali. All this was fairly obviously derived from *Scènes de la Vie de Bohème* and Dumas' *La Dame aux Camélias*, as Du Maurier himself candidly admitted – except for the character of Svengali. Svengali too had his precursors and progenitors – Shylock, for instance, and Dickens's Fagin – but he was a highly original creation. He was a villain, physically repulsive with his long greasy locks, heavily lidded eyes, yellow canine teeth, and hoarse rook's caw of a voice, but he had more vitality and eloquence than the 'good' characters, and his virtuosity as a pianist was far more credible than were the alleged gifts of Little Billee as a painter. Du Maurier in fact manifested a similar ambivalence towards the Hebrew race in real life, voicing the conventional English distaste for their collective presence in large numbers, while at the same time befriending individual Jews and admiring their artistic and intellectual gifts. Indeed Little Billee was said to have some Jewish blood in his ancestry, the narrator commenting that *'most of us have a minimum of that precious fluid in our veins'*.

As he turned the pages he came across the remarkable speech in which Svengali, enraged by Trilby's indifference to his overtures, tried to frighten her with a vision of herself as a corpse in the Morgue.

'But you are not listening, sapperment! Great big she-fool that you are – sheep's head! Dummkopf! Donnerwetter! You are looking at the chimney-pots when Svengali talks! Look a little lower down between the houses, on the other side of the river! There is a little, ugly grey

building there, and inside are eight slanting slabs of brass, all of a row,
like beds in a school dormitory, and one fine day you shall lie asleep
on one of those slabs — you, Drilby, who would not listen to Svengali,
and therefore lost him! . . . And over the middle of you will be a little
leather apron, and over your head a little brass tap, and all day long
and all night the cold water shall trickle, trickle all the way down your
beautiful white body to your beautiful white feet till they turn green,
and your poor, damp, muddy rags will hang above you from the ceil-
ing for your friends to know you by; drip, drip, drip! But you will
have no friends . . .'

The picture he drew of the poor girl's naked corpse was a remarkable transposition of the nude as *beau idéal* into a kind of gloating
memento mori, and it was significant that the death with which Svengali
prophetically threatened Trilby was by drowning, the traditional end
of the fallen woman in fiction. By associating this idea with his
villain Du Maurier ruled it out as a possible fate for his heroine,
and strengthened the audience's sympathetic identification with her,
in spite of references to her liaisons with several artists in the past
(something, by the way, that would surely have been much more of
a stumbling block to a conventional prig like Little Billee than her
sitting 'for the altogether'). His review in *Harper's* had in fact provoked
a letter from a righteous American matron chiding him for not
condemning the heroine on this account (he had forwarded it to
Du Maurier for his amusement) but on the whole it was surprising how little protest there had been from the notoriously puritanical American reading public. The novel had provoked much
discussion in the press, and even apparently sermons from pulpits,
but it had not been widely denounced. It had helped no doubt to
make the story acceptable that the heroine died before there was
any possibility of the hero marrying her.

He picked up the third volume (the second, in which Little Billee
made his name as an artist in England, but failed to heal his broken
heart, was the most tedious of the three) and turned to its closing
pages. After the death of Svengali in the middle of a concert,
attended by Little Billee and his friends, which caused her to lose

her ability to sing, Trilby sank into a slow decline. Then one day she was shown a portrait of the evil genius which was enough to reassert his spell over her: she produced one more flawless vocal performance, of Chopin's Impromptu in A flat, and fell back dead on the pillow. Little Billee followed her to the grave not long after in a passage of typical authorial insouciance. 'There has been too much sickness in this story, so I will tell as little as possible of poor Little Billee's long illness, his slow and only partial recovery, the paralysis of his powers as a painter, his quick decline, his early death, his manly, calm and most beautiful surrender – the wedding of the moth with the star, of the night with the morrow.' Was ever a writer's duty to his tale and his readers so shamelessly shirked? And yet, and yet – the public loved it. The manuscript itself had been bought for a huge sum by the London Fine Arts Society, and was to be exhibited at their premises under glass on payment of a shilling as if it were a first Folio of Shakespeare or the holograph of *The Pickwick Papers*. A mystery!

He snapped the book shut, and returned the three volumes to the book table. He had managed to pass an hour since breakfast. It was time to walk to the Haymarket and secure his seat for *An Ideal Husband*.

Because of the length of his excursion he was obliged to leave Tosca behind and endure her whimpering and reproachful looks as he left the flat – Smith would give her a run later. He walked through Kensington Gardens and across the Park to Piccadilly, muffled up in greatcoat, gloves, scarf and hat. It was a cold, grey morning with, as his servant had promised, a biting wind, but he was glad of the exercise. There was ice on the Serpentine, but it was thin and transparent as glass, and there were notices warning would-be skaters and sliders of the danger. Keen equestrians were trotting their mounts up and down the Row, riders and horses sending clouds of condensed breath into the cold atmosphere. There was a sleety precipitation in the air, and he squinted anxiously upwards, assessing the threat of the sky. 'Shall we have snow?' he asked a park attendant who was sweeping the footpath. 'I shouldn't think so, guv'nor,' the man said. 'Nuffink to worry about, anyways.' 'I'm glad to hear you say so,' he said. 'Good day.' At the gates on Park Lane he passed a legless beggar sitting on a little wheeled pallet, and dropped a half-crown into his upturned cap. 'Fanks, sir, you're a Christian,' said the man, seizing the coin and biting it – thus displaying rather unchristian suspicion. But after all it must have seemed an astonishingly generous donation to the poor wretch, whose cap had previously contained only a few coppers. It was not every day of the week that he was passed by a playwright nervously awaiting the first-night performance of his play and superstitiously eager to bribe Providence by all available means to achieve a favourable outcome.

He walked the length of Piccadilly to the Circus, where Alfred Gilbert's pretty monument to Lord Shaftesbury, erected a couple of years ago, still retained its pristine silvery gleam in spite of the sooty London atmosphere – apparently because it was made of aluminium. He was reminded by his recent encounter with the beggar that, according to the artist, the winged figure leaning forward, grace-fully balanced on one foot, to release an arrow represented the Angel of Christian Charity, though it was widely believed to be the young god of profane love, a confusion that must be embarrassing to the pious philanthropist's shade, though appropriate to the nocturnal character of this part of the West End. He turned down Haymarket and passed between the great columns of the Theatre Royal's hero-ically proportioned portico to purchase his ticket at the box office within. He asked for a seat in the front stalls, and at the end of a row, so that he could slip out before the performance ended if need be, but he had to be content with one situated well towards the back of the auditorium, for apparently the house was nearly sold out. It looked as if Oscar had scored another 'hit'.

From the Haymarket it was a short distance along Pall Mall to the Reform. It was always balm to the spirit to enter the extrava-gantly spacious premises, modelled on a Roman palazzo – indeed he had chosen the club more on account of its architecture than its membership. In the library, a vast hushed high-ceilinged room smelling of old leather, he wrote a brief letter, dated 'Saturday, noon', to Marion Terry: 'I don't want to worry you – on the contrary; so this is a mere word on the chance that I didn't say a couple of nights ago *distinctly* enough that your business at the end of Act I – your going and leaning your face against the pillar of the porch – couldn't possibly be improved . . .' Ever since he had recalled it in the watch of the night he had been troubled by the thought that she might at the last moment – actors were such fickle and impulsive creatures – decide to omit or change this expressive gesture. He would have the letter delivered to the stage door of the St James's, where she would find it on her arrival later that afternoon. Although he could easily drop it off himself on his way home, he had somehow conceived the idea that, just as it was said to be unlucky for a bride-groom to behold his bride in her wedding dress before she entered the church porch, so it would be inauspicious for him to set eyes on the St James's, all bedecked with posters and placards for the premiere of *Guy Domville*, until he arrived that evening at the appointed hour, and for this reason he had carefully skirted the vicinity of King Street on his morning walk. He had not felt the same inhibition at Southport when *The American* was first performed – but he was still a comparative novice in the ways of the theatre then; he had not yet acquired a feeling for its protocol, its superstitions, and its codes, nor a full understanding of what was at stake in the launch of a new play. Nervous as he had been that day, it was nothing to the growing panic he felt now. Imagine, he had actually gone calmly to sit among the audience at the opening of *The American*! They would have to chloroform him to make him do the same tonight.

He gave the letter and a shilling to a porter with instructions for its delivery, and proceeded to the dining room. For luncheon he ate mulligatawny soup, steak and kidney pie, and sherry trifle, with a half pint of the club's claret. He sat alone, studiously avoiding the eye of anyone else who entered, in case it was an acquaintance who might feel it his duty to inflict his company. Heavy with his repast, he returned to the library, picked up a copy of the *Saturday Review* and sank into a deep armchair near the fireplace. He started to read a leading article protesting against an Indian import tax on British cotton goods but almost at once lapsed into a blessed slumber, and woke half an hour later with a start, wishing it had been longer.

He retrieved the *Saturday Review*, which had slipped from his grasp to the floor, and turned to the arts and book pages. He noted that the journal had acquired a new theatre critic, writing under the initials GBS. It must be the young Irish journalist, George Bernard Shaw, who used to write so amusingly about opera for *The World* under the same initials. Elizabeth Robins knew him and said he was clever but not to be trusted. He was certainly clever – his little book, *The Quintessence of Ibsenism*, was proof of that – and possessed of a caustic wit. He was reviewing a melodrama by Sydney Grundy called *Slaves of the Ring*, whose absurdities he mercilessly anatomised, concluding: 'It is not a work of art at all; it is a mere contrivance for filling a theatre bill, and not, I am bound to say, a very apt contrivance even at that.' Elizabeth said Shaw had ambitions himself to be a playwright, and had had a play put on with some success the previous spring, when he had been abroad. What would Shaw think of *Guy Domville* – for presumably he would be at the theatre tonight to review it? What would William Archer think of it? What would any of them think of it? At least they could not deny that it was – or strove to be – a work of art.

He felt a welcome inclination to move his bowels, and went downstairs to the lavatory, a dank, dripping chamber that seemed like a sanitary afterthought to the rest of the building, being meanly proportioned and lined with institutional white tiles. While washing his hands there he had an absurd conversation with another member similarly engaged, who observed that it was a great day and an exciting prospect and how he wished he could be there, and Henry, assuming he was referring to the first night of *Guy Domville*, spoke at some length about his nervous anticipation of the event before he realised the man was referring to a rugby football match between England and Wales that was being played that afternoon in Swansea.

It was nearly three o'clock. If he walked home, not too briskly, that would consume another forty-five minutes. He collected his hat and coat and stick from the cloakroom and set off down Pall Mall, then cut across Green Park and into Hyde Park. The beggar had gone, no doubt to consume his half-crown in drink, and the horse-riders had departed from the Row. The cloud-filled sky, which had never allowed a glimpse of the sun all day, was growing darker already with the approach of evening. By the time he reached Kensington Palace, there were lights in its windows. He really must go and see the State Apartments that had been opened to the public by the Queen a few years ago, but it was always the way: when something was on your doorstep, you kept putting it off. Go now? No, he was not in the mood, and he thirsted desperately for a cup of tea.

Mrs Smith brought his tea and a buttered muffin to the study, with some more letters which had been delivered while he was out, including one from Edward Warren, his fellow godfather to Guy Millar. To reply to the messages of his wellwishers seemed the best way to pass the remaining hour or two before he must go and dress, and he accordingly lit a lamp and settled himself at his desk for this purpose. He began with Warren, to whom he wrote: 'I am in a state of trepidation out of all proportion (I won't say to my possible fate) but to the magnitude of the enterprise of the work. One can have a big danger, in the blessed theatre, even with a small thing.' That, ultimately, was the root cause of his perturbation: the consciousness that soon he would be judged, in an unprecedented blaze of publicity, and in the presence of his friends and peers, on the evidence of a work which did not belong to his primary field of artistic expertise, and which was mediated in a form over which he had limited control.

Smith knocked and put his head round the study door to enquire about his evening dress. 'White tie, I presume, sir?'

'Of course, Smith. Thank you.' If he was to take a bow in front of that audience he had better look the part.

2

IN his practice as a novelist and short story writer, Henry had developed a firm faith in the superior expressiveness and verisimilitude of the limited point of view. He believed the author of fictional narratives should represent life as it was experienced in reality, by an individual consciousness, with all the lacunae, enigmas, and misinterpretations in perception and reflection that such a perspective inevitably entailed; and if this function were to be shared by several characters in the course of a novel, it should be passed from one to another, like a baton in a relay race, with some regularity of plan. The antithetical method was well exemplified by *Trilby*, in which the authorial narrator, in Thackerayan fashion, took out his puppets from the box, and set them capering, and told you in his own confiding ruminative voice exactly what they were all thinking at any given moment, and awarded them marks for good or bad motives, in case there should be any danger of the audience having to make some interpretative effort on its own part.

But when he looked back later on the day which seemed, as he lived it, the longest he had ever known, he felt that neither of these narrative methods, and certainly not the one he himself favoured, would do satisfactory justice to the ironies, the follies, the enigmas, the queer conjunctions and coincidences of those hours, especially the later ones, after darkness fell. He moved through them in a kind of trance, his thoughts a confused mixture of hopes and fears and reverie, with no knowledge of what was happening in the place that concerned him most. It was only afterwards that he was able to piece together the whole story from what other participants told him – Alexander and the other actors, his friends in the audience, and persons who were unknown to him at the time, whom he only met months or years later, or whose memories of the occasion were passed on to him at second hand by mutual acquaintances, or unexpectedly encountered in memoirs and biographies long after the event. In retrospect he was aware that as he crossed and recrossed the space between De Vere Gardens and Piccadilly during that interminable Saturday, as he sat at his desk in his study, while dusk thickened outside the window, writing letter after unnecessary letter, as he sat in the Theatre Royal Haymarket with the laughter of the audience breaking in waves over his inattentive head – while this story, his story, with its drastically limited point of view, was proceeding, other connected stories were in progress, other points of view were in play, at the same time, in parallel, in brackets as it were.

[George Alexander was the first member of the cast to arrive at the theatre, but in his capacity of manager rather than actor. His wife Florence always made sure that he rested during the day at their home in Knightsbridge before a first night, but he was a perfectionist who hated to delegate tasks and he found it impossible to keep away from the scene of his operations for very long. By late afternoon he was in his office, going through the advance booking figures with his business manager, Robert Shone. Shone reported that the Libraries had taken sixteen hundred pounds' worth of tickets, which was reasonably encouraging. The stage doorkeeper interrupted them, bringing a telegram, 'No Reply,' just delivered.

'Another well-wisher,' Alexander commented with a complacent smile as he opened the envelope. His desk was already littered with cards, letters and telegrams. His expression changed as he read the message.

'What's the matter?' Shone asked.

Alexander slowly read out the words pasted to the slip of paper: *'WITH HEARTY WISHES FOR A COMPLETE FAILURE TONIGHT.'*

'Good God!' Shone exclaimed. 'Who sent it?'

'There is no name,' Alexander said, passing him the telegram.

Shone examined the document. 'It was sent from the Sloane Square Post Office,' he said. 'I'll make enquiries.']

To Minnie Bourget he wrote: 'It is five o'clock in the afternoon and at 8.30 this evening *le sort en est jeté* – my poor little play will be thrown into the arena – like a little white Christian virgin to the lions and tigers.' He conveyed his thanks to the unknown Mrs Wharton for her sympathetic good wishes, though not for alerting Minnie to the imminent premiere. 'I hoped *you wouldn't* hear of this little adventure save in the event of its being a success,' he concluded, 'but now I make haste to get this note off to you before my possible dishonour becomes actual.' He took a large envelope for this letter to enclose with it one of the bright red playbills for *Guy Domville*. It occurred to him that William and Alice might also be amused to receive such a souvenir of the event, and dashed off a short note to them to accompany it. 'I stick this florid "poster" into an envelope this tremulous afternoon to help beguile the hours until – 8.30 – and to bring my trepidation home to you. The omens, thank God, are decently good. But what are omens? *Domine, in manus tuas!* This is a time when a man wants a religion. But my hand shakes and I can only write that I am your plucky, but, all the same, lonely and terrified Henry.'

[Being in every respect a thoroughly up-to-date theatre, the St James's was equipped with a telephone, by means of which Robert Shone was able to speak to the postmaster at Sloane Square Post Office. He reported his findings to Alexander. 'Apparently two ladies sent the wire. They gave no names of course. The girl in the cage queried the wording, but they insisted it was correct.'

'What did they look like?'

'They were both wearing hats with veils, so it was hard for her to tell, but she thought one was youngish, the other middle-aged, both well-dressed and well-spoken.'

'Hmm. Who the devil could they be?'

'Somebody who doesn't like Henry James?' Shone suggested.

'But the wire was addressed to *me*,' Alexander pointed out. 'They could be actresses with a grudge, one of them anyway. Somebody I turned down at an audition perhaps.'

'But you didn't audition for this play,' Shone said.

'No. Well, somebody who thinks they should have been offered a part, and wasn't. Or somebody who asked for an interview and was refused – I'm always getting letters from actresses begging to see me. You know what it's like, Bob. It could be somebody I've completely forgotten about.'

The two men silently contemplated the mystery for a few moments. Both were made vaguely uneasy by it: any first night was risky and unpredictable enough without the added stress of anonymous ill-will transmitted by wire. 'I want you to keep this to yourself, Bob,' Alexander said at length. 'Not a word to the cast, and whatever you do don't mention it to James. The man is already a complete bag of nerves.'

'He won't be in tonight,' Shone said. 'He told me he would come behind at the end.'

'What's he going to do with himself?'

'He said he's going to see *An Ideal Husband*.'

'*Is* he?' Alexander was intrigued, for he had hopes of persuading Oscar Wilde to write another play for the St James's, to follow up the success of *Lady Windermere*. He added: 'I wish I could join him,' and the two men laughed together, perhaps more heartily than the quip merited, to relieve their tension. Alexander had no such wish, of course. He looked forward to commanding the stage as Guy Domville. It was a meaty role, and required three changes of costume, all becoming, with a particularly fine pair of riding boots in the third act.]

At six thirty, in full evening dress, he sat down in the dining room to eat Mrs Smith's Welsh rarebit and rasher, tucking a large napkin into the neck of his shirt to protect its starched front. The phrase, 'the prisoner ate his last meal . . .' crossed his mind. He asked Smith to pour him a glass of dry sherry to accompany the collation, which the man did with a flourish, sweeping the decanter round in a great arc before arresting it over the glass and taking out the stopper. Smith's gestures tended to become more and more baroque as the day proceeded, no doubt in proportion to the amount of liquid refreshment he had imbibed himself. He caught a whiff of drink on the man's breath and resolved, not for the first time, to speak to him about it – but not tonight, not tonight.

He glanced at the clock on the mantelpiece, calculating his immediate timetable. He would take a hansom to the Haymarket – he had walked enough that day, and an omnibus would not match the importance of the occasion. So if he left at 7.15, or just before, that should allow ample time to get to the Haymarket for eight. There was no curtain-raiser to *An Ideal Husband*, because it was a four-acter. Fortunate Wilde! He was not in favour of curtain-raisers – if they were very good they could make the main play seem disappointing, and if they were very bad they could put the audience into a disgruntled mood. Which category Field's farce might fall into he couldn't say, not having seen any rehearsals, but in any case its principal function was to give the quality customers their customary three entr'actes, during which to mill about and gossip and display their finery. In consequence his own play, the action of which divided naturally into three acts, had had to be cut to the bone to avoid an over-long evening. It was the intrusion of such purely institutional considerations that made the theatre such an infuriating medium for an artist to work in.

[In King Street the people waiting outside the theatre in two long lines for the cheap unreserved seats in the gallery and the pit were getting restless. Those at the front had been there for several hours, and all were feeling the cold. They stamped their feet and blew on their hands, and banged on the doors for admission, though they were well aware that these would not be opened until half an hour before the first curtain-up. Many of them knew each other by sight if not by name – they were regular attenders at first nights at the

234

St James's, dedicated admirers of George Alexander, who had first attracted their allegiance when he was a young leading actor in Irving's company. They sometimes referred to themselves jocularly as 'Alick's Army'. There was much chaff and chat between them, and much speculation about the author of the night's main entertainment. ''Enery Jimes − oo's 'e, then?' 'Dunno, we never 'eard of 'im before.' 'Oo's Guy Domville?' ''E must be the 'ero, coz Alick's playin' 'im − it sez so on the poster.' 'Good old Alick!'

Two buskers in ragged overcoats, one playing a battered fiddle, the other singing and holding out his cap for coins, passed along the lines. The man with the cap sang in a loud hoarse voice a popular music hall song:

> *'Where did you get that hat?*
> *Where did you get that tile?*
> *Oh, isn't it a nobby one,*
> *And just the proper style!'*

A cheer went up as the doors to the gallery entrance were opened and the crowd surged forward. Just inside the gallery entrance a young man sitting on a high stool behind a cramped counter took their shillings. Grumbling, joking, jostling, they climbed the four flights of uncarpeted stairs to the 'gods', hurrying to claim the best seats.]

He inspected himself in the glass on the wall of the hallway, tweaked his bow tie and smoothed his beard. The evening suit, freshly pressed, looked well. Smith held out his black overcoat. He plunged his arms into the sleeves and pulled in his stomach as he buttoned it up. It was getting to be a dangerously tight fit, and there was no way of 'letting out' an overcoat. He smoothed the black kid gloves over his fingers, and put on the silk top hat which Smith handed him, checking its angle in the mirror.

'No need to wait up for me, Smith,' he said. 'I shall be very late.'
'Very well, sir.'

'Good evening, then.'

'Good evening, sir,' said the man, holding open the front door of the apartment. 'I trust it will be a very enjoyable one.'

[All the seats in the gallery and pit at the St James's were occupied by now, and the stalls were beginning to fill up. In row J the young critic of the *Pall Mall Gazette* looked around with interest and attention, for it was still a novel experience to him to be seated in a theatre, in the stalls, wearing evening clothes, at a first night. Herbert Wells had been the *Pall Mall*'s drama critic only since Wednesday. The editor, Harry Cust, had promised him some time ago that he should have the first staff appointment on the paper that became vacant, and it happened to be drama. He had told Cust candidly that, apart from pantomimes and the occasional Gilbert and Sullivan, he had only been to the theatre twice in his life, but Cust seemed to think this was an advantage. 'Just what I want,' he had said. 'A fresh view. Here are your tickets for this week – Oscar Wilde tomorrow, and Henry James on Saturday. Something for you to cut your teeth on.' Having already acquired considerable facility as a freelance journalist, Herbert had no doubts about his ability to rise to this challenge, but he was conscious of the limitations of his wardrobe. 'Should I wear evening dress?' he asked. Cust, who was son and heir to the Earl of Brownlow, was clearly surprised by the question, and answered, after a pause, 'Yes, of course.' So he had hurried round to a tailor in Charles Street who he knew would give him credit and the man had run him up a suit of evening clothes in twenty-four hours, just in time for *An Ideal Husband* at the Haymarket. Pretty smart work, and Jane had said that it made him look very handsome as she tweaked his white tie and saw him off from their lodgings with a kiss. But not every man in the stalls tonight was wearing evening dress – he caught sight of someone in a brown Norfolk jacket suit taking his seat. It was George Bernard Shaw, who had just started reviewing plays for Frank Harris in *The Saturday Review*. He recognised the head of fiery red hair, and the matching beard like a tongue of flame, having heard him speak at Fabian meetings years ago when he was a student. It was typical of his fearless radicalism to ignore the theatre dress code. Herbert felt a little less smug about his new evening clothes.]

He hailed a hansom on Kensington Gore and asked to be taken to the Haymarket, but, finding he was a little early, alighted in Piccadilly opposite Hatchard's and walked from there. He soon regretted the decision. The pavements around Piccadilly Circus were thronged with the usual promiscuous Saturday night crowd – silk-hatted mashers and Cockney couples, flower-sellers and newspaper vendors, bold young women walking arm in arm and calling out saucy invitations to the shy young men who stepped aside to let them pass. These were what might be called amateur whores, as much in search of a good time as money. But when he turned down the Haymarket the prostitutes trying to catch his eye or deliberately bumping into him to solicit his custom became a serious nuisance. Three of them practically ambushed him, barring his way as he approached the pillars of the Theatre Royal. 'Feeling lonely, handsome?' 'Which of us d'you fancy then?' 'Only half a sovereign for a short time,' they pestered.

'Kindly let me pass,' he said with dignity.

'Oooh, don't be like that, sir!'

They clustered round him, pawing his clothes. He smelled the stink of their cheap perfume and bad breath and recoiled.

'Oi, let the gent alone, you gals! Get lorst!' A young man in a cloth cap and a long threadbare overcoat with a moulting fur collar interposed himself and shooed the women away. Henry was about to express his gratitude when his rescuer added: 'He's not interested in your sort – are you ducky?' and winked suggestively. There was a little gang of youths behind him, dressed in similar motley garments, looking on and grinning. The women moved away jeering and laughing. 'Ain't you a friend of Oscar's?' said the young man.

'No, I certainly am not,' he said. 'Excuse me' – and he pushed past.

'Well, if you see him, give him my love!' the young man called after him. 'Charlie's the name.'

It was a relief to pass under the classical portico and into the foyer with its glittering chandelier and civilised throng. His heart was beating fast from this unpleasant encounter and not until he had deposited his hat and coat in the cloakroom and taken his seat in the auditorium did he feel tolerably calm again. Field's farce would be well under way by now, and the last cabs and carriages would be pulling up outside the St James's with those members of the audience, the most affluent and sophisticated, who had chosen to omit the curtain-raiser.

['Botheration!' George Du Maurier exclaimed, taking out his watch in the cab, and inspecting it by the light from the gaslamps in the street. 'We've missed the curtain-raiser.' The journey from Hampstead in the local hackney carriage had taken longer than usual, and now they were stuck in a long line of vehicles in Regent Street.

'Never mind, dear,' said Emma mildly. 'We'll be in time for Henry James's play, won't we?'

'But I like a farce,' Du Maurier grumbled. As both of them knew, the real reason for his discontent was that, having paid for two plays, it irked him to get less than full value for his money. The sudden surge of income recently generated by the success of *Trilby* had made little difference to his parsimonious habits. 'Hoskins is a hopeless driver,' he said. 'He sticks to the main roads which are always clogged with traffic, whereas your London cabby knows all the best routes through the side streets . . .'

'But he's very safe and reliable,' said Emma.

'I'm sick of these endless journeys in and out of town in this draughty old rattletrap!' Du Maurier burst out petulantly. 'We should move into Town – I mean permanently, not just for a few months every year. We can afford it now, after all.' It was typical of Du Maurier that he could more easily contemplate a large expenditure of money than a small one.

'Well, I don't know, Kiki,' Emma murmured. 'You would miss the Heath so.'

'There are parks in town to walk in. Flat parks. The hills of

Hampstead are getting too much for me. I'm gasping for breath by the time I get home.'

'Well, I know, but—'

'Now that Gerald is doing so well, we'll want to go to the theatre more often. And it's such a beastly bore having to fag back to Hampstead afterwards.'

'I keep hoping that it's just a phase he's going through,' Emma sighed. 'That one day he'll tire of it, and go back to a respectable job.'

'Not a chance, Pem. As soon as I saw him as that waiter in *The Old Jew* I knew he'd found his *métier*. There was nothing to the part on paper, but he squeezed a laugh out of every line!' He chuckled, his good humour returning at the memory. 'Now I come to think of it, that was almost exactly a year ago to the day – January the sixth. Let's hope James's first night is equally successful!']

'Going on to the Hartlocks' tonight, Margaret?'

'I suppose so. Are you?'

'Yes. Horribly tedious parties they give, don't they?'

'Horribly tedious! Never know why I go. Never know why I go anywhere.'

'I come here to be educated.'

'Ah! I hate being educated!'

'So do I. It puts one almost on a level with the commercial classes, doesn't it?'

From the very opening lines of *An Ideal Husband* he knew he had made a mistake in coming to see it. He couldn't enter into the spirit of the piece, he couldn't respond to the jokes, and he couldn't follow the plot, because his thoughts were elsewhere, with another play – or at least half of his thoughts were, or all his thoughts for half the time. It was as if he were receiving information from two sources at once, only one of which really interested him. He heard the words spoken by the actors, he recognised them as English, and he heard the answering laughter of his neighbours, but they made no immediate sense to him – only by a laborious effort of recapitulation, putting aside the mental images of his own play (on which the curtain would be rising at any moment), could he recall a line of Wilde's and understand why it might have been thought funny, by which time the dialogue had moved on and he was still more at sea. He sat rigid in his seat, with a fixed blank expression, not moving a muscle, as if turned to stone, while all around him people rocked in their seats and shook their shoulders and nudged each other delightedly.

[At the St James's *Too Happy By Half* had finished to friendly applause, and latecomers, including the Du Mauriers, were taking their seats, smiling and waving to old friends and acquaintances, as the orchestra played the 'Guy Domville Prelude', a medley of pleasant old airs evocative of the last century put together by the theatre's musical director and conductor, Walter Slaughter. In row G, Cécile, the drama critic of *Woman*, stroked his moustache and tapped his feet in time to the music – for Cécile was actually a young man called Arnold Bennett, the assistant editor of that weekly journal of moderately feminist tendencies (motto, '*Forward, but not too fast*'). As well as commissioning and editing articles and short snippets on subjects like 'The Professional Girl at Home', 'Do Rich Women Quarrel More Frequently Than Poor?' and 'How to Keep Parsley Fresh', he wrote a regular column about theatrical entertainments called 'Music and Mummery', under the name of 'Cécile', and a weekly book review under the name of 'Barbara'. It was that kind of magazine – you had to be versatile to work for it.

Walter Slaughter brought the overture to an end with a flourish, and turned, bowing, smiling, to receive the audience's polite applause. The house lights dimmed. Electrification made that effect easy to achieve, though Alexander was not tempted to imitate the growing fad of plunging the auditorium into near-darkness during the performance. He knew that the kind of fashionable West End audience for whom he catered liked to see each other and be seen throughout the evening, and not just in the entr'actes.

The orchestra struck up again, a quieter strain to introduce the first act, and the audience fell expectantly silent. Arnold Bennett took out his notepad and pencil. The curtain rose and a little murmur of approval ran around the auditorium. He wrote in shorthand in his notebook: '*Excellent set, old garden, very pretty, flowers look real.*' Being able to write shorthand was a very useful accomplishment for a theatre critic. Sometimes he thought that acquiring this skill was the cleverest thing he had ever done. Without it he would never have got the job of solicitor's clerk that had brought him to London – he might still be working in his father's office in Hanley, yawning with boredom as the clock ticked slowly through the long day and the smoke from a hundred pot-banks drifted over the blank street outside the grimy window. Instead of which he was sitting in a London theatre being paid to watch a play by Henry James. He greatly admired, even if he did not always enjoy, Henry James's novels and stories, and regarded him as a supreme technician in the art of fiction, an art in which he nourished ambitions of his own (there was a half-finished novel in a drawer at his Chelsea lodgings and he had already had a short story accepted for publication in *The Yellow Book*, to which James himself was a contributor). He looked around, wondering if he might spot the author in the audience – though even if he did he wouldn't dare to speak to him, because he suffered from a stammer which was apt to make him tongue-tied when he most wished to be eloquent.]

He thought of walking out of the theatre – since he was seated at the end of a row it would be simple enough – but where could he go? Not back to De Vere Gardens, obviously – the Smiths would think he was out of his senses; not to the pub with the ticking clock, already eliminated as a possible bolt-hole; not to the Reform where some acquaintance was sure to buttonhole him and enquire why he wasn't attending his own first night; and certainly not to wander round the streets, swarming with prostitutes and blackguards of every description. There was nothing for it but to grit his teeth and try to concentrate on the piece being played before him. The plot seemed to concern a smooth English politician, with a priggish wife, who had done something dishonest in the past, in spite of which one was invited to sympathise with his plight when threatened with exposure by some unscrupulous adventuress, and approve of the efforts of an effete aristocratic friend to rescue him. The effete aristocrat, evidently modelled on his creator, was unable to open his mouth without uttering a paradox or an epigram.

'I love talking about nothing, father. It is the only thing I know anything about.'
'You seem to be living entirely for pleasure.'
'What else is there to live for, father?'

The audience chuckled. Meanwhile the first act of *Guy Domville* would have begun. Picturing the scene, the pretty garden set, the simultaneous entrances of Frank Humber by the wooden gate and of Fanny, the maid, from the house – *'You're wanted, sir! Excuse me, sir; I thought you were Mr Domville.' 'Isn't Mr Domville in the house?' 'No indeed, sir, I came out to look for him,'* – he realised that the St James's was the only place where now – now that it was too late – he wanted to be! What a fool he was!

[The first act went very well. As it unfolded, Elizabeth Robins, sitting with Mrs Hugh Bell in the absent Henry James's box at his invitation, felt hugely relieved on the author's behalf – not to mention her own, for she recalled how exhausting it had been, the process of repairing his wounded feelings after the disappointing reviews of *The American* and the cancellation of *Mrs Jasper's Way*, and she would be glad to escape a repetition of that duty. She was a great admirer of Henry as a novelist and critic, and felt privileged to call herself his friend, but she had always laboured under a certain embarrassment in their relationship, which was inseparable from their mutual involvement in the theatre – namely, in the deepest recesses of her heart she doubted whether he really had the dramatic gift. The plays he read to her or showed to her in various stages of composition were always in principle performable – the plots were well-constructed, the dialogue easy on the ear – but they lacked something which she could best describe as a real passion for the theatre as a medium of artistic expression. He was fascinated by it, but at the same time he despised it, and brought to it only his second-best ideas (often they were second-hand too). Henry's attitude to the theatre sometimes reminded her of an elderly uncle who had decided to play some children's game with his little nephews and nieces, which he did with an elaborate show of seriousness and solemnity, squatting down to put himself on their level, diligently learning the rules of the game and doing his best to beat them at it, and then became seriously, disproportionately competitive, so that he ended up spending hours in this pursuit that would have been better dedicated to something more appropriate to his talents.

But the first act of *Guy Domville* made her doubt her own judgement. It was some time since he had read it to her. It had been much improved in the meantime, and it was beautifully acted, especially by Alexander and Marion Terry. The elegance of Henry's language, which sometimes made his lines seem stilted and artificial, seemed appropriate to the period of the action, and the action itself was intriguing. There was a certain amount of coughing in the gallery at one point, but she could sense the whole house attending closely and appreciatively to the concluding scenes. When Marion Terry, left alone on the stage, with her hopes dashed as suddenly as they had been raised, poignantly laid her face against the pillar of the porch, and the curtain came down at the end of the act, the applause was too loud and spontaneous simply to be attributed to the large number of the author's friends in the audience.

'Well, wasn't that wonderful!' Florence Bell said into her ear, clapping energetically.

'Wonderful,' Elizabeth agreed. 'What a pity Henry isn't here to see it.'

'And to hear the applause!'

★　★　★

'Well done, my dear,' Alexander murmured to Marion Terry as she came into the wings.

'Was it all right, Alec?' she asked. 'The business at the porch?'

'It was perfect,' he said.

They, and the other members of the cast, dispersed to their dressing rooms, exchanging pleased smiles, but no more words. All knew the act had gone well, but it was inviting bad luck to crow openly about it. Besides, Alexander reflected, the second act was a much trickier proposition.

'Well, that was delightful, I must say,' said George Du Maurier to Emma, as the lights in the auditorium were turned up to their full brilliance, and the applause faded to be replaced by a hum of conversation. 'Did you enjoy it, dear?'

'Very much. Such a pretty set! Do you think the flowers are real?'

'I really didn't notice them, Pem. I was attending to the play.'

'Yes, the play was very nice too.'

Du Maurier laughed. 'I hope you won't congratulate James on the flowers when we next see him.'

'Don't be silly, Kiki, of course I won't.'

'Shall we stretch our legs in the entr'acte?'

Moving up the aisle in a slow-moving stream they ran into Tom Guthrie, known to readers of *Punch* as the humorist 'F. Anstey'.

'Hallo, Du Maurier. What d'you make of it?'

'I think it's a very distinguished piece of dramatic writing.'

'Yes, it's distinguished, all right. But caviare to the general, I fear – there was a good deal of coughing behind me in the pit. By the way, I hear *Trilby* is going to be staged in America. Are you writing the play yourself?'

'No, no, a man called Paul Potter. Very experienced, I'm told.'

'So you'll be raking in even more shekels.'

'Alas, no. I don't own the dramatic rights.'

'Ah. Still, it will be good publicity for the book, I daresay.'

'Oh yes.'

'Not that it needs it.' Guthrie moved off to greet another friend.

'Everybody thinks I'm a millionaire since *Trilby* came out,' Du Maurier grumbled.

Most of the audience in the stalls chose to 'stretch their legs' like the Du Mauriers, and filtered out into the bars and the foyer in search of refreshment or their friends. A few men, however, remained in their seats, their heads bowed, writing in notebooks balanced on their knees. These, Herbert realised, must be his fellow critics, recording their impressions of the first act. George Bernard Shaw did not linger long, jumping to his feet after a few minutes and striding up the aisle. Herbert followed suit, hoping to find an opportunity to introduce himself, but in the foyer he was surprised to run into Harry Cust and a colleague, encased in boiled shirts and evening suits. Cust grinned and greeted him a little sheepishly. 'What do you think of the play?' Cust asked.

'You must wait and see,' he replied.

'Don't forget to use the red envelope when you post your copy,' Cust said.

'No, I won't,' Herbert said, adding: 'Do you go to many first nights?'

'It depends,' said Cust, and his companion stared down at his shoes.

'Were you at the Haymarket on Thursday?' Herbert asked.

'Well, yes, we were as a matter of fact.'

Herbert realised that the two men had come so that they could cover for him if he failed to produce a usable review.

'A smart evening suit, that, Wells,' Cust remarked. 'Is it new?'

'No, I've had it for years,' Herbert said.

Mrs Alexander and her guest, the actress Lily Hanbury, did not leave their box in the interval. It was Florence Alexander's special box, one which was always reserved for her on first nights, commanding an excellent view of both stage and auditorium.

'A wonderful set, Florence,' said Miss Hanbury, 'and beautiful costumes, as usual. Did you have a hand in the dresses?'

'I did take some period drawings to Savage and Purdue to give them some ideas. And as usual I approved the materials and the colours, to make sure they would go with the scenery.'

Florence Alexander, who had been an actress herself in youth, took a keen interest in her husband's business. In his early days as a manager she had helped to economise on production costs by designing the actresses' costumes, even sewing some of them herself. She also kept a watchful eye on the stage management, and personally checked before first-night performances that all the props were in place. First nights were always a strain – so many things could go wrong – but this one was going very well. How handsome Alec looked in his sober clerical costume!

'The flowers look quite real,' said Miss Hanbury.

'They *are* real!' Florence laughed. 'They're all growing in little pots and have to be watered daily.'

'Goodness! What perfectionism.'

'What do you think of the play?'

'I think it's quite wonderful, so far.'

The patrons in the gallery and the pit were somewhat less enthusiastic about the first act than those in the stalls and lower boxes. They would have liked more action and less talk, and some of the talk had been obscure to them. There was however general satisfaction that Guy Domville had decided against becoming a priest – 'if only,' someone remarked, 'so that Alick can get out of that dreary black suit' – but there was much debate among the female spectators about whether he didn't realise that the good-looking young widow was in love with him, or was prevented from reciprocating by knowing his friend was in love with her. Obviously they would marry in the end, so there was speculation about how the rather nice friend would be compensated for the loss of the widow. 'My money's on the heiress, what was mentioned at the end,' somebody said. Another thought the maid, Fanny, would turn out to be another heiress and so eligible to marry the gentleman. The women ate oranges and cakes that they had brought with them in brown paper bags, and passed bottles of ginger beer to each other. Most of the men went out in search of stronger refreshment, and returned in a merrier mood, hoping for more robust entertainment in the second act.]

'Some tea, Lady Markby?'

'No thanks, dear. The fact is, I have promised to go round for ten minutes to see poor Lady Brancaster, who is in very great trouble. Her daughter, quite a well-brought-up girl, too, has actually become engaged to be married to a curate in Shropshire. It is very sad, very sad indeed. I can't understand this modern mania for curates. In my time we girls saw them, of course, running about the place like rabbits. But we never took any notice of them, I need hardly say. But I am told that nowadays country society is quite honeycombed with them. I think it most irreligious . . .'

The speech went on for several minutes longer. The speaker, Lady Somebody-or-Other, had no apparent function in the play except from time to time to deliver such speeches, which were entirely irrelevant to the action. The audience didn't seem to mind this in the least, for they tittered or chuckled or laughed uproariously at the end of every sentence. The play was well into its second act, which meant that the second act of *Guy Domville* would be just beginning. *'MRS DOMVILLE'S villa at Richmond. MRS DOMVILLE and GEORGE ROUND discovered.'*

['The reason of my "wicked return", ma'am, is simply the respect I owe you, and the respect I owe to my cousin, your too amiable daughter.'

'Have you forgotten that I informed you six months ago how you could best express that respect?'

'By keeping out of your sight — by permitting you to forget my existence and encouraging you to hope I had forgotten yours? I obeyed your command, ma'am; I immediately joined my ship. But my ship came back last week.'

How quickly the mood of an audience could change . . . how swiftly their hard-won interest and attention could be dissipated. Elizabeth Robins's nervous system was finely attuned to recognise the signs, and she felt her spirits rapidly sinking, like a barometer at the approach of a storm, within a few minutes of the curtain rising. It was a fatally misconceived way to begin the second act, with two characters unfamiliar to the audience, and only briefly referred to in the first, having to remind each other of things that had happened in the past which they both knew very well but the audience didn't. There was an epidemic of coughing throughout the theatre, much more noticeable than before, which was a sure sign of impatience and inattention. The actors heard it of course, and were unsettled by it. Mrs Edward Saker in particular showed signs of nerves in the part of Mrs Domville. She was wearing an elaborate crinoline dress, combining rich materials of variegated pattern, ornamented with numerous frills, flounces and furbelows, and a very extraordinary hat. Elizabeth presumed that the hat must have been modelled on some old illustration, but she had never seen anything quite like it before. It looked more like a gigantic muff, or a small pouffe such as one might rest a gouty foot on, than a hat. It was made of black fur and roughly cylindrical in shape, but wider in diameter at the top than at the bottom. It appeared to be at least two feet high, and the flat top was decorated with a bunch of long black plumes which waved and nodded at every movement of the actress's head. It was a hat that required a great deal of assurance in the wearer, an attribute which was visibly deserting Mrs Saker as the scene proceeded. There was more suspense in the audience about the next movement of the hat than about the development of the plot. How was it secured? Would it tip forward? Would it fall off? Elizabeth could see people in the stalls and circle turning their heads to whisper comments which made the recipients smile, and when a voice from the gallery sang out the well-known refrain, *'Where did yer get that 'at?'* there was a good deal of laughter in every part of the house. Whatever dramatic illusion was left in the scene was shattered. Elizabeth had a dreadful presentiment that Mrs Saker's hat was going to have the same unfortunate effect on *Guy Domville* as Edward Compton's coat had had on *The American*.

Florence Alexander, sitting in the next box to Elizabeth Robins, was both angry and mortified. How could people be so cruel, and how could they be so philistine? She felt like standing up and shouting to the barracker that high, elaborate headdresses for ladies were extremely fashionable in the late eighteenth century. But of course she didn't. Perhaps, a little inner voice whispered to her, the costume *was* over-ambitious. It certainly took some wearing, and she had had her doubts at the dress rehearsal about whether Rose Saker was equal to it, but had suppressed them. Now the actress's confidence was quite gone, and she goggled at Alec with panic-stricken eyes when he made his entrance. This affected his performance in turn, and he began to overact the part of the eager bridegroom in a desperate attempt to draw the audience's attention back to the play. Florence could hardly bear to watch. In fact she closed her eyes and listened, waiting with fingers clenched for Mrs Saker's exit. But the scene that followed went just as badly.

'Why does Alexander open his mouth on one side like that? It makes his face all crooked,' John Singer Sargent whispered to his companion Graham Robertson.

'Because he's rattled,' Robertson whispered back, 'and I don't blame him. Do you understand what this scene is about?'

'No, I was hoping you would tell me in the next entr'acte,' Sargent muttered.

The scene brought together Guy Domville, ostensibly eager for his imminent wedding to Mrs Domville's daughter, Mary, with Lieutenant George Round, Mary's true lover, who had been sent packing months before by her mother and Lord Devenish, but had returned in the forlorn hope of reclaiming his sweetheart. The point of the encounter was that Guy should discover this attachment, of which he had been completely ignorant, give up his claim to Mary, and assist the lovers to elope. The playwright had decided that the hero, puzzled by Round's presence, should endeavour to ascertain his intentions by getting him drunk, while Round for his part was trying to allay Guy's suspicions by the same method, so both men were toasting each other and pretending to get drunk while in fact surreptitiously disposing of their liquor by pouring it into flower-pots, vases and other handy receptacles. Since the play was evidently not intended as a farce, the audience – at least those members of it occupying the dearer seats – hesitated to laugh at this improbable business. But since both characters were evidently honest and honourable gentlemen, and a few straight questions and answers would have cleared up all misunderstanding between them, there seemed to be no dramatic point in their contrived attempts to deceive each other. The drinking scene, in short, was completely redundant. It was George Alexander's misfortune to apprehend this flaw in the play only at the moment of performing the scene in public for the first time, as he sensed the tide of bafflement and incredulity flowing across the footlights from the auditorium and surging round his feet. He came off the stage (to permit George Round to try and persuade Mary to elope) to find Mrs Saker having barely suppressed hysterics in the wings. 'Give her smelling salts, somebody,' he snarled. 'She's got to go on again in a minute.' He closed his eyes and took deep breaths, trying to calm himself for his next entrance. *'Hearty wishes for a complete failure tonight.'* There was a serious danger of the curse being fulfilled.

The author's friends applauded loyally at the end of the act, but the note of real enthusiasm that had marked the reception of the previous one was missing. They exchanged uncomfortable smiles and glances as they rose from their seats and shuffled out of the auditorium into the foyers.

In the gentlemen's lavatory Edmund Gosse found himself

standing at the urinal beside William Norris. 'Not such a good act as the first,' he said.

'No,' said Norris. 'But there seems to be a rowdy element in the gallery. They're not giving the play a fair chance. Is James here?'

'No,' said Gosse. 'He's coming along at the end.'

'Just as well, perhaps.'

'Yes,' said Gosse. He was thinking to himself how fortunate it was that James had cancelled their original plan. He wouldn't have relished going out to that pub to tell him how the second act had gone. Recalling the wag who had called out, *'Where did you get that hat?'* he couldn't suppress a disloyal smile. 'I didn't know you were in town, Norris,' he said, buttoning his fly.

'I came up specially. I believe we're both lunching with James tomorrow, by the way.'

'Oh, will you be there? Good,' said Gosse. He had introduced Norris to James and was rather surprised at how well they seemed to get on – James had stayed with him in Torquay the previous summer and had written enthusiastically about the visit. Norris was a dull decent man who turned out dull decent novels in a sub-Trollopian style that James could not possibly admire. When questioned on this topic James had simply answered: 'I find his company soothing.' Which, on reflection, might be just what was required at lunch tomorrow.]

A good many people beside himself stayed in their seats at the third interval. He glanced at his watch. Ten past ten. The third and last act of *Guy Domville* would soon be starting. *'The White parlour at Porches. Door from the hall left; door to the bookroom right. MRS PEVEREL is seated by the fire. Enter FANNY from the hall with a letter on a tray.'* Suppose he were to get up and leave now, hurry over to the St James's and slip into the back of the stalls to watch it? He certainly had no interest whatsoever in staying here to find out whether Sir Robert Chiltern would escape the disgrace he so richly deserved. But he would be late for the beginning of the act at the St James's, and might disturb the performance of that pretty first scene. He had better stick to his original plan. *Guy Domville* would end at about eleven. He would leave *An Ideal Husband* at a quarter to the hour, whether it was over or not, and *tant pis* if he caused a disturbance in the process.

[At first Elizabeth Robins entertained hopes that the third act would rescue the play from disaster. The curtain rose on a quite exquisite set, a parlour so comfortable and elegant and perceptibly solid that one would have been glad to live in it oneself. And the first scenes, between Mrs Peverel and Fanny, and Mrs Peverel and Frank Humber, re-evoked the charm of the first act. The actors playing these parts had been resting in their dressing rooms throughout the second act, and were unscathed by its rough passage. They performed with delicacy and poise and began to win back the audience's sympathetic interest. But with the appearance of Lord Devenish (who was now, for his own reasons, eager to further a match between Guy and Mrs Peverel), shortly followed by the hero himself, it all began to go wrong again. W. G. Elliott had from the beginning been the weakest link in the chain of performers, tending to overplay the villainy of his character; now his sneers and leers became increasingly grotesque. George Alexander, still struggling to recover his poise after the traumas of the second act, was mannered in his gestures and strained in his diction. It didn't help that the motivation of his character became increasingly complex and casuistical at this stage of the story. Guy had come back to declare his love for Mrs Peverel, but, on discovering that Frank Humber had been alerted to this intention by Devenish, changed his mind yet again, and decided to go into the priesthood after all, even though his friend gallantly urged him not to. The stalls and circle listened respectfully to his reasons, but the gallery and the upper boxes had lost all interest and belief in the story. A low mutter of irreverent commentary and snatches of inappropriate laughter filtered down from the upper levels of the theatre, to join similar noises from the pit. Some of those seated in the stalls or lower boxes looked up or over their shoulders disapprovingly, and a few hissed 'Ssshh!' but without much effect. Elizabeth Robins and Florence Bell exchanged alarmed glances. The atmosphere in the theatre was turning ugly.]

'Gertrude, is it love you feel for me, or is it pity merely?'
'It is love, Robert. Love, and only love. For both of us a new life is beginning.'

As the curtain came down, he leapt to his feet and hastened from the auditorium, propelled like a ball from a cannon by the explosion of clapping. Attendants loitering in the corridors stared as he burst through the Exit doors before they could open them. He could still hear the muffled waves of applause as he retrieved his hat and coat from the cloakroom, and not until he was outside on the Haymarket pavement did he shake off the sound of success at his back. He crossed the road and plunged down Charles II Street, ignoring the women who called softly to him from shadowy doorways, or swayed their hips and plucked at their skirts as he passed them under the gaslamps. What a cynical, meretricious play! The ideal husband a swindler and a hypocrite, whom his priggish wife had to forgive only because she had compromised herself. And he was supposed to be a Minister of the Crown. The ending might have been justified in a bitter satire on political corruption, but the play was essentially a sentimental comedy. And they loved it – the audience loved it. They arched their collective backs and purred with delight, they rolled over and waved their paws in the air while Oscar tickled their tummies with his facile wit.

He was halfway across St James's Square when the full import of his own thoughts hit him, with a force that was almost physical and brought him momentarily to a halt. If *An Ideal Husband* was the kind of thing that pleased the contemporary West End audience, then *Guy Domville*, with its old-fashioned manners and decorous language, its morally fastidious hero and suffering, reticent heroine, its genuine ethical dilemmas and final endorsement of self-sacrifice and renunciation, certainly wasn't. Although over the last days and hours he had made himself almost ill with anxiety, it was only now that he really believed in the possibility of failure, and he continued on his way at a slower pace, his heart heavy with foreboding.

[On the stage *Guy Domville* was creeping towards its conclusion. For most of the author's friends in the audience, it could not come too soon – they longed for it to be over, for the wretched actors to be put out of their misery, for the snipers in the gallery to be deprived of their target, and for their own discomfort to be relieved. 'Please God, let it end soon,' Elizabeth Robins prayed silently, and she willed the actors to quicken their pace. But some perverse impulse seemed to make Alexander do the opposite, slowing the tempo of the final scene, and drawing out his last speeches with a sonorous, soulful delivery. It should of course have been his big theatrical moment, when Guy Domville finally renounced the world in favour of higher things, and selflessly commended his friend and the woman he loved to each other's care – and if the play had worked its spell up to that point it *would* have been such a moment, but the spell had been irretrievably broken long before. The insistent repetitions of diction and cadence in the dialogue, intended to give the scene a moving elegiac tone, only offered further provocation to the disaffected sections of the audience. There was one phrase in particular, *'the last of the Domvilles'*, that had been uttered several times throughout the play, and frequently in the final act, and when Alexander solemnly enunciated it yet again, with a new, heavy emphasis, at the beginning of his long final speech – *'I'm the* last, *my lord, of the Domvilles'* – a voice called out loudly from the gallery: 'And it's a bloody good job y' are!' Elizabeth Robins covered her ears against the laughter this sally provoked. She had no great affection for Alexander, but she didn't like to see a fellow-actor suffer humiliation. She hoped against hope that Henry would arrive too late to share it.]

He entered the theatre by the stage door, with a nod to the doorkeeper, and, being familiar with its geography by now, threaded his way through the dimly lit passages, smelling faintly of gas and drains, that led to the backstage area. He had cut it fine. As he approached the wings he could hear Marion Terry uttering her penultimate line, *'It was a dream, but the dream is past!'* He came to a little huddle of actors, Esmond, Evelyn Millard and Irene Vanbrugh, in their costumes as Round, Mary and Fanny, waiting to take their bows after the final curtain. They turned as he approached and, after showing him faces momentarily blank with surprise at his apparition, smiled in greeting. Was it his own apprehension that made their smiles seem forced? 'Has it gone well?' he whispered. Esmond raised a warning finger to his lips to enjoin silence – or to avoid replying? On stage Alexander was backing slowly, and rather awkwardly, towards the parlour door on the opposite side. *'Be kind to him,'* he said to Marion Terry – though it sounded like *'Be keynd,'* for his voice was strangely strangled – and *'Be good to her,'* he said to Herbert Waring. He paused on the threshold, said once more, *'Be good to her,'* and slowly closed the door. A moment later he reappeared in the wings opposite, dabbing at the perspiration on his brow with a handkerchief. He caught sight of Henry across the stage, where the other two actors were exchanging their final lines – *'Mrs Peverel – I shall hope!' 'Wait!'* – and shot him a glance that he was unable to interpret. Then the curtain came down, and there was the sound of applause such as he had never heard before. It was loud, and long, but mixed in with the sound of clapping were other noises, shouts and yells and whistles that might have expressed enthusiasm or might have been the ejaculations of an angry mob for all he could tell. The curtain went up again and the actors took their bows, first as an ensemble, and then singly. From where he was standing he could see a box whose occupants – he thought he recognised the Burne-Joneses – were applauding vigorously. When Mrs Saker curtseyed at the front of the stage, her black plumes nodding, a section of the audience seemed to strike up a song, and she hurried from the stage as pale as death, passing Henry without a glance or a greeting. What was going on? He looked around for someone to ask, but there was nobody near whose eye he could catch. The curtain came down again, and a stage-hand held it open in the middle for Alexander to step out and take his usual solo bow. There was a storm of applause which sounded genuinely warm and lasted for two or three minutes. And then with unspeakable relief he heard cries of 'Author! Author!' So it had gone well, after all.

[Elizabeth Robins immediately saw the danger. The cries of 'Author!' had come first from the gallery, and were then taken up enthusiastically by Henry's friends in the stalls and circle, but the two groups had entirely different motives for wanting to draw him out into the open. The clapping continued. The cries of 'Auth-or! Auth-or!' became more insistent. She could see Alexander hesitating, glancing into the wings. Surely he would not be fool enough to expose Henry to this divided and volatile audience after such a flawed, unhappy performance?]

He saw Alexander beckoning him, taking a few steps towards the wings with hand outstretched, and an encouraging smile on his face. He took a deep breath, straightened his shoulders, and stepped forward into the dazzle of the footlights. Alexander shook his hand and drew him to the centre of the stage, and as he turned to face the audience . . . as he turned to face . . . as he turned . . .

[As Henry James turned to face the audience, and prepared graciously to bow, a barrage of booing fell from 'the gods' on his defenceless head. 'Boo! Boo! Boo!' There was also some hissing, and jeers and catcalls, but it was the long vowel sound of 'oo' that dominated the cascade of sound. 'Boo! Boo!' James looked stunned, bewildered, totally unable to understand what was happening, or how to react. He seemed paralysed, canted forward in the act of bowing, his pale plump face and bald brow thrown into relief by the fringe of dark beard and his black evening clothes. His mouth opened and closed once or twice, slowly and silently, like a fish in a bowl. 'Boo! Boo!' His outraged friends and supporters responded with more vigorous applause and cries of 'Bravo!' – which only provoked the booers to louder efforts.

'This is intolerable!' John Singer Sargent exclaimed, jumping to his feet. He felt a powerful impulse to clamber over the seats in front of him and leap up on to the stage to rescue his fellow countryman from this insult.

'Why are they making that noise, Kiki?' Emma said, clutching Du Maurier's arm in fright, and impeding his efforts to clap.

'I don't know – well, I *do* know – but it's unfair, it's cruel,' he said. 'They're a lot of cads. Poor James!'

'This is dreadful!' Florence Bell cried to Elizabeth Robins, raising her voice above the uproar. 'What's the matter with Alexander? Why doesn't he take Henry off?' Alexander was standing just behind and to the side of the author, with an embarrassed, hangdog expression on his face, shifting his weight restlessly from foot to foot.

'I don't know,' said Elizabeth grimly. 'Why did he bring him on?'

Perhaps it was only two or three minutes, but it seemed to his friends like an hour that Henry James stood there, buffeted by the storm of noise, until, with a kind of helpless shrug, he turned on his heel and fled into the wings, followed sheepishly by Alexander.

The gallery went on booing, the stalls went on applauding. Philip Burne-Jones stood up in his box and clapped his hands ostentatiously in the direction of the upper levels of the house, calling down a further salvo of boos and catcalls.

Arnold Bennett wrote in his notebook in shorthand: *'A battle between the toughs and the toffs.'*]

He blundered into the wings, in shock, dazed by the noise and still dazzled by the footlights. He knocked over a piece of stage furniture, and stood still, uncertain where to go, what to do, as Alexander came up to him.

'I'm sorry, Henry,' he muttered.

'Why did you expose me to that – that – infamous treatment?'

'I didn't expect it,' Alexander said. 'You heard the calls of "Author!"'

'You were under the impression the play was a success, then?' he asked sarcastically.

'Not exactly. The first act went like a dream, but things began to go wrong in the second. We must cut the drinking scene. It doesn't work.'

'Cut the drinking scene!' he exclaimed. 'Is that the only thing those – those – those *barbarians* – is that why they're making that appalling noise? Because the drinking scene didn't work?'

'No, but—'

'I have never been so insulted in my life,' he said bitterly.

They listened to the continuing hubbub in the theatre.

'It's not very pleasant for me, either,' said Alexander. 'I'm not used to failure.' A thought seemed to strike him. 'In fact, we may be the victims of some kind of cabal.'

'What?'

'I had a telegram this afternoon, *"Hearty wishes for a complete failure."* Unsigned of course.'

'*What?* Who would . . . ?'

'I've no idea. Some enemy, obviously.' He turned his head at a new surge of noise in the auditorium. 'I must put a stop to this. Excuse me.'

Alexander went back on to the stage, while Henry withdrew deeper into the wings.

Alexander came forward to the footlights, centre stage, and held up his hands in a deprecating gesture. The booing stopped, and there was only the sound of applause, from all parts of the house, and cries of '*Speech! Speech!*' Alexander indicated that he would respond, and silence fell.

'Ladies and gentlemen: in my short career as a manager I have met with so many favours at your hands that these discordant notes tonight have hurt me very much . . .'

A voice from on high called out: 'T'ain't your fault, Alick, it's a rotten play,' and there was laughter and a chorus of ''Ear, 'ear' from the same quarter.

'I can only say,' Alexander continued, 'that we have done our very best; and if we have failed, we can only try to deserve your kindness by trying to do better in the future.'

He bowed, and there was another round of applause.

'What a toadying speech,' Du Maurier murmured.

'What a grovelling performance,' Sargent muttered.

'Alec has saved the day,' Lily Hanbury said encouragingly to Mrs Alexander.

'The day, perhaps,' said Florence. 'But what about the run?'

At a signal from Alexander, Walter Slaughter led the orchestra into the National Anthem. The audience rose to its feet and stood in silence until the last bars faded away. The eventful evening was over, but they had plenty to talk about on the way home.

Herbert pushed his way through the throng, and collided with a young man of about his own age, and not dissimilar appearance, knocking from his hand a notebook covered with shorthand hiero-glyphics. 'I beg your pardon,' he said, picking up the notebook and thrusting it into the hand of the stranger, who must, he presumed, be a critic too.

'That's – that's – that's—' stammered the young man. Herbert did not stay to hear the rest of the sentence, but hurried forward. He was conscious of behaving rudely, but he had his sights fixed on another critic. He got to the foyer just in time to see the back of George Bernard Shaw disappearing through the swing doors, and caught up with him in King Street, striding briskly towards St James's Square.

'Mr Shaw!'

Shaw turned, lifting his chin and jutting his beard challengingly. 'Yes, sir?'

'May I introduce myself? Herbert Wells. I've heard you speak many times – back in the 'eighties I used to go to those meetings at William Morris's house in Hammersmith.'

Shaw grinned. 'Did you, indeed?' he said, in his tenor Dublin voice. 'In that leaky old conservatory – I remember it well.'

'And we're fellow-contributors to *The Saturday Review*.'

'What's this you said your name was?'

'Herbert Wells. I write as "H. G. Wells".'

'Ah, yes, I've read some of your pieces, here and there. Interested in science, aren't you?'

'Very.'

'So what attracted you to *Guy Domville* – I presume you were there tonight?'

'Well, as a matter of fact I'm reviewing it, for the *Pall Mall Gazette*.'

'Are you indeed? And how long have you been doing that?'

'I only started this week.'

'And *I* only started last week, so we're both beginners, you might say.'

'But you were an opera critic before that. You know something about the drama—'

'I do. I think I may say in all modesty that I know more about the drama than most of the eejits who write about it for the news-papers – no offence, young man.'

'None taken. I know very little. I wondered what you thought about the play tonight – and the booing.'

Shaw looked at him quizzically. 'Where do you live, Mr Wells?'

'Mornington Crescent.'

'I'm going in that direction myself. We'll walk together, if you like.'

In the foyer Gosse ran into Norris, buttoning up his overcoat. His expression was funereal.

'A bad business,' Gosse said.

'It was horrible.'

Both men were uncomfortably aware that they had unintentionally collaborated in their friend's humiliation.

'If I had known the gallery would behave so disgracefully,' Gosse said, 'I wouldn't have called out "Author!"'

'Quite,' said Norris. 'Neither would I.'

'James will be terribly cut up.'

'Do you think we should try and find him?' said Norris. 'Look after him?'

'No,' said Gosse. 'I happen to know that he's giving supper to the company. It won't be a very cheerful occasion, I fear. We must do our best to buck him up tomorrow.'

'Yes, indeed.'

They bade each other goodnight and parted. Neither of them had any inclination to discuss the play.

'The second act was hopeless,' Shaw said as they walked side by side up Shaftesbury Avenue. Herbert, who was only five and a half feet tall, had trouble keeping up with his long-legged stride. 'The drinking scene was a nonsense – but Alexander should have seen that in rehearsal, and done something about it. The play never really recovered – neither did the actors. But the first act was charming. And what a pleasure to hear language like that spoken in a London theatre. Henry James uses words like a poet, even though it's written as prose.'

'But do people actually talk like that?'

'Did people talk in blank verse in Shakespeare's day?' Shaw retorted. 'I'm not saying it's a great play, mind you. It's flawed, it has its *longueurs*, it deals with a very narrow strip of human life. But it's written by an artist! Which is more than you can say for nine-tenths of the plays on the West End stage.'

'Why did they boo it, then?'

' 'Twas the people in the gallery who booed, and the pit and the cheap upper boxes. They didn't understand or appreciate the play – how could they, when they've been fed for decades on a diet of crass melodrama and coarse farce? They had no patience with the fine moral scruples of Guy Domville, and when he denied them a happy ending by going into the priesthood after all, 'twas the last straw! The stalls were more respectful, but I doubt if they enjoyed it or understood it any better. A lot of them were Henry James's friends – too many for his own good, perhaps. Maybe the gallery decided there was an upper-class claque in the stalls, so they decided to set up a rival commotion. Alexander should have known better than to bring James on at the end.'

'It seemed to me an act of revenge,' said Herbert.

Shaw chuckled. 'You may be right.'

'Does it happen very often – booing like that?'

'Not very often. I was booed at the first night of *Widowers' Houses* – though whether they were booing the play or the speech I insisted on making was not altogether clear to me.'

It was news to Herbert that Shaw was a playwright as well as a journalist, but he thought it prudent to disguise his ignorance. 'How many plays have you written?' he asked cunningly, as they turned up Charing Cross Road.

'Several, but only two have been staged. They're generally considered too controversial, and likely to incur the wrath of the censor. I've just written a new one, called *Candida*. Wyndham wept over the last act when he read it, but he told me it would be twenty-five years before the London stage was ready for such a subject. Then I offered it to Alexander—'

'You mean George Alexander?'

'The very same. He said he would do it if I would make the hero blind.'

'Why?' Herbert laughed incredulously.

'He thought it would make the character more sympathetic. He was thinking of playing the part himself, you see. Of course I refused.'

'Aren't you in a rather delicate position,' Herbert ventured, 'reviewing plays put on by the managements you hope to interest in your own work?'

'I considered that question carefully when Frank Harris offered me the job,' Shaw said. 'But I am incorruptible. And, besides, I need the money. What about you, Mr Wells? Do you support yourself by writing?'

'I'm trying to. I used to be a tutor in a correspondence college, but I chucked it in.'

'Are you married?'

'I'm in the process of getting divorced, while living with the woman I love,' Herbert said, hoping this would impress the free-thinking Shaw.

'That sounds expensive,' the Irishman commented dryly.

'I'm confident of earning a living as long as my health keeps up,' said Herbert. 'I've just sold a serial story to *The New Review* for a hundred pounds.'

Now Shaw *was* impressed. 'Congratulations! I'll look out for it. What is it called?'

'*The Time Machine,*' said Herbert.

'An intriguing title,' said Shaw.]

So it was over. He had come to the dead end of the road, the dry bottom of the well, the rock wall at the end of the tunnel. Failure. He had made a bargain with Fate − 'one more year' − and Fate had kept him waiting for the full term, kept him clinging hopefully to the rope ladder that led to success, before severing its strands with a single malicious stroke, sending him tumbling into the abyss. His play was a failure − there was no evading that fact. Alexander's talk of a cabal, and the mysterious malevolent telegram, had given him hope for a moment that he had become innocently involved in some vendetta against the actor-manager, but as soon as he heard the booing die down and the applause swell when Alexander went back on to the stage to make his bootlicking speech he knew that it was not 'Alick' that the *canaille* in the gallery had wanted to savage, but himself. *Guy Domville* had been his last throw of the dice − '*le sort en est jeté*' − and he had lost. He didn't intend to risk another humiliation like that. The premonition of failure he had experienced as he crossed St James's Square had not prepared him for being pilloried by a jeering mob in the presence of almost everybody he knew in London. The memory of that awful moment, the ululating crescendo of noise that greeted him as he turned to confront the sea of faces, *'Boo! Boo! Boo!'* made him flush even now, as he walked through the cold dark streets that skirted Green Park. The prostitutes did not bother him any longer: something about the stony set of his features, the unswerving deliberateness of his pace, must have conveyed the pointlessness of accosting him.

He turned into Piccadilly. A hansom slowed as it overtook him and the driver glanced hopefully in his direction. Should he take it? No, he wanted to walk. He would walk the whole way home, along Piccadilly, Knightsbridge, the Kensington Road and Kensington

Gore. He was tired, but he wished to be even more tired, totally exhausted so that he would fall asleep as soon as his head touched the pillow. And before that he wanted time to reflect, time to taste the bitter dregs of defeat to the end, to abandon himself to private, solitary misery. For the past hour or more he had felt as if he were coming round from chloroform, numbed but aware that a horrible pain was lurking somewhere just beyond the threshold of consciousness, waiting for him to become fully sensate. Now he confronted it, gripped it, abandoned himself to it.

Alexander, when he came off the stage for the last time, had hinted that no one would be surprised or offended if he cancelled the supper for the actors, but he had insisted on going through with it. It had been a gruesome occasion. Mrs Saker had sent her apologies – Alexander had muttered some incomprehensible explantion concerning her hat. Several others had made excuses to leave early. He had gone through the motions of being a host, he had made conversation, though he had no memory of what he said, and he had even attempted an occasional joke. Marion Terry had very sweetly tried to cheer him up, assuring him that Mrs Peverel was the best role she had ever had, and Elliott drank too much wine and told an off-colour story that was received in silence. Nobody mentioned the booing. Alexander deliberately took a seat at the opposite end of the table from himself, and spoke to him only when the party broke up, about cutting the drinking scene in Act Two. He had listened and nodded without taking in a word the man was saying, but he had promised to deliver a revised scene on Monday morning, for the cast to rehearse and perform in the evening. He wondered now if he would be able even to glance at the text of the play, let alone revise it, without being overcome with nausea. *'Boo! Boo!'*

He supposed he would grit his teeth and do it. For the sake of the actors, and for the sake of professional honour, he would make one more, one last 'cut' in his play, already scarred and bleeding from countless wounds of the same kind. He had no illusions that this surgical tinkering would rescue the piece from commercial failure; and even if by some miracle it did, that would not affect his determination never to expose himself again to such a rude rejection as he had experienced that night. It was bitter to reflect how much time and energy he had wasted on the effort to become a playwright. Five whole years! Five years, for which he had nothing to show but one half-success and one complete failure on stage, and drawers full of unperformed plays in multiple drafts. The endless rewritings, the countless letters and telegrams and meetings, the hopes raised and dashed and then raised again, that had occupied five years, and come to virtually nothing in the end. What vanity! What a waste! The line he had heard Marion Terry utter as he came into the wings seemed to sum up his whole career as a dramatist: *'It was a dream, but the dream is past!'*

A thin cold rain began to fall from the dark sky. The gaslamps stretched out before him along an almost deserted Piccadilly, casting pools of light on the pavement, with patches of darkness between them. He walked on grimly towards Kensington.

3

THERE commenced a slow convalescence of the spirit.

He woke well before first light on Sunday morning with a horrible feeling of depression and was instantly reminded of the cause. There was no hope of going back to sleep, so he lay there, like the survivor of a shipwreck cast up on the cold shingle of a deserted beach, too exhausted and demoralised to crawl above the tide line, scarcely caring whether he lived or died, letting wavelets of dismal thoughts break over him. What most distressed him was that his humiliating failure was known, or would very soon be known, to everyone in his large circle of acquaintance. There was not a person whom he would meet, or with whom he would correspond, in the next few weeks, who would not be aware that he, Henry James, had been loudly booed on the stage of the St James's Theatre. The event would be reported in every newspaper; it would be discussed in clubs and drawing rooms and servants' quarters; gossip about it would cross frontiers and seas. His every social encounter, and every exchange of letters, would be constrained by mutual embarrassment about whether to mention the subject or ignore it, and if the former, how to treat it.

His first ordeal of this kind came very soon, in the form of the lunch he had arranged for that day (which seemed in hindsight an act of hubristic folly) specifically to garner impressions of *Guy Domville*. Nothing could have been less welcome, but, like the funereal supper for the actors the night before, it must be endured. William Norris was the first to arrive. He shook Henry's hand and looked at him with anxious, sorrowful eyes. 'My dear chap,' he said. 'I will say one word about last night, and then no more. You have written a wonderful play – full of poetry, feeling, and moral seriousness. The ruffians who hooted it last night condemned themselves as illiterate. Of course, you will be feeling nothing but pain now, but time will heal it. You are a great writer.'

'Thank you, William,' he said, sincerely.

'And now let us talk of other things.'

But that was easier said than done. Young Philip Burne-Jones arrived, still fizzing with excitement and indignation at the events of the night before. He had stayed on at the theatre and got into an argument on the pavement outside with some men coming out of the gallery, and was eager to tell Henry of this adventure as a token of his support. It didn't seem to occur to him that his host might prefer to pass over the whole fiasco in silence. He was fond of Philip, who had done a very passable portrait of him the previous year – in profile, sitting at his desk with a quill in his hand, gazing into space as if in search of the right word – but he was a rather wild, undisciplined young man, who had caused his father much grief by his taste for high living and late nights, sometimes in the company of the Prince of Wales's dubious entourage. He saw the rumpus in the theatre as a skirmish in the war between culture and anarchy – 'a deliberate attempt by a gang of underbred rowdies to spoil an evening of civilised entertainment,' as he put it. Not until Gosse said loudly, 'Perhaps we should change the subject,' and glared at him, did he let go of it. Gosse deftly led the conversation on to other topics: the latest gossip about Oscar Wilde, Lord Alfred Douglas and the Marquess of Queensberry, the obituaries for Christina Rossetti, who had just died, the controversial court-martial trial of Captain Dreyfus, and, inevitably, the extraordinary success of *Trilby*.

Mrs Smith's roast leg of lamb with mint sauce was unanimously praised, and he signalled to Smith to be generous with the claret, so the mood of the party became quite jolly. Sturgis amused them by describing how Du Maurier's novel had been subjected to the vulgarest commercial exploitation in America. Apparently 'Trilby' boots and shoes were widely advertised in the press, illustrated with engravings of the heroine's naked foot 'after' Little Billee's famous drawing on the wall of the Paris studio, and a Broadway caterer had moulded ice-cream in the same shape. 'There is also, I understand, a "Trilby Hearth-brush" and even a "Trilby Sausage", but whether they are also shaped like feet I couldn't say,' said Sturgis, to general laughter.

He attended only fitfully to the conversation, but threw in the odd remark when it seemed apposite, and evidently managed to give the impression of someone in full possession of his faculties, for Gosse said quietly to him on leaving: 'I'm very glad to see you so calm, Henry. I know what it's like to be the object of public insult, and I remember what good counsel you gave me at the time.' He was referring to Churton Collins's devastating attack on his published Clark Lectures, *From Shakespeare to Pope*, years ago in the *Quarterly Review*, showing them to be full of egregious factual errors. Gosse was a good fellow, and a clever one, but he had a genius for inaccuracy which Collins had pounced on and made the occasion for a violent and controversial attack on the state of English literary criticism. His advice to Gosse on that occasion had been to avoid reading the newspapers until the affair was forgotten, and he intended to follow it himself.

He broke this resolution, however, the very next morning. He had spent Sunday evening removing the drinking scene from Act Two of the play and writing new dialogue to perform more straightforwardly the same dramatic function. It had been arranged that a messenger would call at 9 a.m. to collect the manuscript and take it to the theatre, where it would be copy-typed for the actors so that they could rehearse the emended scene when they came in at eleven o'clock. He couldn't face attending the rehearsal – he doubted in fact whether he would ever set foot in the St James's again – and sent his MS to Alexander with a covering note, saying: *'This is the best I can manage in the time available – use it as you think fit.'* When it had gone, there was nothing to do after breakfast but retire to his study and brood.

Smith had placed *The Times* on his desk, with a quantity of letters considerably greater than the usual Monday morning post. A number of his friends who had been at the theatre on Saturday had hastened to send him messages of support and sympathy. They all said more or less the same things — *'enjoyed the play enormously — scandalous behaviour of the gallery — shameful speech by Alexander — hope you will not be discouraged from giving us more fine plays'*. It was kind of them, but the cumulative weight of their pity was oppressive, and he skimmed rather than read the letters. He picked up *The Times*, and leafed through it to check whether it contained a review of *Guy Domville* — only, he told himself, in order to be prepared to turn over the page quickly when he came to it. There *was* a review on page 13, placed next to an article on 'Stockfeeding Value of the Farm Crops of the UK', and he found himself unable to resist running his eye down the long column of print to get the gist. It was unfavourable. The anonymous critic began by referring to the controversial reception of the play on the first night, and sided unequivocally with the gallery. *' "The drama's laws the drama's patrons give." It is vain to insist upon the literary merits of an unsuccessful play or to question the popular verdict that has condemned it.'* The writer commended Alexander for promising in his curtain speech to do better in future, though the failure was not his fault. *Guy Domville* was not a good play. *'In every scene, almost in every line, it tells of painful and misdirected effort.'* The dialogue perhaps had literary quality, but *'apt and vital it is not; and the actors can do nothing with their text but recite it like a well-conned lesson'*.

Dismayed, he let the paper drop. If he had retained any spark of faith in his play, any lingering hope that discerning theatregoers, other than his own interested friends, would appreciate its merits, they were crushed out under the vindictive heel of this nameless assailant. If *The Times* sided with those hooligans in the gallery, then there was no place for him in the English theatre. *'Painful and misdirected effort'* — the words stung like a slap across the face, but they could be the epitaph on his career as a playwright. It had indeed been painful, and it had manifestly been misdirected. He had wasted five years on the futile quest for an illusory Grail — five years in which he had neglected the art of which he *did* have some acknowledged mastery. And if he returned to that now, who would be interested? He had published no new novel since *The Tragic Muse*, and the sales of that and its predecessors had been pitiful in the last couple of years – no more than twenty copies of any title. Magazine editors had virtually ceased to solicit him for contributions. He was in serious danger of extinction as a literary figure, not to mention bankruptcy.

He was overwhelmed by a feeling of total hopelessness, and for the first time in his life he felt the real seduction of the idea of suicide. He had always believed that consciousness was the supreme value, but what did it profit a man to be conscious if it was only of failure, humiliation and regret? This gloomy train of thought made him think of Fenimore, who had evidently come to the conclusion that there was no further possibility of joy in her life, and had rationally acted upon it. He shuddered at a mental picture of her lying crumpled in a moaning heap on the cobbles of the Ramo Barbaro – but there were easier paths to oblivion than that. Drugs, opiates. To cease upon the midnight with no pain . . . And that made him think of Alice, who had paradoxically refused the offer of a Lethean draught, though she had every justification for taking it and believed in principle that suicide was no sin but a valid human choice.

He went to the cabinet where he kept her journal in a locked drawer, and took it out. It was not a document that he cared to leave lying around for prying eyes to light on. When he received his copy the previous spring from Kathleen Loring, one of four she had had privately printed for herself and Alice's surviving brothers, reading it had been as disturbing as reading Fenimore's notebook – indeed in some ways more so, for its references to himself were much more explicit. He was astonished and not a little embarrassed to find the casual small talk with which he had entertained his invalid sister – some of it mildly malicious at the expense of his acquaintance, and some self-revealing – scrupulously recorded in its pages. He was impressed by his sister's lively prose style, but had been horrified by Katherine Loring's proposal to publish the journal as it stood. His counter-proposal was that a carefully edited version, with all compromising personal references removed, should be published, and then the original copies burned. The matter remained unresolved.

He found the passage he was looking for under the date August 5th, 1889, when Alice was living in Leamington Spa. It referred to the death of William's friend, the English psychologist Edmund Gurney. *'They say there is little doubt that Mr Edmund Gurney committed suicide. What a pity to hide it, every educated person who kills himself does something towards lessening the superstition. It's bad that it is so untidy, there is no denying that, for one bespatters one's friends morally as well as physically, taking them so much more into one's secret than they want to be taken. But how heroic to be able to suppress one's vanity to the extent of confessing that the game is too hard.'* What an extraordinarily sharp mind she had possessed, his little sister! He had underestimated her insight and her wit when she was alive. He seemed to feel she was addressing him from the other side of the grave in this passage – to the same effect that their father had addressed *her* years before on the same topic – turning him against the idea of suicide in the very act of seeming to commend it. Did he want to reveal to his friends the true depths of his despair? Did he want to admit to the world that the game was too hard? Probably not.

It was a mercy anyway that Alice had not lived to witness the ignominious collapse of all his theatrical ambitions – she would have felt the disappointment almost as keenly as himself. He turned the leaves of the journal, looking for the references to his dramatic ventures. The first mention of *The American* was on March 25th, 1890. *'H. seems cheerful about his play and to be unable to grasp my flutterations about it. What a "state" I was in when he told me six months ago as a great secret that he had embarked.'* There was a long entry on January 7th, 1891, summarising his report of the first night at Southport: *'it was delightful to hear and see him flushed with the triumph of his first ovation . . . am so thankful that the dear being has had such a success. The "first nights" to come, we shall be less quivering about.'* He was reminded of many moments of excited expectation that had turned out to be ill-founded or illusory – for example, *'H. came in, a few days ago, all heated from a most sympathetic interview with Hare, who not only accepts play number two, Mrs Vibert, which H. wrote before Christmas for Miss Genevieve Ward, but accepts it with enthusiasm and calls it a "masterpiece of dramatic construction".'* Even Alice had perceived his tendency to become over-confident at the slightest encouragement, and his failure to appreciate the inherent treacherousness of the stage as a medium for his work. This last entry continued: '*I was surprised to find that H. didn't seem to see how much more dependent this play will be, for success, upon the actors than* The American.' As he reread these and similar passages they seemed to recapitulate his whole dramatic career in a condensed and ironic form, but he was also struck by Alice's enthusiastic identification with his campaign to conquer the English stage. She regretted that he had not begun it a few years earlier, when she might have been strong enough to attend a performance. But, she said, in one of the last entries in the journal, in September 1891, '*I shall, after all, have seen a bit of* The American; *for Harry brought a sample of Madame de Cintré's ball dress the other day, he having been to choose it, with Mrs Compton.*' Reading this, he shed tears.

The only comfort of a limited sort he could draw from the journal was that Alice had no word of criticism of him personally – on the contrary she frequently praised him for his patience and kindness, in terms that made him almost blush: '*I have given him endless care and anxiety but notwithstanding this and the fantastic nature of my troubles I have never seen an impatient look upon his face or heard an unsympathetic or misunderstanding sound cross his lips.*' He didn't deserve such praise. The reason he had been kind to her was because she gratified his egotism – she was so devoted, so admiring, so eager for his success, and she didn't compete with him – that was the key. Whereas he had failed Fenimore because she *did* compete. He had used her in the same way that he used Alice, as a confidante, as a counsellor, as a source of moral support in times of professional difficulty; but he had never given her the same support in return, he had never poured over her anxieties and self-doubts the healing balm of total, unqualified, extravagant praise, such as all artists needed occasionally. He flushed as he recalled her disappointment at his article, 'Miss Woolson', her all too justified resentment of its meagre, grudging praise, its prim reservations, its patronising tone. How much of that might be traced to simple jealousy because she had sold forty thousand copies of *East Angels*, and he only eight thousand of *The Portrait of a Lady*? And lately he had caught himself treating George Du Maurier in the same ungenerous spirit. As long as their friendship had been a complementary one of author and artist it had been harmonious and enjoyable, but since Du Maurier became an author too the relationship had subtly changed, at least as far as he himself was concerned. It was being eaten away from within by the worm of envy and jealousy.

He found himself engaged in what Roman Catholics called an examination of conscience, which a Monsignor of his acquaintance had once explained to him was part of the preparation for Confession, accusing himself of selfishness, envy, jealousy, resentment, and a corresponding lack of generosity, humility, magnanimity and fortitude. The very day's newspaper seemed to confirm this harsh self-judgement. There was a report in *The Times*, almost certainly written by Morton Fullerton, of 'The Degradation of Captain Dreyfus', which described how the unfortunate man had been paraded before three thousand troops, and a crowd of civilian spectators pressed against the railings around the barrack square, to hear the sentence declaimed by General Darras in a loud voice: *'Dreyfus, you are unworthy to bear arms and we degrade you!'* And then an adjutant stripped him of his epaulettes, plume and red stripes, and broke his sword in two under his heel (it had been filed through beforehand). *There* was a spectacle to put his own petty humiliation on the stage of the St James's in perspective! *'Dreyfus held his head high and protested his innocence: "Vive la France! Je jure que je suis innocent."'* He was inclined to believe the man's claim. He certainly admired his courage and dignity under extreme duress, beside which his own response to rejection seemed merely sulky.

And in the correspondence columns there was more food for thought: a letter from Sidney Colvin forwarding a long report of the death and burial of Robert Louis Stevenson in Samoa, by his stepson Lloyd Osbourne. Samoan chiefs had come from all over the district bearing fine mats, each one of which had taken a woman a whole year to weave, in which a great man had to be wrapped according to Samoan burial practice. *'They kissed his hand one by one as they came in. I wrote down the speech of one of them that came and* threw himself on his knees beside Louis. He was an old, worn-out man, and his crying made it hard for him to speak. "I am only a poor black man and ignorant. Others are rich and can give Tusitala the parting present of rich things. I am poor and can give nothing this last day that Tusitala receives his friends. And yet I am not afraid to come and take the last look at my friend's face. We were in prison and he cared for us. The day was no longer than his kindness. You here are great folk and full of love. Yet who is there here so great as Tusitala? Who is there more loving-compassionate. What is your love to his love? Oh Tusitala, this is the last time I see your face till we meet in God together." '

This extraordinary testimony brought tears to his eyes once again. How had Louis managed to inspire such devotion from these people of a totally different race and culture after only a few years of living amongst them? He did not deceive himself that he would ever be mourned in the same heartfelt way, but he resolved to be a better man in future, more humble and less self-centred. He would accept his failure in the theatre philosophically, he would re-dedicate himself to the solitary craft of fiction, he would seek perfection in it without concern for fame or greed for material reward, he would purge himself of envy and jealousy. It was too late to make amends to Fenimore, but he would seek out George Du Maurier and renew their old, easy companionship.

He made this 'firm purpose of amendment', as the Romans called it, at half past three in the afternoon. At four o'clock came a telegram from Alexander, saying: 'NEW SCENE EXCELLENT WELL DONE MANY THANKS COME AND SEE FOR YOURSELF TONIGHT ALEC.' Instantly he felt a little thrill of gratification at praise for a professional task skilfully accomplished, and an irresistible urge to see his handiwork performed. Would this be inconsistent with his resolutions? He persuaded himself that it would not.

He went to the St James's that evening wearing ordinary clothes and sat in the gallery, whose other occupants followed the play attentively and with apparent pleasure. He had to admit that the second act did not suffer by the omission of the drinking scene – indeed it progressed smoothly and naturally. The theatre was nearly full, and at the end the cast were warmly applauded, taking several curtain calls. He mingled with the outgoing crowd on the stairs and in the main foyer, and overheard several approving comments on the play. Afterwards he went behind and spoke to Alexander, who said it had been 'a good money house', meaning they had given away very few complimentary tickets, and passed him copies of a couple of reviews, by Archer in the *World* and Clement Scott in the *Telegraph*, which were much more sympathetic than the one in *The Times*. Both praised the first act highly – Scott called it *'one of the most beautiful human documents that has been committed to the care of the stage for some time'*. He began to wonder whether the play might not turn out to be a success after all, until Alexander sounded a cautionary note.

'I think a lot of people came tonight because they were curious to see what all the fuss was about on Saturday,' he said. 'We can't rely on that kind of interest to fill the theatre for long.'

'They seemed to enjoy what they saw,' he said.

'They did indeed, and if they urge all their friends to come we may be able to keep it going. But advance bookings are weak, and the reviews are, to say the least, mixed.'

'*The Times* was beastly, but these are not bad,' he said, holding up the cuttings from the *World* and the *Telegraph*.

'There were some others I didn't think you'd want to see,' said Alexander ominously. 'We shall depend on word of mouth. I'll keep you informed of how it goes.'

As he walked back to Kensington he regretted the impulse that had sent him to the theatre. Already he felt himself being drawn back into the sickening, exhausting maelstrom of emotion that seemed to swirl around every theatrical project, generating an endless, soul-destroying alternation of hope and dejection. How soon he had lapsed from his high resolve of the afternoon! He vowed once again to put his failure behind him, to renew his allegiance to the muse of fiction, to strive to be a better person, to possess his soul in peace. But it wasn't easy, it wasn't easy.

★ ★ ★

The next two days were largely occupied in answering the letters that continued to pour in by every post from friends and well-wishers, a task both painful and gratifying. On the one hand he was thus constantly reminded of the horrible experience of the first night; on the other he was moved by the apparently genuine enthusiasm of so many of these correspondents for *Guy Domville*. One of the most painful letters he had to write was to William and Alice, in which he was obliged to act as his own defendant, because they had no direct knowledge of the play – though they would certainly have heard indirectly about the *débâcle* of the first night. Ever since he had compared American social and cultural life unfavourably with that of Britain in his book on Hawthorne, back in 1880, the American newspapers had conducted a vendetta against him and his works, and would have reported the booing episode with glee. In any case his brother and sister-in-law would have observed that he hadn't, as promised, cabled them on Sunday about the first night, and drawn the obvious conclusion. 'Even now it's a sore trial to me to have to write about it,' he confessed at the outset of his letter, '–weary, bruised, sickened, disgusted as one is left by the intense, the cruel ordeal of a first night that – after the immense labour of preparation and the unspeakable tension of suspense – has, in a few brutal moments, not gone well. In three words . . .' But as usual he required a lot more than three words to describe the event and its effect on him. He began the letter on Tuesday evening and finished it on Wednesday morning.

The next day he had a welcome break from London and letter-writing, when he fulfilled an engagement to visit a relatively new friend, Arthur Benson, at the home of his father, Edward White Benson, the Archbishop of Canterbury. He had met Arthur Benson, who was a master at Eton, at Frederick Myers's house in Cambridge, and soon added him to the little confraternity of clever, deferential and well-read young men whose company he valued. Arthur's younger brother Edward, who had literary interests too, was also at home for the Christmas vacation. The archiepiscopal residence at Addington, in Kent, was nobly proportioned and comfortably appointed, and its atmosphere of donnish

Anglicanism was soothing to his bruised spirit – the very words 'archiepiscopal residence' sounded like a benediction as he pronounced them silently to himself. There was however no possibility of forgetting all about *Guy Domville* for the duration of his brief visit: his hosts had read the review in *The Times*, and in various tactful ways offered their sympathy. The Archbishop was less lively company than his sons, but over a cup of tea beside a glowing log fire in the drawing room, as the light faded on the level lawns outside the long windows, he mentioned a story of a haunting, recently told to him, which caught and held Henry's attention. It concerned a pair of bad servants in a country house, a man and a woman, who had corrupted two young children in their care, and then died, but reappeared as ghosts, beckoning to the children from battlements and across water to join them, so that they would destroy themselves. It was only a sketchy anecdote, clumsily narrated, but he thought it had possibilities as the basis for a short story and made a note of it when he returned to London the next day.

His notebook was bulging with ideas for stories and novels waiting to be written, and he meant to write them. It was, he was sure, the only way forward. Produce! produce! he urged himself. But he hung back, he hesitated to begin. He sat at his desk and wrote in his notebook: *'I take up my own old pen again – the pen of all my old unforgettable efforts and sacred struggles. To myself – today – I need say no more. Large and full and high the future still opens. It is now indeed that I may do the work of my life. And I will.'* But he laid the pen down again. He was not ready. His confidence in himself as a writer had been badly damaged, and the worst thing he could do would be to rush into some new work of fiction which might turn out to be another disappointment.

It was difficult, in any case, to turn his back decisively on the drama as long as *Guy Domville* continued to play at the St James's and its future remained uncertain. Favourable reviews continued to appear and were passed to him by friends: an intelligent one from George Bernard Shaw in the *Saturday Review*, which addressed directly and effectively the philistine arguments of *The Times*, and was marred only by rather fulsome praise of Alexander's performance; one in the *Pall Mall Gazette*, by a writer whose name, H. G. Wells, he did not recognise, which described the play as 'finely conceived and beautifully written', and another by a female critic in a magazine called *Woman* who found 'the behaviour of the pit and gallery inexplicable', and concluded: 'The setting of the last act, "the white parlour" at Mrs Peverel's home, Porches, was one of the most perfect stage interiors I have ever seen.' This typically feminine gush of enthusiasm for the décor made him smile, but the review was not imperceptive.

From these sources, and from conversations with friends like Gosse and Elizabeth Robins who had been present at the first night, he began to reconstruct the sequence of events which had led up to his own unsuspecting appearance at its deplorable climax: the universally applauded first act which seemed to presage a great success; the hesitant beginning of the second act, the rude mockery of Mrs Saker's costume by the gallery and pit, the consequent collapse of her confidence and its disastrous effect on the other actors; the growing hubbub of jeering and barracking as the third act drew to its close. Information about the mysterious telegram received by Alexander had leaked out, and there was speculation in the press that the performance had been maliciously disrupted by a hired claque. Someone who had been present wrote a letter to the *Pall Mall Gazette* claiming that the upper boxes were filled by men who looked far too rough to be able to afford four shillings for a seat and who returned after the entr'actes behaving as if they had been treated to strong drink. Nothing was ever proved, however, to confirm these suspicions, and the memory of how warmly Alexander was received when he went back on stage to make his grovelling curtain speech convinced him that the hostility of the gallery and pit had been mainly directed at himself and his play. But what became more and more obvious, as the total picture became clearer, was that Alexander had betrayed him by inviting him to take a bow, as surely as Judas betrayed Jesus with a kiss in the Garden of Gethsemane. The image of Alexander smilingly beckoning him to come out of the dark wings into the glare of the footlights was as vivid to him as if it had just happened, but the smile now seemed vulpine. He must have been well aware that, despite the friendly applause from the more expensive seats, the play had gone badly in the last two acts, and that the cries of 'Author!' from the gallery and the pit were not expressions of enthusiasm, but on the contrary a device to lure him out of hiding in order to hurl abuse. Yet Alexander had led him into the trap, presumably out of some malicious impulse of revenge, a desire to make him share something of the discomfiture that he and the other actors had endured for the past hour or two. Perhaps he hadn't anticipated the intensity of the storm of booing that ensued, Elizabeth Robins conceded, but he couldn't for a moment have supposed that Henry would receive a unanimously warm ovation from that audience.

It had been a treacherous act, but he couldn't prove it, and in any case he would not demean himself by accusing Alexander directly. Relations between them continued cool and businesslike. He did not attend any further performances, but towards the end of January he called at the theatre one morning at Alexander's request, to be told by the manager that he was taking the play off at the end of its fourth week, on February 2nd. 'I'm sorry, Henry,' he said. 'I'm just as disappointed as you, but we're simply losing too much money, and there's no sign of an upturn in box office takings — isn't that right, Bob?' Alexander turned to his business manager, Robert Shone, whom he had invited to the meeting for support. Shone had graduated to his present position from that of stage manager, and had taken some pains to dress and equip himself for the part. He wore a dark three-piece suit bristling with pens and pencils, and had a big ledger open on the table in front of him.

'I'm afraid so,' said Shone, nodding gravely. 'We're averaging less than forty per cent paying customers.'

'And how much might I expect to receive by way of royalties in the end?' he asked.

Shone peered at his ledger through a pince-nez and sucked his teeth. 'I would estimate about two hundred pounds. Perhaps a little more.'

It seemed a paltry reward for so much work and worry and suffering. His face was evidently eloquent of this reflection, for Alexander said: 'I shall lose fifteen hundred myself.'

'More,' said Shone dolefully.

'Every play is a gamble,' said Alexander. 'You never know whether you will win or lose. I've been lucky in this theatre so far, but . . .' he shrugged and left the sentence unfinished.

'I'm sorry to have been responsible for your luck running out,' he said coldly.

'We're counting on Oscar to restore it,' said Shone, perhaps indiscreetly, for Alexander glanced frowningly at him.

'Wilde?' he said, surprised. 'Has he written another play already?'

'It's one that Wyndham has had under option for some time,' said Alexander, 'but he's not in a position to put it on, so he let me have it. It's called *The Importance of Being Earnest*. A good title, don't you think?'

There was to be no end, it seemed, to the exquisitely ironic twists in the story of his failure as a dramatist. He had walked from a performance of one successful play of Wilde's to experience the humiliation of being booed, and now another, sure to be equally to the public taste, was being hurried on to the stage of the St James's to replace his own rejected piece.

On Saturday the 2nd of February, when *Guy Domville* was due to have its thirty-first and last performance, he wrote to William of having lived through 'the four horridest weeks of my life'. It was a long, confessional letter, and reading it over he realised how far he still was from purging himself of all the negative emotions that had plagued him ever since the first night. 'Produce a play and you will know, better than I can tell you, how such an ordeal – odious in its essence! – is only made tolerable by great success, and in how many ways accordingly non-success may be tormenting and tragic, a bitterness of every hour, ramifying into every throb of one's consciousness.' He did not feel he was exaggerating his pain.

He had decided to attend the last performance that evening, to make his adieux to the cast and, he hoped, finally to lower the curtain on this unhappy chapter of his life. But when he got to the theatre Shone was waiting in the foyer to tell him they were extending the run by another week, since Wilde's play would not be ready for another two. He obviously felt himself to be the bearer of good news, but to Henry it was only an unwelcome anticlimax, another obstacle to freeing his soul from the poisonous tentacles of the theatre. He derived little pleasure from the evening. Only Marion Terry had preserved the original delicacy of her performance. The rest of the acting had already become coarse and mechanical, including Alexander's over-explicit interpretation of the hero. 'Oh the mutilated brutally simplified, massacred little play!' he ejaculated in a postscript to William the next day.

He shared with his brother the irony that *Guy Domville* continued to provoke far more letters of praise from people who had seen it than any previous work of his, in any form. He did not tell William, however – he did not tell anybody – that one of these letters was from Ellen Terry, who had attended the first night to support her younger sister. She commiserated with him about the bestial behaviour of the gallery, complimented him on *Guy Domville*, and asked if he would consider writing a one-act play for her. She was going to do a tour in America with Henry Irving later in the year and was seeking a suitable curtain-raiser. This was a hard test of his resolution to renounce theatrical ambitions. Although he was not himself an uncritical admirer of Ellen Terry, she was the most celebrated actress of her generation on the English stage. She must have new plays pressed upon her daily by petitioning playwrights, and whatever she approved was sure to be performed. He could not bring himself to reject her flattering proposal out of hand, so replied in noncommittal terms, and agreed to meet her.

Ellen Terry received him in a small reception room at the Lyceum where refreshments were served to visiting royalty and other dignitaries during entr'actes, and indeed the interview was rather like an audience with a Queen of the stage. Although she must be, he calculated, nearly fifty years of age, she was still handsome, and the famous voice, at once crystal-clear and faintly husky, was just as spellbinding in quiet intimacy as it was in the theatre. It was impossible when face to face with her not to think of her scandalous and sensational personal life – the disastrous marriage to Watts when she was still virtually a child, and the separations, divorces, liaisons, marriages and children that had followed, not always in the conventional order. All this, including her current relationship with Irving, was well known among those who belonged to her world, but Ellen Terry never made the mistake, as Wilde had, of encouraging scandal. On the contrary she conducted herself with admirable discretion and impeccable outward propriety, and Henry, who more and more believed that only an elegant and resourceful system of benign social lying kept civilisation from being destroyed by human passions, respected her for it. She had forgotten or forgiven or perhaps had never been aware of his dissenting reviews of her much-lauded performances as Goldsmith's Olivia and Shakespeare's Portia in the distant past. She was charming, persuasive, and prepared to wait patiently till the summer for her play. Weakly he agreed to think further about the matter, and almost as soon as he got home had an idea for a comedy with a part so perfect for Ellen Terry that it took all his moral strength to stop himself from sitting down and incontinently beginning to write it. Instead he made a brief, rather shamefaced note of the idea, and directed his thoughts sternly back to prose fiction.

Browsing through the pages of his notebook, that precious mine of unworked, richly-veined deposits of raw story-stuff, he was particularly taken with two ideas for novels – one about a widowed father and his daughter, greatly attached to each other, who both married at the same time, then discovered that their respective spouses were in fact lovers, but managed to redeem the ugly situation by nobility of soul and social cunning; the other – over which the spirit of Minny Temple hovered – about a beautiful rich young woman who contracted a fatal illness which threatened to deprive her of the experience of love, and was exploited by friends poorer and less scrupulous than herself. But the possible narrative development of these ideas remained vague and amorphous, and he shrank from embarking upon any major project without a more detailed map by which to navigate. If you made up a story as you went along, there was always a danger that it would go in too many different directions, inhabit the consciousnesses of too many characters, touch on too many themes, to achieve unity and concentration of effect. That, he had to admit, had happened in the composition of his last two full-length novels, *The Princess Casamassima* and *The Tragic Muse*. And that perhaps was why he had been tempted to try his hand at dramatic representation, with its inherent formal constraints.

But this reflection prompted another. Suppose one were to apply to prose narrative the method he had used in developing his ideas for plays, namely, the scenario – the detailed scene-by-scene summary of an imagined action? Then one would have a model, as it were, of the novel or tale in a virtual form; one could take the measure of its structure as a whole, assess its unity and symmetry, and make any necessary adjustments, before commencing the process of composition proper. And then, he thought with gathering excitement, might not the dramatic principle itself, of presenting experience scenically – 'showing' rather than 'telling' the story, through the confrontation and interaction of the characters – might this not give prose fiction the kind of structural strength and elegance it so often lacked, while the narrative artist remained free to *add* the priceless resource, denied to the dramatist, of being able to reveal the secret workings of consciousness in all its dense and delicate detail? He was so pleased with this *aperçu* that he immediately committed it to his notebook, and commented: 'Has a *part* of all this wasted passion and squandered time (of the last 5 years) been simply the precious lesson, taught me in that roundabout and devious, that cruelly expensive, way *of the singular value for a narrative plan too* of the (I don't know *what* adequately to call it) divine principle of the Scenario? If that *has* been one side of the moral of the whole unspeakable, the whole tragic experience, I almost bless the pangs and the pains and the miseries of it.'

He did not, however, immediately put this new compositional method, so luminously promising in theory, to the test of practical application; and the very next day the positive, hopeful mood it had engendered was disturbed by reading an ecstatic review in *The Times* of *The Importance of Being Earnest*, which had just opened at the St James's, with Alexander in the leading male role. This favourable reaction was shared by all the critics he read subsequently, with the solitary exception of George Bernard Shaw, and by all his acquaintance who had been to see the play. It seemed to be Wilde's biggest 'hit' to date – some were calling it his masterpiece. Wilde had embarked on his playwriting career at about the same time as himself, and, he suspected, with the same mixed motives – to make much-needed money and at the same time bring some literary distinction to the debased English stage – and he had therefore always regarded him as more of a personal rival than any other contemporary playwright. It was time to admit defeat: at every point, and by every scale of measurement, Wilde had outreached him. Morton Fullerton had once quoted to him a chilling epigram of Wilde's which was painfully apropos: *'It is not enough that one succeeds – others must fail.'* It was evidently his own destiny to add this extra savour to Oscar's triumph.

But then, suddenly, towards the end of February, when 'House Full' notices were being placed nightly outside the St James's, Wilde's success was clouded by scandal, and before long his fortunes were in steep and irreversible decline. The Marquess of Queensberry, whose outrage at Wilde's alleged seduction of his son had been the gossip of London clubs for weeks, publicly denounced Wilde as a sodomite, and Wilde sued him for libel. Queensberry was committed for trial, which began on April 3rd at the Old Bailey amid intense public interest and journalistic frenzy. Wilde lost the case, and was shortly afterwards arrested and charged with sodomy and indecency. The public mood turned decisively and viciously against him. Philistine England was eager to get its revenge for decades of enduring Wilde's barbed witticisms and aesthetic anathemas, and few dared to defend him now, or to be seen patronising his work. Wyndham closed *An Ideal Husband* in mid-April, while Alexander removed Wilde's name from the advertisements and playbills of *The Importance of Being Earnest* in a desperate effort to keep it running.

The trial of Wilde began on the 26th April. After several days of damaging and unspeakably sordid evidence, the jury failed to agree and a retrial was ordered; but whatever the result of the second trial might be, Wilde was now irretrievably disgraced. Alexander took off *The Importance of Being Earnest* on the 10th of May. Wilde was tried for a second time at the end of the month, found guilty, and sentenced to two years' hard labour. It seemed unlikely that his 'masterpiece' would ever be performed again.

Henry did not derive any *Schadenfreude* from this sudden reversal of his rival's fortunes. He found most of the published comment on the case, and the general satisfaction at the result, unpleasantly vindictive and often nauseatingly hypocritical. But he thought Wilde was ultimately responsible for his own downfall by the recklessness of his conduct, right up to and including his refusal (so it was said) to flee to the Continent when he had the opportunity. That was not the heroism of a man determined to accept his punishment, but the arrogance of someone who thought he could evade it indefinitely. Wilde had consistently flouted the constraints which society wisely imposed on deviant sexual behaviour, and his overweening vanity had convinced him that he could do so with impunity. Henry felt pity for the man, but not empathy – affected by the spectacle of his downfall, but detached from it. Like an ancient tragedy, its effect was cathartic, purging pity and fear, as Aristotle said – in his own case, self-pity and fear of the future. At last he felt able to accept the humiliating failure of *Guy Domville* and move on.

In mid-May, between the two trials of Oscar Wilde, he began work on a new work of fiction, using the method of the preparatory scenario that he had adumbrated in his notebook. Its 'germ' was not the story of the two children haunted by former servants which he had most recently entered there, but an anecdote told to him at a dinner table two years ago, about a widow and her son who fell out concerning the ownership of a house full of beautiful 'things' which the mother appreciated and the son merely coveted. He planned to tell the story from the point of view of a character

who was not in the original source at all – the mother's companion, a young woman at once finely sensitive and humanly fallible.
His working title for this tale was 'The House Beautiful', a phrase
of Walter Pater's which Oscar Wilde had appropriated for the title
of one of his most popular public lectures.

George Du Maurier had been among the first of his friends to write
to him, with characteristic sensitivity and tact, after the opening night
of *Guy Domville*, deploring the behaviour of the gallery and expressing his admiration for the play, and he wrote again, supportively and
sympathetically, when its run was prematurely terminated. Henry
replied warmly to both letters, and they exchanged words briefly at
a noisy crowded private view at the Grosvenor Gallery in February,
but it was not until the beginning of March that he carried out his
'firm purpose of amendment' to the extent of walking up to
Hampstead to have a long and confidential chat with his old friend.
He deliberately chose a weekday, rather than a more gregarious and
family-dominated Sunday, and luckily it was a fine and unseasonably
warm one. It would be best, he decided, not to attempt to disguise
his own bafflement at the success of *Trilby*, but to bring the subject
out into the open and frankly address it. Accordingly as he climbed
the last steep hill to New Grove House, he prepared a speech which
he delivered as soon as Du Maurier came into the hall to greet him.

'Will you take off your coat and rest for a while,' Du Maurier
asked, 'or would you like to take a walk on the Heath at once?'

'Let us take our walk, *cher ami*,' he said. 'Let us find our old familiar seat, and sit down and endeavour to discover – if it is in any
way possible to arrive at a solution – endeavour to discover some
reason for the success of *Trilby*. I mean of course,' he added hastily,
for the prepared speech sounded a little ungracious when uttered,
'not its success with discriminating readers – which could have been
foreseen – but with so many thousands to whom the very word
"discriminating" would be a novelty and a puzzle.'

'With all my heart,' Du Maurier said, laughing. 'But I must warn
you that I have no ready explanation myself.'

Du Maurier continued to be as surprised as anyone by the popularity of his book and appeared to be more bothered than gratified by it. Correspondence was a great headache. 'I get at least five letters a day from American readers – Harper forward them, you know – and it's a frightful bore having to reply,' he said, as they walked down the hill to the Heath, their sticks clicking on the pavement almost in unison, and the now aged Don hobbling along just ahead of them.

'You ought to get a secretary to answer them for you,' Henry said.

'Well, Pem does take care of some of them.' Du Maurier gave a little chuckle. 'I think she's rather brusque with my more ardent female admirers. It seems to me very extraordinary that people appear to think that having bought a book entitles them to write a private letter to the author asking all kinds of personal questions and giving all kinds of information about themselves in which one can have no conceivable interest.'

'You could always just ignore them,' Henry said.

'Yes, I could, but I wouldn't feel happy about it. I was taught that it's bad manners not to answer a letter, and I can't shake off the habit of a lifetime.'

'What kind of things do they say?'

'Oh, the usual tosh about how wonderful the book is, and how they sat up all night to finish it, and how they cried when Trilby died. Quite a lot of them seem to think the characters are real people, or were. I've had at least three letters complaining that they couldn't find Little Billee's paintings in the National Gallery.' (Henry laughed and struck the ground with his stick.) 'A number of clergymen have offered to explain the error of my freethinking ways and to convert me to their particular brand of Christianity.' ('Inevitably!' Henry exclaimed.) 'And I had a letter from a gentleman in Virginia asking very earnestly what exactly was the relationship between Trilby and Svengali when he paraded her around the concert halls of Europe as La Svengali.'

'And what did you tell him?'

'Oh, that she was only under his spell when she was singing, and that otherwise their relationship was that of father and daughter. He wrote me an effusive letter back, saying that I had saved his sanity – the idea of the odious Jew having his wicked way with Trilby had been driving him mad.'

'And was it really a father-and-daughter relationship – in your own imagination, I mean?' Henry asked.

'Oh yes, of course.' Du Maurier looked surprised, even shocked, at the suggestion that anything else could have been the case.

'But at the beginning of the story Svengali seems to have designs on Trilby,' Henry pointed out. 'He rebukes her for ignoring his overtures and threatens her with dreadful consequences. Once he had her in his clutches wouldn't he use his mesmeric powers for – for purposes other than musical?'

'Goodness me, Henry, what an imagination you have! You're as bad as Maupassant! No, no, Trilby would never have submitted to him, mesmerised or not. It would have killed her. There could never be another man in her life after Little Billee.'

He was amused by Du Maurier's denial of the logical consequences of his own story, but did not pursue the point. They reached the Bench of Confidences and sat down in the pale spring sunshine. A few crocuses showed their buds timidly in the long grass. 'In spite of this immense – this intrusive and often fatuous correspondence – you must nevertheless be gratified by the enormous success of *Trilby*?' he said.

'Well of course, the tin is very welcome, though I haven't made as much as everybody seems to think, for reasons you know. But as to the fame and the celebrity – well, frankly it appals me – it almost frightens me. You feel you have no control over your own life any more. Did you know all kinds of products are being sold in America with the name 'Trilby' attached to them – like shoes and hearthbrushes and kitchen-ranges? Entirely without permission, of course.'

'I didn't know about the kitchen-ranges,' said Henry, 'but I hear there is a Trilby sausage.'

'God in heaven!' Du Maurier exclaimed. 'That's a new one. I wish you hadn't told me.'

'I'm afraid it's a very American kind of vulgarity,' said Henry.

'One of the less amiable consequences of our enthusiasm for democracy and capitalism.'

'I keep getting invitations to go to America, offering me huge fees for a lecture tour, but I've no intention of accepting them.'

'No, you mustn't,' said Henry firmly. 'The journalists there would eat you alive. But it's interesting that – if I'm not mistaken – *Trilby* has been even more successful in America than in England.'

'Absolutely. In fact when the book came out here – if you remember – the reviews were not at all enthusiastic. It was reading in the newspapers about the *Trilby* boom in America that made people here curious to read it. Then they didn't care what the reviewers had said.'

'And you have no theory to account for its extraordinary appeal?'

'No – have you, Henry? You seem to have given a lot of thought to the matter.' He smiled to show the question was gently teasing rather than sarcastic.

'Yes, I have,' Henry admitted. 'Obviously the character of Trilby herself is crucial. You've done a very remarkable thing, Kiki. You have created a heroine who is – or at least *was*, at one stage of her life – no better than she should be, and the Anglo-Saxon reading public has taken her to its collective heart. I can't think of a precedent. Thomas Hardy tried it here with his Tess, George Moore with his Esther Waters. All they got for their pains were brickbats and denunciations from the custodians of morality.'

'But I make it clear that she's essentially innocent – a victim of her appalling upbringing,' said Du Maurier. 'She had no conventional moral education. She went with those artists in her youth out of simple generosity – she really didn't see there was anything wrong in it. And her dreadful mother encouraged her. It's only when she sees how upset Little Billee is at discovering her sitting for the figure that she develops a sense of modesty. From that moment on, she is chaste.'

'Yes, it was very clever of you to place all her sexual indiscretions in the past, and focus on her posing in the nude in the main story,' Henry said. As was his wont when thinking aloud with a walking stick in his hand, he began to scratch lines in the earth, using the stick as if it were a pen. He recalled Fenimore when he first met her in Florence, fresh from the Midwest, confessing her '*difficulty in appreciating the nude*'. 'I think the great American public finds that a tremendously daring and shocking thing to contemplate – a woman disrobing in front of men – but not *too* shocking. It's something they can forgive her for, especially as Trilby promptly gives it up on falling in love with the hero. So one might perhaps say that her sexual sin is – I mean of course in the consciousness of your readers – her sin is, as it were, *displaced* on to her posing for the figure, and thus made redeemable.'

'That's all too subtle for me, Henry,' said Du Maurier, shaking his head, 'and as far as my being "clever" goes, I just wrote the whole thing spontaneously, as it came to me. But I must admit that American readers – the ones that write to me, anyway – are uncommonly interested in Trilby's sitting for the figure. A gentleman in Chicago offered me ten thousand dollars for a signed drawing of Trilby in "the altogether".'

'Ten thousand dollars!' Henry exclaimed. 'And did you oblige him?'

'Certainly not,' said Du Maurier.

'I admire your principle,' said Henry. 'In your position I admit I should be tempted.'

'It's not just principle,' said Du Maurier, with a laugh. 'I should have to hire a model to sit for the figure, and Emma wouldn't allow it.'

'Really?'

'Yes, Pem is a very prudish soul, God bless her.' Du Maurier paused, and made a small inarticulate sound, an exhalation of breath that was half wistful sigh, half amused grunt, as a memory seemed to rise from the past. 'When we were first married I asked her one day if she would sit for me – *pour l'ensemble, tu as compris?* But she wouldn't. I promised her the drawing would be for my eyes only, and that she could destroy it if she didn't like it, but it didn't make any difference. Nothing would persuade her. And she was quite right, of course,' he concluded.

'Why do you say that?' Henry asked.

'The relationship between artist and model should be quite impersonal, like doctor and patient. Otherwise . . . inappropriate feelings are likely to arise. And I mean arise.' Du Maurier gave a sly sidelong glance to see if the *double entendre* was appreciated. Henry was aware that he had something of a reputation in the *Punch* coterie for risqué quips of this kind, but was seldom a recipient himself. He dutifully smiled, and said: 'I'm told that Leighton's house has a special side-door for the models, which is, I suppose, a little like a doctor having a separate entrance for his surgery.'

'Quite so. By the way, you mustn't let Pem know I told you about that episode in our early married life,' said Du Maurier.

'My dear chap, of course not,' Henry said.

As it happened, Emma was not feeling well that day, and retired to bed shortly after they had finished their dinner. When she had gone, Du Maurier picked up a second bottle of his favourite claret from the sideboard and, with a wink to Henry, carried it into the studio, where a cheerful fire glowed in the hearth. Wine after dinner was an indulgence that Emma seldom allowed him these days.

'*Fi! de ces vins d'Espagne,*' Henry quoted, as Du Maurier filled his glass.

'Indeed – though this cost me more than *quatre sous*,' said his friend. He seated himself at the piano, and played a few jaunty bars of the song, singing the words:

> '*Fi! de ces vins d'Espagne.*
> *Ils ne sont pas faits pour nous . . .*'

then stopped. 'I mustn't disturb poor Pem.'

'Play me the Chopin piece that Trilby sings just before she dies,' Henry said.

'The Impromptu in A flat? Yes, that's quiet enough. You won't expect me to vocalise the notes as she does, I hope?' He found the sheet music and played the piece, very effectively as far as Henry could tell.

'Bravo!' he said, when Du Maurier had finished.

Du Maurier shook his head as he got up from the piano stool and seated himself in an armchair. 'I made several mistakes.'

'Well, I wouldn't notice. You remember the occasion all those years ago when you offered me the story of Trilby?'

'Of course – how could I ever forget? That conversation started me on my career as a novelist—'

'And I said I couldn't do it, because I didn't have the musical knowledge? Well, I was quite right – the book is saturated in music. That's part of its charm.'

'But it's also a frustration, because you can't make your readers *hear* the music in their heads, unless they happen to know it already,' said Du Maurier. 'Now there's going to be a play of *Trilby* in America. I rather dread to think what they will do to the story, but at least the audience will be able to hear the music.'

'Trilby will sing? She will sing the Chopin Impromptu?'

'Yes – I presume so. Why not?'

'Well, you describe her voice – under Svengali's spell – as having a unique, unprecedented range and beauty – and we believe you. But it's asking a lot of an actress to live up to your words.'

Du Maurier frowned. 'Hmm. I hadn't thought of that.'

'I'm sure they'll find a way round it,' Henry said reassuringly. 'Theatre is all illusion – like any art. You remember that little anecdote you told me – the one I *did* work up into a story – about the genteel couple who offered themselves as models? The "real thing" in art is never the real thing.'

'I remember it well.' Du Maurier began to roll himself a cigarette. 'When I read your wonderful story I was worried that the couple concerned might read it too, and recognise themselves. You had them off so well, I could hardly believe you had never actually met them yourself.'

'Ah well,' said Henry, allowing himself a certain complacency, 'when you have been at the game as long as I have, a little information goes a long way. Do you think you will write another novel?'

'I'm already writing one,' said Du Maurier.

This was news to Henry and not entirely welcome, but he congratulated his friend.

'I think it will be the best thing I've done so far, but it's going slowly. I always have to start a story by drawing on my own experience and memories, but that unpleasant business with Whistler has made me nervous.'

Henry knew about this affair, but was curious to hear Du Maurier's account of it. 'I was in Italy at the time, you know,' he said. 'There was a lawsuit, wasn't there?'

'Yes, Whistler recognised himself in the character of Joe Sibley in the *Harper's* serial, and took offence. You know what a prickly character he is — and litigious as the devil. He sued Ruskin once for a bad review, remember? Anyway, he complained to the newspapers, complained to my club, complained to my publishers — complained to everybody — and threatened to sue me for libel. It completely spoiled any pleasure I might have taken in the success of the serial. In fact there were moments when I thought I might have to withdraw the whole thing. In the end I agreed to drop the character from the book version, and invented another one to take his place.'

'You *had* portrayed Whistler then?'

'I couldn't deny the resemblance. And I suppose I did make Joe Sibley out to be a bit vain and arrogant. But I thought Jimmy Whistler would take it like a good sport. After all, we were pals once. And none of the others took offence.'

'The others?'

'My other friends in the *Quartier Latin*. Armstrong, Lamont, Poynter . . . and the rest. They could all recognise bits of themselves in my characters, but they didn't mind. Some more wine?'

'No thank you. And Trilby herself? Did she have a real-life counterpart?'

Du Maurier filled his own glass and smiled. 'People are always asking me that. No, she's a figment of my imagination.'

'What about Svengali?'

'He too.'

'Really? He's such a wonderfully vivid character. You never knew anyone like him?'

'Well, there was someone – I tell you this in strict confidence—'

'Of course.'

'Did you ever hear of a man called George Lee?'

'No.'

'He was a music teacher, who developed a new technique for teaching singing – allegedly based on anatomical principles. He wrote a book about it. He rented a house at the less fashionable end of Park Lane, in the late 'seventies and early 'eighties, where he gave lessons and held musical soirées. I used to go sometimes.'

'Was he Jewish?'

'No, Irish, but he looked like a gypsy. A dark complexion, thick black hair worn long, and black whiskers. Handsomer than Svengali, but the same type.'

'Did he mesmerise his pupils?'

Du Maurier laughed. 'Not as far as I know, but his teaching method certainly seemed to work best with women . . . He was very friendly with George Bernard Shaw's mother – she was a protégée of his in Dublin, and followed him to London. Some people say Shaw looks remarkably like Lee. I shouldn't be telling you this, Henry. The danger of the second bottle.'

'You can rely on my discretion, *cher ami*. But Svengali's mesmerism, his Mittel-European Jewishness – where did *they* come from?'

Du Maurier tapped his temple with a forefinger. 'Out of my head. Out of books. Out of dreams.'

'And nightmares . . . ?'

Du Maurier nodded assent. They were both silent for a few moments, staring into the fire. Then Henry took out his watch and said he must go. Du Maurier put on his coat and accompanied him a little way down the hill until Henry pleaded with him to go back, on the grounds that he himself would be in Emma's black books otherwise. He stood still on the pavement watching his friend slowly climb the gradient until he disappeared into the misty gloom. A frail, bowed, rather sad figure he looked. One would never have guessed that he was one of the most famous authors in the world.

★ ★ ★

Du Maurier's fame only increased as time passed. Henry went back to Hampstead in April, on a Sunday this time, and found the gathered family in high excitement at the reported success of the stage adaptation of *Trilby* which had recently opened on Broadway to ecstatic reviews and was already sold out for weeks. Furthermore Beerbohm Tree had seen it on his last night in New York before returning to England from a tour, and had bought the play for a London production, with the intention of playing Svengali himself.

'The role is perfect for him,' said Henry. 'It will be a tremendous success, I'm sure.' His firm purpose of amendment was certainly being tested to the limit: that Du Maurier should triumph on the stage as well as the page with *Trilby* was a little hard to take. 'You will soon be as rich as Croesus, my dear chap,' he said, forcing a smile.

As usual Du Maurier was at pains to minimise his earnings. 'I don't own the American stage rights,' he said, 'and I sold the British rights to somebody for a footling sum. But Beerbohm bought them back and I have hopes that he may pay me a small royalty.' He added: 'I intend to use my influence to get Gerald a part, anyway.' That thought seemed to give him more satisfaction than anything else. Charles Millar later gave Henry a more promising account of this business. It seemed that Tree had offered a very reasonable percentage and Paul Potter had also agreed to share royalties on the play.

It was a fine sunny day, and they went on to the Heath in a great crowd – children, grandchildren, perambulators, dogs – and scattered in different directions. Henry and Du Maurier found themselves alone on Parliament Hill, looking down at London, spread out before them in a brown haze of coal-smoke, as they had on one of their earliest walks.

'I have some news, Henry,' Du Maurier said. 'We're moving to London.'

'You mean – permanently? Good heavens, when?'

'As soon as it can be managed. It's time. The children are all grown up. New Grove House isn't really convenient for a couple of old codgers like Pem and me. And now people have found out where we live, they come up here and stand in the street and stare at the windows.'

'What people?'

'Readers of *Trilby*, I suppose,' said Du Maurier.

'How very impertinent,' he said, genuinely shocked. 'But where will you move to?'

'We've found a suitable house in Oxford Square – near the Park, you know. And if people track us there and stare at the windows there'll be a constable handy to move them on.'

'Well, I don't know what to say, Kiki! It's the end of an era. Hampstead won't be worth visiting without you.'

'You and I will see more of each other, anyway, old chap.'

'That's true, though . . .'

'Though what?'

'Ironically enough – *I'm* thinking of moving *out* of London,' he said.

'Good Lord! Where?'

'I don't know. I've only just had the idea.' In fact it had been growing inside him ever since the first night of *Guy Domville*, but in a quiet, secret fashion, hardly acknowledged even by himself. He had certainly not mentioned it to a single soul before. But now it filled him with certainty. He wanted to get away from London, away from people, parties, plays (especially plays); away from the constant jostling for attention and success; away from the noise and the traffic, the sooty fogs of winter and the foetid heat-waves of summer. He wanted a little house somewhere quiet and green, with perhaps a strip of blue sea in the offing, where when you drew the curtains of a morning and raised the sash windows you breathed in fresh air scented with cut hay or a hint of brine, not the odours of coal-smoke and ordure, and heard the sounds of rooks cawing or sea-gulls mewing instead of the rattle of carriage wheels and the cries of tradesmen. He wanted peace and quiet in which to write, and to be able to take Tosca for a walk over the fields when the day's work was done.

'Anyway, I daresay it will take me some time to find the right place,' he said.

4

'THIS is a little *démodé* "crescent" hanging over a green green garden that hangs over a blue blue sea. Over all hangs my balcony – and over my balcony hangs a beautiful striped awning. No sound but the waves licking the honey-coloured sand.' So he wrote to Anne Thackeray Ritchie, sitting on his balcony at the Osborne Hotel, describing the scene before him like an artist painting a landscape *en plein air*. It was the quiet, somnolent hour after luncheon; at another time of day he might have been obliged to add a few more sounds to the gentle lapping of the waves – the faint cries of children on the beach, the muffled shrieks of bathers plunging into the sea from their wheeled cubicles. But, although it was August, and Torquay was full of visitors, the beach at Meadfoot Sands was never crowded or noisy. It was perhaps too long and strenuous a walk from the centre of the town for ordinary holidaymakers; and in any case most of them seemed to prefer the diversions and amenities of the harbour, the Royal Terrace Gardens, and the promenade that stretched westwards towards Torre Abbey. As for the Osborne itself, like most superior hotels in Torquay it had its high season in the winter, when the rich and leisured were drawn to the resort by its famously mild climate. At this time of the year it was half-empty and surprisingly cheap, a blessedly peaceful retreat for an author still convalescing from a grievous blow to his self-esteem.

He had stayed here briefly the previous summer, at the suggestion of William Norris, and liked the place enormously. *Démodé* it might be, but it was comfortable and, in its idiosyncratic way, elegant: a perfect Georgian crescent of white stucco terraced houses such as one would not be surprised to find in Bath or Cheltenham, but here standing strikingly alone in its own grounds. It was as if a street of townhouses had taken flight like a flock of birds, soared over Vane Hill, and alighted in a graceful arc on the grassy brink of the sea.

Originally it had been an exclusive residential development, but a number of the units had later been joined together to make a hotel, named somewhat opportunistically after the Queen's summer residence on the Isle of Wight. The crescent was screened and sheltered at the rear by trees, mostly Scotch firs, though palm trees and other exotic flora also flourished in this warm humid nook of south Devon; and further back steep, densely green hills rose up to meet the sky, with red-roofed villas and curving carriageways fleetingly visible between their leafage. Perhaps the setting pleased him so much because it reminded him of the hills around Florence. He occupied a very pleasant suite of south-facing rooms, with an uninterrupted view of the sea, for the road that ran along the back of the sands was sunk out of sight beneath the lip of the Osborne's gently sloping lawn. A giantess of a chambermaid, at least six feet tall (she might have sat for one of Du Maurier's duchesses), kept the rooms in excellent order, and ran his bath for him in the mornings. The food was decently adequate – one could expect no more from an English hotel.

It had been a happy last-minute thought to settle here for the summer after weeks of vacillation. He had decided against going to Italy – he had no wish to reawaken painful memories of Fenimore or be jostled by the vulgar tourist hordes, and in any case he could hardly justify the expense of such a trip given the present state of his affairs. So he had dallied in London through May and June, distracted by the usual packed calendar of the Season, and by some particular social responsibilities of his own. Daudet came over from Paris for an extended visit at the beginning of May and he had felt obliged to put himself out for this venerable *cher collègue*. He escorted him down to Dorking to meet George Meredith, and the two old men embraced movingly on the station platform, though both were so enfeebled that he feared they would topple over, locked in each other's arms, and roll under the wheels of the train. Later he gave a dinner in Daudet's honour at the Reform, attended by Du Maurier and every other distinguished French-speaking guest he could scratch together in London. It went off well, though a certain anxiety attended the event because Daudet's control of his bladder was unreliable (the consequence no doubt of libertinage earlier in life) and he required some means of relieving himself at frequent intervals throughout the meal that would not entail a long walk to the lavatory under the main staircase. He was accommodated by the provision of a chamber pot behind an arrangement of screens at one end of the private dining room, and any embarrassment was spared by the rest of the party talking together with particular loudness and animation whenever the guest of honour had abruptly to retire behind them.

The weeks passed, June turned into July, London grew increasingly airless, smelly and dusty, and still he had made no plans for getting away. It had to be a place where he would have some company – otherwise he would become lonely and depressed – but also be independent and have time and space in which to work. If the Du Mauriers had been going to Whitby he might have braved the rigours of its climate again, but even Kiki and Emma were shirking it for once, having both been quite ill there the previous summer. They were talking of Folkestone, which did not entice him. He thought of going back to the Tregenna Castle Hotel at St Ives, where he had stayed comfortably the previous summer as a kind of satellite guest of Leslie and Julia Stephen in their damp and draughty seaside house, but Julia's lamentable recent death ruled that out. Even if the family went to Cornwall as usual this year, he didn't know them well enough to intrude on their grief, and in any case the idea of having to keep the lugubrious and taciturn Leslie Stephen company without the presence of the enchanting Julia, and with those unnervingly clever long-nosed young girls, Vanessa and Virginia, closely observing him in order (he suspected) to make fun of him behind his back, was not to be contemplated. But by association St Ives and the Stephens made him think of Norris and Torquay, for it was Stephen, when he was editor of the *Cornhill*, who had first encouraged Norris to write fiction, and it was on his way to St Ives the previous summer that he had broken his journey to stay in Torquay. On receiving this inspiration he had immediately wired the Osborne with a request for accommodation and conveyed his intentions to Norris, who declared himself delighted at the prospect of seeing him for an extended period. He had taken the rooms for the remainder of July and the whole of August, and he thought he might well decide to stay longer – perhaps even look for a house of his own in the vicinity. Meanwhile he was growing more at peace with himself and the world by the day.

These days had a regular and soothing rhythm. The morning was dedicated to work, namely, the one-act play commissioned by Ellen Terry. He felt a little foolish at breaking so soon his vow to forswear the theatre, but in the end the temptation had proved irresistible, and it was easier to make an accommodation with his conscience in Torquay than it would have been in London. He told himself that, after all, only a short play was required and it would not occupy him for very long; that he would be dealing directly and confidentially with an actress who possessed a formidable power of patronage; and that if the piece did not please her he could easily turn it into a short story and nobody would be the wiser. Having convinced himself with these arguments he suspended work on 'The House Beautiful' (which was, in truth, proving more difficult than anticipated) and began to write a comedy provisionally entitled *Mrs Gracedew*. The eponymous heroine – the role designed for Ellen Terry – was a rich and handsome American widow with an enthusiasm for historic English country houses such as 'Summersoft' (a kind of Osterley) where the play was set. In the course of a single afternoon she was to rescue the house from the philistine to whom it was mortgaged, restore it to its rightful owner, and agree to marry him, while at the same time sorting out the matrimonial future of the philistine's daughter. Her benign intrigue required her at one point to pretend to be a guide 'showing' the house to a group of gawping tourists, a comic set piece which he could imagine Ellen Terry carrying off brilliantly. Altogether he was very pleased with the rapid progress he was making with the play.

The afternoons were for catching up on correspondence, reading, and taking lessons in riding a bicycle. He had purchased a machine from a shop in the town, and a young man called John Plater came out to give him instruction for an hour each day. Hilly Torquay was not an ideal place for a beginner, but the Meadfoot Road that ran along behind the beach for nearly a mile was flat and straight and seldom busy. He was now able to ride up and down its whole length without falling off, and his purple bruises were beginning to turn yellow. His waistline, he was pleased to note, had already been reduced by this regular exercise. After it, if he was very heated, he sometimes took a second bath; then between five and six he would walk up the hill to Norris's villa, 'Underbank', and take tea with him.

This was really the only time of day when they could conveniently meet, since Norris played golf every morning and wrote his novels between the hours of two and five every afternoon, but it was opportunity enough. They usually ran out of things to say to each other after ten or fifteen minutes, and sat very contentedly in long contemplative silences after that. If Norris's daughter Effie were present she would fill up their intermissions by talking about horses and hunting, the only subjects which appeared to interest her. She was a big, blonde, red-cheeked young woman of twenty-three, the very epitome of the healthy, hearty English maiden, as instinctive and unreflective as a fine animal – as, indeed, a horse. He found it useful to think of her when evoking the character of Mona Brigstock, the energetic but aesthetically insensitive rival of the heroine in 'The House Beautiful'. Effie was Norris's only child and only companion, her mother having died some fifteen years earlier in circumstances on which Norris did not elaborate, and into which Henry did not enquire.

Norris was the son of a colonial Chief Justice, and had been educated at Eton and the Inner Temple. He had been called to the Bar, but had no inclination to practise law. Instead, he chose to live the life of a country gentleman, and since the mid-'eighties had taken up, rather as if it were an enjoyable and modestly lucrative hobby, the writing of novels about English gentlefolk – mainly their courtships, marriages, and wills. Norris turned out these books at the rate of one or sometimes even two a year, three-deckers with not very many words to the page, perfectly adjusted to the circulating library system which was his principal market. They were things to marvel at, these novels, for totally lacking any distinctive flavour. Henry compared them in his mind to cups of tea brewed in a pot from which the tea leaves had been accidentally omitted in the process of preparation, and served to people who were either too polite to comment or didn't actually like tea. The pot, and the cups, were of unexceptionable design, the water was of exactly the right temperature, and flowed freely from the teapot's spout, but the beverage was completely transparent and tasted of nothing. They were novels for people who liked to have a novel always to hand, but did not much care for the reading process itself. You could put them down as easily as you picked them up, and five minutes after you finished one you wouldn't remember a single word of it. Naturally he had never conveyed this opinion to Norris himself. Their friendship depended on a tacit agreement not to discuss each other's work. Norris was the perfect English gentleman – it was what made his company so restful – and a disapprobation of anything that might resemble 'talking shop' was entirely consistent with his character. Norris's private word to him before lunch, on the morrow of the first night of *Guy Domville*, had been the only occasion on which he had explicitly complimented Henry on his writing, which was why he had been genuinely moved by it.

After he had spent his hour with the Norrises he would leave them to change for dinner – a ritual they observed religiously even in the summer months – and return to the Osborne to dine contentedly alone, with a book propped up on his table. Once he accepted an invitation to dinner at Underbank, but found the meal overtaxed their collective ability to maintain a three-cornered conversation, and pleaded the pressure of work to excuse himself thereafter. And indeed he did sometimes put in another hour after dinner, going over what he had written in the morning and revising it, before retiring and falling asleep lulled by the faint whisper of waves breaking on the shore. His residence at the Osborne was proving, as he wrote to Anne Ritchie, both productive and restorative.

He owed her a letter, but what had prompted him to write was the association in his mind of Norris with Leslie Stephen, whose sister-in-law she was by his first marriage. He concluded the letter, signed and sealed it, and took it to the hotel's reception desk to be posted. A message for him had just arrived from John Plater, his bicycling instructor, apologetically cancelling the afternoon's lesson. He was downcast for a moment, then reflected: why should he not take a spin on his own along the sea-road? He had managed well enough on his last outing. Accordingly he changed into plus-fours and Norfolk jacket, put on a soft cap, and fetched his bike from the stables at the back of the hotel where it was kept. Rather than entertain other guests by attempting to mount the machine on the carriage drive in full view of their windows and balconies, he wheeled it out of the hotel grounds and on to the Meadfoot Road. After one false start and a few alarming wobbles, he got the bike under way and pedalled stoutly.

It was a pleasant, sunny afternoon, with a light breeze from the south that, augmented by his movement through the air, stirred his beard and cooled his cheeks agreeably. As always he felt exhilarated by the surge of speed compared with mere walking. In a few minutes he had travelled half a mile. What a wonderful invention it was! So simple, and so ingenious. Why had it taken mankind so long to realise that, given a certain momentum, a human being could balance indefinitely on two wheels? The combination of Momentum and Balance was the secret – and one might draw an analogy here with the art of fiction: momentum was the onward drive of narrative, the raising of questions to which the audience desired to know the answers, and balance was the symmetry of structure, the elimination of the irrelevant, the repetition of motifs and symbols, the elegant variation of—

At this point in his reverie a very small perambulator suddenly rolled out of a side alley in front of him, pursued by a young woman and a little girl. He braked hard, his front wheel locked and skidded in some loose gravel on the road, the bicycle overturned and he tumbled to the ground. The woman – she appeared to be a nursemaid – helped him rise to his feet. The little girl, aged about five, looked on from the side of the road with round eyes and a pale face.

'Are you all right, sir?' the woman asked anxiously.

'I think so,' he said, feeling himself, and flexing his limbs. He had grazed his hand – the left one fortunately, not his writing hand – and he would have a fresh bruise tomorrow on his shin, but otherwise he seemed to be all right. He picked up his bicycle. The handlebar was twisted slightly on its axis, but the machine did not appear to be seriously damaged.

'That was very careless of you, Miss Agatha, letting go of your pram,' the maid scolded the little girl. 'You might have killed the gentleman.'

'I hardly think so,' he said, smiling to reassure Agatha, whose lower lip was trembling. 'It was partly my own fault. I omitted to apply the back brake before putting on the front one.' It was a lesson Plater had often impressed upon him. 'But Dolly may have suffered worse injury, I fear,' he added. The perambulator had overturned in the road and the doll was sprawled face down, like the victim of a crime.

'Oh, don't mind that, sir,' said the maid, picking up the doll and righting the perambulator. 'As long as *you're* all right.'

'Quite all right, thank you,' he said. 'Good day to you.' Plater always insisted that he got back on the bike immediately after a fall (*'Else you'll lose your nerve, Mr James'*), so he valiantly remounted and pedalled away.

He interpreted this mishap as a warning against hubris – not only with respect to bicycling, but also (to extend the analogy which he had been developing when it happened) with respect to the literary life. He was very pleased with his new play, now called *Summersoft*, but reminded himself, when he dispatched it to Ellen Terry in the middle of August, of how many unforeseen obstacles and unexpected resistances might prevail against it. The wisdom of adopting this philosophic attitude was quickly confirmed. Ellen Terry wrote back after a few days to say that she liked the play, but would not be able to perform it in America as the programme for the tour was already decided and her departure imminent. She wished, however, to acquire the rights for a production next year.

He decided to go up to London at the end of the month to ascertain in person and in more detail her opinion of the play and its prospects, and to stay on for a week or so to take care of other business and social obligations. He had agreed to meet the Benedicts, mother and daughter, who were returning to America from England, and help them on their way (he did so purely out of piety to Fenimore's memory, not to say as a penance, for he found their company tedious). He had a longstanding invitation, which could not politely be deferred for much longer, to visit the Humphry Wards at their grand new country house in Hertfordshire. He also intended to call on the Du Mauriers at their new address in Oxford Square, but on the very day of his departure from Torquay he received a letter from Folkestone, where they had finally decided to take a holiday of some weeks' duration, expressing a hope that they might see him there. Du Maurier didn't seem to be enjoying himself very much: his health was indifferent, his nerves irritable, and he was fretting about Tree's forthcoming production of *Trilby*. Henry dashed off a hurried reply, promising to pay '*Carino Kikaccio mio*' a brief visit before he returned to 'this sweet and soothing spot for which I have a really you-and-Whitby-like tenderness'. He added: 'I am very sorry indeed to hear that you have been nervous and unwell but we will change all that; just wait till I get hold of you. I've wondered about your theatricals and you must tell me all.'

Pressed for time by preparations for her American tour, Ellen Terry was able to grant him only a very brief interview in her box at the Lyceum one evening, but she was encouragingly complimentary about *Summersoft* in general terms, and, as always, gracious and charming. The following day she sent him a cheque for £100 for the rights in 'your Gem', and renewed her promise to produce the play on her return. 'It will seem a long year,' he replied, gratefully acknowledging the payment, 'but art *is* long, ah me! At all events, if the Americans are not to have the Gem, do excruciate them with a suspicion of what they lose.' As he sealed the envelope he reflected that he had very little real hope that she would ever perform the play – and was rather pleased to note that he was not in the least depressed by this thought. Perhaps he had at last achieved detachment from theatrical ambitions.

The following weekend he made his promised visit to Folkestone to see the Du Mauriers. Why they had chosen this resort for their summer vacation, when they could afford to go anywhere in the world, was something of a mystery, but they had never been an adventurous couple and it was probably the safe banality of the place that had attracted them. They had based themselves in a modest private hotel on the high cliffs to the west of the town, known as the Leas, which had been extensively developed to attract visitors. There was a broad and immensely long promenade, a zigzag path that led down to the shingly beach hundreds of feet below, a pretty iron bandstand, and a terrace from which you could see the long arm of the harbour wall and watch the cross-Channel steamers, small as toy boats on a pond, going in and out. Gardens and lawns were neatly laid out along the clifftop between the promenade and the rows of dignified white stucco houses and hotels. It was Bayswater-by-the-Sea.

He and Du Maurier spent a good deal of time strolling up and down the promenade and hanging over the balustrade of the terrace as they talked, since walking down the path to the beach entailed an exhausting climb back or an uneasy ascent in the creaking Sandgate Lift. They were usually alone, for Emma found the exposed and shadeless promenade uncomfortable in the exceptionally hot weather. Du Maurier himself was still, as he had described himself in his letter, out of sorts, and seemed to derive little zest from the continuing success and fame of *Trilby*. Total sales of the novel in England and America, he informed Henry almost gloomily, were approaching a quarter of a million. It was the most requested book in the history of the Chicago public library system. The New York stage version was a hit, and some twenty other productions had been mounted or were in preparation elsewhere in the United States. Advance booking at the Lyceum for Tree's production was unprecedented. A new town in Florida had been named Trilby.

'My dear Kiki, this is tremendous,' Henry said. 'I congratulate you on your success.'

Du Maurier shrugged. 'It's not just success – it's a "boom", and there's something freakish and unnatural about the phenomenon, in my opinion. Why me? Thackeray never had a boom – *you* never had a boom, Henry—'

'And never will,' he interpolated.

'Well, that may be a blessing in disguise. When I was young I used to dream of being a famous painter – I mean, a really famous painter, like Leighton, say, or Burne-Jones. And I think I could have carried it off if it had happened, because I've always thought of myself as an artist. Writing novels was a kind of afterthought when my sight began to fail. Of course I made them as good as I could, but I would rather have been a successful painter than a successful novelist. Painters don't have booms.' He added after a pause: 'Not yet, anyway – who knows what the future holds?'

'How is the new novel progressing?'

'Very slowly. It's another of the drawbacks of a boom – you know all the critics are waiting for you to fall over your feet next time, so you keep rewriting.'

'What is it to be called?'

'*Soured by Success*,' Du Maurier said with a wry smile. 'No, it's called *The Martian*. Don't ask me to explain.'

They had reached the eastern end of the promenade, where there was a statue of William Harvey, a native of the town, who had discovered the circulation of the blood. 'There's a man who has done more for humanity than any of us,' said Du Maurier sententiously, 'and never had a boom.'

Later, over tea in the hotel lounge, Henry asked about the forthcoming stage production of *Trilby*, in which Kiki took a proprietary interest, but in a curiously arm's-length fashion, as if he hoped it would succeed but was slightly ashamed of it. 'It's an awfully simplified version of the story, I'm afraid – but I suppose it has to be,' he said defensively. Tree was obviously anxious to have his approval of the production: he had shown him Potter's script and invited him to collaborate on improving it, and had involved him in the crucial casting of Trilby. Du Maurier had championed a little-known actress called Dorothea Baird, whose family were friends of Charles Millar, and after offering some resistance, Tree had agreed. Miss Baird was apparently physically perfect for the part, even down to her large but shapely feet, and had auditioned extremely well, but now Du Maurier was feeling the burden of responsibility for the choice and awaiting the verdict of the public with apprehension.

'Exactly as I felt when we cast Elizabeth Robins for Claire Cintré in *The American*!' Henry exclaimed. 'Have you seen her in rehearsals?'

'No, no, I don't go,' said Du Maurier. 'But Gerald says she's very good. He's playing Dodor, the dragoon, you know – a character based on his uncle, so he shouldn't have any difficulty with the role. He's being paid four pounds a week, which he spends in a day. But I make him an allowance, because he keeps me informed of what's going on. And he's made some improvements in the play.'

'Gerald has?' Henry was surprised.

'Yes, though he makes it seem as if Tree thought of them himself.'

'I think your son will go far in the theatre, Kiki.'

'I think so too,' said Du Maurier, smiling.

Trilby was due to open in Manchester in a week's time, and would have a short provincial tour before going to London. Du Maurier said he wouldn't be going to the Manchester first night, but was sending Charles to see it and report back. 'I'm surprised you can keep away,' said Henry. 'I know I couldn't.'

'I can't face the botheration. I shall have to go to the London opening, I suppose – that will be quite enough to cope with. I hope we'll see you there – shall I reserve seats for you? It's the 30th of October.'

'It's very kind of you, Kiki, but I'm not sure that I'll be back in London by then,' he said quickly. 'I'm going to stay on in Torquay while De Vere Gardens is being electrified.' This was true: he had decided to have the flat redecorated while he was away – it was long overdue – and had taken up an advantageous offer from the landlord to share the cost of installing electric light at the same time. In no circumstances, however, would he have contemplated attending the London premiere of *Trilby*. It was likely to be a huge success, with Du Maurier no doubt being induced to share the rapturous applause at the end, and the contrast with the first night of *Guy Domville*, and his own ignominious role in it, would be too bitter to bear. It was hard enough to conceal his envy at the amount of money Du Maurier must be earning from his book. A quarter of a million copies! He wrote to Gosse on his return to Torquay that Du Maurier was in low spirits 'in spite of the chink – what say I, the "chink" – the deafening roar – of sordid gold flowing in to him. I came back feeling an even worse failure than usual.'

In due course he received word from Du Maurier that, according to his son-in-law's report, the Manchester premiere had been a triumph. Tree had mesmerised the audience and Dorothea Baird had charmed them, and the auguries for London were most propitious. It was easier to respond enthusiastically in writing than in person. 'I most heartily and ecstatically rejoice, my dear Kiki,' he wrote back, sitting soberly at his desk in the Osborne, 'and clap my hands, I perform fandangos, *je me livre à toutes les extravagances de la joie la plus folle. Allons*, it's all exactly as it should be.' But, to ensure that he would not be able to attend the London first night, he invited Jonathan Sturges to come down to Torquay and stay at the Osborne for a week at the end of October.

With *Summersoft* in cold storage he returned to work on 'The House Beautiful', now retitled 'The Old Things', but with some anxiety. It was not that he lacked faith in the potential of its subject or the elegance of its form. The problem was that the tale kept growing longer and longer without getting any nearer its conclusion. Originally he had proposed it to Scudder, editor of the *Atlantic*, as one of three short stories the magazine had gratifyingly offered to commission, each to be of approximately ten thousand words. But the 'scenario' itself had soon exceeded this limit, and by the time Scudder had agreed an additional 5,000 words, the manuscript stood at 25,000. It was obviously threatening to turn into a short, or even medium-length, novel. He put it aside and began another story, called 'The Awkward Age', about young girls 'coming out' in a decadent London society setting, but that too soon developed the rhythm and scope of a full-length novel. He put *that* aside too, and in desperation dashed off a lightweight story called 'Glasses' to keep Scudder happy, then went back to 'The Old Things', which the editor had shown some disposition to take as a serial.

The Indian summer continued into October. A delicate pearly mist enveloped the hills in the early morning, but burned away by midday to leave a clear blue sky, and at night the reflected moon made a silver pathway on the calm sea. With some regret he gave up biking: the hills in the neighbourhood were too steep for him and he was bored with riding up and down the Meadfoot Road. He walked for exercise, and one day encountered little Agatha again, accompanied by her nursemaid, and trailing a puppy on a lead which she had just been given for her fifth birthday. He stopped and chatted for a while about the care of dogs, to show he bore no ill feeling for the accident. He missed Tosca, who was being looked after by the Smiths, and felt a little guilty at having left her to endure the noise and disturbance that would be caused by the electrification of the flat.

The weather was still holding when Jonathan Sturges came down. As always the brave and resourceful style with which he bore his crippled state, hopping nimbly about on his sticks, was an example and a reproof to one's own selfish discontents, but he was unusually melancholy. It seemed that he had fallen in love with a woman in France, and had, in the gentlest possible way – but no less wounding for that – been rebuffed. There was absolutely nothing to be done about it, or said. All one could do was to offer general kindness and comfort, like a silent handclasp. Only once did a note of something like bitterness escape Sturges's lips, and then in the most allusive and oblique way. He was talking one evening before dinner, as they sat in Norris's garden, smoking cigarettes and watching the changing colours of the sunset in the sky, of meeting William Howells a year and a half ago, at a party in Whistler's garden in Paris. Howells had been much taken with the glamour and elegance of the company and the setting, all the more because he was about to leave Paris prematurely and return to America on account of the death of his father. In the course of their conversation he seemed to be suddenly seized by a prophetic insight and, putting his hand on Sturges's shoulder, had said something like: 'You are young, you are young – be glad of it and *live*. Live all you can – it's a mistake not to. It doesn't matter so much what you do – but live. This place makes it all come over me. I see it now. I haven't done so – and now I'm old. It's too late. It has gone past me. You have time. Live!' After quoting this speech Sturges crushed his cigarette under his heel and added wryly: 'All very well to tell me to "live!" It's not so easy when you can't move a yard without these.' He grasped the two sticks that were leaning against his seat and raised them languidly in the air like clipped and useless wings.

It certainly seemed a tactless remark by Howells, but clearly his old friend had been so consumed by the sense of having let life slip through his fingers that he hadn't reflected on the plight of the young man whom he was addressing. Henry was deeply struck by the poignancy of the anecdote, and perhaps because he was closer to Howells's age identified with him rather than with the younger participant in the scene. For a scene was what it very rapidly composed itself into in his mind: an old high-walled Paris garden, the swish of ladies' skirts over the lawn, the tinkle of fine china and glassware, the fragrance of cigars, the brilliant, witty, civilised talk . . . and looking on, taking it all in with a hungry late-awakened appetite, the grizzled, middle-aged American. It was surely a *sujet de roman*. What had brought him there – not Howells of course, but the fictional hero who began at once dimly to stir in his imagination – and what had precipitated this soul-searching utterance? He recorded the anecdote in his notebook the next morning, with a tentative sketch of the fictional story that might grow from this seed.

The date of this entry was the 31st October. His long sojourn in Devon was coming to an end – the next day he would accompany Sturges, who was far from well and needed to see a specialist, back to London. He had enjoyed his time at the Osborne enormously, but he had not made any effort to look for a house of his own in the locality. Charming as the place was, it was just too far from London to be convenient, and too hilly to be explored by bicycle. He must seek his ideal country retreat elsewhere, next summer.

Returning to London was less disagreeable than he had anticipated. Tosca's ecstasy at seeing him again was gratifying, and the bright appearance of the redecorated rooms at De Vere Gardens under the new electric lights was a considerable compensation for the shortening of the days and the pollution of the air. One of his first social calls was at the Du Mauriers' newly acquired house at 17 Oxford

Square, which also enjoyed electric lighting but seemed quite gloomy in comparison. He gathered from Emma that Kiki had been delighted with the electricity at first, all the more because of his poor sight, and kept the house in an almost dazzling blaze of light until the first bill came, after which, in spite of all the money pouring in from *Trilby*, he had several of the sconces turned off. It was a substantial and well-appointed town house, and in comfort an undoubted improvement on New Grove House (which had never even had a proper bathroom), but it lacked character. Neither Kiki nor Emma seemed quite at ease in it, and the familiar furniture they had brought with them from Hampstead looked shabby and out of place. In Hampstead the studio had been the centre of the house – a room for music-making and reading and entertaining as well as a place to work. In Oxford Square there were more rooms, each dedicated to a different function in the bourgeois way, and Kiki and Emma circulated dutifully from one to another according to the time of day without looking really at ease in any of them.

But Beerbohm Tree's production of *Trilby* was the talk of the town. Dorothea Baird had become a star overnight, and all the critics had acclaimed Tree's performance as Svengali, with the exception (especially interesting to Henry in the light of his conversation with Du Maurier earlier that year) of George Bernard Shaw, who condemned it as crudely melodramatic. His dissenting opinion, however, had no effect on the demand for tickets at the Lyceum. 'I may solicit your help in that connection, Kiki,' said Henry.

'Just say the word. But you needn't rush – Tree predicts it will run for a year,' Du Maurier said, with the air of bemused fatigue that was now becoming habitual with him. There was obviously no end in sight to the *Trilby* boom. Royalty itself had succumbed: the first night had been graced with the presence of the Prince and Princess of Wales, and Du Maurier had been invited to the Royal Box and presented.

'Did they enjoy the play?' Henry asked.

'The Princess said she didn't like Dorothea Baird having bare feet, which suggests that she hasn't read the book.'

'She must be the only person in England who hasn't, then,' said Henry. 'What else did they say?'

'I can't remember anything else,' said Du Maurier. 'I wasn't quite the ticket that evening.'

'You were ill, Kiki,' said Emma, 'and should have been tucked up in bed by rights. But he made the effort,' she said, turning to Henry, 'because people would have been so disappointed.'

'And did you make a curtain speech?' he asked.

'I did, but I can't remember that either.'

'He made a very nice speech,' said Emma loyally, 'complimenting Dorothea Baird and thanking Mr Tree and making a joke about Gerald, and everybody laughed and clapped.'

'And how is Gerald?' Henry asked.

'Having the time of his life,' said Du Maurier, smiling, 'and praying that Tree will fall ill one day so that he can step into the breach. But I told him that that kind of luck only happens once.' He was referring to an already legendary feat of Gerald's during his first professional engagement, as a waiter in *The Old Jew* at the Garrick, in which John Hare played the title role. Gerald had observed his performance so closely and was so familiar with his lines that when Hare suddenly became ill he was able to take over the role the very same night. His son's involvement in *Trilby* was the only thing about it that seemed to give Du Maurier any real pleasure. He was still grinding away at *The Martian*, and in spite of being now nearly blind continued to contribute to *Punch*, drawing on a very large scale so that he could see what he was doing. As it happened, shortly after this meeting he produced one of his best cartoons for a long time. The cross-hatching was rather coarse, and the drawing of the figures lacked subtlety, but the composition was strong and the joke a good one. Entitled 'True Humility', it depicted a smooth, eager-to-please young curate taking breakfast with his bishop and family. The caption was: *Right Reverend Host.* 'I'm afraid you've got a bad egg, Mr Jones!' *The Curate.* 'Oh no, my lord, I assure you! Parts of it are excellent!'

Henry no longer 'took' *Punch* – he hadn't for years – and relied on seeing it at his club or in the houses of friends. He was shown the cartoon by Edward Warren, when he dined with him and his pretty wife Margaret at their little house in Westminster soon after his return from Torquay, and they chuckled over it together before the meal. He liked this couple very much and was godfather to their first child, repeating the baptismal link with which their acquaintance had begun. Warren was doing well in his architectural career, and was also something of an artist. A pencil-and-wash picture of a curious old building, recently executed and displayed on the wall of the sitting room, particularly caught Henry's eye. The building was of red brick with stone detailing, and had a large handsome bow-fronted window on the first floor, but a humble wooden door at ground level such as one might see on a stable or barn. 'This is charming,' he said. 'What is the building?'

'It's the Garden Room of Lamb House, in Rye,' Warren said. 'A kind of Georgian gazebo, I suppose one might call it. The house itself is somewhat older, and probably the finest in Rye.' He and Margaret had spent the summer in a cottage at Playden, just outside Rye, and were full of enthusiasm for this corner of East Sussex. In fact they had written to Henry urging him to come and sample its attractions, but comfortably ensconced in the Osborne he had politely demurred. Now, over dinner, he listened to their enthusiastic description with keener attention, explaining that he would be looking for a place to retreat to during the summer months of next year.

'Blomfield's cottage at Playden would be the very thing for you,' said Warren, and the more he heard about it the more promising it seemed. Reginald Blomfield was a friend of Edward's and a respected architect. He was building a number of private houses on a site called Point Hill overlooking Rye and the Romney Marshes, and had a summer place of his own there which Edward thought he would be very willing to let Henry rent cheaply in the early summer.

'And are there roads through the Romney Marshes – where one might ride a bicycle?' he asked.

'Absolutely! Flat roads that go on for miles. And charming villages with wonderful old churches to explore.'

'It sounds like just the place I'm looking for,' he said, and Warren promised to make enquiries on his behalf.

At the end of the meal Margaret left them at the table to finish the wine while she went to check that her infant was sleeping soundly upstairs. Warren asked him what he was writing, and he told him about *The Old Things*, which the *Atlantic* had mercifully agreed to take as a serial, and which he hoped to finish by the end of the year. 'And will you write any more plays?' Warren asked. 'I do hope that beastly experience last January hasn't put you off.'

He hesitated for a moment to break the vow of secrecy he had imposed on himself as regards *Summersoft*, but he was relaxed by the good food and wine and the warmth of the hearth fire at his back, and he desperately wanted at least *one* other person in the world to know that he had been commissioned by Ellen Terry to write a play for her, and had completed the task to her satisfaction. No confidant could be more reliable and discreet than Warren. 'Well, strictly for your ears only . . .' he began, and briefly related the history of the play and its prospect of production next year.

Warren was impressed and delighted. 'That's wonderful, James! What a splendid riposte to your critics!'

'It may of course never reach the stage,' he said. 'I've learned not to rely on theatrical promises.'

'Even so, this proves that it wasn't only your friends who admired *Guy Domville*,' Warren said. 'Ellen Terry must have been really impressed when she saw it, in spite of the loutish behaviour of the gallery.'

'That was indeed – at the time – a small reassuring thought to salvage from the *débâcle*,' he admitted.

'It really was a very good play, you know, Henry,' Warren said kindly. 'You should be proud of it.'

He meditated his response to this remark for a moment. 'It was, shall we say, good in parts,' he said. 'Like the curate's egg.' It took Warren another moment to place the reference, then he threw back his head and laughed heartily. Henry, pleased by his own witticism, joined in the laughter. It occurred to him later, recalling this convivial moment as he walked home, that if he was able to make a jest at the expense of *Guy Domville*, then the wound its failure had inflicted on his soul must finally be healed.

5

IN the late spring of the following year, 1896, he moved into the Blomfields' cottage at Playden, having rented it for three months at a very moderate rate. He was hugely pleased with his situation, which was superior even to the Osborne both scenically and in amenities. The cottage was perched on the edge of Point Hill, a high escarpment which rose abruptly from the level plain of the Romney Marshes and faced the sea a few miles away. From the terrace, where he spent many hours, and dined most evenings due to the uncommonly fine weather, he enjoyed a view that might have been painted by some Italian or Flemish master. To his right the town of Rye, girdled with an ancient wall, conical in outline, and surmounted by its medieval church tower, was reminiscent of the picturesque hill towns in the background of old religious pictures that often drew one's eye away from the martyrdoms or miracles in the foreground. Immediately below him the River Rother uncoiled itself lazily towards the sea, and to his left the marshes, which were in fact lush fields grazed by sheep and cattle, spread out in a hazy expanse punctuated with clusters of trees and the occasional church steeple. Long ago, in the Middle Ages, when the sea had covered most of this land, Rye had been a flourishing port. But the sea had withdrawn, dykes had been built to prevent its return, and the marshes drained. Rye had been left high and dry, connected to the sea only by a narrow channel, and a similar fate had been suffered by two other Cinque Ports (as they were collectively known), Winchelsea and Old Romney. But the decline of their commercial importance had largely preserved them, and the whole area, from the disfigurements of the Industrial Revolution, making this pocket of southern England a kind of historical-geographical anomaly, a delightful secret known only to its natives and a small confraternity of occasional residents from outside (Ellen Terry, for instance, had a cottage in Winchelsea).

The Blomfield cottage was a modest bungalow, but quite large enough for his needs, and he was well looked after by the local servants. For company he had brought Tosca with him, and a singing canary in a cage, the gift of a female friend. He also brought his bike, and used it to explore the Romney towns and villages in the afternoons. The mornings, as usual, were dedicated to work. He put the finishing touches to *The Old Things*, which began appearing in the *Atlantic* in April (it finally amounted to about 75,000 words), and started work on another, shorter serial for the *Illustrated London News*, called *The Other House*, based on his unperformed play about the murder of a child by a jealous woman. He had never written for such a popular magazine before, nor had he ever written about murder before. It was the closest thing in his *oeuvre*, he supposed, to a 'sensation novel'. But it was well paid, and cost him little effort – he kept closely to the original dramatic structure, and merely expanded it with additional dialogue and some scene-setting descriptions. He was becoming pragmatic, to use one of William's favourite words, about his writing career. If he couldn't make money from the theatre, then he must make it where he could.

He enjoyed strolling around Rye – its steep and narrow cobbled streets were unsuitable for cycling – browsing in the bookshops, pricing items in the curiosity shops, lounging on the ramparts of the Ypres Tower, and reading the inscriptions on the gravestones in the churchyard. St Mary's was a Norman church much added to and restored, with Gothic flying buttresses, an eighteenth-century clock with mechanical moving figures to strike the hour, and a recently installed, rather beautiful window of the Nativity designed by Burne-Jones and fabricated by Morris. From the parapet of its square tower you could see for twenty miles. It stood inside a churchyard studded with ancient graves and hemmed on four sides by quaint little clapboard cottages. One day, strolling off this square into West Street, he recognised with a little thrill of pleasure the distinctive shape of the Garden Room that Edward Warren had sketched. It was attached to its parent, Lamb House, at a right angle in the cobbled grass-grown roadway, which descended steeply to the High Street. The architecture of the main house was plainer than the garden extension, but very pleasing to the eye: a solid, honest English gentleman's residence of mature red brick, with seven sash windows, a handsome canopied front door with a fine brass knocker, and three stone steps down to the pavement. It was an immensely attractive house, and he coveted it instantly. He lingered in the street for some time, and peered impertinently through a ground-floor window, though without being able to glimpse more than a corner of a snug wallpapered parlour. The top of a large mulberry tree visible over the wall between the gazebo and the main house hinted tantalisingly at the existence of a spacious garden. He enquired at the nearest shop, an iron-monger's, as to whether Lamb House was likely to be available for rent, and received a discouraging reply. It was owned by a Mr Francis Bellingham, a retired banker and former mayor of Rye, who occupied it with his wife and son, and the presumption was that the son would take it over when his parents died. Disappointed, he nevertheless left his name and address with the ironmonger and begged to be informed if the house should unexpectedly become available in the future.

His lease of the cottage on Point Hill ran out at the end of July, and he was unable to extend it, since the Blomfields would be spending the rest of the summer there. He liked the area so much, and was so reluctant to return to London in the dog days, that he looked for another place to rent in Rye, and discovered that a house near the church known as the Old Vicarage was luckily available. It was scruffier than the Blomfields' cottage, and lacked the latter's modern plumbing, but it was more spacious, and had a little back garden from which you could see a segment of the same view, and look up at the gulls wheeling and crying overhead. Here he began work on a new story, which showed every sign of growing into a novel, about a little girl called Maisie who became the victim, witness and pawn of her adulterous parents and their respective lovers; the technical feat of presenting a depraved adult world through the eyes of a perceptive but innocent consciousness was proving peculiarly fascinating.

He brought the Smiths down from De Vere Gardens to look after him – and so that he could keep a closer eye on Smith, who had made alarming inroads into his modest cellar in his absence. He suspected that the man was in a permanent state of mild inebriation, but it was difficult to accuse him because he artfully disguised the symptoms under the habitual extravagance of his professional manner, swooping and twirling around the dining table, producing dishes and carafes out of the air like a conjuror, or standing to attention at the sideboard with glazed eyes and impassive countenance while his master and guests consumed their food. A writer called Ford Madox Hueffer, a tall slender young man with centre-parted yellow hair, who was staying with relatives at Winchelsea and had asked to meet him on the strength of an alleged admiration for his work, came to lunch and had been so discomposed by Smith's idiosyncratic style of serving food, swinging each dish round from behind his back like a discus and arresting it inches from the recipient's top waistcoat button before lowering it to the table, that Henry had openly reprimanded the man, but it made no difference. Smith's aloof bearing seemed to convey the message: *'If you wish to be waited on by an earl's butler, you must tolerate a degree of eccentricity.'* Hueffer was the grandson of the painter Ford Madox Brown, one of the more respectable members of the Pre-Raphaelite group, whom Du Maurier had brilliantly satirised in *Punch* in the parodic illustrations and doggerel verse of his 'Legend of Camelot'. Henry had so relished this piece at the time that he had committed much of it to memory, and he was still able to recite some lines about Rossetti's women:

> *'O Moses what a precious lot,*
> *Of beautiful red hair they've got!*
>
> *How much their upper lips do pout!*
> *How very much their chins stick out!*
>
> *How dreadful strange they stare! They seem*
> *Half to be dead and half to dream.'*

The verses still made him laugh, even if young Hueffer's amusement was more restrained.

●

Not long afterwards he received a worrying letter from Du Maurier, who unwisely had gone back to Whitby once again with Emma and the family, exposing himself to its frigid blasts of North Sea air and pitting himself against its unforgiving inclines. His health had evidently suffered in consequence, though he characteristically covered this information with a joke: 'It's only when struggling uphill that one realises how fast one is going downhill.' His old friend and hero, Millais, had died of cancer earlier in August, and he had been invited to be a pall-bearer at the funeral in St Paul's Cathedral, but he had had to excuse himself and was not even well enough to attend the service. Knowing how devoted Du Maurier had been to Millais, Henry took this to be a grave indication of his state of health. He had finished *The Martian* at last, but was still working on the illustrations, and thought his good eye would just about see him through this task. Henry replied with sympathetic concern and urged him to moderate his usual rigorous Whitby regime.

The next thing he heard was that, on his return to London in September, Kiki had been told by his doctor that he had overstrained himself by climbing too many steep hills, and was ordered to spend three weeks in bed, to which he had submitted with much reluctance and grumbling. When he next had occasion to run up to London, Henry went to see him in Oxford Square. Outside the house he met Tom Armstrong, Du Maurier's old chum from 'Trilby' days in Paris and now the distinguished head of the College of Art in Kensington. He was bent on the same mission, so they saw the invalid together, sitting on upright chairs beside his bed. Kiki's appearance was a shock. He was haggard and hollow-cheeked, and seemed thinner than ever in his nightshirt with a shawl round his bony shoulders. He was suffering from several symptoms, trivial individually, but collectively debilitating: acute dyspepsia, infected gums, and a wheezing asthmatic cough, not helped by his insistence on continuing to smoke in spite of the doctor's advice. 'Life really isn't worth living without the occasional smoke, especially when you can't take solid food,' he said with a naughty grin, puffing away at one of his hand-rolled cigarettes, and brushing the ash off his blankets in case Emma should see it.

They chatted about the success of *Trilby*, which had just ended its long run at the Lyceum and set off on another provincial tour preparatory to going to America – it seemed that in spite of having numerous productions of their own the Americans craved to see Tree's already legendary performance. Henry had seen the play the previous winter, and found it, as he expected, a vulgar but tolerably entertaining version of the novel, with much prurient emphasis on Trilby's sitting 'for the altogether' in the first half, and some lively singing and dancing, notably a *cancan* in the Christmas party scene in which Gerald flung himself about the stage in his dragoon's uniform with perspiring abandon. Tree had built up the character of Svengali into a dominating presence – a capering, gloating, eye-rolling, yellow-fanged, greasy-locked villain, who manipulated all the other characters like puppets. Henry remarked that the actor pronounced the name 'Svengali' with a long 'a', making it sound much more sinister than Du Maurier's own pronunciation, which rhymed with 'alley'.

'Yes,' said Kiki, 'and now everybody says "*Svenghaali*", like Tree, so I suppose *I'll* have to as well. I hardly feel the story belongs to me any more. It's got out of my control. Did you know there's now a man's hat called a Trilby, like the one Dorothea Baird wears in the first act?'

'Yes, indeed,' said Tom Armstrong, 'and selling like hot cakes, I was told in Lock's.'

'There's no such hat in my book, of course,' Kiki grumbled.

The presence of Armstrong, whom Henry did not know very well, prevented any really intimate personal conversation, a circumstance which he deeply regretted later, for this proved to be the last occasion when he saw his friend alive. The end came with shocking suddenness a few weeks later – or at least it seemed sudden to Henry, who had been hard at work in the seclusion of the Rye Vicarage. At the beginning of October he and his retinue returned to De Vere Gardens, and he found a note from Emma telling him that Kiki's condition had worsened. When he enquired what would be a convenient time to see him she wrote back to say that he was really too weak to receive visitors. A new specialist had been called in who had diagnosed an ominous-sounding condition called 'matter around the heart'. A few days later, Kiki was dead. He was sixty-two.

It seemed that, like Alice, Du Maurier had expressed an unconventional wish to be cremated. Henry learned that his corpse made the same railway journey to Woking, attended by a small party of relatives who brought back the ashes for interment in the churchyard of Hampstead parish church a few days later. In spite of Du Maurier's well-advertised agnosticism, Canon Ainger had agreed readily to hold a funeral service and presided himself, assisted by two other local clergymen. It was a cool, blowy October day, with leaves drifting down from the trees and carpeting the footpaths. Inside the church the urn containing Du Maurier's ashes had been placed on a bier at the foot of the chancel steps, covered in wreaths. The pews were packed with mourners: distinguished artists and writers, *Punch* colleagues, Hampstead neighbours, old friends from the student years in Paris, and, occupying the first two or three rows, the extended Du Maurier family, all in deep mourning apart from Guy, resplendent in his Captain's dress uniform: the men grave, the women struggling to suppress their tears, and the two grandchildren who were deemed old enough to attend awestruck. It was an emotional occasion. Ainger spoke eloquently about his old friend and walking companion, and some of Du Maurier's favourite music was played on the organ, Schumann's 'Der Nussbaum' and Schubert's 'Serenade' and 'Adieu' – or so it said in the order of service. Henry did not recognise any of the tunes, though he remembered vividly the mild March evening years ago when they had passed beneath an open window in Porchester Square from which issued the sound of a male tenor voice and an accompanying piano, and Kiki had stopped and, lifting his finger, said: 'Ah, Schubert's Serenade!'

The bier was carried in solemn procession to the New Churchyard on the other side of Church Row, the original one having long been filled up with generations of the dead going back centuries. Ainger read the last prayers of the funeral service over the open grave, 'I am the resurrection and the life . . .' The urn was lowered, and the grave filled in. Du Maurier's daughters wept quietly, clinging to each other, but Emma was stronger, standing straight-backed with a grandson on each side, clasping their little hands in hers, her face inscrutable under its veil.

Ainger had invited the family and friends to his house afterwards for some refreshment. 'You *will* come, won't you, Mr James?' Emma said to him in the churchyard as he took her hand in both of his own, and held it and squeezed it. She preserved her customary formality of address even at this emotional moment, while he himself was almost lost for words.

'My dear Emma – if I may presume – do please call me Henry – this is – this is—' He shook his head helplessly. 'So sad,' he concluded lamely. 'How do you bear it so bravely?'

'I've known in my heart for some time that Kiki was not going to get better,' she said. 'It was not such a shock to me as for others.'

'He was a dear, dear friend, but to you—'

'He was a wonderful husband. We had a very happy life together. I thank God for that.'

'You see how much he was loved,' he said, gesturing at the crowd of mourners milling around outside the church.

'Yes, he had many friends. But you were very special to him . . . Henry.' She hesitated over the first name and blushed a little as she pronounced it. 'He always considered himself privileged to call such a distinguished writer his friend.'

'Nonsense,' he murmured.

'It's true.'

Among the first people he spoke to at Ainger's house was Gerald, who had come up that day from Bristol where *Trilby* was playing. He was in the conservatory, smoking a cigarette, sucking the smoke into his lungs as if his life depended on it. 'I saw the Governor just two days before he died,' he said. 'He was very frail. The last thing he said to me, looking up from the pillow, almost in a whisper, was:

"*Si c'est la mort, ce n'est pas gai.*" ' Perhaps because Gerald was an actor, repeating these words seemed to have a powerful emotional effect on him, and his eyes suddenly filled with tears. He hastily wiped them away and blew his nose on his handkerchief. 'At least I was able to tell him how well the *Trilby* tour was going.' He grinned as he added: 'But I didn't tell him that Tree is thinking of dropping the fourth act. I thought it might upset him.'

'You mean – Trilby won't die?'

'No, she'll marry Little Billee. A happy ending.'

'Oh, I know all about happy endings!' he said. 'Your poor father has at least been spared that – seeing his book travestied.'

'But Tree has a point,' Gerald said, 'I mean, once Svengali's spell has been broken, and he's dead, why shouldn't they marry?'

'It would take too long to explain, my dear boy,' he said. 'But the fact that you ask the question tells me a lot about the younger generation.'

Gerald smiled. 'I must be going, Mr James,' he said. 'Must get back to Bristol for the evening performance.'

As they shook hands and Gerald departed, Du Maurier's publisher Clarence McIlvaine came up to Henry, a schooner of sherry in each hand, and gave him one of them. 'I don't really like sherry, but it's all there is – apart from coffee and tea,' he said. 'At a time like this one needs whisky.' They exchanged some platitudes about the funeral service, and then McIlvaine moved quickly on to business. He was a Princeton graduate who had done very well in publishing in a comparatively short time. He had been chosen to set up Harper's British imprint with James Osgood in 1890 to exploit the new Copyright Act, and had recently become the sole head of the firm after Osgood's untimely death. 'I'm glad to say that Du Maurier delivered his new novel before he died,' he said. 'It's called *The Martian*.'

'Yes, I know,' said Henry.

'You've read it?' McIlvaine asked, cocking an eyebrow.

'No, I know nothing about it except the title.'

'Ah. Well, we're serialising it in *Harper's*, starting in the next issue – we've brought it forward as a kind of tribute. There will of course be tremendous public interest in his last book. I recall you wrote us a very helpful piece for the weekly magazine, about *Trilby*, when we were running it in the monthly, and I was wondering if we could persuade you to do something similar again.'

'Oh,' he said, pursing his lips and frowning. 'Perhaps this is hardly the moment . . .'

'What I had in mind was a kind of obituary article – a personal piece, you know, drawing on your close association, surveying his remarkable late career as a novelist, up to and including *The Martian*. Nobody could do it as well as you, James.'

'Well, I don't know,' he said, warming to the idea somewhat. He hesitated because it would take time and energy away from his own creative projects. On the other hand he felt an urge and an obligation to pay tribute to his dead friend, and this would be an appropriate opportunity. 'How long a piece?' he asked.

'As long as you like,' said McIlvaine. 'It would be for the monthly *Harper's*.'

This was an incentive. He had learned by now that it cost him more effort to trim his work to fit a preordained limit than to let it find its own natural length. 'I've already contracted to write a "London Letter" once a month for *Harper's Weekly*,' he thought it prudent to point out.

'No matter. We'd pay a hundred dollars per thousand words up to a ceiling of, say, five hundred.'

This was generous. 'Very well,' he said.

'Excellent! I'll let you have proofs of *The Martian* as soon as they're available.'

'What's it like?'

'Interesting.' McIlvaine's enigmatic expression made him think he should have asked this question earlier. 'More like *Peter Ibbetson* than *Trilby*.'

'Oh, well, that's all right,' he said, relieved. 'I always preferred *Peter Ibbetson*.'

'But *Trilby* was the best seller.'

'I detest that barbarous Americanism!' he said emphatically.

'"Best seller"? What's the matter with it?'

'It confuses quality with quantity in a single word,' he said, 'and it's a solecism – I mean, the way it's used. I understand that the American newspapers now publish something called "best-seller lists", numbered from one to ten.'

'That's right – *The Bookman* started it, and it caught on. It's a darned good idea.'

'But how can there be more than one best seller? "Best" means "better than all the others".'

McIlvaine thought about this for a moment. 'You're quite right, of course, James – in principle. But as regards *Trilby* . . . it really *is* our best seller. I mean, we've never sold so many copies of a single book before in the company's history. And since Harper is one of the biggest general publishers in the world, and if you forget about pirate publishing in the old days, for which nobody knows the figures anyway . . . it's quite possible that *Trilby* is the best-selling novel ever.'

'Good God!' Henry said.

'A solemn thought, isn't it? Can I get you another sherry?'

'No thank you,' he said. 'I need some air.'

In fact it was at least another half an hour before he managed to escape from the reception. As he pushed his way through the crowded drawing room and hallway he was accosted by numerous friends and had to exchange greetings and words of condolence with them. He had to say goodbye to the three Du Maurier sisters, Trixy, Sylvia and May, and renew acquaintance with his godson Guy Millar, now aged seven, to whom he covertly slipped a half-sovereign, enjoining secrecy with a finger raised to his lips. The last person he spoke to was Emma, to whom he confided that he was to write an appreciation of Kiki for *Harper's*. 'That's wonderful, Henry,' she said. 'I shall look forward so much to reading it.'

He took the shortest route to the Heath, and then made his way to the old Bench of Confidences. There he sat down to calm his thoughts, which had been stirred up, first by the emotions of the funeral and then by McIlvaine's rather crass but undeniably interesting intervention. The best-selling novel ever! The *Trilby* phenomenon became more and more inexplicable – at least, no literary analysis could account for it. At some critical point in the novel's reception the momentum of sales had taken on a life of its own – the more people who read it, the more people there were who 'had to' read it; and just when interest might have been expected to flag, it was revived by the success of the stage adaptation. No wonder poor Du Maurier felt that he had lost control over his own work, that it no longer belonged to him. It was as if he had released a kind of genie from the bottle of his imagination, which swelled to alarming proportions and beat its chest and roared and danced and pranced and went whirling round the globe, returning to bury him under a suffocating heap of correspondence, newspaper gossip, and coin. No story could illustrate more vividly the vanity of human wishes, or the perils of answered prayers, as far as authors were concerned. Apart from the first few months when it was being serialised, before Whistler started complaining, poor Kiki had seldom shown any sign of enjoying the success of *Trilby*, and the wealth it brought had come too late to give him any real satisfaction. Charles Millar had a revealing anecdote of lunching at Oxford Square, when a servant brought in a registered letter which Kiki opened at the table. He had glanced at the contents and passed the envelope to Emma without a smile or flicker of interest, saying wearily: 'Another cheque from Harper's, my dear.' It was, Millar discovered later, a cheque for seven thousand pounds. Of course Kiki had the satisfaction of knowing that his family would benefit from his windfall in the future – but he would much rather have lived to share more of that future.

There were several lessons to be drawn from these reflections, some of them almost embarrassingly obvious insofar as they applied to his own literary ambitions, but the one he took most earnestly to heart was the most banal: the primacy of the gift of life itself. Kiki was dead. There was a Kiki-shaped hollow space in his world which would never be filled up. But it would, over time, be less and less noticeable. It was shocking – shocking, but there was no point in denying it – how sooner or later we accustomed ourselves to the deaths of others, even dearly loved friends, even parents and siblings. Spouses and children might be a different matter – he couldn't be sure, never having had or lost one himself – but about other forms of bereavement he could speak honestly and with conviction. However deeply and sincerely one grieved for the dead, they gradually and inevitably occupied less and less of one's conscious thoughts as time passed. He had written a story a couple of years previously, 'The Altar of the Dead', about a man who tried to arrest that process by taking over the altar of a Catholic chapel and dedicating candles to his deceased friends – he had begun it in the year of Fenimore's death, while actually staying in her old Oxford lodgings, and it had been in part a way of coming to terms with her tragic end – but when he had occasion to reread it recently there seemed something unnatural and unhealthy about his chief character's behaviour of which he had not been fully aware when he wrote it. One should remember the dead, yes, but also let them, slowly, gently, go. He would distil and preserve his memories, his friendship, and his love for George Du Maurier in a memorial essay, which should be as fine and eloquent as he could make it, and then he would move on to complete and perfect his own *oeuvre* in the years that were left to him, in that *'certain splendid "last manner"'* of which poor Dencombe, the hero of another story, had only dreamed.

As usual, this resolution was more easily formulated than carried out. First there was a purely physical impediment to the furtherance of his literary plans. Since the spring he had become increasingly troubled by a pain in his wrist, obviously caused by spending seven or eight hours a day at his desk with a pen in his hand, and by October it had become unbearable. It was not 'writer's cramp' of the familiar kind, which usually eased after a short respite, nor the more exclusive variant known as 'Trollope's thumb', named after the prolific Postmaster. It was more like rheumatism, an excruciating inflammation of the joints and tendons of the wrist which controlled every movement of the hand. His doctor told him that only extended rest, for weeks or months, would cure the condition

– an unthinkable course of action. He tried writing with his left hand, and the results looked like the efforts of an idiot child under the influence of alcohol. The only solution was to hire a secretary.

This idea came initially from William, who suggested that he might give his hand some relief by dictating his correspondence – as he himself did at Harvard, with much economy of time and effort. Henry couldn't imagine himself adopting this method except for the most impersonal business letters, but he remembered that Du Maurier had composed his novels by dictating them to Emma, and he thought to himself: why shouldn't I do the same, using a stenographer? Accordingly, after making some enquiries, he obtained the services of William MacAlpine, a young Scot for whom the epithet 'dour' seemed inappropriate, as suggesting too lively and excitable a temperament, but who was extremely competent in taking dictation and typing. At first MacAlpine took his dictation in short-hand and transcribed it on his own typewriter at home; but before long Henry purchased a Remington machine for De Vere Gardens and dictated straight to the typewriter, with an immediate improvement in efficiency. MacAlpine made fewer mistakes – indeed, hardly any – and was able to leave the day's work behind for Henry to read over and annotate in the evenings, ready for revision the next day. Sometimes he paced up and down the study as he dictated, and sometimes he lay at ease on his chaise longue. He found the click-click of the keys soothing rather than distracting, and MacAlpine was so silent and impassive that he almost forgot it was a human being with a consciousness of his own who was taking down his words. He was aware that his sentences were becoming longer and more intricately wrought under this new regime, but the stammer that so often afflicted him in social situations when he had some-thing urgent and important to say did not trouble him. There was no hurry or pressure. He could form the sentences, order and rearrange the clauses, select the words, all in his mind, or as it were in the air, holding them there for contemplation before he uttered them; and later, with the transcript in his hand, he could dictate the passage again, adding and inserting new units of sense to thicken the richness of meaning.

With the aid of this new system of composition he finished *What Maisie Knew* in December and placed it with a Chicago magazine which began serialising it in January. He corrected the proofs of *The Spoils of Poynton*, the much-revised book version of *The Old Things*, which would be published in February – the first ripe fruit, as he saw it, of his new fictional method. Now his desk was cleared and he was free to write his essay on George Du Maurier, for which McIlvaine was pressing him – four instalments of *The Martian* had appeared already in *Harper's*. But he hesitated, he stalled, he procrastinated. He made his commitment to the monthly 'London Letter' an excuse for putting off the Du Maurier article. But the real problem was that *The Martian* was a great disappointment – in fact, not to put too fine a point on it, *The Martian* was embarrassingly bad. The narrator, supposedly writing at some date in the near future, was a dull conventional Englishman called Robert Maurice who had been a schoolmate of the hero of the tale, the gifted, handsome, aristocratic Barty Josselin. Clearly Kiki had based these two characters on the English and French aspects of his own personality and life history. Thus Maurice studied chemistry at London University, while Barty Josselin studied art in Antwerp, where his hopes were dashed by losing the sight of one eye. (Henry was amused to note that this happened while Barty was painting 'an old man', not a young girl in the altogether.) It was at this point that the story lurched into the supernatural-scientific-prophetic mode that had been the undoing of *Peter Ibbetson*, but in a clumsier and even less credible fashion. Barty was rescued from suicidal despair by the intervention of a female spirit calling herself 'Martia', a native of the planet Mars, whose inhabitants, she explained, were morally and intellectually far superior to human beings and able to inhabit a multitude of physical forms. She had come to Earth in a shower of shooting stars a hundred years ago, and existed in a variety of guises, animal and human, until she adopted Barty. Having revealed her existence to him in letters which he discovered by his bedside on waking, she later took the form of one of his children by his adoring Jewish wife, Leah. (An interesting ethnic detail, this, perhaps intended to compensate for the prejudicial portrait of Jewishness in

Svengali.) Martia also dictated to him in his sleep a series of brilliant visionary books, with titles like *The Fourth Dimension* and *Interstellar Harmonics*, which made Barty into a world-famous author – not surprisingly, since according to Maurice: *'He has robbed Death of nearly all its terrors; even for the young it is no longer the grisly phantom it once was for ourselves, but rather of an aspect mellow and benign.'* And, the narrator asked rhetorically: *'To whom but Barty Josselin do we owe it that our race is on average already from four to six inches taller than it was thirty years ago, men and women alike?'* Reaching this point in his set of galley proofs, Henry gave a great guffaw of irrepressible derision and flung the sheets to the floor, startling Tosca, who was dozing beside the fire at his feet, and causing her to jump up and waddle across the room, barking crossly. 'Oh dear, oh dear, Tosca,' he said, as he picked up the scattered sheets and put them in order, 'what on earth can we say about this nonsense?'

The answer was, nothing, except that it was a poignant index of Kiki's physical and mental decline in the last two years. He would not be the only reader to think so: the chapters published in *Harper's* had already provoked some cruel comments in the press, and several friends had spoken privately to him of their disappointment at the new book – what would they make of Martia when they came to her? The traders in reputations in the literary marketplace who were, as Kiki himself had prophesied, hoping he would take a fall after the success of *Trilby*, would enjoy sneering at *The Martian*. He had no wish to give them encouragement, but he could not in honesty defend the book either. It was impossible to cancel his agreement to write the article since he had rashly told Emma about it; so he put off writing the piece, but continued to brood on its subject.

A memoir of Du Maurier by Felix Moscheles, *In Bohemia with Du Maurier*, published not long after his death, contained much food for thought. He knew of Moscheles, though he had never met him – he was a moderately successful artist and the son of a famous musician, a friend of Browning's (whose portrait he had painted), a British citizen of European Jewish descent and cosmopolitan education. He had been a fellow student of Du Maurier's at the Academy of Art in Antwerp, and a close friend in the difficult years that

331

followed. Du Maurier had not cultivated the relationship in later life, and his occasional allusions to Moscheles in Henry's hearing were somewhat dismissive. In his book, however, Moscheles presented himself, in slightly cloying fashion, as a devoted friend. In a brief prefatory note he described how he received the news of Du Maurier's death while correcting the proofs of his book in Venice. *'My world, resplendent with sunshine, was suddenly lost in darkness. The most loveable of men, whose presence alone sufficed to make life worth living to all those near and dear to him, was gone from amongst us.'* A whiff of insincerity seemed to rise from this bouquet of clichés. It was a very short book, lavishly illustrated with slapdash humorous pen-and-ink sketches and holograph poems by Du Maurier, recording episodes from their years together in Flanders. Moscheles had evidently preserved these papers, together with letters from Du Maurier, and one could not avoid a suspicion of his 'cashing in' on the *Trilby* boom by publishing this material at the present time. As the title of his book implied, he maintained that the atmosphere of the early chapters of Du Maurier's novel, and the character of Trilby herself, derived from Du Maurier's experiences in Belgium as well as Paris, and his own style mimicked that of *Trilby* with its lyrical nostalgia, local colour, facetious nicknames and arch humour. Moscheles claimed in his preface that Du Maurier had 'cordially endorsed' the project, and even assisted him in correcting the proofs, but Henry wondered if Kiki had in fact been less than enchanted with it, and whether the correcting of proofs hadn't entailed some argument, for it was in many ways a compromising document. He had heard indirectly that the Du Maurier family were displeased by its publication, and was not surprised.

The most interesting revelation in the book concerned a young girl called Octavie, whom the youthful Du Maurier and Moscheles nicknamed 'Carry', and who Moscheles strongly hinted was the model for Trilby. They met her in Malines, where Du Maurier was living after suffering his detached retina. She was the seventeen-year-old daughter of a tobacconist who had just died and she ran the shop with her mother. She was pretty, blue-eyed, with abundant brown curly hair and 'a figure of peculiar elasticity'; and 'her soul was steeped in the very essence of Trilbyism', by which Moscheles seemed to mean the unconventional, unselfconscious freedom of manners exhibited by Du Maurier's young heroine. The two young men found her very attractive, and they formed a kind of flirtatious threesome, with Du Maurier and Moscheles pretending, or perhaps not altogether pretending, to be rivals for her affections. Moscheles noted that he was at a disadvantage in this competition because he was still continuing his studies in Antwerp, and could only spend the weekends in Malines, whereas Du Maurier had Carry all to himself in the intervening weekdays. What particularly interested Henry was that the sketches depicted Moscheles as having a black beard, long black hair and a prominent hooked nose, and often playing the piano *con brio* to entertain Du Maurier and Carry; also that Moscheles admitted to having experimented successfully with mesmerism at that period of his life.

The idyll ended when Du Maurier moved on to Düsseldorf and Moscheles went back to England. The later story of Carry was a sad one. After several unsatisfactory liaisons with other men she met a doctor who married her and took her to Paris, but he died shortly after giving her a son. 'What can have become of Carry once more cast adrift in Paris to fight the battle of life in this hard ever-love-making world?' Moscheles asked rhetorically. He added: 'We never knew,' but the hint in 'ever-love-making' was obvious. Henry began to form a theory about the genesis of *Trilby*. Du Maurier might well have felt guilty in later life about the way he and Moscheles had exploited the seventeen-year-old Carry's innocent availability and later left her to fend for herself. Suppose she had become Du Maurier's mistress during those weekdays when Moscheles was out of the way, perhaps with the collusion of her widowed mother (which was how Trilby had first 'fallen'), perhaps through his persuading her to sit for him in the nude. Might he not have projected his guilt on to a demonised version of his Jewish friend, Svengali, while idealising Carry as Trilby, and portraying himself as the chaste and chivalrous Little Billee? Might Kiki's hints about George Lee being the model for Svengali have been merely a device for concealing the true source of the novel?

There was something else of interest in Moscheles' book, which pertained to Du Maurier's astonishing boom late in life. The young men had a third friend at the Antwerp Academy whose initials were T.A.G., leading them to adopt the soubriquets 'Rag', 'Tag', and 'Bobtail'. There was a poem addressed 'To Bobtail' (Moscheles) by 'Rag' (Du Maurier) reflecting on the unpredictability of their respective futures, which ended:

> Yet who shall be lucky, and who shall be rich?
> Whether both, neither, one or all three;
> Is a mystery which, Dame Fortune the witch,
> Tells neither Tag, Bobtail, or me!

Moscheles returned to this verse later in his book, and modified it:

> Who was to be lucky and who to be rich,
> Who'd get to the top of the tree;
> Was a mystery which
> Dame Fortune the witch,
> Was to tell Du Maurier and me.

It seemed to Henry that, underlying Moscheles' protestations of friendship, there was running through the whole memoir a strain of envy provoked by Du Maurier's eventual success, and perhaps resentment at having been 'used' as the model for Svengali. There was no way by which he could verify these theories, and even if they were true there was no way he could expound them in his article, but they helped to keep his thoughts about Du Maurier simmering at the back of his mind while he worked on other things.

The other things were mainly his London Letters for *Harper's Weekly* – reviews of the latest books, plays and exhibitions – well-paid hack work, essentially. He couldn't settle to anything more substantial while the quest for some permanent refuge from London remained unresolved through the spring and summer. The public hysteria and disruptions to life in the capital caused by the preparations for the Queen's Jubilee made him all the more eager to get away, if only temporarily. He thought of going back to Rye, but neither the cottage at Point Hill nor the Vicarage was available, and he couldn't face the bother of looking for an alternative and probably being disappointed with what he found. He went to Torquay briefly, and the Osborne was as agreeable as ever; but it had nothing new to offer, and neither did Norris's conversation. He escaped the Jubilee at the last moment by going down to Bournemouth, taking MacAlpine and the Remington with him, and had a tolerably pleasant time there, tinged with melancholy memories of two dear departed invalids whom he associated with the resort, Alice and Louis. He cycled a lot, and bought a machine for MacAlpine so that he could have company (if one could call that silent presence company) on his rides. Then came a pleasant and intriguing surprise: a letter from Elly Emmett, née Temple, Minny's sister, who was spending the summer in Dunwich on the Suffolk coast with her three daughters, and invited him to visit them there. The idea of meeting these American cousins, in a part of England he had never visited before, was an enticing one, and he accepted promptly, asking Elly to find accommodation for himself and MacAlpine for the month of August.

It was a poignant experience to see Elly again after so many years, and to reflect that Minny might also have turned into a thick-waisted, heavy-hipped, grey-haired matron if she had lived as long. Her three daughters, all in their early twenties, were however dazzlingly beautiful and, in spite of some defects of education and manners, irresistibly charming – to all, that is, except MacAlpine, who retained his granite impassivity in the face of their girlish efforts to tease and flirt with him. They reminded Henry of Minny in their fearless curiosity and appetite for life, and sometimes they seemed like modern reincarnations of Daisy Miller in their cheerful disregard for conventional proprieties and lack of awe for their elders and betters. They had bicycles too, and accompanied him and MacAlpine on long explorations of the flat unpaved roads of Suffolk. He deplored their slovenly American speech and took it upon himself to correct them. Once he overheard them mimicking him, 'Not "*jool*", Edith – "*jew-el*". Not "*Yeah*" – "*Yes*",' and giggling hysterically together; but in his presence they pretended to be mortified by his criticisms – 'Oh, cousin Henry, you're so *crool*' – '*Cru-el*, Rosina' – and he derived a certain subtle pleasure from admonishing them.

He found the Suffolk countryside, with its sleepy villages and old watermills and bird-haunted estuaries, attractive in a quiet, unostentatious way, and it was certainly good cycling country in dry weather. For a while he toyed with the idea of looking for a cottage in the area, but decided that without the stimulating company of the cousins it would be almost too quiet to bear, and it was inconveniently distant from London, with poor communications. His dream of finding a nesting place somewhere in the country remained unfulfilled. But his temporary residence in Suffolk was so refreshing and restorative that he felt at last able to address himself to the article about George Du Maurier.

It was time. *The Martan* had finished running in *Harper's*, and had been published as a book, to almost universally unfavourable reviews (Du Maurier's premature death had at least spared him the distress of reading them). He could pass over it lightly, taking his readers' knowledge of it for granted, and concentrate on the aspect of his subject that really interested him: the paradox that Du Maurier's astonishing success with *Trilby* had seemed to cause him more distress than joy, and what the whole phenomenon implied about contemporary culture and society. In the little parlour of their rooms at the Dunwich inn he dictated to MacAlpine a long article in which he surveyed Du Maurier's life and evoked his character, throwing in personal reminiscences where appropriate, but emphasising that no one could hope to equal the man's evocation of these things in his own novels. *'I have read with even more reflection than the author perhaps desired to provoke the volume devoted by Mr Felix Moscheles to their common experience in Flanders and Germany,'* he said, in a passage intended to make the memoirist feel uneasy, and to give the Du Mauriers some comfort, *'as to which what most strikes me is the way in which our friend himself has been beforehand with any gleaner.'* After paying tribute in a general, impressionistic way to the charm of Du Maurier's novels, he suggested that the success of *Trilby* constituted a uniquely interesting case. '*The charm was one thing, and the success quite another, and the number of links missing between the two was greater than his tired spirit could cast about for. The case remains, however; it is one of the most curious of our time; and there might be some profit in carrying on an inquiry which could only lead him, at the last, in silence, to turn his face to the wall.*' In that last phrase he felt he seized and held his theme: it was *Trilby* that had killed Du Maurier – or, rather, the monstrous explosion of 'publicity' which the novel had provoked. The passage that followed was the apocalyptic climax of his article, and cost him most effort – a whole morning's dictation, and further polishing by hand that evening. The following day he dictated the revised version to MacAlpine:

'*What I see certainly is that no such violence of publicity can leave untroubled and unadulterated the sources of the production in which it may have found its pretext. The whole phenomenon grew and grew till it became, at any rate for this particular victim, a fountain of gloom and a portent of woe; it darkened all his sky with a hugeness of vulgarity. It became a mere immensity of sound, the senseless hum of a million newspapers and the irresponsible chatter of ten millions of gossips. The pleasant sense of having done well was deprived of all sweetness, all privacy, all sanctity. The American frenzy was naturally the loudest and seemed to reveal monstrosities of organization; it appeared to present him, to a continent peopled with seventy millions, as an object of such homage as no genius had yet elicited. The demonstrations and revelations encircled him like a ronde infernale. He found himself sunk in a landslide of obsessions, of inane, incongruous letters, of interviewers, intruders, invaders, some of them innocent enough, but only the more maddening, others with axes to grind that might have made him call at once, to have it over, for the headsman and the block. Was it only a chance that reverberation had come too late, come, in its perverse way, as if the maleficent fairy of nursery-tales had said, in the far past, at his cradle: "Oh yes, you shall have it to the full, you shall have it till you stop your ears; but you shall have it long after it will bring you any joy, you shall have it when your spirits have left you and your nerves are exposed, you shall have it in a form from which you will turn for refuge – where?"* He *appears to me to have turned for refuge to the only quarter where peace is deep, for if the fact, so presented, sounds overstated, the element of the portentous was not less a reality.'*

MacAlpine tapped out the last words, and looked enquiringly at Henry.

'That's all for the time being, MacAlpine,' he said.

'It's powerful stuff,' said MacAlpine.

Henry stared, then turned his back and smiled to himself. It was the first time the man had ever vouchsafed a comment on anything he had dictated. He was pleased, but it was not a habit he wished to encourage.

Reading the finished article through for the last time, before sending it off to *Harper's*, he realised that it was as much about himself as about Du Maurier – about confronting, defining and refining his own literary ambitions, and finally exorcising the demon of envy which had threatened in the last two years to mar his pleasure in their long friendship. In that, at least, he had succeeded, and he only hoped that others would see it as a worthy tribute to Du Maurier, and find in it evidence of the tenderness and affection he had always felt for him. It was reassuring that Edward Warren thought so. He came over to Dunwich one day from Felixstowe, where he was renting a house for the summer, and Henry showed him the carbon copy. Warren was particularly moved by a passage near the end about his last visits to Du Maurier in Hampstead and *'the gradual shrinkage, half tacit, half discussed, of his old friendly custom of seeing me down the hill. The hill, for our parting, was long enough to make a series of stages that became a sort of deprecated register of what he could do no more; and it was inveterate enough that I wanted to re-ascend with him rather than go my way and let him pass alone into the night.'*

'Wonderful, James,' Warren said, after reading this aloud. 'A wonderful image – Du Maurier passing into the night. It will make his wife cry, but they will be healing tears.'

'I hope so,' he said.

It was almost the end of his stay in Dunwich. He had extended it into September, and the countryside was touched with the first signs of autumn, which seemed appropriate to his elegiac mood. Warren had brought his bike with him from Felixstowe and together they bumped over the rutted, dusty tracks between fields of amber corn waiting to be harvested, and orchards heavy with ripening apples. They discussed the pros and cons of Suffolk as a place to acquire a country retreat, agreeing that the balance went against it, and Henry wistfully recalled the tantalising attractions of Lamb House.

Two days later he returned to London, and found waiting for him a letter from the ironmonger in Rye:

> Dear Mr James,
>   If you are still interested in Lamb House I wd. advise you to come down here as soon as possible as it is to let on a long lease. Old Mr Bellingham died last winter and Mrs Bellingham likewise in June and young Mr Bellingham is going to Canada to make his fortune in the gold rush. Hoping this finds you well,
>   Yrs sincerely,

The signature was illegible. Henry gave a hoot of incredulous laughter as he read this missive, at the sheer implausibility of its contents, the novelistic contrivance to which Fate had been reduced, killing off the senior Bellinghams in quick succession and dispatching the son to join the Klondike gold rush, in order to offer him the house of his dreams, whose presumed unattainability he had been lamenting only a few days ago. He felt both excited and afraid at this singular turn of events. He had a lively premonition of all the financial and legal liabilities, the problems and distractions, that acquiring the house would entail, but he saw also the impossibility of *not* accepting such a gift from the gods, unless it turned out to have some insuperable and catastrophic flaw. His destiny could hardly have been more clearly indicated if a giant hand had come out of the clouds with a finger pointing peremptorily to East Sussex. He immediately wrote to Warren asking if on his return to London the following week he would accompany him to Rye to survey the house and advise him. But two days later he was overcome with panic at the thought of losing the house in the meantime, and wired Warren that he was going down to see it on his own.

6

THE sun woke him early, shining through a gap in the curtains. It rose over the church, and on a clear morning there was always a brief moment when it directed a bright beam straight down West Street, into the King's Room and on to his pillow, if he had neglected to draw the curtains fully together on retiring. They were made of Irish linen, self-lined and greeny-blue in colour, contrasting pleasantly with the oak-panelled walls. He had chosen the material himself, but gratefully left the supervision of their manufacture to Margaret Warren. How would he have managed the immensely complex task of moving into Lamb House without the Warrens? But then, without the Warrens, he might never have set eyes on the place, or known of its existence. His friendship with this couple had acquired a special warmth from the shared sense, equally agreeable to all three parties, that fate had determined their intimate involvement in his acquisition of Lamb House. Although he had been thrilled by his first inspection of the property, which more than confirmed the hoped inspired by his earlier covetous glances from the street, he would never have had the nerve to sign the lease – for twenty-one years, no less – without Warren's approval and enthusiastic support a few days later. Still, he was glad that he had bolted down to Rye to view the house on his own, so that his first impressions of it were unconditioned and entirely personal.

It was almost exactly a year ago that he had ascended the three stone steps and crossed the threshold for the first time. He vividly recalled moving through the house as if in a dream, because the rooms so perfectly fulfilled his vague desires in their size and disposition: the handsome square hall; the cosy drawing room to the left, opening on to the garden, the quaint little parlour to the right, which he immediately assigned as a writing room for guests; the arched staircase that led up to the light and airy Green Room (so-called because of its painted panelling) which overlooked the garden through one window, and afforded a fine view towards Winchelsea through the other, and the master bedroom, known as the King's Room because George the First had slept there for four nights, having been driven ashore on nearby Camber Sands by a storm (with what instant relish he had anticipated boasting to William and Alice of this royal association and teasing their republican prejudices); then the garden, with the ancient mulberry tree spreading its shade over a broad flat lawn, bounded by flower-beds and an old brick wall whose rich hues of red, pink and purple, peeping through the leaves and branches of vines and climbing fruit trees, were like smudges of paint on an artist's palette; and finally – well, not finally, but it was the climax of his tour – the Garden Room which Warren had sketched, thus planting in him the first seed of yearning for this place. It had been added by James Lamb, the mayor of Rye who built the main house, as a banquet-ing room, but it offered itself immediately to his excited vision as the perfect study, at least in the summer months (in the winter he could retreat to the Green Room), removed from domestic distrac-tions, elevated above the garden on one side and the quiet street on the other, with room for two large writing tables, one for himself and one for MacAlpine, and ample space for pacing up and down, and for an armchair and a chaise longue beside the fireplace where he could recline and reflect. Paradise!

That was his overwhelming impression on that first afternoon – that he had somehow found his way back to the Garden of Eden through the big green door with the brass knocker in West Street – and it was a fancy that often recurred, especially when he took a turn around the garden after a good morning's work, with Tosca snuffling happily at his heels. But he had needed Edward Warren's assurance that paradise was structurally sound, and his expert advice on how to make it even more perfect. It was Warren who had perceived that the rather lurid wallpaper in the downstairs parlours concealed fine oak panelling which, now restored to view and freshly varnished, enormously enhanced the dignity and historic atmos-phere of the house; and it was he who had seen where a bathroom might be introduced, and what other modern improvements might be made to the sanitary arrangements and the kitchen facilities, without damage to its architectural integrity. That work, and the supplementary painting and decorating and carpeting and curtaining, had taken a frustratingly long time to accomplish, and he hadn't been able to move in until June, some nine months after he signed the lease, but already he felt completely at home, and determined to stay in Lamb House till the end of the year. He had, in the meantime, managed to sub-let De Vere Gardens, staying at the Reform when business necessitated an overnight trip to London.

The curtains stirred gently in a little puff of sea-scented air that blew into the room through the partly-opened window, carrying with it the plangent cry of a gull. The church clock struck seven. He did not repine at having woken early. He was content to lie there, just enjoying the simple sensation of happiness, in the chamber where a king saved from drowning had lain nearly two centuries ago. The charming story was that the mayor's wife had yielded her bedroom to the King in spite of being heavily pregnant, and had given birth the same night to a son, to whom the monarch, being detained in Rye by a snowstorm, had acted as godfather two days later, and made a present of a silver-gilt bowl and a hundred guineas (the boy was of course christened George). It was pleasing to trace the motif of christening which had linked him to the Warrens from their first acquaintance back to the early history of this house which he had so miraculously come to possess with their help. Of course he didn't actually own it, but the lease would not expire till 1918, which should cover most, if not all, of the years remaining to him, and he was already resolved to take any opportunity that might arise before that date to buy the freehold.

He heard footsteps on the landing outside, probably the house-maid going down from her attic bedroom to kindle the kitchen fire. He could summon her and ask for his hot water to be brought as soon as it was ready, but he felt no urge to rise early and disturb the normal timetable of the house. Part of the euphoria he felt at this moment was the consciousness that the day ahead of him was entirely at his own disposal, free from all social obligations and distractions, available for uninterrupted work and quiet private recreation. Gosse had gone back to London the day before and, much as he had enjoyed his company, there was inevitably a slight sense of strain involved in the entertainment of visitors, of whom he had already had several since June. It was always pleasing to receive them, and to register, as much by the expressions on their faces as by their words of congratulation, their admiration of his new residence; but this gratifying response only spurred him on to be a host worthy of the house, and he spent far more time thinking about and attending to the needs of his guests than he had ever done in London. So it was always also a secret relief to see them go, and to relish the prospect of an interval of selfish peace until the next one was due.

Gosse, to do him justice, had been no trouble, happy to spend his mornings reading and writing in the small parlour while he himself was dictating to MacAlpine in the Garden Room. He had brought his bike with him and they made some quite long excursions into the Romney Marshes, which was perfect cycling country – miles of flat, unfrequented roads winding between fields of grazing sheep and leading to sleepy old towns and villages with extraordinary churches – one the size of a cathedral in little Lydd, and another like something out of a fairy-tale, with shutters on the windows and a free-standing conical steeple made of wood, in Brookland. The most memorable of these trips, however, had been to New Romney to visit H. G. Wells, who was convalescing there at the home of an exceptionally kind and caring doctor, having been taken ill with a severe kidney complaint while making a bicycle tour of the East Sussex coast with his wife.

Their mission had been a delicate one: the Royal Literary Fund, having heard that Wells might be in need of financial help, had asked Gosse to make a confidential assessment of the young writer's needs without letting him know that his case was under consideration. Gosse knew Wells slightly and his pretext for calling on him was to introduce Henry, who remembered his intelligent review of *Guy Domville* with gratitude and was pleased to cooperate. Wells had since made a stir with a scientific romance called *The Time Machine*, which he fully intended to read one day, and some similar tales in the same vein, but one of the things they learned on their visit was that he was currently engaged on a realistic novel of contemporary life called *Love and Mr Lewisham*. Another was that Wells was in no great financial need – indeed he was sufficiently solvent to talk of building himself a house somewhere on the East Sussex coast as soon as he should have recovered his health. He was very interested in domestic architecture, and raged eloquently against the meanness and inconvenience of the typical modern British house, with its cramped rooms and interminable staircases, its inefficient heating and inadequate sanitation. He aimed to build the first house in England that would have an *en suite* lavatory for every bedroom, an eccentric ambition which suggested that he would not find Lamb House *sympathique*. Henry nevertheless invited him to call when he felt fit enough to do so. Although they had no interests in common except books and bicycles, he was impressed by the courage and self-belief of the young man, and his refreshing lack of reverence for the tried and the tested. He was the very embodiment of the new scientific age, glorying in visions of inventions that would transform everyday life. When Henry described how he was dependent on dictation as a method of composition, Wells predicted that before the end of the next century there would be machines that would take dictation and instantly transcribe your words on to a screen for revision and emendation and print them out on a typewriter without any human agency. How he and Gosse had laughed! Wells's charming little wife Jane – his second apparently, in spite of his youth – who gazed adoringly at her husband as he held forth, had looked quite hurt by their lack of respect.

He was rather pleased that Wells was thinking of settling in the area, confirming other evidence that it was becoming a popular habitat for authors. Ford Madox Hueffer had rented a farmhouse near Hythe, where he apparently collaborated with the interesting Polish expatriate Joseph Conrad on literary projects, and Stephen Crane, the brilliant young American author of *The Red Badge of Courage*, whom he had met briefly in London, was coming to live at Brede, on the other side of Rye, when he returned from reporting the war in Cuba. His wife Cora had already taken an enormous ramshackle house there. It was regrettable that the morals of these literary folk (Conrad excepted) were somewhat lax – Wells had lived with Jane for some time while waiting for his divorce, there was gossip about Hueffer's relationship with his sister-in-law, and it was rumoured that Cora had been a brothel madam in the far West before she met Crane. He was anxious to establish his credentials as a thoroughly respectable citizen in the eyes of deeply conservative Rye; but as long as he was careful not to get personally involved in these scandals it was all grist to a novelist's mill.

The remarkable relaxation of moral standards in English society that had taken place in recent times, and the freedom with which such matters were discussed in sophisticated circles, was in fact a central theme of the novel on which he was presently engaged, *The Awkward Age*, and he was enjoying projecting something of himself into the character of Mr Longdon, the elderly country-dwelling bachelor whose old-fashioned values provided a measure of the decadence and cynicism of the metropolitan set in which he found himself, and provoked his compassionate interest in the plight of two young girls making the difficult transition from the schoolroom to marriage in this milieu. It was an idea he had started developing as a short story and put aside when it showed a stubborn determination to be a novel. Now he was writing it as a full-length serial for *Harper's Weekly*, with such facility and confidence that he had agreed to their starting to run it in October even though he was some distance from finishing it.

Nothing had been more striking, or more gratifying, about his acquisition of Lamb House than its liberating effect on his creative imagination. Almost immediately after signing the lease he had begun dictating *The Turn of the Screw*, which showed every sign of making more of an impression than anything he had published for years. The impetus had been partly – indeed mainly – mercenary. Slightly panicked at the thought of the expenditure to which he had committed himself, he had leafed through his notebook in search of something that might tickle the reading public's jaded taste, and decided that a ghost story, inspired by Archbishop Benson's anecdote about the two haunted children, was most likely to perform the trick. In that regard it had exceeded his expectations. The novella-length tale, serialised in *Collier's* in the first few months of this year, had elicited a large postbag of complimentary letters from friends and strangers alike, but it was clear from the tenor of the correspondence that he had touched a deeper level of response in his readers than a mere pleasurable shudder. There was something peculiarly chilling about the idea of an adult couple corrupting the innocence of two young children, and then coming back from beyond the grave to claim their souls, but he had instinctively known that to underline the evil, to make it luridly explicit, would diminish its effect. The tale 'worked' because the nature of the corruption was never specified, and the supernatural manifestations were domesticated to its idyllic country house setting – they might even be (as the down-to-earth housekeeper Mrs Grose hinted) the fevered imaginings of the susceptible young governess who was its narrator and sole centre of consciousness. As his more perceptive readers recognised, he had contrived that every uncanny incident in the story was capable of two explanations, one natural and one supernatural, and it was the undecidability of the narrative, sustained to the very end, that more than anything else kept them on the rack of suspense. Several wrote to him pleading to be put out of their misery by an authoritative explanation of the 'true' nature of the case, requests which he had found elaborately polite ways to evade. He anticipated receiving more such entreaties when the tale was published in book form next month, paired with another long short story to plump out the volume, 'Covering End'.

This was a recycling of his play *Summersoft*, which Ellen Terry had hung on to for three years without showing any signs of getting it produced. That he had been able to shrug off this disappointment, and put the material to profitable use in another form, surely demonstrated that he had finally weaned himself from the Theatre. But he had learned lessons as well as tasted bitterness at that treacherous bosom, as *The Awkward Age* demonstrated, consisting very largely of 'scenes' which might, without much adjustment, be performed on a stage that could accommodate ten or twelve hours' traffic instead of the statutory two or three. Editors were apt to complain (or alleged that their readers complained) that his stories contained too much analysis and introspection, that they were slow-moving and insufficiently 'slick', and sometimes hinted that these defects might be mended by increasing the proportion of dialogue to narration, as if there were not many significant moments in life from which dialogue was axiomatically excluded (such as, for instance, a man lying alone in bed musing on his good fortune). But if they wanted dialogue, he would give them dialogue – *The Awkward Age* contained little else – and see how his critics liked it. Probably no better than his internalised narrative mode, he thought wryly.

He was resigned now to never being a really popular author, or producing a 'best seller', like poor Du Maurier. Something had happened in the culture of the English-speaking world in the last few decades, some huge seismic shift caused by a number of different converging forces – the spread and thinning of literacy, the levelling effect of democracy, the rampant energy of capitalism, the distortion of values by journalism and advertising – which made it impossible for a practitioner of the art of fiction to achieve both excellence and popularity, as Scott and Balzac, Dickens and George Eliot, had done in their prime. The best one could hope for was sufficient support from discriminating readers to carry on with the endless quest for aesthetic perfection. *'Who was to be lucky and who to be rich,/Who'd get to the top of the tree?'* He would never be rich, but when Lamb House fell into his hands he had felt blessed with good luck, and there was more than one tree from whose highest branches one might look down with a satisfying sense of achievement.

The future seemed to stretch before him bright with hope and possibility, like a great calm ocean under the morning sun. He some-times figured Lamb House as a ship of which he was the captain, steaming into the future, with MacAlpine as first officer and his little band of servants as crew; this bedroom was his cabin, the lawn was the main deck, and the Garden Room the bridge. Somewhere ahead a great project awaited him: three major novels, as analytical, introspective and deliberately paced as he cared to make them, but also as deep, as daring and as beautiful as only he *could* make them. The elements were already stored in his notebook. One about the grizzled American overcome by a vision of lost opportunities in the Paris garden, urging his young companion to 'Live all you can!';

another about the sick heiress betrayed by love and her friends; a third about the father and daughter who overcame the destructive power of passion by their goodness and cunning. He was not ready to begin them yet, but he felt a serene inner certainty that he would write them in Lamb House.

After breakfast he interviewed Mrs Smith in the drawing room as usual. Since there were no guests, either in residence or expected, there was little to discuss as regards the day's menu, and he approved her prudent suggestions for 'using up' ingredients left over from entertaining Gosse.

'Is there anything else?' he asked, as she seemed disposed to linger.

'Well, yes, sir, there is,' she said, twisting the strings of her apron a little nervously. 'I was wondering whether you've ever thought of getting a house-boy.'

'A house-boy?' he echoed her with some surprise. 'Do we need one?'

'It would be useful, Mr James. Someone to run errands and do odd jobs around the house – helping Alice with polishing the knives, for instance. Cleaning boots. Bringing in the coals. There's all manner of things to be done in a big old-fashioned place like this. I don't like to ask George Gammon to do much – he's got his work cut out in the garden.'

'That is true,' he acknowledged. His friend Alfred Parsons, a landscape painter who was also expert at designing gardens, had produced a comprehensive plan for the improvement of the Lamb House acre-and-a-half which would keep Gammon fully occupied for years. But he suspected there was another reason for the suggestion. Smith's drinking had got worse since the move to Rye – he seemed to pine for the bustle and noise of London, and missed the electric light and other modern conveniences of De Vere Gardens. He was frequently 'poorly', a euphemism for drunk or recovering from drink. To cover his delinquencies Mrs Smith had to perform many of her husband's duties, and pass on some of her own to the parlourmaid or the housemaid, so there was probably some stress in the lower ranks of his little crew which a boy might relieve.

'Hmm,' he said. 'How much would I have to pay a house-boy?'

'Four shillings a week, sir,' Mrs Smith said promptly. 'And his meals. But he wouldn't live in.'

'You sound as if you have someone in mind, Mrs Smith,' he said.

She blushed. 'Well, yes, sir, I have. Mrs Noakes who lives round the corner in Watchbell Street, a very decent woman, lost her husband recently and is left with six young children. She's desperate to find some work for her eldest, Burgess.'

'Burgess? An unusual name. How old is he?'

'Fourteen, I think, sir. A nice lad.'

Henry thought for a moment. 'Very well, Mrs Smith, you may invite Mrs Noakes to bring her son for an interview one day.'

'Thank you, sir.' Mrs Smith still lingered. 'You wouldn't like to see them now, by any chance?'

'*Now*? My goodness, are they in the house, then?'

'They're sitting in the kitchen, sir. Sarah Noakes brought him early and asked me to ask you. She's that desperate.'

He sighed. 'Very well, I suppose I might as well get it over with. I promise nothing till I've seen the boy, mind you.'

'No, sir. Thank you, sir. I'll fetch them straight away.'

He detained her as she turned to leave. 'You're sure that four shillings is enough?'

'It's the usual rate round here,' said Mrs Smith. 'You can always raise the wages if he gives satisfaction.'

'Very true.'

A few moments later, Mrs Noakes entered the room with her son, curtsied and thanked him effusively for seeing them.

'This is Burgess, sir, my eldest. A very willing boy, sir. You won't regret having him to work for you.' She thrust her son forward. The boy gave a shy smile and looked down at his boots. He was slightly gnome-like in appearance, with a snub nose, plump cheeks, a deep upper lip, and a head of dense wavy hair, but his most salient feature was his extremely small stature.

'He's very small, Mrs Noakes.'

'Small, but strong, sir. My poor dear husband was the same.'

'Is he really fourteen?'

'Nearly,' Mrs Noakes said, evasively.

'And he's left school?'

Mrs Noakes shrugged. 'He's had to. I've got five younger ones to feed.'

'Can you read and write, Noakes?' he asked the boy.

'Yes, sir,' said Noakes.

'Can he, sir?' Mrs Noakes echoed rhetorically. 'If ever I needs to write a letter, Burgess does it for me. He has a lovely neat hand. And he reads the newspaper to me beautiful.'

'Does he – does he do the police in different voices?' he said with a chuckle.

'I beg your pardon, sir?' Mrs Noakes looked puzzled, as well she might.

'Nothing – nothing. A literary allusion. As you may know, I am an author by profession—'

'Yes, sir, Mrs Smith said.'

'And so I require a certain degree of peace and quiet in the house and garden when I am at work, or reading. Are you a quiet boy, Noakes?'

'Quiet as a mouse,' Mrs Noakes cried.

'Please let the boy answer for himself, Mrs Noakes.' He looked Burgess Noakes in the eye. 'Do you, for instance, *whistle*?'

The boy thought about this question for a moment, and then replied: 'Well, I does whistle – occasional, like – but I can stop m'self.'

There was undoubtedly something rather engaging about him, unimpressive as his appearance was. They discussed the nature of his duties for a while, and Burgess Noakes professed himself able and willing to perform them. Henry asked if he had any questions to ask himself.

'Will I be able to go to the club?' he said.

'What club is that?'

'The Rye Athletic Club,' said Mrs Noakes. 'He's in the Boys. Mad about it.'

'I'm sure you can have some time off for recreation,' Henry said. 'You'd have to arrange that with Mrs Smith. And what sports do you pursue, Noakes?'

'Football and boxing,' said Noakes.

'Boxing?' He could not conceal his surprise. 'Aren't you a little small for that?'

'Bantamweight,' said Noakes.

'Ah, yes. Bantamweight . . . In London this summer I saw the Fitzsimmons–Corbett fight, at the cinematograph,' he said. 'It was most exciting. Did you happen to see it?'

Burgess's eyes widened. 'I wish I did!' he said.

'The cinematograph ain't come to Rye yet, sir,' said Mrs Noakes.

'That was the heavyweight championship, was it not?'

'Fitzsimmons is a light-heavy but he's the best boxer in the world,' said the boy, suddenly animated. 'Dropped Corbett in the fourteenth, 'e did.'

'Well, it was certainly satisfying to see the smaller and more skilful man win.' It was time to draw the interview to a close, before the conversation became too technical. 'Very well, Noakes,' he said, 'I will take you on a month's trial.'

He accepted Mrs Noakes's tearful thanks, and directed them to make the necessary arrangements with Mrs Smith, whom he summoned with the bell. He looked at his watch: it was ten minutes before ten, the hour when he usually began work.

He passed out through the French windows into the garden, with Tosca at his heels. It was a clear, crisp sunny September day. He took deep breaths of the salty air, and waved to MacAlpine who was standing at the foot of the Garden Room steps, smoking a pipe. He took a turn around the lawn, and greeted George Gammon, who was hoeing a flower-bed, and promised him crocuses, tulips and hyacinths in the spring. He waited, politely turning his back, while Tosca completed her toilet in the appropriate part of the garden, then quickening his step he made his way to the Garden Room. He had reached that point in *The Awkward Age* where Nanda was speaking to Vanderbilt in the garden of Mr Longdon's country house, and he intended to base his description of this setting on his own garden. He looked forward immensely to the morning's work.

PART FOUR

THE second day of 1916 at Carlyle Mansions is inevitably something of an anticlimax after the excitements of the first, though more telegrams and letters of congratulation arrive from home and abroad (and will continue to do so for days to come). Mrs James recognises the distinguished names appended to some of these messages – William Dean Howells, for instance, Logan Pearsall Smith, Ellen Terry – and permits Theodora, who calls to enquire if her services are required, to identify some of the less familiar: Jean Jules Jusserand, French Ambassador to the United States; the French Academician Paul Bourget and his American wife, Minnie; Elizabeth Robins, the actress and producer; Mr and Mrs Edward Compton, who produced and performed in Henry's first play, and their son, Lieutenant Mackenzie, Royal Marines, who cables his congratulations from the British Legation in Athens and signs himself 'Monty'.

'You may know him better as Compton Mackenzie, the novelist,' Theodora says.

'Oh, you mean *Sinister Street*? Peggy told me not to read it because I would be shocked.'

'Mr James admires it greatly,' says Theodora, who has learned by now not to use the familiar 'HJ' in conversation with Mrs James. 'And this note is from Ford Madox Hueffer, who published an excellent novel last year called *The Good Soldier* – better than *Sinister Street*, in my opinion, though it didn't receive anything like the same attention.'

'No, I haven't heard of it,' says Mrs James. She is impressed in spite of herself by both the quantity of the messages and the quality of the senders. Henry himself however seems to have lost interest in his honour. He closes his eyes with a bored expression when she reads out the messages to him, and brushes her hand aside impatiently when she tries to show him the names and signatures attached to them. Eventually she gives up this unrewarding effort, and tells Burgess to wheel Henry's couch to the window in the sitting room, where the view of the passing boats, tirelessly cleaving the brown water of the Thames, and Burgess's patient attendance, have their customary calming effect.

The next day Mrs James's daughter Peggy arrives, having set off from New York on Christmas Eve. That she was prepared to brave wintry seas and U-boat wolf-packs to see her dying uncle is a measure of her affection for him. They have had a special relationship ever since 1900, when she was left at a boarding school in England while her parents traipsed around the Continental spas in search of a cure for her father's heart ailment. She spent two Christmases and other holidays at Lamb House during that time, and Henry used to meet her occasionally in London and take her out to theatres and museums and the cinematograph, doing his kind best to mitigate her homesickness. Sadly, she inherited the James family's tendency to depression, and as a young woman suffered a nervous breakdown very like her Aunt Alice's at a similar age, apparently triggered by her brother Billy's marriage. Her recovery was helped by going back to England and enjoying Henry's society again, and she was actually thinking of settling there when the war broke out and obliged her to return home. The uncle who waved her off on the boat train in 1914 was, in spite of his years, and his anguish about the war, a dapper, assured, alert man-of-letters. Now she sits beside the couch where he lies like a small beached whale, helpless, stricken, and confused, and sympathetically squeezes his limp hand. He seems pleased but unsurprised by her presence.

'I'm very glad to see you, Peggy,' he says. 'I hope your father will be in soon. He is the one person in all Rome I want to see.'

'He thinks he's in Rome today,' Mrs James explains superfluously. 'Yesterday it was Dublin. Tomorrow it might be New York.'

Mrs James is very glad indeed to see her daughter installed in the flat. At last she has an ally, a compatriot and a member of the family, to help in the management of the crisis. Peggy, for instance, completely supports her attitude to Theodora Bosanquet, and is outraged to learn that the secretary has been corresponding regularly with Edith Wharton. 'The way that woman and her husband carried on before they got divorced was an offence to decent society,' Peggy says fiercely. 'Especially her flagrant affair with Morton Fullerton. We should have nothing to do with her.'

'I quite agree,' says Mrs James. 'Though it appears that she has done Henry some favours in the past. She is of course very rich.'

'We don't need her money – or Miss Bosanquet's interference,' says Peggy.

So poor Theodora is frozen out of the household even more pointedly than before. Edith Wharton, guessing from the paucity of information Theodora is able to transmit that something of the kind must have happened, writes to offer Theodora a job as her secretary. Theodora thinks it over carefully. At first glance it seems inviting, an opportunity to enter a glamorous cosmopolitan world of staterooms and motor cars and first-class hotels that she has so far only glimpsed from outside – it seems to be the very direction in which Lambert Strether's injunction, *'Live all you can,'* was pointing. But in the end she declines the offer. One interview with Mrs Wharton had been enough to give her the measure of that lady's formidable personality. To be her secretary would mean being her slave, however cushioned by luxury, and their values are ultimately incompatible. Theodora is a convinced Christian with an interest in mysticism (the oriental as well as occidental traditions), and although less censorious of unconventional behaviour than Peggy James, is at heart just as unsympathetic to Mrs Wharton's style of life. Accordingly she politely declines the post, pleading the inadequacy of her French, though in fact she is perfectly competent in the language. When the time comes – and it cannot be far off – that her employment by HJ is terminated, she believes she will have no difficulty finding work in some Government department for the duration of the war. Meanwhile she intends to stay at her post, even if she is prevented from doing anything useful. When Mrs James gives Theodora her monthly salary she returns the cheque on the grounds that she has not been allowed to earn it, but the old lady, evidently feeling some contrition for her behaviour, insists she accept the money.

All through January Henry's state appears to be stable – 'like a tired child' is Alice's descriptive phrase in a letter home, 'but comfortable, tranquil'. He is physically weak but not in pain, and his delusions are gentle, kindly ones. He speaks of having tea with Carlyle and his father round the corner in Cheyne Row as if it happened yesterday. Sometimes, perhaps as a result of gazing at the tugs and barges and launches moving ceaselessly up and down the river beyond his window, he imagines he is on a ship, and once, on being told that Burgess Noakes is out on an errand, says: 'How extraordinary that Burgess should leave the ship to do errands.' He has addressed his servant by his first name ever since he came back from the war, but now he occasionally refers to him as 'Burgess James', as if he has mentally adopted him as a kind of son. Only when Burgess is absent for any considerable length of time does he become fretful. Sometimes his hand moves over the counterpane of his bed as if writing words in that extravagantly large loose scrawl that his family know so well from his letters.

The days pass so quietly, and the routine of the household develops a rhythm so smooth and regular that the two James ladies feel able to venture out occasionally for some relief and recreation. One evening they go to see *Peter Pan* at the Duke of York's. Mrs James has never seen it and is curious to do so, and Peggy is privately of the opinion that it is just about the only entertainment in the West End that can be relied on not to bore, offend or shock her mother. Alice is enchanted, and enthuses about the play to Edmund Gosse who calls next day to enquire about Henry. She mentions that she didn't hear the line which Henry quoted on New Year's Day about death being an awfully big adventure, and Gosse says it has been cut from the play because of the war.

'I can understand that,' says Peggy drily.

'Barrie himself is dreadfully cut up about the death of George – you know, the eldest of the boys he adopted,' says Gosse.

'No,' says Mrs James. 'I don't know anything about it.'

'I remember hearing something,' says Peggy. 'But please tell us, Mr Gosse.'

'Ah. Well, they were Sylvia Llewelyn Davies's boys – that's George Du Maurier's daughter, Sylvia,' says Gosse, settling back in his seat. He enjoys telling stories like this one. Henry is asleep in his bedroom and they are having tea in the sitting room. 'She married Arthur Llewelyn Davies, a barrister, and they had these five boys. Barrie met the two eldest in Kensington Gardens with their nanny, when they were quite little, and took a fancy to them. Used to tell them stories and play games of imaginary adventures – that was how he got the idea for *Peter Pan*, in fact. He soon became a close friend of the family. He had no children himself, you see – but that's another story . . .'

'Wasn't there a divorce?' says Peggy.

'Yes, a very painful business for Barrie . . . The Llewelyn Davieses became a kind of surrogate family for him, and everything was fine until Arthur got a dreadful cancer of the jaw when he was in his forties, and died after a ghastly operation failed. Then Sylvia died, of cancer too, just a few years later. So Barrie became guardian to the five orphans. Doted on them, sent them to Eton, Cambridge, everything . . . The eldest, George, was killed in Flanders last March. Sniper's bullet. He was twenty-one. It happened just a week or so after Sylvia's brother, Guy Du Maurier, was killed – on the same front. Guy was a professional soldier, a Lieutenant Colonel. Thank God poor Emma didn't live to hear about it.'

'Emma?' Alice is bewildered by this stream of unfamiliar names.

'George Du Maurier's widow. She saw her two eldest daughters die before her – Sylvia and Trixy, both lovely girls. It would have been too cruel if she'd lived to hear about Guy and George Davies as well. But she passed away herself in January last year.' He sighs and the ends of his grey moustache seem to droop even more than usual in sympathy with this sad story. 'A tragic family, especially when you think how gay and vital they all were when they were young. I knew them well – so did Henry of course. But now it seems all families are potentially tragic . . . My own son, Philip, is in Flanders . . .'

The two women murmur their sympathy.

'He's not fighting, thank God, he's a doctor with an ambulance unit. But it's dangerous work, near the Front.'

'I don't understand what this terrible war is about,' says Mrs James.

'I don't think anyone understands what it was about orginally,' says Gosse, 'but now it's quite clear what we're fighting for – we *must* resist German aggression. Henry saw that very clearly from the beginning. It's been marvellous, the support he's given to this country in its hour of need. I was very honoured that he asked me to be his sponsor when he applied for British citizenship.'

A frown of disapproval passes across Mrs James's face at this last phrase, but she contents herself with saying: 'Well, I'm old enough to remember the Civil War, and all the fine young men who were killed then. I just hope America has the sense to keep out of this one.'

'Henry would, of course, disagree with you vehemently,' says Gosse.

'Well, it wouldn't be the first time,' says Mrs James.

There is a pause in the conversation.

'I think perhaps I should leave you now,' says Gosse, rising to his feet. 'I take it that there is no possibility of Henry's being able to receive his honour from the King at Buckingham Palace?'

'None at all, I'm afraid,' says Mrs James, and Peggy concurs.

'Very well, I'll pass that on to the appropriate quarter,' says Gosse. 'No doubt some arrangement can be made to confer the honour here.'

So on the 19th of January Lord Bryce, former British Ambassador to the United States, and a personal friend of Henry's, comes to Carlyle Mansions to deliver the insignia of the Order of Merit at Henry's bedside. The recipient is barely conscious throughout the simple ceremony, and Mrs James has to make a brief and rather awkward speech of thanks on his behalf. She feels ill-at-ease in this role, and not just because of her republican principles. She doesn't know quite what to make of the fuss that is being made about Henry's O.M., and the deluge of telegrams and letters from prominent persons that it triggered. She has always considered that she was married to the more distinguished of the two brothers. William's international fame as a philosopher and psychologist had come relatively late in life, but it never faltered. Whereas Henry had struggled to maintain his early success as a writer – at least, his letters were always full of complaints about poor sales, stupid reviews, and the indifference of the reading public to his work. Why he ever expected to be a best-selling author was a mystery. The unreadability of his later books – anything later than *The Portrait of a Lady* as far as she herself was concerned – was something of a family joke. William more than once urged him to write more simply and directly if he wanted to attract more readers, but instead Henry's style grew more and more elaborate and obscure, and he had ruined his early work by revising it for the New York Edition, which, not surprisingly, had been a complete flop. As to his doomed attempt to make himself into a playwright, the less said about that the better. By any objective standards, his career, taken all in all, has been a story of failure and disappointment, but the way people have reacted to his O.M. would make one think he was a Great Writer, as eminent in his own sphere as William in his. Alice is puzzled and irritated by the paradox. She loves her brother-in-law, of course – she wouldn't be here in war-worn London if that wasn't the case – but she can't bear to see him put on a pedestal at the same level as her dear William.

At the end of January Alice's son Harry arrives at Carlyle Mansions. He is a lawyer by training, an administrator by temperament and choice. Manager of the Rockefeller Medical Foundation in New York at the outbreak of the war, he has been working in Europe ever since as a member of the Rockefeller Commission for the relief of non-combatants. He is a vigorous energetic bachelor in his midthirties, striking in appearance, with hair already going white, but a black moustache, and a strong, jutting jaw-line. He immediately assumes executive control of the household, and although his mother has been given power of attorney over Henry's affairs she defers to her son's judgement in most matters. He has much the same attitude to his uncle's literary status as she has: pleasure in the credit it brings to the family, mingled with some bafflement and scepticism about the artistic value of his writings, and a pragmatic concern to protect their monetary value. His brisk, practical, masculine leadership disperses some of the volatile emotional atmosphere that has accumulated in a space occupied mainly by women. Since it is obvious that Henry is not going to recover, Harry sees no point in waiting sentimentally for the end to come before beginning the formidable task of sorting out his estate. The immediate beneficiary is Theodora, who is soon given work to do, making lists of Henry's manuscripts, and thus gains access to the flat again. Harry himself goes down to Lamb House and makes inventories of its contents. He finds a bundle of letters from George Du Maurier in a cabinet drawer in the Green Room, and brings them back to London.

'I don't understand why there aren't more letters, either here or in Rye,' he says to Theodora, after his return. 'Uncle Henry must have received hundreds – thousands – in his lifetime, many of them from famous people. They would be valuable.'

'He burned them,' says Theodora. 'He burned them in the garden at Lamb House.'

'Why?'

'He was depressed. It was late in 1909, just before you came over to see him.'

'Oh, yes,' says Harry, remembering. His father was still alive then, and had been so alarmed by the despairing tone of the letters he was receiving from Henry that he dispatched Harry across the Atlantic to discover what was the matter. Harry had found his uncle prostrate, unable or unwilling to get out of bed, and scarcely able to take nourishment. He sat by his side, holding his hand, distressed and embarrassed as Henry sobbed and mumbled scarcely intelligible sentences about the futility of his life, the total absence of hope and joy, and how he longed for an end to the pain of consciousness, all mixed up with obscure references to Aunt Alice and 'Fenimore', who Harry thought must be Constance Fenimore Woolson. When he reported by letter to his father, William diagnosed a nervous breakdown of possibly suicidal severity, and set off immediately with Alice for England, passing Harry's returning ship in mid-Atlantic. They took Henry away from Lamb House to Bad Nauheim, and by midsummer he had fully recovered, more by virtue of their kindness and company than the waters of the spa. It was William whose condition deteriorated, and he died shortly after getting home, tenderly accompanied by Henry as well as Alice, the brothers' roles now reversed, and by the invaluable Burgess Noakes. Harry had met the little party off the boat at Quebec, in pouring rain, and escorted them by rail and road to the family's country house at Chocorua, New Hampshire, where his father died a week later. 'Yes, yes, it all comes back to me now,' Harry says to Theodora. 'But I didn't know he had destroyed all his letters. Why?'

'I think he had lost the will to live, at the time,' she says, 'and he didn't want to leave any private papers behind. He has an obsession about privacy. He hates the idea of people prying into his life after he is dead.'

'What about the letters he received since then?' Harry asks.

'I believe he burned them too, when he went down to Lamb House last October. Kidd told me he had a big bonfire of papers in the garden.'

'So these letters from Du Maurier are something of a rarity?'

'They're probably the only complete – or fairly complete – set of letters from one of his friends in existence.'

'What a shame,' Harry sighs. 'He knew so many distinguished people.'

'He knew everybody,' says Theodora.

They fall silent, both struck simultaneously with the uncomfortable realisation that they are already speaking of him in the past tense.

* * *

The letters from George Du Maurier are all out of sequence, and pages from different letters are mixed up, as if they were bundled together carelessly or hastily, so after dinner that day Harry asks his mother and sister if they would like to put them in order. They find the task interesting, though the letters themselves are rather less so, except for the little sketches which rather endearingly illustrate them. Du Maurier was obviously a nice man, and devoted to Henry, but not a great mind, nor a great prose stylist, to judge from the correspondence. He was humbly deferential to Henry's literary knowledge, and dutifully reported his reading of French authors recommended by his friend in conversations on Hampstead Heath. *'It is often my custom of an afternoon to sit on the bench where we talked of Flaubert and Zola and Daudet,'* he wrote early in their relationship. He praised Henry's novels generously, but the shorter nonfiction pieces were clearly more to his taste: *'when dealing with people and places your work is more delightful than that of anyone else I can think of.'* The warmth of their friendship is obvious from the letters – *'I'm told you are coming on Sunday – hooray!'* he wrote, typically, in September '88 – but its chemistry remains elusive.

Then Mrs James makes an unexpected discovery: a letter, dated September 23rd, 1910, not from Du Maurier, who had long been dead by then, but from his widow, to 'My dear Mr James', evidently thanking Henry for a letter of condolence he had written on the death of her daughter, Sylvia. *'I quite know how sincerely and deeply you must feel for me in this very great sorrow that has come to me, and I was so glad to get your kind letter so full of sympathy,'* it begins. Having heard the sad history of Sylvia very recently, Alice finds it easy to enter into Emma Du Maurier's situation and to empathise with her – especially when the letter goes on to refer to the death of her own beloved William. *'It was on my way home from Devonshire on August 29th that I read in the papers of your brother's death, and I do feel very grieved for you dear Mr James, for I know how devoted you were to each other and this great sorrow came to you at a time when you were less able to bear it.'* Immediately this releases a stream of poignant memories for Alice, of the spring and summer of 1910 – Henry's nervous breakdown, their errand of mercy to Europe, the stressful return journey to America, William's sudden decline and death in his beloved house in New Hampshire. Henry had stayed on after the funeral to keep her company, so . . .

'Henry must have received this letter at Chocorua!' she exclaims. 'How very extraordinary.' She passes the letter to Peggy.

'Yes, I remember Uncle Henry mentioning Sylvia's death at the time,' Peggy says when she has perused the letter. 'Don't you?'

'No. And if he did, I wouldn't have paid any attention – I had enough grief of my own to cope with. What was Sylvia Du Maurier – or Sylvia Something-Davies – to me?'

But now it is different. Going to see *Peter Pan*, hearing from Edmund Gosse the story behind it, finding this letter written at the time of her own husband's death, addressed to the brother-in-law who now lies dying in another room, reading Emma Du Maurier's slightly wistful account of Barrie's offer to take care of the orphaned Davies boys – *'I am too old to be really of any use to them. He is unattached and his one wish is to look after them in the way Sylvia would have wanted,'* and knowing that the eldest boy, George, was killed in the war five years later at the age of only twenty-one – the convergence of all these circumstances seems to make a kind of pattern, linking up separate lives and deaths in a way that novels do, with an effect of contrived but irresistible pathos. Alice finds herself unexpectedly weeping.

'What's the matter, Mother?' Peggy asks anxiously.

Mrs James shakes her head, sniffs and wipes her eyes with a handkerchief. 'I don't know. It all seems so sad.'

'Mrs James is crying,' Minnie reports to the kitchen. 'I never seen that before.'

'The doctor was here this afternoon,' says Joan Anderson. 'He must have told her something.'

'I don't think so,' says Burgess. 'Mr James was just the same as usual today.'

'He can't last much longer, though,' says Joan. 'I heard the nurses saying.'

'Sayin' what?' says Minnie.

'Saying that,' says Joan. 'And then – what will happen to us?'

At last the subject, the question secretly pondered by all of them for weeks, is out in the open, on the table for discussion.

'You'll be all right, Joan,' says Burgess. 'There's always work for a good cook.'

'What about yourself?' says Joan.

Burgess shrugs. 'I s'pose I'll report back to the regimental depot.' He has heard nothing from the War Office about a discharge.

'They'll never send you back to the Front, will they?' says Minnie.

Burgess doesn't hear the question, or perhaps pretends not to hear it.

'I'll get a job in a factory,' says Minnie. 'A munitions factory.'

'Minnie – you'd never!' says Joan Anderson, shocked.

'Why shouldn't I?' Minnie says defiantly. 'The pay's good – and I'd be doing my bit for the war effort.'

'But they're terrible places, those factories,' says Joan. 'I've got a niece who tried it once – she couldn't stand it. The swearing, the smutty talk, the goings on. And you have to wear trousers.'

'I wouldn't mind wearing trousers,' Minnie says.

'It's dirty, dangerous work, Minnie,' says Burgess. 'It's not for you.'

'What *is* for me, then?' she says, looking him directly in the eye. 'What do you think I should do, Burgess?'

He strokes his moustache thoughtfully. 'You could train to be a nurse,' he says. 'You'd make a good nurse.'

'Yes, Minnie, you've had plenty of practice,' says Joan Anderson.

'True enough,' says Minnie. 'But I don't like the sight of blood.'

'Ah, well, that *would* be a drawback in a field hospital,' says Burgess, nodding.

The next morning Burgess is sorting out the morning's first delivery of mail in the kitchen when he comes across an official envelope from the War Office addressed to himself. He freezes so suddenly that Minnie, who is preparing Mrs James's breakfast tray, notices.

'What is it, Burgess?'

He is staring at the envelope, lying on the deal table, as if it is an unexploded bomb. Minnie comes over and sees what it is.

'Oh, Burgess!' she exclaims. 'It's your discharge! Open it!'

'Maybe it is, and maybe it isn't,' he says.

Joan comes across from the kitchen range to look. 'Open it and see.'

'I'll open it for you, if you like,' says Minnie.

'No, I'll do it.' He rips open the envelope, unfolds the letter inside and quickly scans it. 'Discharged on medical grounds,' he says, looking up, and grins.

Minnie screams, throws her arms round him and kisses him.

'Here, steady on!' he says.

Minnie sits down abruptly on the nearest chair and bursts into tears. Joan Anderson gives Burgess a hug.

'I must tell the old toff,' says Burgess.

The night nurse is getting ready to go off duty, and the day nurse has not yet arrived. Burgess tells the night nurse to go, and sits down beside the bed. The curtains have been drawn back, and a cold grey light slants through the north-facing windows from an overcast sky. The author is lying on his back, with his eyes closed, breathing regularly, the sheet and blanket turned down neatly under his chin by the nurse. He seems to be asleep, but who knows?

'Mr James, sir,' Burgess says quietly, 'my discharge has come through.'

The author opens his eyes, looks up at Burgess and smiles faintly. 'Burgess,' he murmurs.

'My discharge came through, sir,' Burgess repeats, a little louder. 'I got the letter this morning. I thought you'd like to know.' The author closes his eyes again. 'And I want to thank you, with all my heart,' says Burgess. 'First for getting me the extended leave, and now this. I'd be dead by now if they'd sent me back to the Front. Dead, or crippled, or doolally. And that's the truth.' He is not sure whether his master hears or understands or even whether he is fully awake, but it doesn't matter. He can feel the tension that has gripped him ever since he returned to England, the fear of being sent back to the Front, uncoiling inside him like a powerful spring. He has never told anybody about what it was really like, but the time has come to unburden himself, and it suits him to have a patient, silent listener who will not interrupt or ask questions or pass comment.

'It weren't gettin' wounded that was the worst part. In a way that was the *best* part. We'd just relieved the Second Battalion in the trenches near Cambrin. There was no real fightin' at the time, but the Huns lobbed over the occasional mortar bomb just to be aggravatin'. One landed in my trench after breakfast one morning. I didn't know what hit me till I woke up in the field ambulance and the orderly said something I couldn't hear, but he smiled so I knew I couldn't be hurt too bad. He gave me a cigarette, and it was the best fag I ever smoked. I thought to myself: "I'm going to get out of it. I'll be sent home." And I was, thank God.

'No, the worst part was two weeks before that, the battle of Aubers Ridge. That's what they called it in the papers. We didn't know what it was called at the time. It weren't much of a ridge — just a gentle slope risin' up out of the plain, nothin' like Point Hill at home. Our orders was to clear the Huns out of the trenches in front of it and occupy the high ground. It was the first real action we saw in the Fifth Battalion. The first and the last for a lot of the lads. We didn't know it, but up till then it'd been a cakewalk for us — a lot of marchin' and just a bit of shellin' and sniper fire. Mostly we was kept in reserve while the Second Battalion did the fightin' — they're Regulars of course. A tough lot. "The Iron Regiment," the Germans call 'em. Anyway, this time we was in support of the Second. They was to go over the top first, and we was to be the second wave — "mopping up", that was what Captain Courthope said we'd be doin'. Some 'opes. Captain Courthope was OC "C" Company, which I was in.

'It was the 9th of May, a Sunday, a beautiful Sunday morning. Not a cloud in the sky as the sun came up. You could hear the birds singing. Then at half past five all hell let loose as our artillery started shelling the German lines. The idea was that the barrage would destroy the German defences, kill 'em in their trenches and dugouts, blow away their wire, and all we would have to do was to run across No Man's Land and . . . finish 'em off. There was only three hundred yards of No Man's Land. Three football pitches. That's what Captain Courthope said, to encourage us like. Three football pitches laid end to end – even with a rifle and pack you could cover it in under a minute, he said. And when the whistles went for the attack, and the men went over the top, with the officers waving their red marking flags like linesmen, you might have thought it *was* a game, and looked for the ball . . . But it weren't a game.

'The artillery barrage didn't work, you see. Don't know why – whether the gunners' aim was out, or there was something wrong with our shells, failin' to explode, as was said afterwards – but as soon as the Second Battalion went over the top and charged they were cut down by machine guns and rifle fire. It was murder. Nobody got within a hundred yards of the German trenches – they were spread out across No Man's Land, dead, or dyin', or takin' what cover they could find in craters and behind trees. And then the German artillery started poundin' our positions. The First Aid post took a direct hit. The noise was terrible. I was shakin' with fear, I don't mind telling you, and I wasn't the only one. The man beside me filled his pants – beggin' your pardon, sir, but I could smell it. We moved up from the second line of trenches to the first, and mustered there, with fixed bayonets. I was in the fourth platoon of "C" Company. The first three platoons went over the top, and we got ready to follow. Lieutenant Haigh raised his whistle to his lips, and I thought to myself: "Well, Burgess, this is it." And then Captain Courthope came up and I heard him say to Lieutenant Haigh: "Don't take your platoon over. There's no point. It's a bloody shambles." It was his own decision to hold us back, and it saved my life – I'm sure of that. A little while afterwards the order came from battalion HQ to retire but it would have been too late if we'd already gone over the top. The other three officers in "C" Company was killed, and scores of the lads, many of them pals of mine. And it was still only seven o'clock in the morning . . . I remember look-ing at my watch and thinking to myself, if I was at home now, I'd just be getting up and havin' a wash and a shave, and then goin' down to the kitchen to have a bit of breakfast with Minnie and Joan, with plenty of time before I have to wake Mr James . . . And didn't I wish I *was* at home!

'After a while we was relieved, and regrouped in the rear trenches. They told us we were goin' to support another attack in the late afternoon. Waiting for *that* wasn't funny, I can tell you. But the first wave failed again – a few brave lads got to the German trenches, but none of them came back, so they called off the attack. At about six o'clock in the evening the order came to return to our billets at a place called Gonnehem – "Gone 'ome", we called it. The battalion marched off in good order, singin' "Sussex by the Sea" – the regimental song, you know. The C.O. complimented us afterwards on our spirit. But we had something to sing about. We'd survived. Not like the poor sods dead in No Man's Land. The battalion lost two hundred men that day, killed, missing or wounded. And what did we gain? Sweet Fanny Adams. Not a yard of ground, at the end of the day. Like Captain Courthope said, it were a bloody shambles.'

There is a discreet tap on the door.

'That'll be the day nurse,' says Burgess. 'Thank you for listening, sir. I hope I didn't upset you, but I needed to get it off my chest.'

'Thank you, Burgess, that will be all,' the author murmurs, without opening his eyes.

'So what are you going to do now, Burgess?' says Joan Anderson, a few days later.

'Do?' says Burgess, looking blank.

'When the old man . . . pops off.'

'Oh. Soon enough to think about that when it happens,' he says.

'It can't be long,' says Joan. 'He had a bad night last night.'

'Don't you be so sure,' says Burgess. 'Don't write him off yet.'

'Oh well, if you don't want to talk about it . . . I'm going out shopping, to see what I can scrape together for dinner,' says Joan, a little huffily. She goes out of the kitchen, leaving Burgess and Minnie together. They are polishing the cutlery. Burgess applies the polish and rubs it vigorously into each item, removing the tarnish marks, and then hands it to Minnie to buff with a clean duster.

'I might look for a job as a gentleman's valet,' says Burgess, after a minute or two of silence, broken only by the soft clash of the knives, forks and spoons as Minnie sorts them into matching groups on the table. 'But I'll be lucky to find another master like Mr James.'

'You don't want to settle down, then? Get married and raise a family?' Minnie says boldly.

'No,' says Burgess, shaking his head. 'I'm not the marryin' kind.' Another long silence follows before he continues. 'I remember Mr James sayin' to me once – we were in a train, in America – "the cars" they call 'em out there. Very comfortable they are – seats like armchairs . . . I remember him sayin' to me – I don't know why he was in such a confidin' mood, but on those long journeys he would get talkin' sometimes . . . I remember him sayin': "I decided long ago that I would never marry, Noakes" – he still called me Noakes in those days. "A writer shouldn't have any ties – except to his art." That's what he said. And I reckon it applies to being a good servant, too. You have to be dedicated. It's a vocation.'

'There are servants who are married,' says Minnie.

'Yes, but it always causes problems. Take the Smiths – they were at Lamb House before your time. He was the butler, she was the cook. It seemed like a good arrangement, but Smith was a terrible drunk – he was always tippling Mr James's wine.'

'Yes, I heard,' says Minnie.

'It was a disgrace. But his wife covered up for him. Mr James had to get rid of them in the end, but it went on far too long. Smith could never have got away with it if they hadn't been married. Now you and me, Minnie, we make a good team because we're independent. Everything between us is open and above board. We're professionals.'

'Did they have any children – the Smiths?' she asks.

'No, thank God. That's another tie. I saw what it did to my poor Ma, left with six kids to bring up when my old man died. That's why she took me out of school and got me the job at Lamb House – she was desperate to get me earnin' a bit. She told the old toff I was fourteen, but I was only twelve. I don't blame her, mind. I've had a good life working for Mr James, a good life and an interestin' one . . . Two bachelors together. We were well matched.'

'But what about love, Burgess?' Minnie bursts out.

'Oh, that,' he says. 'You mean girls, women?'

'Yes.'

'I was always shy with girls, when I was young,' he says, after a pause for thought. 'I preferred sports in my spare time. I'd rather be down at the athletic club than chasing girls, any day. And when I saw what happened to some of my mates – getting girls in the family way, having to get married, having a brood of kids they couldn't support . . . I reckoned I was better off on my own. And later on in the Army it was the same. The lads with wives and sweethearts was twice as miserable as those of us who was single – missin' 'em, wonderin' if they would ever see 'em again – or wonderin' what they might be getting up to at home. I was glad I was a bachelor, like Mr James.'

'But if everybody felt like you and him, the human race would come to an end,' says Minnie.

'Not much risk of that, I reckon,' says Burgess with a grin.

'I love you, Burgess,' says Minnie.

'This deafness of mine is a real curse,' he says. 'Apart from that, I consider myself a lucky man. I'd better do that knife again, Minnie, don't you think?'

Suddenly the kitchen door swings open, and Mr Henry James Jr bursts in. 'Burgess – Mr James has taken a turn for the worse, and Dr Des Voeux's phone seems to be out of order,' he says. 'Would you run round to his house and ask him to call?'

'Certainly, sir,' says Burgess.

And so, on the 25th of February, the death-watch begins. Henry's last words to Alice, before he lapses into semi-consciousness, are: 'Stay with me.'

'Of course, Henry,' she says, and stays at his side for hours before weariness compels her to retire. The other members of the household take it in turns to sit with him and relieve the nurses through-out that day and the next. Burgess in particular spends long hours at the bedside, watching his breathing, straining to hear the unintelligible words he occasionally mutters. On the 27th the nurse summons Mrs James because the patient's breathing has become irregular, but the crisis passes. On the 28th he is unable to take nourishment. At four in the afternoon, as darkness falls outside the windows, he begins breathing in short gasps. Dr Des Voeux, who is in the room with Alice and her children, says quietly: 'This is the end.' But it isn't, not quite. The relatives gathered round his bed are physically and emotionally exhausted. They long for the inevitable end to come. But the author's fingerhold on life is extraor-dinarily tenacious. He will not let go until he has to.

. . . while for me, as I conjure up this deathbed scene, looking at it as through the curved transparency of a crystal ball, perhaps the most poignant fact about Henry James's life is that, having suffered professional humilia-tion and rejection in mid-career, culminating in the débâcle of Guy Domville, *and having then triumphantly recovered his creativity and confidence, and gone on to write his late masterpieces, those foundation stones of the modern psychological novel,* The Ambassadors, The Wings of the Dove, *and* The Golden Bowl, *he had to suffer the experience of catastrophic failure all over again, little more than a decade after the first ordeal. The three major novels, written at Lamb House and published in quick succession between 1902 and 1904, in an astonishing, prolonged surge of creative power, were received for the most part with respectful bafflement or blank indiffer-ence. Sales of each book were just a few thousands. This was dispiriting enough, but what plunged him into depression, hypochondria, and near suici-dal despair – what reduced him eventually to the gibbering, weeping, bedrid-den wreck his nephew Harry discovered on arriving at Lamb House early in 1910 – was the total failure of the New York Edition of his collected works, on which he had laboured for many years, selecting, revising and proofreading the texts, and prefacing them with richly meditated accounts of their genesis and composition. The majority of the twenty-four volumes were published in 1908, and his royalty payment at the end of the year from this*

source amounted to just $211. This discovery, he told a correspondent, 'knocked me flat'. The critical reception of the edition was equally disappointing – only Percy Lubbock's review in the TLS hailed it as a literary landmark, and for the most part it was simply ignored by the press. There was an additional sting in knowing that many of his literary friends who had disapproved on principle of his extensive revision of the early work, such as Edmund Gosse, would feel vindicated by the outcome. As another year passed with no improvement in the fortunes of the edition he became convinced that the whole project had been a gigantic folly, which would ruin him financially and bury his reputation. By a cruel twist of fate this experience coincided with a revival of his theatrical ambitions and hopes, which at first offered relief from his depression but only exacerbated it when they were once again dashed. In 1908 the distinguished actor-manager Johnston Forbes-Robertson offered to produce an extended version of the one-act play Henry had written long ago for Ellen Terry, now entitled The High Bid, but after trying it out in Edinburgh he decided to put on Jerome K. Jerome's The Passing of the Third Floor Back in London instead. This was a sensational hit and ran for three years, while The High Bid received only five matinee performances. Two other plays commissioned at about the same time didn't get even that far. The cumulative weight of all these disappointments was too much to bear. It was in the mood of black despair they induced that he made the first great bonfire of his correspondence in the garden at Lamb House, watched by his awed and uncomprehending servants. It was essentially an act of revenge against the uncaring, unsympathetic literary world that had scorned or ignored his work. If they didn't want his novels, he would do everything in his power to ensure that they didn't get his life – he would rather vanish entirely from the literary landscape than become one of those 'interesting' minor figures who live on in biographies and collections of letters and footnotes to the works of more eminent writers. He derived some temporary relief from this drastic act, but before long he was plunged into acute depression again.

He recovered in due course, thanks largely to the care of his brother and sister-in-law, and wrote more books, notably the volumes of autobiography, A Small Boy and Others and Notes of a Son and Brother, which were warmly received by a literary world now inclined to cherish him as the venerable relic of an earlier era. But he completed no further major fictional project, and more and more of his books went out of print. It was just as well he did not know that the surprisingly generous advance he received for The Ivory Tower *had come out of Edith Wharton's royalties by her secret arrangement with Scribner's.* He must have felt, when 'the distinguished thing' presented its visiting card, that, in spite of the admiration of his friends and the young disciples to whom he was cher maître, in spite of the Order of Merit and the congratulations it provoked, in spite of his own belief in the value of his work, and in the difficult aesthetic path he had carved out and strenuously followed – in spite of all this, he must have felt that he had failed to impress his vision on the world's collective consciousness as he had hoped to do at the outset of his literary career.

It's tempting therefore to indulge in a fantasy of somehow time-travelling back to that afternoon of late February 1916, creeping into the master bedroom of Flat 21, Carlyle Mansions, casting a spell on the little group of weary watchers at the bedside, pulling up a chair oneself, and saying a few reassuring words to HJ, before he departs this world, about his literary future. How pleasing to tell him that after a few decades of relative obscurity he would become an established classic, essential reading for anyone interested in modern English and American literature and the aesthetics of the novel, that all his major works and most of his minor ones would be constantly in print, scrupulously edited, annotated, and studied in schools, colleges and universities around the world, the subject of innumerable postgraduate theses and scholarly articles and books (and of course biographies – but it wouldn't be tactful to mention them, or the fact that he would be adopted by a branch of academic criticism known as Queer Theory, whose exponents claim, for instance, to find metaphors of anal fisting in the Prefaces to the New York Edition). And what fun to tell him that millions of people all over the world would encounter his stories in theatrical and cinematic and television adaptations, that The Turn of the Screw *would be made into an opera by one of the greatest of modern British composers,* and that although his plays would, alas, remain unperformed, the novels and stories would provide coveted roles for some of the greatest actors and actresses in the world; and that film and TV tie-in editions of these books would sell in large quantities.

It was his misfortune to consort with, and often befriend, writers far more popular than himself whose success only aggravated his own sense of failure, but time has rectified the balance. Of his peers and contemporaries probably *only Thomas Hardy is more widely read today (I don't count as either a peer or a contemporary little Agatha, who knocked him off his bike in Torquay, where there is now a statue of her by the harbour, and who still sells five million books a year though she's been dead for a quarter of a century), whereas Mrs Humphry Ward is almost totally forgotten and even George Du Maurier is slipping out of the collective cultural memory. Everybody knows what the name 'Svengali' signifies and what a trilby hat is and what 'the altogether' means, but not many people, I find, especially young people, know where these terms come from. 'You only contributed one word to the English language,' I would tell HJ, 'but it's one to be proud of: "Jamesian".'*

A silly, self-indulgent fantasy, of course. And even if the other impossible conditions were met, I would be too late. He is beyond hearing or understanding now. Every active cell of his body and his brain is dedicated to drawing the next breath . . .

At six o'clock he exhales three sighing breaths at long intervals, the last one very faint, and peacefully expires. Dr Des Voeux checks his pulse and pronounces him dead. Alice and her daughter embrace and comfort each other. Harry goes to the kitchen to tell the servants. Minnie bursts into tears and covers her face in her apron; Joan Anderson wipes her good eye as well as the chronically weeping one; Burgess goes very pale, coughs, and says, in a voice husky with emotion: 'Beggin' your pardon, sir, but could I ask a favour?'

'Of course, Burgess, what is it?'

'Could I shave Mr James – for the last time, like? I think he would have wanted me to. Better than some stranger doin' it.'

Harry looks a little taken aback by the request, but quickly agrees. 'Certainly – I'm sure your instinct is right, Burgess. But not yet – tomorrow morning perhaps.'

'Yes, sir. Thank you, sir,' says Burgess.

'And . . . I've got something else to discuss with the three of you,' Harry says, looking at them rather strangely, one by one. 'But that can wait till tomorrow too.'

* * *

The next morning, after the breakfast things have been cleared, Mr James summons the three servants to the dining room, and invites them to sit down at the big polished table with him.

'I expect you've been giving some thought to what you will do in the future,' he says. 'I want you to know that we – I mean my mother and sister and myself – are very aware of what good and faithful servants you have been to my uncle, over many years, and especially in these last few months. We are very grateful. And we'd be very glad if you would stay on here as long as there is work to be done, while we settle my uncle's estate, and so on. Of course you are quite free to give notice at once if you wish—'

'Speakin' for myself, sir, I've no such wish,' says Burgess quickly, and the two women murmur their agreement.

'That's good to know,' says Harry. 'I've reason to believe that my uncle has generously left Lamb House to me, and it would be an immense weight off my mind if you would look after the property until I decide what to do with it. I can't actually live there – as long as the war continues my work will be in Europe, and after-wards I'll be going back to America – so I can't give you any long-term guarantee of employment. But I had a timely letter yesterday from my younger brother, Billy, which I want to share with you. You may recall that Billy and his wife spent part of their honey-moon at Lamb House a few years ago, when my uncle kindly lent it to them—'

'Oh yes, I remember Mr Billy!' says Minnie. 'And Mrs Billy.'

'They certainly remember you – all of you – very warmly. I mentioned in a recent letter my concern about what would happen to you all after my uncle passed away, and – well – in a word, they've offered to take the three of you, to work for them as butler, cook and maid, in their house in Cambridge, Massachusetts. They have another house on Cape Cod. My sister-in-law is a wealthy woman. I'm sure the terms of employment will be generous. But you don't have to make any decision immediately,' he says, as they gape disbe-lievingly at him. 'Think it over. Take your time.'

★ ★ ★

'Well, I don't need any time to make up *my* mind,' says Burgess, when they get back to the kitchen. 'Just think of it, eh? America!' The gleam in his eye shows plainly enough that the idea of putting so many thousands of miles between himself and the Western Front is irresistible. 'What about you, Joan?'

'I'm game,' says Joan.

'What about you, Minnie?' he says.

'I don't know,' she says. 'It's a long way.'

'You'd love it,' he says. 'They know how to live out there, I can tell you. There's space. There's food. Steaks, enormous – you've no idea. Ice-cream, as much as you can eat. Piped heat in the winter – no fires to lay every mornin'.'

'I don't know,' she says again.

'Go on!' he says. 'Don't break up the team, Minnie. You, me, and Joan – we could do well for ourselves in America.'

'Yes, go on, Minnie,' says Joan. 'Nothing ventured, nothing gained.'

Minnie hesitates. 'You seem to want me to come very bad, Burgess,' she says.

'Course I do,' he says. 'It wouldn't be the same without you, Minnie. We're mates.'

She looks at him silently for a moment. 'Well, all right, then,' she says. 'I'll give it a try.'

'Good for you, gal!' says Burgess, clapping his hands. 'I'll tell Mr Harry we're all of a mind to go. But not till the funeral's over. First things first. Which reminds me,' he says, adjusting his features to a more serious, even solemn, expression, 'I've got to shave Mr James this morning.'

'I don't know how you can do it, Burgess,' says Joan Anderson, with a little shudder. 'Shaving a corpse.'

'I don't mind that,' Burgess says. 'I wouldn't let anybody else do it. He taught me how to shave him, you see. He said I had a very gentle touch. I never cut him once. It's a way of sayin' goodbye.' Suddenly tears are pouring down Burgess's cheeks. 'Sorry – I don't know what's the matter with me,' he says huskily, taking out a hand-kerchief, wiping his eyes and blowing his nose. Minnie goes over, puts her arm round his shoulder, and gives him a squeeze. Now that she has given up her romantic dreams it suddenly seems easier to do that.

'There's nothing to be sorry for, Burgess,' she says. 'I'll get you a jug of hot water and a clean towel.'

Later that day Theodora calls at the flat to offer her condolences. She had come round to Carlyle Mansions the previous evening to enquire about HJ but met in the lobby a neighbour who had already heard of the author's death. Theodora, not wishing to intrude on the grieving family, left a note for Mrs James and went to the Post Office to cable the sad but not unexpected news to Edith Wharton. She does not mention this to Mrs James and Peggy, who are noticeably warmer in their manner towards her, and thank her for all she has done for Henry. 'Would you like to see him?' Mrs James asks. 'One has a great tenderness for the body of a person one knew well in life, I think.' Theodora says she would, and is shown into the drawing room by Minnie Kidd.

Henry James is laid out in his coffin, covered with a black pall, and there is a white cloth over his face which Minnie folds back to reveal his immaculately shaven face. He looks very fine, like a work of art in ivory wax, perfectly peaceful, but dissociated from everything that was his personality. She understands what Mrs James meant about feeling a tenderness for the body, because the spirit that inhabited it isn't there to care for it any longer. Theodora, who is an active member of the Society for Psychical Research and sometimes attends séances in this capacity, reflects that it would be an interesting experiment to try one day to contact the spirit of Henry James. Authentic messages from HJ about the afterlife would be well worth having, and inauthentic ones would be easy to identify, since no medium could possibly fake his style.

Some six years earlier, Henry James wrote an essay entitled 'Is There a Life After Death?' which he must have dictated to Theodora Bosanquet, so she

would have had a good idea of his views on the subject. It was published in
Harper's Bazaar, *January–February 1910, along with contributions on the same*
theme by other writers, including William Dean Howells, which were collected
into a book, published by Harper, called In After Days. *Since Henry was in*
the grip of a paralysing depression in February 1910, we must suppose that he
wrote the essay in a period of relative calm in 1909, a break in the gathering
storm clouds of gloom, for it is an eloquent and optimistic piece of writing.

Leon Edel, who made himself the world's greatest authority on the life
and work of Henry James, summarises the essay, in his monumental biog-
raphy, as follows:

> If one meant physical life, he believed there was none. Death
> was absolute. What lived beyond life was what the creative
> consciousness had found and made: and only if enshrined in
> enduring form.

Actually, that was not quite what Henry James said. It was what you
might expect him to say on the subject; it was what you might hope
he would say, if you were a convinced materialist and a professor of
literature; but it is not what he in fact said. 'Is There a Life After
Death?' begins: 'I confess at the outset that I think it is the most
interesting question in the world, once it takes on all the intensity of which it is capable' — *hardly the sentiments of someone who*
thinks that death is absolute. But like all James's writing, and espe-
cially his later work, the essay is very difficult to summarise. His prose
is in fact designed to defeat paraphrase. It is like a fine-spun web, flex-
ible and delicate, designed to catch meaning rather than to express it.
You have to negotiate the web, spread yourself over it, experience *it,*
to get the meaning. Stand back from the web, and you can hardly trace
its structure, its threads are so fine; try to condense it, and you risk
destroying it. Still, we will try. He says that contemplating the question
can have two possible effects:

> the effect of making us desire death . . . absolutely *as* welcome
> extinction and termination; or the effect of making us desire
> it as a renewal of the interest, the appreciation, the passion, the

large and consecrated consciousness, in a word, of which we have had so splendid a sample in this world.

He himself was familiar, and would soon be familiar again, with the first effect, but the essay consists largely of an exploration, and eventual affirmation, of the second, in which death is seen as the portal to an extension, not an extinction, of consciousness. He frankly acknowledges, however, the absence of any firm evidence for such a hope. We must resign ourselves, he says,

to the grim fact that 'science' takes no account of the soul, the principle we worry about, and that we are abjectly and inveterately shut up in our material organs . . . Observation and evidence reinforce the verdict of the dismal laborator-ies and the confident analysts as to the interconvertibility of our genius and our brain — the poor palpable, ponderable, probeable, laboratory brain.

For him orthodox religion offers no firm foundation from which to chal-lenge this view; neither is he impressed by the claims of spiritualism to access life beyond the veil. The dead are conspicuous by their absence and their silence. So what gives him any confidence in the possibility of personal immortality? Simply 'the accumulation of the very treasure itself of consciousness', *an accumulation heightened and refined by the circum-stance of being an artist:*

It is in a word the artistic consciousness and privilege in itself that thus shines as from immersion in the fountain of being. Into that fountain, to depths immeasurable, our spirit dips — to the effect of feeling itself, *qua* imagination and aspiration, all scented with universal sources. What is that but an adven-ture of our personality, and how can we after it hold complete disconnection likely?

In other words, he finds the interaction between his developing individual consciousness and the world it inhabits so rich and rewarding that he cannot accept that the sense of self thus produced is just a cruel trick played by Nature which will be rudely exposed at death. He emphasises that this is not 'a belief' (a word he has been careful to avoid) but 'a desire'. There is in fact an implication running through the entire essay, an idea which some speculative theologians have since found attractive, that we will get the afterlife we desire (and no afterlife at all if we don't desire it). The essay concludes:

And when once such a mental relation to the question as that begins to hover and settle, who shall say over what fields of experience, past and current, and what immensities of perception and yearning, it shall *not* spread its wings? No, no, no – I reach beyond the laboratory brain.

Interesting, somewhat surprising stuff – and it encourages a different and more pleasing fantasy than the one I indulged in earlier: the spirit of Henry James existing out there somewhere in the cosmos, knowing everything I wished he could know before he died, observing with justifiable satisfaction the way his reputation developed after his death, totting up the sales figures, reading the critiques, watching the films and the television serials on some celestial video player or DVD laptop, and listening to the babble of our conversation about him and his work, swelling through the ether like a prolonged ovation.

Henry, wherever you are – take a bow.

Acknowledgements, etc.

This kind of book cannot be written without the help of other books, and other people. My biggest single debt, inevitably, is to Leon Edel – not only for his indispensable biography, *Henry James: a life* (1984), but also for his editions of Henry James's *Letters* (1974–84), the *Complete Plays* (1949), *Guy Domville* (1961), and *The Diary of Alice James* (1964); also for *A Bibliography of Henry James* (with Dan H. Laurence; 3rd edn. 1982 revised with James Rambeau). Among other biographical studies of James, I profited particularly from Lyndall Gordon's *A Private Life of Henry James* (1998), Philip Horne's *Henry James: a Life in Letters* (1999), R. W. B. Lewis's *The Jameses; a family narrative* (1991), H. Montgomery Hyde's *Henry James at Home* (1969), Simon Nowell-Smith's *The Legend of the Master* (1947), and Robert L. Gale's *A Henry James Encyclopaedia* (1989).

My main sources of information about George Du Maurier were Leonée Ormond's comprehensive and lavishly illustrated biography, *George Du Maurier* (1969), his granddaughter Daphne Du Maurier's *The Du Mauriers* (1937) and *The Young George Du Maurier: A Selection of his Letters 1860–67* (1951), C. Hoyer Millar's *George Du Maurier and Others* (1937), and, going further back in time, Felix Moscheles' *In Bohemia with Du Maurier* (1896), J. L. & J. B. Gilder's *Trilbyana: the Rise and Progress of a Popular Novel* (New York, 1895), and R. H. Sherard's profile, 'The Author of *Trilby*' in *The Westminster Budget* (Dec. 1895). It was Daphne Du Maurier who discovered that the alleged aristocratic strand in the family's history was a fiction concocted by George Du Maurier's paternal grandfather, Robert Mathurin-Busson, who was an ordinary artisan with no claim to either the name or estate of Du Maurier, and fled from France to England to escape, not the Revolution, but a charge of fraud. George Du Maurier died in blissful ignorance of these facts. He must have known that his English maternal grandmother, Mary-Anne Clarke, had been a famous Regency courtesan and the mistress of Frederick Duke of York, who supported herself and her (legitimate) daughter Ellen in exile in Paris on an annuity obtained by threatening to publish her compromising memoirs and the Duke's love letters; but he did not, it seems, share this knowledge with his friends. It was his son, Gerald, who allowed the name Du Maurier to be used for a well-known brand of cigarettes.

Other published sources from which I gleaned valuable information and ideas include: Clare Benedict, ed., *Constance Fenimore Woolson* (1932); Andrew Birkin, *J. M. Barrie and the Lost Boys* (rev. edn. 2003); Theodora Bosanquet, *Henry James at Work* (1924); Joseph Francis Daly, *The Life of Augustin Daly* (1917); Margaret Drabble, *Arnold Bennett* (1974); Daphne Du Maurier, *Gerald: a portrait* (1937); Richard Ellmann, *Oscar Wilde* (1987); James Harding, *Gerald Du Maurier* (1989); Michael Holroyd, *Bernard Shaw, Vol. I, 1856–1898: The Search for Love* (1988); Compton Mackenzie, *My Life and Times* (1963–1971); G. D. Martineau, *A History of the Royal Sussex Regiment* (1955); A. E. W. Mason, *Sir George Alexander and the St James's Theatre* (1935); Michael Millgate, *Testamentary Acts* (1992); Harry T. Moore, *Henry James* (1974); Daniel Pick, *Svengali's Web: the Alien Enchanter in Modern Culture* (2000), and Introduction to *Trilby*, Penguin Classics edition (1994); Lyall H. Powers, ed., *Henry James and Edith Wharton: Letters 1900–1915* (1990); Elizabeth Robins, *Theatre and Friendship: Some Henry James Letters and a Commentary* (1932); Miranda Seymour, *A Ring of Conspirators: Henry James and His Literary Circle 1895–1915* (1988); Alison Smith, *The Victorian Nude* (1996); John Sutherland, *Mrs Humphry Ward* (1990); Elaine Showalter, Introduction to *Trilby*, Oxford World's Classics edn. (1995); Ann Thwaite, *Edmund Gosse: A Literary Landscape 1849–1928* (1985); Edith Wharton, *A Backward Glance* (1933); H. G. Wells, *An Experiment in Autobiography* (1934); Ruth Bernard Yeazell, ed., *The Death and Letters of Alice James* (1981).

I was fortunate to be assisted in my researches by three couples who were or are custodians of Lamb House, now the property of the National Trust, who facilitated my access to the house, and generously helped me with information, documents and introductions: the late Graham Watson (who was my first literary agent) and his wife Dorothy; Hilary and Gordon Brooke; Sue Harris and Tony Davis. Burgess Noakes's great-niece, Mrs Diane Davidson, kindly answered some questions and supplied me with some useful documents.

Peter Davison, Michael Holroyd and John Sutherland helped me by answering specific enquiries. Alan Readman of the West Sussex Records Office supplied useful information and photocopied documents concerning Burgess Noakes's war service. Kathy Chater did some research for me in the East Sussex County Records Office. I am grateful to the staff of the London Library (an invaluable resource), the British Library, and the Houghton Library of Harvard University – especially Jennie Rathbun of the latter institution, for helping me to obtain photocopies of the Henry James–George Du Maurier correspondence, most of which is unpublished, and some letters of Burgess Noakes. Bernard Bergonzi, Maurice Couturier, Joel Kaplan and Sheila Stowell, Mike Shaw and Jonathan Pegg, all read the first complete version of the novel and made helpful comments and corrections, as did my wife Mary. My editors at three different publishing houses, Geoff Mulligan, Paul Slovak and Tony Lacey, gave me very useful notes for my final revision of the text.

In my brief authorial prologue I state that, although 'nearly everything that happens in this story is based on factual sources . . . I have imagined some events and personal details which history omitted to record'. Some readers may wish to know more about the nature and extent of these additions to my sources, so here is a summary of the significant instances.

Since I was unable to find any verbal description or photograph of Minnie Kidd, I was obliged to invent her personal appearance. Her unrequited love for Burgess Noakes is a speculation, partly encouraged by the fact that she wrote frequently to Noakes when he was serving as a soldier in Flanders, and that Theodora Bosanquet and Edith Wharton concurred, in their correspondence, in hoping he would get a medical discharge 'for Kidd's sake' (though by that they probably meant the assistance he gave to Minnie in looking after HJ). James did allude to 'The Beast in the Jungle' when Minnie came to his assistance at the time of his stroke, but her attempt to read the story is my addition. The telegram from Alexander congratulating James on his O.M. is a matter of record, but Gerald N Maurier's is not.

Although we know that James was shocked by the morals of Wagner's entourage in Italy in 1880, and subsequently broke off relations with Zhukovski, Leon Edel says that 'we can only guess what happened at Posilippo' – so I have guessed. Du Maurier's encounter with the Protestant minister in Malines, which he relates to HJ, is my invention, though it is consistent with his circumstances at the time and his subsequent views. The excursion of HJ and Du Maurier to Staithes is not based on any record, though HJ did join his friend in Whitby that summer, and the walk to Staithes was a favourite of Du Maurier's. HJ's brush with the prostitutes and the louche young men outside the Haymarket Theatre on his way to see *An Ideal Husband* is my invention. Du Maurier's encounter with Tom Guthrie and Edmund Gosse's conversations with William Norris in the St James's Theatre on the same evening are imagined, though all were present at the first performance of *Guy Domville*. The actions and reactions of the other named characters that night are more closely based on recorded fact. The Chicagoan's offer of $10,000 for a signed drawing of Trilby in the nude is my only embellishment of the true story of the *Trilby* 'boom'. Agatha Miller, better known by her married name of Agatha Christie, was living in Torquay, and reached her fifth birthday, when HJ was residing at the Osborne, but the encounter between them is a fancy of my own. Exactly when HJ hired Burgess Noakes as house-boy is uncertain; I have favoured the earliest possible date, the autumn of 1898, for structural reasons. It was my idea to send Peggy James and her mother to see a performance of *Peter Pan*. I believe Burgess Noakes must have been present at the battle of Auber's Ridge; drawing on the 5th Battalion's war diary for facts, I have imagined how he observed and survived it. The offer of Billy James and his wife to employ Burgess Noakes, Minnie Kidd and Joan Anderson may not have been conveyed quite so soon after HJ's death as I have presented it.

In the course of my researches I learned some facts about the subsequent lives of Henry James's servants which may be of interest to readers of this book. It would appear that the trio went to America to work for Billy James and his wife Alice (née Runnels) in September 1916. Burgess returned to England and was married in 1930 to Ethel May Chapling. According to Mrs Davidson, Ethel was not much liked by his family, who suspected her of marrying Burgess for his money, and he said later it was 'the worst thing he ever did'. From 1934 they lived at a cottage in Peasmarsh, near Rye, where Burgess raised greyhounds. The marriage was evidently childless. Ethel died around 1960, and Burgess subsequently moved back into Rye, where he died in 1975, at the age of 89. According to an obituary in *The Sussex Express and County Herald* he went back to America on several occasions to visit members of the James family, and he seems to have been in regular correspondence with Mrs Alice Runnels James – there are three letters from him to her written in 1956, the year before she died, in the Houghton Library at Harvard. In one he says he hopes to make a day-trip to some unspecified place to see Minnie, who is suffering badly from arthritis, and in another that he has had a letter from her and that things are very difficult for her as she has to look after an older sister, '82 or 3 I think who lives in the same building and who she feels responsible for, she says her relations take no notice of their old aunts and all are doing fairly well. She was too good-natured and let them sponge on her when she came home from America.' I infer that Minnie Kidd never married.

I first made a note about the relationship between Henry James and George Du Maurier as a possible subject for a novel in November 1995, but I did not begin serious research on it until five years later. I started writing the novel in the summer of 2002. In November of that year, by which time I had written about 20,000 words, I read a review in the *Guardian* of a new novel by Emma Tennant, entitled *Felony*, which (I gathered) is in part about the relationship between Henry James and Constance Fenimore Woolson. To avoid being distracted or influenced by this work, I decided not to read it, or any other reviews of it; and I have not yet done so. A few weeks after I delivered the completed *Author, Author* to my publishers in September 2003, I learned that Colm Tóibín had also written a novel about Henry James which would be published in the spring of 2004. I leave it to students of the Zeitgeist to ponder the significance of these coincidences.

D.L.

Birmingham, November 2003

FOR THE BEST IN PAPERBACKS, LOOK FOR THE

In every corner of the world, on every subject under the sun, Penguin represents quality and variety—the very best in publishing today.

For complete information about books available from Penguin—including Penguin Classics, Penguin Compass, and Puffins—and how to order them, write to us at the appropriate address below. Please note that for copyright reasons the selection of books varies from country to country.

In the United States: Please write to *Penguin Group (USA), P.O. Box 12289 Dept. B, Newark, New Jersey 07101-5289* or call 1-800-788-6262.

In the United Kingdom: Please write to *Dept. EP, Penguin Books Ltd, Bath Road, Harmondsworth, West Drayton, Middlesex UB7 0DA.*

In Canada: Please write to *Penguin Books Canada Ltd, 90 Eglinton Avenue East, Suite 700, Toronto, Ontario M4P 2Y3.*

In Australia: Please write to *Penguin Books Australia Ltd, P.O. Box 257, Ringwood, Victoria 3134.*

In New Zealand: Please write to *Penguin Books (NZ) Ltd, Private Bag 102902, North Shore Mail Centre, Auckland 10.*

In India: Please write to *Penguin Books India Pvt Ltd, 11 Panchsheel Shopping Centre, Panchsheel Park, New Delhi 110 017.*

In the Netherlands: Please write to *Penguin Books Netherlands bv, Postbus 3507, NL-1001 AH Amsterdam.*

In Germany: Please write to *Penguin Books Deutschland GmbH, Metzlerstrasse 26, 60594 Frankfurt am Main.*

In Spain: Please write to *Penguin Books S. A., Bravo Murillo 19, 1º B, 28015 Madrid.*

In Italy: Please write to *Penguin Italia s.r.l., Via Benedetto Croce 2, 20094 Corsico, Milano.*

In France: Please write to *Penguin France, Le Carré Wilson, 62 rue Benjamin Baillaud, 31500 Toulouse.*

In Japan: Please write to *Penguin Books Japan Ltd, Kaneko Building, 2-3-25 Koraku, Bunkyo-Ku, Tokyo 112.*

In South Africa: Please write to *Penguin Books South Africa (Pty) Ltd, Private Bag X14, Parkview, 2122 Johannesburg.*